James Luke Meagher

The Festal Year

Or, The Origin, History, Ceremonies And Meaning Of The Sundays, Seasons, Feasts

And Festivals Of The Church During The Year, Explained For The People

James Luke Meagher

The Festal Year
Or, The Origin, History, Ceremonies And Meaning Of The Sundays, Seasons, Feasts And Festivals Of The Church During The Year, Explained For The People

ISBN/EAN: 9783741192159

Manufactured in Europe, USA, Canada, Australia, Japa

Cover: Foto ©Andreas Hilbeck / pixelio.de

Manufactured and distributed by brebook publishing software (www.brebook.com)

James Luke Meagher

The Festal Year

INTERIOR OF ST. PETER'S, ROME.

THE

FESTAL YEAR;

OR,

THE ORIGIN, HISTORY, CEREMONIES AND MEANINGS

OF

THE SUNDAYS, SEASONS, FEASTS AND FESTIVALS

OF

THE CHURCH

DURING THE YEAR,

EXPLAINED FOR THE PEOPLE.

BY

REV. JAS. L. MEAGHER,

AUTHOR OF "TEACHING TRUTH BY SIGNS AND CEREMONIES."

———⋄———

NEW YORK:
RUSSELL BROTHERS, 17, 19, 21, 23 ROSE STREET.
——
1883.

PREFACE.

In the days of the infancy of the Christian Church, when, with a mighty wind, the Holy Ghost in tongues of fire came down on the Apostles, he breathed into them his own divine wisdom, and kindled in their hearts the fire of his love. Thus enlightened with the light of that fire from heaven and moved by the Holy Spirit, the Apostles and the followers of Christ dedicated the year, its days, its times and its seasons to the memory of the Saviour, to the mysteries of our redemption, and to the work of the Spirit of God, in saving the generations of men, as they come and go upon the stage of this world. They took the finest passages and parts of the Old and of the New Testaments, the inspired words of the ancient Patriarchs, the magnificent canticles of the Prophets, the simple yet sublime writings of the Apostles and their successors, and of them formed for each Sunday, Season, Feast and Festival, an Office of praise, of prayer and of thanksgiving unto God. Such was the beginning of that striking and magnificent ceremonial or Liturgy of the Church, called the Latin Rite.

In the following pages will be opened up before you, in a clear and simple manner, the origin, history, meaning and ceremonies of the Christian Year, which the Church uses in her public Services, when her prayers, her praises, and her thanksgivings ascend ever up before the throne of God. Spouse of Christ, and directed by the Holy Spirit, she offers daily unto our Creator a Service and a Sacrifice worthy of the Godhead and worthy of our study.

More than eighteen hundred years have come and gone since Christ, the Saviour, walked this earth, yet by these yearly rites and ceremonies, by these striking forms and figures, by these types and symbols, changing daily as the Sundays and Seasons, the Feasts and Festivals of the year pass by, by these the remembrance and the memory of God's creation and of the Son's redemption are ever kept before the minds of men. Take away the celebration of the Festal Year and soon the works of the Creator and of the Redeemer would be forgotten. Such is the object of the yearly services of the Church, to keep forever bright and green before the world the remembrance of the creation, the redemption, and the salvation of the human race.

We have dug deep into the rich mines of ancient learning and of lore, searched the works of the great Fathers of the Church, read the writings of those master minds, who in the early days of the Christian religion, gathered up the traditions of the Apostles ; we looked over the works of both ancient and modern times in preparing for this work, but with regret we are forced to say that the duties of a parish, added to our poor abilities, have made the book much inferior to what the subject demands, yet we promise you, reader, that you will be well repaid for reading the following pages, and if you find anything to admire in the book, give honor to the Holy Ghost, whose wisdom you will find reflected in the yearly services of the Church.

Feast of St. Luke the Evangelist.

Marathon, Cortland Co., N. Y., Oct. 18, 1883.

CONTENTS.

CHAPTER V.

THE SEPTUAGESIMA SEASON.

CHAPTER VI.

THE LENTEN SEASON.

CHAPTER VII.

THE HOLY WEEK SEASON.

CHAPTER VIII.

THE EASTER SEASON.

CHAPTER IX.

THE AFTER-PENTECOST SEASON.

THE FESTAL YEAR.

CHAPTER I.—THE DIVISION OF TIME.

REASONS RELATING TO THE DIVISION OF TIME.

Let me lay before you, reader, the times, the seasons, the feasts and the festivals of the year. Let me take you back among the writers of the past and show you the origin, the history and the meaning of the rites and services of the Christian year. Let me tell you how the Apostles and the followers of our Lord dedicated the hours, the days, the weeks, the months and the seasons of the year to the memory of Christ, by which, from generation to generation, His coming, His life, His wonderful works and His awful death are brought before the minds of men.

And Thou, O Holy Spirit, who guided the prophets of olden times, wilt Thou guide me now? Thou who moved upon the waters[1] on the morning of creation, move now my mind and pen to show Thy face as seen in these wonderful rites and ceremonies. Thou whose guiding hand directed the Church in celebrating the festal year, wilt Thou direct me now, that I may clearly and worthily show forth the beauties of the Christian feasts and festivals? Be with the reader going through this book; open his mind to see the truth; inflame his heart that he may love, so that, guided by knowledge and inflamed by love, he may rest at last in God, the fountain of all knowledge and of love.

To prepare the reader to understand the festal year, we will first treat of the different parts into which time is divided. But what is time? Time is a part of duration. If we study the duration of beings, we find one without

---

[1] Gen. 1. 2.

a beginning or an end, having no first or last. There never was a time when He was not; time will never come when He will not be. That being is God. Thus looking back we find his duration lost in the past without a beginning; looking ahead we find his duration lost in the future without an end. Not only that, but with God there is no past or future; with Him all is present. That is His eternity,[1] revealed by Jehovah in the olden days of the splendors of the Egyptian kingdom, when the children of Israel dwelt in the land of Gessen. When God called Moses from the burning bush He said, "I am who I am."[2]

If we consider again the duration of beings, we find some stamped with the image of the Godhead—creatures brought forth from nothing, but to last forever—to be as immortal as God Himself—created to sing forever the praises of the Lord. They are creatures having reason and free will; they are angels and men. There was a time when they were not. A time will never come when they will not be. They have not the duration of eternity in the past, but they will have the duration of eternity in the future. They were made to the image and to the likeness of God. Their duration is called their age. Of them the Royal Prophet speaks where he says, "Thou enlightenest wonderfully from the everlasting hills."[3]

If we examine still the duration of beings, we find others brought from nothingness and dark night on the morning of creation, when God created the world. They are the material things of the universe. Once they were not; again they will not be. Their duration is called time. They were made by the Creator when, in the beginning, "God created the heaven and the earth."[4]

Thus, eternity is the everlasting, unchanging,[5] ever present duration of God. Age is the never dying, ever living duration of created minds; while time is the duration and the measure of the movements of material things.[6] Material things belong to the mineral kingdom, and as far as science goes to-day everything we see around us is divided into sixty-eight simple substances; but as the knowledge of the human race increases

---

[1] S. Aug., Vol. xii. 31.   [2] Exod. iii. 14.   [3] Ps. lxxv. 5.
[4] Gen. i. 1.   [5] S Aug., Vol. xxvii. 297.
[6] San Severino, Philos. Christ. Compend. St. Aug., Vol. xix. 22

every day, and mind grasps the secrets of nature, these may change in future times.

According to Newton's laws, all pieces of matter attract each other,[1] and that attraction is according to their mass and the distance they are apart. It takes place as though a string pulled each particle toward the larger body. Among the little parts it is called molecular attraction,[2] from the Latin, meaning a little mass, while among the suns and planets it is called gravitation, from the Latin, signifying heavy. What it is, or how it takes place, no one knows, as the very nature of matter is to be dead, without motion—to stay where it is put till moved by another force outside of itself. We find all matter in movement. Nothing in the universe is still. It is God moving the material things of the world to prove that He exists.[3]

Under the influence alone of attraction matter takes the round form, as the rain drops falling from the clouds, as oil dropped in the water, as the dewdrop on the flower, as the shining orbs of the sky. If the suns and planets of the heavens were left to this attraction alone, soon they would all come together, being pulled by gravitation the smaller toward the larger, and the systems of the universe would end in one mighty crash, as the worlds would be pulled together with an ever increasing quickness, and but one mighty mass would remain of the fragments of the shining worlds of the sky.[4]

Besides attraction, at their creation God gave each sun and planet two movements—one that of turning around on its own centre, the other a movement around a great central mass. For example, the earth turns around on itself once each day, and around the sun once each year. The earth attracts the sun, and the sun the earth. They come not together, because at the creation God gave the earth a-motion as He launched it into space, so that it whirls around the sun. As when you tie anything to a string and whirl it quickly around, it tries to fly away, but the string holds it fast; thus the attraction of the sun holds the earth. The attraction of gravitation is like the string, while the movement of the earth around

---

[1] Newton's Princip. Rer.   [2] Secchi, Le Unité des Forces Physiques, l. iv., c. 2, 3, 4.
[3] St. Thomas Sum. Theol. P. 1., Q. II. A. 3.
[4] Mitchel, Proctor, Secchi, etc.

the sun tends to hurl us off into space ; but these two
forces having been fixed at the creation exactly the same,
one balances the other, and thus the earth remains at the
same distance from the great central orb of day, the sun.

The whole universe is in motion. The planets swing
in ceaseless movement around their suns, or the smaller
around the larger, all so balanced and so placed, and so
depending on each other, that if one of these great worlds
would cease to be, the grand and magnificent harmony
of the heavens would be destroyed, and the stars and all
the suns and planets would in time fall into some great
centre of the universe; all would come together overwhelmed with one mighty crash. From the researches
of astronomers of our times[1] that will never take place,
and the system of the heavenly bodies has not in it the
seeds of ruin and decay.

Time is the measure of the movements of the heavenly
bodies.[2] The earth goes around the sun, and the moon
around the earth. The movements of these two measure
for us time. The sun and moon, then, regulate the times,
the days, the weeks, the months and the seasons of the
Church.

Time, says Cicero, is a certain part of a year, a month,
a day, or of any other space. But we say that time is
the measure of the motions of the heavenly bodies. As
they move according to gravitation, which is always the
same, they are the most perfect markers of time.

Looking over the histories of the past, we find the
oldest account of an instrument to mark time to be given
in the Bible, where Isaias the prophet cried to the Lord,
"and He brought the shadow ten degrees backward
.... in the dial of Ahaz."[3] That was the sun dial, by
which the shadow of a stile marked upon a dial the hours
of the day. Again, we find the record of the sun dial
among the Romans, for we read of the one made by
Curser, more than three hundred years after the days of
the kings of Juda, when Isaias was foretelling the coming
of the Lord. The first machinery made to measure
time was a clock moved by the dropping of water. It
was used by the Egyptians under the Ptolemies, still
more improved by Clesibius of Alexandria, till carried to

---

[1] Leverrier. [2] See St. Thomas, Sum. Theo., P. 1, Q. x. 1. S. Aug., Vol. iii. p. 86.
[3] IV. Kings xx. 11.

the noble mansions of Greece and Rome. It marked the time of the masterly eloquence of the ancients, long before the days of the Apostles, for Aristotle, Plato, Demosthenes, Cicero and Pliny speak of the little vessel of dropping water which marked the passing time for these master minds of these olden days. Such was the thing used in the early days of the Christian church to mark the passing hours, even to the ninth century, for we read of one sent to the great Charlemagne as a beautiful gift from the Caliph al Rasched. The hour-glass, early in the Church, took the place of the water glass; but we know not the maker or the date, but we know that it was used till lately, and even now it can be found but only as a toy. They sometimes marked the time by the burning of a candle; and we read of the celebrated one of Alfred the Great, and how by it he divided the day into three parts, one for his religious duties, one for public matters, and the third for sleep. Who made the first clock we know not, some say Boethius, the great Catholic philosopher of the early Church;[1] some say Wallingford, the abbot and superior of the monastery of St. Albans;[2] others, Gerbert, when Archbishop of Magdeburg, who afterwards became Pope Sylvester II.;[3] but we are told by the early writers that in the eleventh century the clock was found in all the monasteries and the convents of Europe, when the tinkling bells of the great clock standing in the halls of the religious houses called the monks and nuns to their prayers, and the tolling of the great bells of the church towers told the people of passing time, or warned them of the hour of mass, or of the moment of the raising of the Host. In the early days the priests brought the clock to England, and the great church of Westminster and the cathedrals of Exeter, of Wells, of Canterbury, and of Peterborough, soon had their clocks to ring out the time for the Catholics of England long before the Reformation (about 1326).

I.—The Hour.

We must first speak of the different parts into which in modern times the hour is divided.

The second is the sixtieth part of a minute, and is tho smallest part of time among English speaking people.

---

[1] 510.   [2] 1326.   [3] 996.

We find no mark of the second in nature. It is only since clocks and watches were improved that they began to put in second dials.

Before that time they called small parts of time moments and instants,[1] which were not fixed in length. Now the second is still more divided into halves, thirds, and quarters, while by the wonderful improvements used in observatories, by electricity, and the transit, with its many spider-webs stretched across the field of vision, the time of the passing of a star can be told to the hundredth part of a second.

The minute is the sixtieth part of an hour. The name minute comes from the Latin, meaning little. We find no mention of the minute in ancient times. Without doubt it was first used when clocks and watches began to measure time, it being so natural to mark the dial off into twelve equal figures, and each figure into five spaces. The sun-dial of the ancients may have been marked the same way, but the earth not moving around the sun at all times with equal quickness, tho length of the days will vary sometimes sixteen minutes during the year when marked by a sun-dial.

The hour is the twenty-fourth part of the day.

From the earliest ages they marked the passing time by dividing the day from sunrise to sunset into twelve equal parts called hours,[2] from the Latin and Greek meaning a part of the day. With them the first hour began at sunrise, and the twelfth ended at sundown. But as the time of sunrise and sunset are not the same at all times of the year, only in the spring and fall, when the days and nights have an equal length, were the hours of the ancients alike.

Of the times when the day was thus divided, history is silent. We know the Jews thus counted time, from many parts of the Bible. One writer, Herodotus, says it was used by the Greeks, who learned the custom from the ancient Babylonians, the most advanced in the knowledge of the movements of the heavenly bodies. Another, Wilkinson, thinks the early Egyptians separated both the day and night into twelve hours. Although the Romans divided the day into twelve hours, as early as history

---

[1] Durondus, Rationale Div. 4. viii. c. v. n. 4.   [2] Polyd. Virgil. III. c. 5.

goes back, they did not thus count the hours of the night till the times of the Punic wars.

We count the hours from twelve at midnight till twelve at noon, and from that till midnight again, a custom we learned from the ancient Egyptians, while the astronomers begin at noon and count twenty-four hours till the next noon. In Rome they count twenty-four hours, beginning at sunset.[1] The Chinese beginning at midnight count twelve hours till the next midnight, one of their hours being equal to two of ours.

From the traditions of the past we learn that Christ was delivered to the Romans the first hour of the day,[2] the third he was scourged,[3] the sixth crucified,[4] the ninth he died, the eleventh his body was taken down from the cross, and the twelfth laid in the tomb.[5] In the early ages of the church they divided the hour into the point, moment, unce, and atom. · The point was the fourth part of the hour, and was like our quarters. The point had ten moments, the moment ten unces, while the unce was made up of forty-seven atoms.

From the times of the Apostles the clergy recited the offices of the breviary, which are called the holy hours. They do not correspond to the hours of the day, but as they were said at regular times, both at night as well as in the day, they took the place of the hours for the clergy before the times of clocks and watches; hence they are called the hours of the breviary.

II.—THE DAY.

The day is the time measured by the turning around of the earth, or the time when one-half of the earth is lighted up by the rays of the sun, and then when the same half is again clothed in darkness till the sun rises again in the east. It is made up of twenty-four hours. That is the natural day. The day then is found in nature. The name, day, comes from the customs of the ancient Romans, who set apart a day of the year for each of their false gods; or again, it comes from the old Greek word meaning two, for thus the sons of ancient Athens called the day and night. As the earth moves around the sun

---

[1] Holy Week in the Vatican, by Pope, p. 2. [2] John xviii. 28. [3] Mark xv. 15. [4] John xix. 14. [5] Durand Rat. Div. L. V. C. I. n. 6.

in the form of an oval, and not with the same speed at all times of the year, watching the movements of the sun in the sky is not a good way of measuring the day, but the average of all the days of the year, measured by the earth going around the sun, is the common day among all nations.

As the fixed stars are so far away that the movement of the earth around the sun is like nothing compared to their distance, the time when a star is in a place in the heavens, and the time when it comes to that point again, is the true time of the turning of the earth, and is called the astronomical day. Since the time of Ptolemy, astronomers begin at noon and count the hours from one to twenty-four, their day being three minutes and fifty-six seconds shorter than the common day.

When the dog-star is in the sky in summer, they are called the dog days. When the sun appears not to move to the north or south in spring and fall, they are called the equinoctial days. When the kings of olden times went out to war, they were called the fighting days. When the forerunner of our Lord was preaching penance on the banks of the Jordan, they were called penance days. When now the children of our church do penance for their sins, they are called fast days. When the church celebrates the feast and the memory of the resurrection of our Lord, they are called Sundays. When we keep the services of the church and celebrate the memory of our Lord, the Holy Virgin, and the Saints, they are called feast days. When the people return again to their work during the week, they are called week days. At length, when the Lord will come in glory to judge mankind, it is called the last day.

The word day again means the space of time when the sun shines on our part of the globe; the part lighted up is day, while the part in darkness is night. The days and nights are the same at the equator, but become longer or shorter as we go north or south, till at the poles the days and nights are nearly six months in length, the day being a little longer in both cases, because the light is turned out of its course by the air through which it passes before reaching the earth.

The day is also made up of three parts—morning, noon and night;[1] but the beginning or the ending of

---

[1] Isidore.

INTERIOR OF ST. JOHN LATERAN, ROME.

these parts of the day are not closely marked. The word morning comes from an old word of northern Europe, and means the early hours of the day. Noon comes from the Latin, and was the hour at which the Romans took their chief meal at three in the afternoon; and as in these latter times we take our midday meal at noon, we call it noon. Evening comes from the old Teutonic word signifying declining, and means the going down of the sun, or the calmness of the declining day, and such is its meaning now.

The clergy of olden times, under the inspiration of the Catholic Church, divided the night into seven parts. They had the Vesper time, for when the evening star "Vespera" looked down so brightly from the sky, the early Christians sang the Vespers—the psalms of praises to the Lord. They had the twilight hour, when they said their evening prayers, when the clergy read the compline. They had the crepuscule, when they retired to their couches. They had the corticine, when all dropped into sleep. They had the midnight, when all was silent, as they had no lights as we have now; the silent night was then in the midst of its course. They had the galicine, when the crow of the cock waked the stillness of their slumbers. They had their matin, when the clergy rose to say or sing in common the matins of the breviary. They had the delicule,[1] when the faint rays of the hidden sun told of the coming day. They had the aurora, when the splendors of the breaking light waked the world with the brightness of the sun, the coming king of day.

Again, following the customs of the Jews, the early Christians divided the time of daylight into four parts: They had the first hour at six in the morning, when their work began, when the clergy recited Prime from the holy office. They had the third hour, when the sun had risen midway toward the highest heavens, when the clergy said Terce. They had the sixth hour at noon, when they had the Office of Sext, while, when the orb of day had gone half way down the western sky, they finished the Little Hours by saying None. Thus in the infancy of the Church was the day devoted to God by the

---

[1] See S. Aug. Ser. ccxxi., in Vig. Pasch.

early saints and martyrs of old, amid the persecutions of the pagan nations when our fathers kept the faith.

But do you think we changed? The same has ever since been carried on by the clergy of the Church. The seven Offices of the Breviary are divided now as in these olden times of martyrs and of saints, for we never change. Matins must be said in the morning, or the day before, by a special favor of the Holy See; Prime and Terce before noon, unless the reciter has a reason; Vespers in the afternoon; but in times of penance, as in Lent, before noon, because, in ancient times, they fasted till the evening, and then they said Vespers, and under the beaming light of the evening star the early Christians broke their fast. Thus we still renew those ancient days of holiness and of saints. We consecrate the hours of the day to Him who came and prayed to His heavenly Father during the hours of the day, and spent whole nights in communion with His Father.

The Jews, beginning the day at sundown, divided it into three series of times: the major hours, the minor hours, and the hours of prayer. The major hours began at six in the morning, and divided the day from morn to eve into four equal hours;[1] the minor hours began at six, and divide the day into twelve equal hours as we do now.[2] Thus, when we know these two ancient ways of counting the hours, we find there is no trouble between the Gospel of St. Mark, where he says, "And it was the third hour and they crucified Him,"[3] for he followed the major way of counting the hours; and the words of St. John, who says, "And it was the parasceve of the pasch, about the sixth hour,"[4] for he followed the minor way of counting the hours. Our Lord, then, was scourged at nine in the morning, crucified at noon, and died at three in the afternoon. The hours of prayer, or as they were called by the Jews, the hours of the temple, were the third hour at nine in the morning, the sixth hour at noon, and the ninth hour at three in the afternoon, when, by the silver trumpets of the temple at Jerusalem, they were called to the services of the law of Moses.

These customs came down from the times of the Patriarchs, for the most ancient traditions of the Jews tell us

---

[1] See Mark xx. 3, 5.   [2] See Matt. xx. 9, John i. 39.
[3] Mark xv. 25.   [4] John xix. 14.

that Abraham, their father, used to pray at the first hour,
Isaac at the third, and Jacob at the sixth.[1] That they
had their times of prayers during the hours of the day
many parts of the Bible prove. David says, "Evening
and morning and at noon I will speak and declare."[2]
Those customs of the Jews are continued to-day in the
Church of God, when the Angelus bell tolls morning,
noon and night to call the people to their prayers, continued again at the prayers said before our three meals.
Thus from the very days of the Patriarchs we trace our
custom of praying three times each day.

In the old law, the sacrifices of the tabernacle and of
the temple were offered up morning and evening, prefiguring the morning and evening services of the Church,
the mass and vespers of our holy faith. In the early
ages of our holy religion mass was said both in the morning and evening, for they followed the customs of the
temple. They all fasted till the evening hour, such was
the fervor of those ancient days.

Some began to celebrate after breaking their fast,
when the Church made laws forbidding mass to be said
unless by priests and bishops when fasting.[3] And again
by other councils[4] they were forbidden to say mass unless
fasting, except on Holy Thursday. This custom of holy
men fasting till evening and then celebrating the mysteries of the mass remained till the twelfth century,[5]
when it went out of custom.[6] Even at that time the
custom was not to celebrate in the evening, as St. Thomas
says, "Generally mass should be said during the day
and not at night."[7] The general custom and law is at
this time not to begin before the aurora or after noon.[8]

The remnants of these times of prayer are found to-
day among the Mahommedans. From their founder they
learned to keep these customs of praying five times each
day—at daybreak, soon after sunrise, at noon, in the
afternoon, and at nightfall, when, after the ceremony of
their washing themselves, learned from the Jewish
temple and from the Catholic Church, they offer up their
prayers to the one God their founder learned to love
from the teachings of our faith, which once flourished in

[1] Zanolini, Dispt. de festis et Sectis Jud. c. viii. [2] Ps. liv. 18. [3] Concil. Agath et
Aurelien. [4] Concil. Carthag. iii., et Matis. ii. [5] Innocent III., Lit. de Temp. Ordinat.
[6] Hallier De. S. Elec, et Ordinat, p. 2., sec. vii., c. I., A. iv. [7] P. 3. q. 83. A. 2. [8] Ru-
brica Missalis.

Arabia. The ecclesiastical or church day begins in the evening and ends on the following evening, a custom coming from the Jewish temple.[1]

III.—THE WEEK.

The word week comes from the old Teutonic tongue, and means the seven days into which all nations had divided time. Amid the grandeurs of ancient Egypt, when the rows of obelisks pointed heavenward on the road leading to the temple of the sun at Heliopolis—when the temples grand and gorgeous of olden Thebes saw the mysterious rites of Isis and Osiris, from beyond the dawn of history their priests had kept the week. Among the half cultured peoples of India, in the olden times, when the religion of Brama was telling of the trinity of the Veda, on the banks of the Ganges, from beyond the ancient age of fable, the people kept the week. Amid the splendors of classic Greece, in the temples and shrines of ancient Athens, among the verdant hills of Thessaly and of Epirus, the Grecian peoples kept their week and called it the hebdomada. The Teutonic tribes of northern Europe, where the Druid rites were carried on before the time of Christ, had their week. In the temples of Rome they kept their week and named each day after one of their false gods. Thus the great writers of remote times[2] tell us that the week of seven days was observed by the oldest nations, and was the remains of the early traditions coming down from the creation that God had made the world in six days, and rested on the seventh.

The Egyptians studying astronomy named the planets after their gods, and to each they consecrated a day of the week;[3] thus they called the days of the week by the names of the planets. As the Egyptians worshipped the sun and fire, the obelisks were cut to signify the rays of the orb of day beaming through the clouds to the earth, and the pyramids were built to be like the shape of a flame of rising fire. The sun and its light then was their chief god, and to his worship was set apart the first day of the week, Sunday. The moon in brightness comes next to the sun ; to her was dedicated the second day of

---

[1] See O'Brien, Hist. of the Mass, p. 144, note. [2] Clemens Alexan., Josephus, Pholo Jud and others. [3] Casius, Hist. Rom. L. 37 C., 18, 19.

The Cathedral, Strasburg.

the week, Monday. The planet Mars shines brightly, morning and evening, in the sky; to him they devoted Tuesday. He was the god of war, but by our fathers of northern Europe he was called Tise or Tiwes, from that comes Tuesday. Mercury was the planet nearest the sun, to him they set apart Wednesday; but as he was known to our pagan fathers as the god of eloquence and of commerce under the name of Woden, the god of the Saxons,[1] from that we have Wodensday, or Wednesday. Jupiter, seen so often as a shining star, by them was adored on Thursday, but by the people of the Teutonic race he was known by the name of Thor, the god of thunder, hence our Thursday. To Venus, the shining evening and morning star, they sacrificed on Friday; but by the ancient people of northern Europe she was known by the name of Frig, or Friga, the goddess of love and of marriage, from whence our Friday. Saturn was supposed by them to be the farthest planet from the sun, and he was worshipped on Saturday.

The Egyptians began their week on Saturday,[2] and from them it is said in ancient times the Greeks and Romans learned to name the days of the week called after their gods, whom they supposed had gone up into heaven and became the shining planets, looking down from on high and guiding the course of the world below.[3]

The week dates back to the time when, "in six days the Lord made heaven and earth, and the sea, and all things that are in them, and rested on the seventh day.[4] All nations of antiquity had held that tradition, till the poets and the priests of the pagan times destroyed the old belief of the people in one God[5] long before the time of Christ, till we read that God commanded Moses that they "should observe the Sabbath day.[6] Some say that the four weeks of each month come from the four quarters of the moon.[7]

That week of creation, when from nothing God brought forth this world by His almighty power—when He arranged all things for the use of man—when He brought the material world to the state of being a place of happiness for the human race—what do these great periods of

---

[1] Cartwright. [2] Dion Cassius Rom. Hist. [3] S. Aug. Enar. in Ps. xciii. n. 3
[4] Exod. xx. 11. [5] St. Aug. Confes. L., proving this, quotes Cicero. [6] Deut. v. 15.
[7] Cosmographie par L'Abbe Menuge, p. 127.

time, these six days of the creation of earthly things, signify? They are but so many figures of the six ages during which God in the Old Testament foretold, arranged and prepared the things of the spiritual world for the redemption of man during the six periods, or the six ages of the world before the coming of Christ. Thus, as man came on the sixth day, the last and most perfect handiwork of God, so Christ came in the sixth day, the sixth age of the world, as the last and the greatest work of God for the salvation of the race. As on the seventh day or age God rested, so all may rest in the bosom of the great Catholic church founded by Christ, our Lord.

The first day or age of revelation was from Adam to the flood, when darkness was upon the mind of man, and but little light beamed upon the patriarchs, the holy ones of old. The second age was from the flood to the call of Abraham, when God called him to be the father of the faithful. The third age was from the call of Abraham to the delivery of the Israelites, when God established with them His covenant, and gave them His rites and ceremonies, to typify the rites and ceremonies of the Church. The fourth age was from the going out of the children of Israel to the building of the temple of Solomon, when God filled him with wisdom to raise a house adorned with beauty and with grandeur to prefigure our churches. The fifth age of the world was from the temple of Solomon to its destruction and its ruin, to tell all people that unless they keep the faith, their churches and their nations will be destroyed and ruined.[1] The sixth age of the world was from the destruction of the temple to the coming of the Lord to found His Church.

And as when God had made all things at the creation of the world he rested on the seventh day, and called it holy; thus when God, who of old brought the world from nothing at the creation, so at the redemption, when he brought the human race from the destruction of original sin by the wonders of his mighty miracles of grace and of prophecy in the time of the Old Testament, and after his death he rested in the tomb. Now all is done. The mind of man can rest in his holy church; and the seventh age of rest is now here. Man can rest, for he has been redeemed.

---

[1] Is. lx. 12.

Reason teaches us there is a God. Reason tells us God must be worshipped. But reason does not say what time we should set apart to the worship of the Almighty.

To the Jews God spoke by the mouth of Moses,[1] and told them to keep the Sabbath—to teach them of the time he was to be worshipped—to keep before their minds that in six great periods of time he made the world, to turn men from the things of this life, to give the people time to rest, and by that to prefigure the rest of their dead redeemer in the tomb, and to tell of the rest of all the good at last in the bosom of God in eternity.[2] How deeply God planted that work in the heart of his people, " Six days shalt thou work, the seventh thou shalt cease to plow and to reap."[3] It was the rest of the Sabbath. The first month, the fourteenth day of the month, is the phase of the Lord . . . seven days shall you eat unleavened bread.[4] " It was the great week of the year, prefiguring Holy Week, wherein our Lord died. "You shall count, therefore, from the morrow after the Sabbath, wherein you offered the sheaf of the first fruits, seven full weeks."[5] It was the week of weeks, to foretell the great solemnities of the Church from Easter to Pentecost." "The seventh month, on the first day of the month, you shall keep a Sabbath;" and again, "upon the tenth day of this seventh month shall be the day of atonement "[6] to prefigure the wiping out of our sins by the blood of our Saviour.

They had the week of years, the seven years of seven years, when the fiftieth was the year of the jubilee,[7] from the Hebrew word signifying a time of joy, when all were delivered from their debts, when all were liberated from slavery, to prefigure our deliverance from sin and from the slavery of Satan. Then the word of the Angel Gabriel to the prophet Daniel came to pass, when the seventy weeks were "shortened upon thy people and upon thy holy city, that transgression may be finished, and sin may have an end, and iniquity may be abolished; and everlasting justice may be brought; and vision and prophecy may be fulfilled; and the Saint of saints may be anointed;"[8] when our Lord

---

[1] Exod. xvi. 23. [2] S. Aug. En., in Ps. xxxvii. n. 1. St. Thomas Sum. Theo. I. 2. q. 100. etc. [3] Exod. xxxiv. 21. [4] Levit. xxiii. 5, 6. [5] Levit. xxiii. 15. [6] Levit. xxiii. 21 27. [7] Levit. xxv. [8] Dan. ix. 24.

would come and finish the works foretold of him
by the great men of old and die for the sins
of mankind. Daniel foretold the time when the temple
and the holy city would be destroyed and desolation rest
in the sanctuary, when the pilgrims and the tourists of
other nations would come and see the ruins of the holy
places, where once the grand temple of Solomon stood
when the Jewish people became a reproach and a mark of
God's anger, and that nation, once the chosen of the
Lord, be scattered to the ends of the earth, to teach
mankind that the wrath of the Lord may fall on nations
as well as on individuals for their sins; to tell and to
proclaim to the world that the things foretold in the
Bible came to pass; to be a living witness against the
infidels, that there was a nation of Jews in olden times,
as the Scriptures say.

The Christians of the first ages kept the week of seven
days, and when errors were increasing in the world, the
Holy See, at the request of St. Boniface, the venerable
Archbishop of Metz, ordered that on Sunday the Mass
of the Holy Trinity be offered up, that is the reason we
say the Preface of Trinity on Sunday; the Mass of Holy
Wisdom on Monday; that of the Holy Ghost on Tuesday;
of Holy Charity on Wednesday; of the Holy Angels on
Thursday; the Mass of the Holy Cross and of the Passion on Friday, as on that day our Lord suffered; and of
the Blessed Virgin on Saturday, for she died on Saturday, the 14th of August, in year 45 or 48.[1] Thus the Church
took the days in the olden times, once devoted to the worship of the false gods of Egypt, of the north of Europe and
of the cultured people of Greece and Rome; she touched
them with her inspired hand and dedicated them to the
honor of God and of His servants. She discarded and
threw from her the names even of the false gods of
ancient times, as it were to blot from the minds of men
the dark stain of the pagan ages.

Thus the Church at her beginning called Sunday, the
Lord's day, Monday the second ferial, Tuesday the third
ferial, Wednesday the fourth ferial, Thursday the fifth
ferial, Friday the sixth ferial, and Saturday the Sabbath,
for she did not wish, nor would she change the name of

---

[1] Life of B. V. Mary, by Orsini, p. 223, note.

Sabbath, in Hebrew rest, ordained by God, but still continues to call it the Sabbath, in remembrance of the day of rest among the Jews, of the law of Moses and of the Sabbath of the Israelites.

Christ was circumcised on Sunday, he rose from the dead on Sunday, and on Sunday the Holy Spirit came down on the Apostles; thus from the beginning of the Church they kept the first day of the week holy[1] in place of the last day of the week, the Sabbath of the Jews, and called it the Lord's day[2] from the very birth of the Church. The oldest inscription calling it thus dates from the year 403.[3] The first civil government to make Sunday a day of rest was that of Constantine, in 321, when he commanded all work to stop in the cities on "the venerable Sunday," but he permitted necessary farming to be done,[4] while, in after years, the Theodosian Code of Laws forbade all public business and lawsuits on that day. From the Church all civilized people learned to keep holy the Lord's day, so that at present it is kept by all Christians, a custom they learned from the Catholic Church in the olden days, when the Lord struck the heart of Constantine and the Emperors of Rome, and showed them the truth of His holy religion.

That they should dedicate the other days of the week to God or to His saints, is but natural, as they wished to turn the minds of the people, soon after the time of Christ, from idolatry; but of all kinds of superstition in those days, the worship of Venus, the goddess of impurity, was the worst. On Friday, the most lascivious, the most immodest and the most impure rites and ceremonies were carried out in her temples, in the streets, and in the woods by the men and women of nearly every part of the ancient world. The early Christians were horrified at the sight of this wickedness. For that reason, from the very days of the Apostles they fasted on Friday, to give an example of self-denial to the pagans and to keep in remembrance the day of the week on which their Saviour suffered for them.[5] Thus, from that early custom, we fast from meat on Friday.[6] Such is the origin and reason why we do not eat meat on Friday.[7]

---

[1] Mayol Ex. 8a. Praecip. Decal nota. [2] Dies Dominica. [3] De Rossi. [4] Am. Cyclo., Sunday. [5] Julius Pollux chron. comt. [6] Billuart Ap. 4. De Abst. et Jej. A. II. n. 6. [7] Const. Apost. l. v., n. 15 et 18 and l. vii. n. 22.

IV.—The Month.

The word month comes from the old Saxon word mona, the moon, and means the time it takes the moon to turn around the earth, being in length twenty-nine days, twelve hours, forty-four minutes and three seconds. The month then is found in nature, and was used by the most ancient nations. It is found among the records of the Chaldeans, in the cuneiform characters in the ruins of the valleys of the Tigris and of the Euphrates. It is found on the banks of the Nile in the remains of the old dynasties of the kings of ancient Egypt. It is seen in the works of the Greeks, in the cultured literature of their oldest authors. It is seen in the works of the Latin writers and in the edicts of their Emperors, regulating the months and the number of their days. It is seen in the legends of the inhabitants of the new world before its discovery by the saintly Columbus. Thus all nations had their months, which they called the " moons ;" for, from the dawn of man's appearance on the earth, he saw the changes of the moon, and measured the month from its turning around the earth.

The oldest history is that of the Hebrews in the Bible. At first they began to call their months the first month, the second, and so on to the twelfth; but by the lapse of time before their captivity in Babylon, they called September Etanim, October Bul, March Abib, and April Sif.[1] These were pure Hebrew words, but after they returned from their exile, in Babylon, the pure Hebrew was lost, they spoke Syre-Chaldaic, and called the month after the manner of the Babylonians ; March was Nisan,[2] April Jiar, May Sivan, June Tamuz, July Ab, August Elul, September Tishri, October Marchesvan, November Chislou, December Tebet,[3] January Scebat, and February Adar. Such were the names of the month among the Jews at the time of Christ.[4]

Some of their months had thirty days and were called full; others were of twenty-nine days and were called not full.[5] At first, the feasts and the sacrifices of the temple were held according to the changes of the moon,[6] till Hillela, a little before the time of Christ, formed their

<hr>

[1] Gen. vi. 11, Exod. xl. ; Numb. ii., I. Par. xxvii., &c.   [2] II. Esdras ii. 1.   [3] I. Par. xxvii. 15.   [4] Esth. viii. 9, Baruch i. 8, Zech. vii. 1, Mach. iv , II. Kings vi. and viii. &c. [5] Gen. vii. 11 and viii. 4.   [6] Zanolini De Fest, et Sect, Jud. c. viii.

cycle by which the phases of the moon in the periods of nineteen years agreed with the revolutions of the earth around the sun. That cycle is followed by them at the present day.[1]

Among the Greeks and Romans the month was known. Cicero thinks its name came from the Latin word, meaning a measure of the days of the month.[2] Macrobius says it is the Greek, meaning a month; others say that the name is from the Latin, meaning to measure, for the month measures the twelve spaces of the year.[3] The Romans, like all the other ancient nations, divided the year into twelve months from their very beginning, but Romulus wanted to begin the year at the first of March, dedicated to the god of war, whom he supposed was his father; and he wanted to have only ten months in the year;[4] but Pompilius, seeing that the revolutions of the moon would not agree with the revolutions of the earth around the sun, added January and February to the beginning of the year, and made the number twelve, as we have them now.

The name January comes from a Latin word, which means a door,[5] for as by a door we enter the house, thus by that month we enter the year. Some say the name comes from Janus,[6] the god to whom the Romans consecrated the first month, who, as he was supposed to begin all things, thus he began the year. February was called thus from a word meaning fever, for in that time of the year the people of Rome were subject to catching fevers. Some say it was named after a Roman festival, celebrated on the fifteenth of the month,[7] when they supposed they purged the souls of their dead from their sins; whence one writer, Isidore, thinks the name is from a Latin word meaning the god guarding the souls of the departed, as to him they sacrificed during this month. Among many of the oldest nations, as the Hebrews, the Romans, etc., March began the year, afterward they added January and February to the year; the latter month being first placed after the former by the decemvirs in the fifth century before Christ (about 450); March was thus called from Mars, the father of Romulus,[8] who, with his brother

---

[1] Talmud. [2] L. II. de Nat. Deorum. [3] Durand Rationale, l. viii. c. iv., n. 1. [4] Ovid I. Fastorum. [5] S. Aug. De Civitate, l. vii., c. vii. [6] S. Aug. C. Faust, l. xviii., n. 5. [7] S. Aug. De Civitate Dei l. viii., c. vii. [8] S. Aug. C. Faustum Man. lxviii. n. 5.

Remus, founded Rome, according to the ancient legends. April was thus named from the Latin word, meaning to open,[1] for then the buds and flowers opened to the light and to the heat of the blooming spring, or as some say, from the Greek, meaning Venus, for to her was this month dedicated among some of the olden peoples. May was named from the elders of Rome, for they were called the majors, in Latin, the elders, or others say from Maja,[2] the mother of Mercury. June came from the juniors, for in the old times of the Roman republic there were the majors, or senators, who remained in the city and attended to the government, and there were also juniors, the young men who went to war; thus May was named in their honor, while June was called in honor of the young men. Some writers say, June was called after the goddess Juno,[3] to whom sacrifices were offered on this month. July was called after Julius Cæsar,[4] who was born in this month, or because in this month he gained his greatest victories, when he conquered Cleopatra, queen of Egypt, with Antonius her husband, in a great naval battle. Before that time July was called the fifth month, being the fifth from March, which then began the year. August was thus named from Octavius Augustus, the first emperor of Rome, who lived in the time of Cicero and the great Latin writers, whence their time is called the Augustinian age of Roman letters. Before that it was called the sixth month, as it was the sixth from March. September was named from the Latin words, meaning many showers, or from the seventh, as that is its number from March. October, from the Latin for eight. November, from the word in Latin for the ninth, and December from the Latin for the tenth,[5] for thus they were numbered from March, which in the beginning began the year. Thus our months came from the manner of naming them in the ancient days of the Romans, and the Church has continued their names and spread them among the civilized nations of the earth.[6]

In the beginning they gave thirty days to each month, making three hundred and sixty days; but when they found they wanted five days to make up the year, they

---

[1] S. Aug. vol. xxviii. 468.   [2] S. Aug. Contra Faust, lxviii., n. 5.   [3] S. Aug. Contra Faust, lxviii., n. 5.   [4] S. Aug. C. Faust, lxviii., n. 5.   [5] S. Aug. C. Faust, lxviii. n. 5.   [6] Durand Rationale Div. l., viii., c. iv.

added one day to January, because it begins the year. Thus, having an uneven number of days, it tells of the unity of God which cannot be divided.[1] They gave another day to March, and for the same reason another to July, while Augustus Cæsar, not liking his month, Augustus, to be shorter than the other, took a day from February and gave it to August. Then, again, the astrologers took a day from February and gave it to December; thus they added five days to the year, leaving February with twenty-eight, and making the year of three hundred and sixty-five days.

There were three days among the Romans in each month which were fixed, and which were called feast days, and regulated the other days. They were the calends, nones and ides. Then the judges held their courts, then the people of the country flocked to the cities.[2] The calends were the first three days of each month, when they held the feasts of June;[3] the nones were the four or the six days following the calends, and were the market days, when they had no feasts;[4] the ides were the eight days which followed the nones, and fell on the 13th or the 15th of the month ; but although the Council of Antioch[5] says they fell on the 10th, this was for another reason. In January, February, April, June, August, September, November and December, the nones fell on the 5th of the month, while on March, May, July and October, they came on the 7th of the month. The ides fell on the 15th day of the last named months, and on the 13th of the first mentioned months, while the following days were numbered from the next succeeding calends, nones or ides. For example, they called February 19th the 11th, before the calends of March.[6] No modern nation follows this way of counting the days of the month. In the beginning of the Church, when her first Pope, St. Peter, dwelt at Rome, following the customs of the Romans, they counted thus the days of the month. As the Church continues her old ways and the manners of the ancients, and always remains the same, we often see to-day this way of counting the days of the months in the book of the Martyrology, in the letters of the Popes, and in the

---

[1] 82 q. I. *Nuptia.* [2] De Con. Dist I. Si quis. [3] Ovid says "Vindicat Ausonias Saturnia Juno Calendas." [4] Ovid says "Nonarum tutela Deo caret." [5] 18 Dist. *Propter.* [6] Cosmographie par L'Abbe Minnge, p. 133.

official Acts of the Pontiffs. For, as in the beginning, the Church adopted that manner of counting the days of the month, she keeps it still to show mankind how we never changed the customs and the manners we received from the times of the Apostles and of the ancient saint.

The months of the year are each set apart to some special devotion, thus : January is dedicated to the Holy Infancy; February to the Holy Family; March to St. Joseph ; April to the Passion of our Lord ; May to our Lady; June to the Sacred Heart; July to the Precious Blood ; August to The Heart of Mary; September to Divine Providence; October to the Holy Angels; November to the Souls in Purgatory; and December to the Immaculate Conception. Thus the Christian Church took the months, among the pagans given up to their false gods, and devoted them to the mysteries of our holy religion.

The word season comes from the Latin, meant at first the time for sowing and for planting, but in latter times it means the four quarters of the year, spring, summer, fall and winter. These seasons are caused by the earth going around the sun, the earth's equator, or a circle around its middle, not being in a line with the sun, but inclined twenty-one and one-half degrees. The sun then appears to pass twice across the equator during the year, in the spring about the 21st of March, called the vernal equinox, meaning the spring-time of equal nights, and in the fall about the 23d of September, called the autumnal equinox, meaning the fall time of equal nights. At these times of the year the days and nights are of the same length—the sun shedding his light the same on both hemispheres of our earth.

The spring is the time when the sun crosses the equator till it stops in its course to the north, beginning at the vernal equinox, March 21, and lasting till the sun begins to return to the south, June 21.

The months of March, April and May make the spring among the people. Summer is the time when the sun begins to return to the south till it reaches the equator, beginning at the end of spring, June 21, and ending when the days and nights are of the same length, September 22. Fall follows summer, and is the time when the sun

St. Mary Major, Rome.

crosses the equator, September 22, till the days are the shortest, about December 21. Winter lasts from the end of fall till the beginning of the spring. Such are the seasons, according to the astronomers, but they are not the same among all nations. In this country the months of March, April and May make the spring; June, July, and August are the summer months; fall comes in September, October, and November, while winter is made up of December, January and February.

The name spring, comes from the plants springing from the ground, as they do at that time of the year; summer comes from an old word of the north of Europe, and signifies the warm time of the year; fall comes from the Saxon word, which means the time of the falling of the leaves from the trees; or its name, autumn, among the Romans, meant the time when nature showered down her abundance upon the earth. The word winter, in the old Teutonic tongue, signifies the season of storms and of winds, and from that it has come to mean the time of snow-storms and of winds among the English speaking people.

From its very beginning the Church divided the Offices of the Breviary into four parts, corresponding to the four seasons of the year. This was to consecrate to the Creator the times and seasons of the year, that from earth to heaven might ascend that prayer of the Church, that universal prayer by the chosen clergy, who plead man's case before the throne of God.

By command of God, the Jews were ordered to fast four times during the year; to dedicate the seasons to the Lord. "Thus saith the Lord of Hosts: The fast of the fourth month, and the fast of the fifth, and the fast of the seventh, and the fast of the tenth, shall be to the house of Juda joy and gladness and great solemnities."[1] Thus the Jews fasted four times during the year, on September 3, December 10, February 13, and on June 17, to sanctify and dedicate to the Lord the four seasons of the year. This custom was followed by the early Christians from the most ancient times. We find that Pope Callistus, in 737, explains the reason in his letter to Bishop Benedict: "As the year revolves through four seasons, we, too, may keep a solemn fast quarterly in the four seasons of the

---

[1] Zach. viii. 19.

year, following the words of the Lord to the prophet Zachary." This fast is called the Quater Tenses, from the Latin, meaning the four times of the year. The Quater Tenses of the year, also called the Ember Days, are held on Wednesdays, Fridays and Saturdays of the week following the third Sunday of Advent, the first week of Lent, Pentecost week, and after the feast of the Exaltation of the Holy Cross, in September.[1] Thus they correspond nearly to the beginning of the four seasons following the 13th of December, Ash Wednesday, Pentecost Sunday, and the 14th of September.[2] In the works of the ancient writers we find that the custom of fasting during the Quater Tenses of the year was introduced by the Apostles, and that when at different times they were falling into disuse, they were restored by Popes Leo and Callistus.[3]

V.—The Year

The year is the time in which our earth completes its movement around the sun. Taking the centre of the sun and the centre of our earth, and referring a line drawn through these centres to the fixed stars, the time of its turning around is called the astronomical year, its length is 365 days, 6 hours, 9 minutes and 9.6 seconds. Taking the path travelled over by the earth, called the anomalistic year, its length is 365 days, 6 hours, 13 minutes and 48.6 seconds. Again, taking the point called the spring time of equal days and nights, called the tropical year, till that point returns again, the year is 365 days, 5 hours, 48 minutes and 4.36 seconds. Thus the year may be of different lengths according to the way we measure it; even then it is not exactly the same, for the earth is always under the attraction of the other planets which may quicken or retard its motion around the sun, and the point from which we measure, the vernal equinox is slowly changing. Of the year we will speak more fully in the following chapter.

---

[1] Missale Rom. De An. et Part. Quot. Tem. [2] Cosmographie par L'Abbé cha. Menuge, p. 132. [3] El Porque de las Ceremonias, c. xxx. Del Adviento, &c.

CATHEDRAL AT SPIRE.

REASONS FOR CELEBRATING THE FEASTS OF
THE YEAR.

Amid the smiling groves of Paradise, when man first came from the creating hand of God, the idea of the Creator was sown in the heart of our first father and mother, and from that moment they knew that they had certain duties to fulfil towards their Creator. Our father, Adam, as the head and the representative of the whole race, sinned against heaven, and by that lost for himself and for us the right to enter that abode of bliss. The grace of God, which would have made us perfect, was taken from us, and therefore we are subject to misery, to suffering, and to death.

Reason teaches man that there is a God, and following the light of his reason, man has always believed in some supreme power over him and ruling his destiny. Thus prayers, services, rites and ceremonies are seen wherever the race is found. The belief in one God, coming from Paradise, spread everywhere throughout the world, till, by the lapse of ages, before the time of Moses, the poets changed that true belief in only one Godhead into the many gods of the pagan nations.[1] Abraham was called[2] to be the father of a new race, the Jews, who were to be God's chosen people, and to be separated from the worshippers of idols. Moses was chosen[3] to receive the revelation from God; to lay down the rites and the ceremonies of the Jewish tabernacle; to prepare the Gentiles for the Church. The Prophets, inspired by the Holy Ghost, foretold the coming, the life and the death of the Son of God. The rites, ceremonies, services, feasts and fasts of the Jewish religion were but so many types and figures of the rites, the services, the feasts, the fasts and seasons of the Christian year. Wonderful was the work of God in preparing the world to receive His Son and the Church He founded for the salvation of the race!

---

[1] Gentilism, by Fr. Thebauld.　　[2] Gen. xil.　　[3] Exod. III.

The same Holy Spirit who moved the Psalmist and
the Prophets to foretell the wonders of salvation, now
guides the Church each year as she offers up before the
throne of God her yearly rites and services. Spouse of
Christ and daughter of the Apostles, our holy Church,
from the time when the followers of our Lord lived upon
the earth, she formed these feasts and fasts, these rites
and ceremonies, and year by year she offers to the Lord
her prayers for the salvation of the world.

The first duty of man towards his Creator is prayer
and sacrifice. God Himself has commanded the kind of
prayer and sacrifice he will receive. He commanded
the Patriarchs how to pray. He directed Moses how to
make the tabernacle.[1] He guided the priests of the Old
Testament in offering their sacrifices. He laid down the
laws of the ceremonies of the Jews.[2] No prayers were
received by God from all the pagan nations. Only in
Israel was man's supplications heard in heaven. One
nation alone, the Jews, could call themselves the people
of the Lord, because he chose them, and because he
told them the services which alone he would receive.
Now there is but one Church founded by our Lord, built
upon the Apostles, wherein there is prayer received by
God. In other churches God is worshipped on Sundays.
Not one quarter of the people ever come near their services, or, if they come, it is not to adore God. In the
fury of the sixteenth century they said in their hearts,
"Let us abolish all the festival days of God from the
land,"[3] and religion, which remained for a long time
among their children, is now dying. Outside of the
Church of God there is scarcely any religion. The world
is rapidly going back to paganism. The pride of man
rebels against his God!

I.—Feasts Among the Pagans.

The word pagan comes from the Latin, and means a
country town; for when Constantine, the Emperor, forbade the worship of idols, the heathens retired to the
little villages, and there, for a time, carried on their
superstitious practices. From that they were called
pagans.[4]

---

[1] Exod. xxvi. [2] Book of Leviticus. [3] Ps. lxxiii. 8. [4] Am. Cyclop. Art. Pagan.

All nations of ancient times, the Jews alone excepted, were pagans—worshippers of idols. As far as we are able to penetrate the history of the pagan nations, we find that all worshipped false gods. Their history before the Trojan war is not certain. It is lost in the mists of fable.[1] Two nations of antiquity left their religious impressions on the others; they are Egypt and Babylon. From the Egyptians the Greeks and the Romans learned their pagan practices. From the Babylonians the people of Eastern Asia derived their religions. The Egyptians adored Isis and Osiris, with many other divinities. They believed the soul would never die. They embalmed the bodies of their dead, with the prayers and the ceremonies of their remarkable ritual. A short time ago many of the bodies of their dead kings were found in a cave in the mountains in a wonderful state of preservation, with records of their funeral rites.

The pagans, feeling in their hearts that they should adore a lord of some kind, worshipped everything. The earth, the sea, fire, water, the sun and moon, the stars and all the planets were adored. Theatres were the first edifices built where the ceremonies of the pagans were carried out.[2] They used to celebrate each year the day of their birth, the day of the dedication of their temples, and the birthday of their gods.[3] Many were the festivals and the feasts they dedicated to their divinities.[4] In their public processions came the priests, the magistrates, fortune tellers, the fifteen heroes crowned with laurel, the vestal virgins who guarded the sacred fires, with the senators and the pontiffs. Among the Babylonians the victories of the army were celebrated. The sculptured winged bulls lined the walks leading to their temples. The great cities sitting on the banks of the Euphrates and the Tigris turned out each festal day to celebrate the ceremonies of their gods. Among the ancient peoples of India the religious days of feasts and of fasts were held each year. On the banks of the Nile temples, grand and magnificent, rose before the time of Moses. The discoveries of to-day are bringing to light these wonders of sculpture and of architecture. By the ancient Mexicans and Peruvians 2,000 gods were worshipped. The tem-

---

[1] Arnobius ad. Gentes, l. 11. [2] St. August. De Civ. Dei, l. vi., c. 66. [3] Lact. l. vi., c. 20. [4] See Arnobius, &c.

ples, the pyramids and the public buildings of these peoples are being discovered in our times. Among all the tribes of the American continent the Great Spirit was adored, and received the sacrifice of the white dog. Every nation and people worshipped some supreme being, showing that by tradition from the garden of paradise came down the idea of a God. Corrupted, it is true, was the tradition, but still the germ of truth was there. In the north of Europe the Druids learned their religion from the Greeks and Romans, and held their feasts each year.

Among the Greeks and the Romans the festivals of the Bacchanalia,[1] the Strenae, and the Saturnalia were kept. The Bacchanalia, held in honor of the god, Bacchus, were brought from Egypt to Greece,[2] and afterwards introduced into the Roman empire. They were held twice each year, on the last of February and on the 15th of August. In these ceremonies, dedicated to Bacchus, men and women ran wild in the streets, the highways, and the country, drunk with wine, dressed in the skins of fawns, mules, and wild beasts, with mitres, garlands of ivy and vine leaves on their heads, and carrying in their hands little lances called Thyrsi; they went through their wild ceremonies to the music of flutes, drums, and rattles. Among the Greeks these rites were called Dionysia, from the word Dionysius, the Greek for Bacchus or orgy, meaning fury, for they were wild with wine and liquor. Their capital, Athens, was celebrated for these feasts, and there, in the spring time each year, they celebrated the honor of their great god, Dionysius, within the city; in the fall of the year they held these ceremonies in the country.[3]

The Saturnalia were held in Rome on the 15th of December, at last on the seven following days by all the people, but by the women on the 1st of March. Then their slaves were treated as their masters. Sometimes the nobles waited on their servants or slaves, and allowed themselves to be told their faults or insulted by their lowest slaves. They said this was done in remembrance of the Saturnian age, of Noe, before the division of land, or the division of society into aristocrats and common people, when all were on a level, the remembrance of

---

[1] S. Aug. xxxviii. 1, 93. [2] Fabri Conciones Dom. Quin, Con. iv, n. 1. [3] Schol in Aristoph., ad. An., 201, 377. Scaliger de Emend, Temp. L. I., p. 29.

which they celebrated.   By the lapse of ages these rites degenerated, so that nothing was seen or heard in Rome but riot, drunkenness and disorder.   Horace calls these feasts the "Liberty of December."[1]   Business was suspended, evenings given up to feasting and banqueting, and days to learned conferences.   The number of persons at each banquet was never to be less than three, in honor of the three Graces, or more than nine, out of respect of the nine Muses.   One was chosen king of the feast, gladiators fought and killed each other for the amusement of the guests, slaves were allowed to sit at the table with their owners,[2] and the masters changed clothes with them, and left them complete control of their houses.[3]   The utmost debauchery and licentiousness were carried on, and society was on the brink of ruin.

The calends of January,[4] or the first days of the new year, were given up to the festivals of Strenia, the Goddess of Presents.[5]   This custom was first introduced by Tatian, King of the Sabins, a friend of Romulus, one of the founders of Rome.   On this day the people carried branches of vervain, cut from the trees of a grove near Rome dedicated to Strenia, which were emblems of good luck for the coming year.   They made presents to their friends, especially of slaves to their masters, vassals to their lords, and subjects to their rulers.[6]

The first converts of the Apostles abhorred these pagan rites.   The Church, by her Popes, her Councils, and her bishops, condemned these ceremonies.   St. Ambrose, St. Austin, and the great Fathers preached against them.[7]   Canons against them were made a part of Canon Law.[8]   With great difficulty were these heathen rites and ceremonies driven from the Christian.   Even in our times we often hear of good luck, fate, the weather, nature, the storm god, fairies, good people, watching the rising sun, and so many of the words and customs which come down to us from the ancient Greeks and Romans, or from the Druid rites and ceremonies of northern Europe.   The Apostles began the feasts of the Church to entice the people from these debaucheries of the pagans.   Led by the Holy Ghost, they instituted the

---

[1] L. II., Satyr, 7.   [2] Rollin Hist. de Rome, t. iv.   [3] Athenaeus and Seneca, Ep. iv.   [4] See St. Aug. Serm. xv., in Octava Nat. Dom. No. 1.   [5] St. Augus. in l. de Civit. Dei, l. iv., c. 16, t. 7, p. 100.   [6] Synmachus L. X. Ep. xx., p. 21.   [7] St. Peter Chrysologus, St. Maximus of Turin, St. Fulgentius, &c.   [8] C. 26 *non obser*, Q. 7 et *Si quis* ib.

feasts, the fasts, the seasons, the rites and ceremonies of the year, to wipe out of the mind of man the remains of these pagan rites and customs we find still so deeply impressed in our nature.

II.—Feasts among the Jews.

From the creation God commanded men to set apart certain days, certain times, and certain seasons to His service and to His worship, that mankind might adore his Creator, and that, as the revolving years rolled by, the works of the Lord might not be forgotten by the children of Adam.

Thus, from the times when, by the creating hand of God, the first man came upon the earth, they kept the Sabbath in remembrance of the glorious rest of the Eternal in the splendors of the skies. After the works of the six great periods of time, called the six days of creation, God's omnipotent power and force itself did not want to rest. God does not tire. God wants no rest; but man, weak and feeble—man condemned to work—man tires with the labors of this life. Man needs rest, and God, in His mercy, knew how much man wants rest. For that reason He laid down the law of the rest of the Sabbath day—rest for man with all his strength and his majesty—rest for woman with all her grace and beauty.

When God created all this universe, he looked from out the boundless eternity he inhabits and saw that all was good.[1] He blessed the seventh day and called it holy.[2] When the children of Adam had scattered over the world—when the cultivation of the earth was in its infancy—the Patriarchs rested on the Sabbath; their temple was the vaulted roof of heaven, their lights the sun and moon, their candles the twinkling stars of sky, their altars stones piled up on the green hills;[3] there, in those olden days, when the dews of the new made world brought life and gladness to the earth, their prayers went up toward heaven—in the hope of the promised Redeemer they prayed to their Lord and their Creator, God.

When, amid the lightnings of Sinai, God spoke to His people, He told them to keep the Sabbath: "Remember ·

---

[1] Gen. i.   [2] Gen. ii. 3.   [3] Gen. iv. 3, 4, viii. 20, xv. 10.

that thou keep holy the Sabbath day. Six days shalt thou labor and shalt do all thy works. But on the seventh day is the Sabbath of the Lord thy God: thou shalt do no work on it, thou, nor thy son, nor thy daughter, nor thy man-servant, nor thy maid-servant, nor thy beast, nor the stranger that is within thy gates. For in six days the Lord made heaven and earth, and the sea, and all things that are in them, and rested on the seventh day: therefore the Lord blessed the seventh day and sanctified it." Thus the Sabbath of the Jews was to be an everlasting sign to them of the creation of the world in six days.[1] "I gave them also my Sabbaths to be a sign between me and them."[2] Thus, in the days of the Prophets, he renewed that command to keep the Sabbath: "Sanctify my Sabbaths that they may be a sign between me and you."[3]

In commanding such an absolute rest from all work, God knew the nature of man, for he made him; and if man had no time for rest—if his hands were to be forever turned toward the earth in work, his soul would turn to earthly things, he could no more look upward toward heaven, his home. The Sabbath was then a time set apart by God, when man was to turn from earthly things to the things of the world beyond the skies, when his thoughts would rise toward heaven and be bedewed by the grace of God.

The Sabbath among the Jews was strictly kept. Silence and repose dwelt in the homes of Israel. They were called to the tabernacle and to the temple by the sounds of the morning trumpets. There they gathered to pray together. They turned their faces toward the altar. They sung the praises of their Lord. The smoke of incense ascended on high. Myrrh and aloes burned on the altar of perfumes. The red blood of the victims flowed on the altar of holocaust. Oil and wine were poured out in sacrifices. The priests placed the new preposition bread on the table in the Holies; the people outside, the priest within; all the children of Abraham bowed their heads in prayer, while from the choirs of priests and Levites, flowed the sweetly sounding songs of poetry. Praises to the Lord ascended toward heaven, ac-

---

[1] Exod. xx. 8, 9, 10, 11.　　[2] Ezech. xx. 12.　　[3] Ib. 20.

companied with the music of the harp, the zither, the psalter, the cymbals and the silver trumpets, all raised the hearts and the souls of the children of Israel toward the throne of their Lord and their Creator, God.

The Hebrews had not only their Sabbath, but their many other feasts during the year, ordered to be kept by the Lord as a remembrance of their history, and to bring before their minds the wonders of their deliverance, in which by the miracles of God's power he led them from the land of Egypt and from the house of bondage.

They had their Sabbath year,[1] which came each seventh year, set apart by the Lord for liberty, for rest and for prayer. They had their year of jubilee,[2] which came at the end of seven times seven years, or at the end of each forty-nine years, that by the seventh day, by the seventh year, and by the seven week of years, they might keep before their minds that in the seven days the Lord created all. These were years of rest given to man and to the earth. What then the earth brought forth belonged to the first who plucked the fruit. The branches bent under their loads, the grapes hung from the vines, the olives dropped from the trees, the grain sprung from the earth, nature was loaded with abundance, and all was owned in common. The poor could take from the fields of the rich, while man and nature rested in these years. The poor, the oppressed, and the unfortunate, rejoiced at the coming of these times, which delivered them from debts, which gave the slaves their liberty, which gave them back their lands, and broke whatever bonds had pressed upon them.

The Sabbath year among the Hebrews began and ended on the first of September,[3] so that they could reap the harvest of the sixth and prepare for the sowing of the seed in the spring time of the eighth year, when the year of rest was ended. Thus, in the midst of the passing times, God set apart these years of rest, that they might learn of the endless time prepared by him for all the good, in the years of the rest of eternity beyond the tomb. That they might see his power, these years of jubilee were years of plenty ; at no other time were the

---

[1] Levit. xxv. 4.   [2] Levit. xxv. 10.   [3] Levit. xxv. 9.

fruits so abundant, the harvest so large,[1] or the earth so plentiful in that land flowing with milk and honey, as the years when the rich and the poor, the high and low, partook of the bounty of their God.

Their Easter[2] came before their other feasts.[3] It was the great anniversary of their flight from Egypt; of the day when Israel was delivered from the house of the Pharaohs,[4] the day which saw their bonds broken; the day when they took up their march toward the promised land[5]—that promised land a figure of our promised heaven. To remind them that their life in this world was but a journey, they were commanded to eat, that day, the paschal lamb.[6] They were told to eat it standing, their loins bound up, their feet sandled, their staffs in their hands, for they were like all men, travellers in this world, travelling toward their home in heaven. The Hebrew word for that feast was the Phase,[7] that is, the Passover—that is the passage, their passage from the slavery of Egypt to the liberty of the Lord; passage that is the passage of the avenging angel, who killed the first-born of the Egyptians whose houses were not marked with the blood of the paschal lamb, a figure of the blood of Christ.[8] They kept that feast the fourteenth of the first month of Ab, our March.[9] They began that feast between the two vespers, when the sun had gone down half way in the western sky, while on the morrow commenced these grand ceremonies in their houses, in their cities and in their tabernacles, and in their temple, which lasted for a week. Each family took a lamb,[10] a lamb without blot or blemish.[11] The head of the family sacrificed the victim; they sprinkled the lintels of the doors of their houses with its blood. The angel saw the blood and passed.[12] They broke no bones,[13] for the paschal lamb was but a figure of the Lamb of God, our Saviour, by whose blood we are saved from the angel of darkness, and because Christ's bones were not broken when he was crucified.[14]

Fifty days from their Easter they held the feast of Pentecost[15] in remembrance of the law God gave from Sinai's top amid the thunders and lightnings of heaven,

---

[1] Levit. xxv. 21. [2] Levit. xxiii. 5. [3] Exod. xii. 11. [4] Dutripon, Concord. Bib. 8. Phase. [5] Exod. xii. 37. [6] Exod. xii. 11. [7] Exod. xii. 11. [8] Exod. xii. 20. [9] Exod. xii. 6. [10] Josephus, Antiq. B. iii. c. x., n. 5. [11] Exod. xii. 5. [12] Exod. xii. 13. [13] Exod. xii. 46. [14] John xix 86. [15] Levit. xxii. 16 ; Josephus Antiq. B. iii., c. x., n. 6.

when Moses entered the cloud, and for forty days lived with Jehovah, when he saw the model of the tabernacle, when he received the tables of the commandments, and when he was told by the mouth of the Lord the way to lay down those grand ceremonies of the people of Israel. From their Easter to their Pentecost were seven weeks, and for that reason they called it the Feast of weeks.

They had the Feast of the Trumpets,[1] both beginning and ending the year. As the day is the most beautiful at its beginning and at its ending, so the Lord appointed the beginning and the ending of the years to be kept holy by his people. At the clarion tone of the silver trumpets, the children of Israel came from their homes; they gathered at the door of the tabernacle and of the temple, and there they offered sacrifices to the Lord for his benefits showered down on them during the year which had passed, and prayed for his grace and his favor for the year which was beginning.

They had the Feast of the New Moon, at the beginning of each month. All were not forbidden to work, but the good and the godly of the Jewish nation gathered at the temple, and at the sound of the trumpets, there they offered sacrifices to their God.

They had the Feast of the Expiation,[2] a day of rest on the sixteenth day of the month of Tizri, our September, which among the Jews began the civil year—a day called in their Hebrew, pardon, for it was given them by God as a day when they were to ask pardon of the Lord for their sins. In those days, taught by Moses, the man of God, they knew that sorrow for sin and repentance for wickedness was the only way of gaining forgiveness. On that day of Expiation Israel, like one man, bowed their heads before the Lord. They waited till a few drops of the blood of the sacrificial victim fell upon their bended forms to wash them from their sins. The High Priest washes not only his hands and feet, as for the other sacrifices, but he plunges his whole body into the laver standing before the tabernacles. Coming forth purified, he clothes himself in robes of white linen,[3] his garments of gold and splendor are laid aside, the splendors of the cere-

---

[1] Levit. xxiii. 24.   [2] Levit. xvi. et xxiii. 27.   [3] Levit. xvi. 32.

monies are seen no more. That day, robed in simple linen, he approaches the altar of his God. He immolates a sacrificial bull and ram for his own sins and for the sins of the other priests. Putting his hands on the victims, he confesses his sins and the sins of his household. He receives from the princes of the tribes, and of the houses of Israel, two goats for sin, and a ram to be offered as a holocaust for all the people. They draw lots to see which of the goats will be sacrificed, which will be set at liberty. The High Priest now takes the fire from the altar of the holocaust, and with it lights the thurible of gold. He pours upon the blazing fire the precious incense of the East, and while the clouds of the sweetly smelling perfumes are wafted heavenward, and fill the Holies with their fragrance, he enters in behind the veil. He penetrates into the sanctuary of the Lord of Hosts, and there he offers up his prayers to the God of his fathers. His prayer is over.

Coming forth he draws near to the altar of holocaust, where he offers the goat on which the lot had fallen as a sacrifice to the Lord; taking the blood of the young bull in a golden vessel, he carries it behind the veil, into the Holy of Holies, where dipping his fingers seven times in the blood, he sprinkles seven times[1] the Arch of the Covenant. He comes again from the Holy of Holies. He takes the blood of the immolated goat and sprinkles the Holy of Holies, the Holy and the Porch with the blood. All this time he is alone in the presence of his God; no priest, no server is with him; the priests, the Levites and the people are without and see him not.

When all these ceremonies are ended, they lead to him the scape-goat,[2] and after having placed his hands on the head of the animal, he confesses his sins and the sins of the whole people, and the scape-goat, loaded with the sins of the priests and the people of Israel, wanders in the wilderness[3] and is seen no more by men; or, according to some, he was pushed off a high precipice and perished.

They had the Feast of the Tabernacles,[4] like the Feast of Corpus Christi among us; the happy feast, the poetic

---

[1] Josephus, Antiq. B. III., c. x., n. 3. [2] Levit xvi. 20. [3] Levit. xvi. 21. [4] Josephus Antiq. B. iii., cx., n. 4; Levit. xxiii. 34.

feast, the feast of flowers, of fields, of joy and gladness, for it is the day of the procession of the Blessed Sacrament. That day among the people of Israel was kept to recall to their minds the times when they dwelt in tents, when they journeyed in the desert, when without cities, without houses, without lands, they travelled in the wilderness, where the hand of the Lord guided them. In keeping that day holy, they were reminded of the times of their march through the country of the Moabites, through the deserts of Arabia, through the lands of the Amalekites; of the pillar of cloud by day, of the pillar of fire by night; of the waters flowing from the rock struck by Moses; of the manna falling from the heavens; of the miraculous flight of quails; of the cure of the brazen serpent, and of the wonders with which, by a strong hand, the Lord led them through the wilderness to the promised land. All these were recalled to their minds by the Feast of the Tabernacles. With joy and gladness, then, the children of Jacob celebrated this feast in the declining days of the fall, when the land was covered with a bountiful harvest, when the descendants of Abraham went forth from their houses of stone, went forth from their cities surrounded with walls, went forth into the green fields, went forth to raise their tents under the twinkling stars of heaven, under the balmy air of Palestine, amid the blooming flowers of the fields, amid the cascades of the mountains, amid the cooling shade of the forests, there they clothed themselves in white.[1] There they sang their songs of gladness, there they chanted their hymns of praises, there their young men went into the woods by the sides of the torrents, there they plucked the branches of the palm trees, the boughs of the olives, the leaves of the wild grapes, the flowers of the valley, and, loaded with their burdens, they ran to their fathers, carrying their burdens, where all the family together lined their tents with flowers, they hung before their doors or spread upon the floors the fragrant boughs, or the green leaves, or the fragrant flowers. Thus they decked their tents and homes, where for seven days and seven nights they dwelt in tents according to the commands of God.

---

[1] Josephus Antiq., B. xiii., c. xi., n. 8.

How beautiful were these feasts of old when Israel
loved the Lord their God. In the plains of Idumia, from
across the banks of the Jordan, from the borders of Moab,
from the hills of Samaria, from every part of the land
of Israel came the long lines of men and women, the
young and old, the rich and poor, the princes and the
leaders of the tribes, all came to the feasts of the year, to
the temple of Jerusalem, and to the sanctuary of the Lord
of Hosts. They carried their first born, they brought
their offerings, they gave their first fruits, all was carried
out according to the law laid down by their leader Moses.

Each morning and evening they gathered around the
altar[1] and sacrificed a lamb.[2] The priests poured out
their libations of wine and of oil; they drew the limpid
waters from the fountain of Siloe, while the high-priest,
robed in the color of hyacinth bordered with the golden
bells,[3] prayed for the sins of his people, while the people
without shook their palms and cried to the Lord, Hosanna! Hosanna! from whence it was called the feast of
Hosanna of Palms.

Again on the 14th day of the month of Adar, they had
the feast of Purim,[4] in remembrance of their deliverance
from Aman.[5] On that day they drew their lots, and before coming to the place they always gave the poor their
offerings, placing them in an urn beside the one wherein
they cast their lots.

In after years they celebrated the day[6] when the valiant
woman Judith cut the head from the wicked Holofernes; and generations after that noble lady of Bethulia
was gathered to her fathers in the tombs of Manasas,[7]
when the day of their deliverance came round, they kept
the feast in her remembrance.[8]

When the centuries rolled by, and the temple built by
Solomon was burned by Nabuchodonosor, and rebuilt by
Darius, when it was dedicated to the Lord, they[9] kept the
feast of the dedication of the temple,[10] of the death of
Nicanor, the 13th day of the month of Adar,[11] of the finding of the holy fire, of the feast of Xylophore, when they
carried in the wood of sacrifice to the temple and held
their sacrifices in honor of these days.

---

[1] Exod. xxix. [2] Josephus Antiq. J. B. iii., c. x., n. 1. [3] Exod. xxviii. 33, 34. [4] Esther ix. 17. [5] Esther ix. [6] Judith xvi. 31. [7] Judith xvi. 23. [8] Judith xvi. 31.
[9] I. Esdras vi. 16. [10] Josephus Antiq., B. vii., c. viii., n. 7. [11] 1 Mach. xv. 36, 37.

Those were days beloved to God and man, days of religion and of patriotism, days when they honored the graves of their forefathers, when they loved the laws of their ancestors, when they honored God in sacrifices and in prayers.

III.—Feasts among the Christians.

When we go from our houses to the church, when we turn our steps to that house of God, to that temple where our forefathers worshipped, where our fathers and our mothers were married, where we were baptized, where our mothers taught us bend our knees in prayer, where the bishop confirmed us, and where each Sunday and holiday we heard the masses offered, as we pass by the way we admire the sunshine decking the landscape, we love the bright leaves with colors of gold, we smell the perfumes of the fragrant air, we admire the tints of the blooming flowers, but above all we more love the church of our fathers, the church founded by our Lord, the church taking the place of the temple of old, the church now saving the fallen race; and before we come to her feasts and to her festivals, we passed through the feasts of the Jews, for they were but figures of ours—they were but like shadowy forms, formed by the Lord in the days of old to prepare the world for the feasts of the church of God—to prepare for these grand and magnificent festivals of the Catholic Church—to prepare for temples grander than Solomon's—to prepare the nations for the salvation of the Gospel.

From the days of the Apostles the Church set apart certain times, certain seasons, and certain days for the worship of the Lord, so that each year, like a living scene, brings before us the life, the mysteries, the doctrines, the benefits, the obligations and the promises of the redemption of the human race by our Saviour Jesus Christ. Such is the Ecclesiastical year. It is to keep before the minds of men the boundless love of God, shown forth from the beginning of the world to the coming of Christ, to remind us of His incarnation, His satisfaction and His glorification, and in the year, his life will be ever shown as well as the redemption, the sanctification and the salvation of the children of Adam. Thus the Christian year is a living gospel of the crucified. Thus Christ is preached to the people ; Christ and His works are ever before their eyes; the Church in her festivals renews forever the life, works, and the death of her founder and her Redeemer, in the feasts, the fasts, and the festivals and the seasons of the year.[1]

The object of the Apostles in the ecclesiastical year was to teach the people the truths of the Christian religion by the many ceremonies and the services of the Church; to keep before their minds the works of the Lord during his life; to let them see in outward forms and rites what they believed in their hearts ; to shower down on them the benefits and graces of the redemption; to restore, to preserve, and to increase in them sanctifying grace, and thus to keep them from sin, make them holy, happy, and give them the aids and the means of attaining heaven.[2]

The chief joyful seasons are Christmas, for which Advent is a preparation; Easter, for which Lent is a preparation; and the After-Pentecost season, lasting till the first Sunday of Advent. At Christmas we celebrate the boundless love of the Father in sending His Son to redeem the world; at Easter we commemorate the unspeakable love of the Son, dying for our sins, and rising from the grave when He redeemed us from the power of the devil; while at Pentecost we yearly renew the memory of the Holy Ghost coming down on the Apostles. Thus these three chief festivals of the year are dedicated to the three most holy persons of the Trinity.

The three fasting seasons are : Advent, the time of prayer and of waiting for the coming of our Lord ; Lent, the time of fasting and of penance for our sins, and the Holy Week, the time of mourning for the sufferings and the death of Christ. The other principal seasons are : Christmas, Septuagesima, Easter, and the after Pentecost seasons. The year then is made of seasons, feasts, festivals, Sundays, fast days and week days.

Sunday, the Lord's day[3] and the Christian Sabbath, is the first day of the week. One day of the week is thus kept holy, because God rested one day;[4] because it is right that man should give one day of the week to the

---

[1] Coffin, Dev. Instr. on the Epist. and Gosp., p. 13. [2] Coffin, Ib., p. 14, Conciones Fabri Dom. 1, post. Epiph. con. vii. [3] S. Aug. Sermo c., lxix. ; De Ver. Ap. Phil. iii. n. 3. [4] Gen. ii. 2.

service of the Lord, and to his soul's salvation; because a day of rest and of prayer is good for man, lest he might be led astray by passion, by the love of the world, or waste his time in work, unless wakened from his forgetfulness of God and called to the service of his Creator. The first day of the week was kept holy by the Apostles,[1] to show that Jews and Christians were not the same; to tell that on the first day of the week the Lord began the creation;[2] to remind us that Christ, on Sunday, was circumcised, baptised, began his public life, changed water into wine, gave the power of forgiving sin,[3] rode into Jerusalem on an ass, rose from the dead, appeared to his disciples, and that on that day the Holy Spirit came down on the Apostles. For these reasons, from the very beginning of the Church, the Apostles set apart the first day of the week, and called it holy to the Lord.[4]

All members of the Church, when they come to the age of reason, are obliged to hear Mass on Sundays and holidays, unless grave reasons prevent.[5] They are obliged to stop all servile work on that day.[6] No other obligation has the Church imposed on the people,[7] as a strict law, but all are to spend the Lord's day in a holy way, as becomes good Christians; but those who cannot be at the Mass are not obliged to say the prayers at Mass in their houses, but they should hear the sermon if they can.

These are what we are to do if we keep strictly to the letter of the law; but any one who looks into the spirit of the Church will see that it is to be kept wholly dedicated to the service of the Lord and to the interest of our salvation. We sanctify the day by assisting at the public services of the Church and at Vespers, if we can.[8] If we cannot go to the Church, we should at home spend the day in prayer, in reading some good book, in making frequent acts of love of God, of faith, hope, charity, and of contrition, and thus prepare ourselves for the temptations of the coming week. Above all, we ask the reader to make a practice of going to Communion one Sunday of every month, or even oftener, as the most perfect way of gaining their salvation. Sunday is broken by unnecessary work and servile labor, by neglecting Mass, by

---

[1] See S. Ang. Epist. lv., n. 21. [2] Gen. 1. 1. [3] Bellarmine T. 11., 1. 2. [4] See Syriac Doc. concerning Edessa Teaching of the Apost. c. 1, &c. [5] C. Mis. 64 De Con. Dist. I., can. 68 and Ex. Jur. Can. passim. [6] Dec. L. 2, Tit. 9, C. I. and many other Councils. [7] Suarez De Relig. T. I. L. 2, C. 16, N. 4. [8] Concil. Trent., ses. xxiv. de Ref. c. 4 et 13.

idleness, intemperance, plays, dances; really it would be better to spend the day at work than to give that holy day up to sinful pleasures.[1] The servile works spoken of here, are the works of manual labor, which cannot be put off 'till another day; while the works which must be done on that day, as the arranging of the house, the care of cattle and the like, are allowed.

Besides Sundays, the feasts to be kept holy like the Sunday are, in this country, the Immaculate Conception, Christmas, New Year's Day, Epiphany, Ascension Thursday, the Annunciation, Corpus Christi, the Assumption and All Saints. Besides these, there are other days not so important, during which the people are not obliged to hear Mass or spend the day as Sunday. They are days dedicated to some mystery of our Lord, to his Mother, or to his saints, but which are commemorated in the breviary, so that each year an office is said to commemorate some truth or some mystery of our holy religion.

The day before the great holiday is called the Vigil, or the Eve, and it is the day we set apart to prepare ourselves for the coming feast. As we should prepare for the celebration of the festal days by works of penance, the eves or vigils of feasts generally are days of prayer and fasting.

And when the joyful day of the feast comes, the time of its celebration is lengthened for eight days, and that is what we call an Octave. All the great feast days of the Church have octaves.

Fasting is of two kinds : fasting from meat and fasting from food. We fast from meat on all Fridays of the year, and we fast from food and meat in Advent, Lent, on Ember days or Quarter Tenses and Vigils. These matters, besides having been regulated by the universal laws of the Church, are left to the authority of the bishops in their diocese to decide who are exempt from these regulations ; but even a doctor can declare persons free from the obligation of fasting, where he sees that they are not strong. The Church is a mother, and never makes laws which her children cannot bear.

That the Church has the power to make and to change the feasts of the year, is seen by the words of the Lord to his Apostles : "Whatsoever thou shalt bind upon earth

---

[1] St. Augustine.

it shall be bound also in heaven, and whatsoever thou shalt loose on earth shall be loosed also in heaven."[1] This power means the making, changing and the regulating of the feasts of the year. As the priests of the old law had the same power, that authority the Church has had from the very beginning; for we see that the Apostles commanded the early Christians not to eat things strangled or to use blood,[2] so that the Jews, who had a prejudice against these things, would not be turned away from joining the Church. When this occasion had passed away, they then changed the law.[3] The mind of the Church in appointing fast days is, that her children, in mortifying their taste, might overcome their evil inclinations; that by fasting they might do penance for their sins; that they might become more fervent in prayer and meditations; that by overcoming their desires they might gain greater strength in God's service, that they might be turned from the pleasures of this world, and thus think of the joys beyond the grave. That fasting is good for the soul is shown by many parts of the Holy Scriptures. For forty days Moses fasted on the Mount;[4] for forty days Elias fasted[5] in his journey; for forty days prophets went without food, and for forty years the people of the Lord lived on manna in the desert; thus the great ones of old fasted to give us an example how to do penance for our sins.[6]

Thus, as we go through the cycle of the year, we find these seasons, these times, these festivals, these days and these anniversaries, like so many yearly scenes of the life of our Lord, of his blessed Mother, of his saints and of his servants, coming ever and ever before our minds, re-calling to us as the years roll by, the works of the crea-tion, the fall of man, the law of Moses, the prophecies, the coming, the miracles, the life, the death, the resur-rection, the ascension of our Saviour, the coming of the Holy Ghost, the preaching of the Apostles, and the lives of the saints and the servants of God, who continue the work of the redemption of the race. Thus, as we keep the anniversary of a great event—as each nation has its holidays, when they celebrate their founding, when they honor their birthdays, when they renew the day of their

---

[1] Matt. xvi. 19. [2] Acts xv. 20. [3] Concil Jerusalem iv. in 52. [4] Exod. xxiv. 18. [5] III. Kings xix. 8. [6] Coffin, Devout Inst. on the Ep. and Gosp., pp. 20 and 21.

birth as a nation, when men keep the anniversary of their marriage—thus the Church, founded by the Saviour, lest the world might forget him, forget him and his works, forget him and his redemption, as the seasons and the years roll on toward the end of time—that Church has from the beginning kept these days, to wake the world from its slumbers, to call the people to her services, to renew the mysteries of the Lord of the mighty ones of old raised by his all-powerful hand, to do the wonders of his power in the saving of the race.

Thus from the days of the foundation of the Church, from the days when the Apostles went forth to spread the light of the gospel to the nations in the darkness of death, they took the year and set apart those times, those days, to renew his coming and his death. For that reason there are two kinds of feasts, one kind falling on fixed days of the year, which change not. They come on the same day of the month, and we can always tell their date. We know that Christmas comes on the twenty-fifth of December, New Year's Day on the first of January, and so of many others. They change not, for they are marked by the motions of the sun. Again, they marked out another kind of feast to celebrate his glories. These feasts happen not on the same times or days as the others. They are the seasons of Advent and of Lent, of Easter, of Pentecost, and of the other changing feasts. They are ruled by the moon, whose movements regulate the changing feasts of the year. Thus the Apostles took the sun and moon to mark the seasons, the times and the feasts of the year, following the work of God, who made the sun and moon "to divide the day and night, and let them be for signs and for seasons, and for days and for years."[1]

IV.—THE PUBLIC OFFICES OF THE CHURCH.

Prayers offered to God are of two kinds—private and public. Private prayers are the supplication offered to God by any one praying in his own name, and for a benefit which he expects alone to receive. Thus when we pray in private—when we kneel down at our bedside, morning and evening—when the whole family prays, or when any number, no matter how many may be present,

---

[1] Gen. i. 14.

it is only a private prayer. It is true they may be heard by God, and the Lord may grant the prayer, as he always hears the words of his creatures, but still it is a private prayer. A public prayer[1] is when the whole Church prays, when the bride of the Lamb offers up her supplications to the throne of grace. Then a private prayer is one offered by any one or by any number of people, while a public prayer is one offered by the whole Church.

The public prayers of the whole Church are called its Liturgy, from the Greek, meaning belonging to the people or a public matter. Liturgy is also called Rite, and means about the same thing. There are nine Liturgies or rites, according to which the public prayers of the Church are held throughout the world to-day. The Latin Rite is the chief, and, as it were, the mother of all the others. In all parts of the west of Europe and throughout the American continent the services of the Church are according to the Latin Rite or Liturgy.

The other Rites and Liturgies will be mentioned in the following pages only in order to better explain the great Latin Rite. All writers say that the Latin Rite was formed by the Apostles at Jerusalem, before their separation, and that it was first brought to Rome by St. Peter, when he left Antioch and came to fix his chair as first Pope in Rome.

The two principal books we will mention belonging to the Latin Rite are the Breviary and the Missal. The breviary is the book containing the public prayers said by all the clergy, either alone or all together, assembled in the choir. The missal, or mass book, is used by the clergy at the masses during the year. The offices of mass and of the breviary form the public prayers of the Church. From every mass offered throughout the world comes the grace of God into the hearts of the people. It is the sacrifice of the Son of God ascending ever up before the throne of God. It is the continuation of the sacrifice of the cross. It is the highest act of man. No tongue can tell the depths of its mysteries. No pen can describe its wonders. No angel can understand its meanings. It is the offering of the human race to the godhead. It is, by its very nature, a public prayer of the

[1] Mentioned by S. Aug. De Unit. Eccl., n. 54, Contra crescon, Don. 1., ill., n. 32, Brev. Col. cum Donat, n. 81, 32, &c.

CATHEDRAL OF FLORENCE.

whole Church.[1] Every mass brings down grace, but the celebrant who offers and the one for whom it is celebrated receive the largest amount of that grace. Those who are present receive more grace than those who are absent, for they assist, take part, and make a part of the congregation.

Every time a clergyman says the Office of the Breviary he prays not as a private, but as a public officer of the Church. His office, then, is a public prayer of the whole Church. He can say his prayers in private like any other person; but the prayers of his breviary are public, for he prays not as a private person, but as the public minister of the whole Church, and the universal Church prays through him. In the Middle Ages many of the good and pious people, at their death, or even while living, left sufficient means to support clergymen for the purpose of offering masses and saying the breviary to honor God, and to bring down the grace of heaven on the people or on the nation.

The origin of the Breviary goes back to the beginning of the Christian religion.[2] In the early days of the Apostles the people used to rise during the night to sing the praises of the Lord. On ordinary days they rose once, and before the great feasts three times.[3] From that custom they called these night watches, nocturns, from the Latin, meaning watches during the night. For that reason the first Office of the Breviary is divided on ordinary days into one nocturn, and on the Sundays and feasts into three nocturns. During the night, with only one nocturn or watch, they sang many psalms, and when they had three nocturns they sang three psalms at each, making nine psalms in all. After the psalms of the first nocturn they read a part of the Old Testament; after the psalms of the second, a lesson from the writings of the holy fathers of the Church; and the psalms of the third closed with a few words from the New Testament with an explanation. In the cathedrals these Offices were sung at regular hours by the canons, clergymen next in rank to the bishops, and from that they were called the Canonical Hours. Some time rolled by and these watches were discontinued in the night, but said in the early

---

[1] See Concil Tredent Ses. xxii., c. vi. [2] El Porque de las Ceremonias, c. xxvi. de las Horas en Particular. [3] El Porque de las Ceremonias Ibidem.

morning; from that they were called Matins, from the ancient pagan name, Matuta Dea, the goddess of morning,[1] sometimes also called Aurora. The lessons began with the Lord's Prayer, and the whole Office of Matins ended with the grand canticle, "Thee, O God, we praise," composed by SS. Augustin and Ambrose. Following the Apostolic times Lauds were called matins, for they were chanted at the Aurora, the break of day; and what we now call Matins were sung or said during the night. In the matins many allusions are made to the night, while in the Lauds, suggestions of the rising sun are given. We find many of the oldest saints mention these Offices. St. Jerome says, "At night we rise twice or three times."[2] Many of the clergy of the religious orders keep these ancient customs, while the clergy who have parishes and the care of souls could not attend to their duties and be disturbed from their sleep to sing. The secular clergy then say these Offices during the day. The Carmelites rise in the early part of the night, the Carthusians a little later, the Mendicants at midnight, the Benedictines and Oisterians after midnight, and many canons at an early hour.[3]

Each psalm of the Office ends with the Doxology, "Glory be to the Father, and to the Son, and to the Holy Ghost.[4] As it was in the beginning, and is now, and will be forever and ever." The whole of the psalms before the lessons were finished by a pious sentence called the "vircicle," because when saying it they turned toward the altar, "versus altar." The bishop, or the one who presided, said the Lord's Prayer, in which all joined.

Matins are followed by Lauds, praises to the Lord, which were sung at the break of day when matins were said at night. As remains of these old customs, Matins and Lauds must be said before Mass unless prevented by some good reason.

Lauds have many beautiful hymns composed by many of the great saints,[5] and as they are very numerous, we cannot give their authors. The Little Hours, Prime, Terce, Sext and None follow Lauds. St. Gregory the Great is the author of the hymn of Prime, and St. Am-

---

[1] Mentioned by S. Ang. De Civit. Dei, l. xviii., c. xiv. [2] Jerome Lit. ad Eustochiam. [3] Canon Pope, Holy Week in the Vatican pp 71, 72. [4] By order of Pope Damasus. [5] El Porque de las Cremonias, c. xxv de las Horas Canonicas.

brose composed the hymns of the three other Little Hours. Vespers,[1] from the Latin, for evening star, is said in the afternoon, followed by Complin, meaning to complete, for by that Office the prayer of the day is completed.

The public Offices of the Church are of different grades according to their solemnity and importance. They are the ferial, the simple, the semi-double, the double, the double of the second class, and the double of the first class.

The word ferial comes from the Latin, and means a day when we are free, or a holiday. Some authors think it comes from the pagan custom of keeping certain days in honor of their gods; but it rather comes from the Jewish law, for we see[2] that they had many classes of feasts during the year which they kept holy. The early Christians called the first day of the week the Lord's day, and named the others, except Saturday, the first ferial, the second ferial, etc., which was confirmed by Pope Silvester.[3] The word ferial means to be free, for the clergy are always free to devote their time to the service of the Lord.[4] A ferial comes when there is no feast celebrated, or no octave, or the Office of the Virgin on Saturday.[5] The ferials are divided into two classes— major and minor ferials. The major offices are either said or at least a remembrance must be made of them. They are the ferials of Advent, Lent, Quatre Tenses, and some of the Rogation days.[6] All the other ferials are minor. The eves of the great feasts are like ferials. The eves are to prepare the people, by fasting and prayer, for the worthy celebration of the following feast. The Eves come from the most ancient times, when the people used to spend the greater part of the night in the churches in prayer and fasting, preparing for the feast. Formerly, on the Eves, all the people fasted, but the obligation was taken away by a decree of Clement XIV.[7] We do not fast on the Eves of Epiphany and Ascension,[8] because they fall in seasons of joy and gladness.

A simple office comes when we celebrate ferial days and on days of little importance. Like the ferials they

---

[1] S. Aug., Epist. xxix. n. 11.   [2] Levit. xxiii.   [3] In Brev. 31 December.   [4] De Herdt S. Lit., vol. 1. n. 23.   [5] Rub. 1.   [6] St. Liguori D. Cærem, Mis., c. v., n. 15, nota 27.   [7] 29 June, 1771.   [8] De Herd, S. Lit., vol. 1, n. 23.

have only one nocturn, and the whole office is made up of the ferial and of the office of the feast celebrated.[1]

The semi-double stands, as it were, half way between the simple and the double. Many of the Sundays and the days within octaves are of this class. They are celebrated with more solemnity than the lower feasts.

The double is the next class of feasts above the semi-double. They are called double, because of their higher dignity. Most of the feasts of the saints are of this class. The feasts of greater importance are named major doubles.

The doubles of the second class belong to many feasts of importance, as New Year's, Feast of the Holy Name, and many of the feasts of our Lord and of his mother.

All the great feasts of the year are doubles of the first class, and they are celebrated with the greatest pomp and grandeur.

The public offices of the Church are regulated by the calendar. The sun regulates the fixed or immovable feasts, which fall each year on the same day of the month; and the moon regulates the changing or movable feasts, which fall on the same day of the week. As the motions of the sun and moon are not regular, but change from time to time, the calendar is the average or mean time of their motions.

In order to understand the matter better, let us go into history before the time of Christ. The moon goes around the earth twelve times in about 354¼ days, while the earth goes around the sun once in a little more than 365 days. The twelve months of moons and the twelve months of the year do not then agree. The twelve months of the Romans made the year of 365 days. Not agreeing with the true year, at length things got so mixed up that, under the pagan priests, who had the regulation of these things, the months of spring once came in the midst of summer.

Meton, of Athens, 439 before Christ, thought that in 19 years the motions of the sun and moon would agree, and he made his calendar according to that; but in these olden times they had no fine instruments to measure time, and soon the time measured by the sun and the time marked by the moon did not agree.

---

[1] De Hert. S. Lit., vol. 2, t. 3, Rub.

Julius Cæsar, 46 before Christ, 708 from the foundation of Rome, aided by the learned astronomer Sosigenes, of Alexandria, added a day to February each fourth year, so as not to disturb the days of the month, but leave them as they were before he had them read bis sexto calends.[1] From that comes our word bissextile, or leap year. But that way was not correct, for it wanted 11 minutes and 9 seconds to make that calendar agree with the true year. That error went on increasing till, at the end of 484 years, the true year marked by the sun was three days ahead of the civil year.

At that time the Catholic Church, following the customs of the Jewish temple, held her feasts according to the time of the moon. They had to know, then, the movements of both the sun and the moon. Among them, as among the Jews, Easter was the chief feast, and on that the other feasts depended. Easter was held by the Jews on the 14th moon nearest the vernal equinox.[2] The early Christians celebrated it at the same time, but not on that day, but the first Sunday following the 14th moon following the vernal equinox, while those who kept it as the Jews were condemned by the Church,[3] because it was not right to celebrate the gladful day of Easter on the 14th moon of March, as on that day our Lord lay dead in the tomb. At that time astronomy not having been as well known as now, the early Christians followed, some the time laid down by St. Hippolitus, others that of Meton.[4] In the year 325 the Council of Nice was called,[5] and decreed three things : that the feast of Easter should be kept on the Sunday following the 14th moon of March, which was followed since the time of the Apostles ;[6] that the moon to guide them in naming the Sunday was never to be either before the 14th or after the 21st of March, the day of the vernal equinox, the year the Council was held, and that the system of Meton was to be followed. Constantine, the Emperor, was present at the Council, and wrote to the absent bishops.[7] From that decree Easter cannot come before the 22d of March nor after the 25th of April.

---

[1] See S. Aug. vol. iii, 240. [2] Exod. xii., Levit. xxiii., Numb. xxviii. [3] Concil. Arl. et Nicae. [4] Zalinger Ap. Hist. c. iv. [5] See Fabri Conciones Dom. xvii., p. Pent. con. vii., n. 1. [6] O'Brien, Hist. of the Mass, p. 328, note. [7] Act. Concil. Nocae. St. Ambrose, Lit. ad. Episcopos Emil.

To know the day on which, in future, to keep the feast of Easter, at that time Victor of Aquitain followed Meton's figures for 532 years, and it went on to the year 533. Then Denis the Little adopted it, and from that it spread through all Christian nations. From that time they began to date the years from the birth of Christ. Before they used to date from the foundation of Rome, from the reign of the Emperor Dioclesian, or from the games among the Greeks called the Olympiads.[1]

But the system adopted by Denis was not correct, for he supposed the year to be made up of exactly 365 days and six hours, and after the end of 19 years, the years marked by the sun and those measured by the moon did not agree, so that at the end of 312 years the new moon appeared a day before the time appointed for it in the calendar. Thus the error went on increasing, because of the want of an exact knowledge of astronomy, till, in the seventh century, the vernal equinox, which comes on the 21st of March, fell on the 11th of the same month, and if things went on in that way, at last we would come to celebrate Easter about the time of Christmas.

A reform was needed. It was proposed by Cardinal d'Ailly. Gerson thought of bringing it before the Council of Constance. Sixtus IV., with the aid of the astronomer Regiomontan, undertook the correction, but did not finish the matter before his death. Thus the matter stood till it was up in the Council of Trent. Knowing that a matter requiring such close calculations of the movements of the heavenly bodies could not be made in an assembly like a Council, they referred it to the Holy See. In 1581, Pope Gregory XIII, with the help of the most celebrated astronomers of his day, aided especially by Lelins, a Roman doctor, and the learned Jesuit, Clavius, gave the last touch to that important work, and thus formed what is called the Gregorian calendar.

Not wishing to, in any way, go against the decree of the Council of Nice, and to keep to the old customs coming down from the times of the Apostles, the Pontiff declared that Easter would be the first Sunday following the 14th full moon of March, which would be the 21st of that month. He gave orders to take ten days from the

---

[1] Craisson, Dis. sur le Calend, n. 29.

4th to the 15th of the month of October, 1582, because the feasts of that time were of less importance than those of any other part of the year.[1] Thus, by the act of the successor of the Apostle Peter, the only one whose voice would be heard by the world, the errors of the past were wiped out, and to guard against it for the future, he decreed that while the cycles of the other ages would be kept, three leap years in every 400 years should be omitted.

How little people know how much they owe to the Church. The old Egyptians, Chaldeans, Persians and Carthagenians began their year at the autumn equinox, Sept. 22. The Greeks and Romans commenced at the winter solstice, December 22. The early nations of Europe began some on March 1, others on January 1, others on December 25, others again on March 25. In France, March 1 opened the year. Some held that Easter was the right time. At the French revolution they changed to September 22, while at the time of the Byzantine empire they began the year on September 1st. Thus, if it were not for the Church, which, at the earliest ages, adopted a fixed time for dating the year, and of the Christian nations being led and taught by her, times and dates would have been so mixed up that it would have brought on a confusion such as the world never saw. It is but one of the many examples of the stubbornness of the hearts of men against the Church, that while all the Catholic nations adopted the Gregorian calendar, for nearly 200 years England refused it.[2] Even to our day Russia refused to receive the calendar of Gregory XIII., because it came from one of the Popes.[3] But last year the Russian government at last adopted the Gregorian calendar, which is now adopted by the whole civilized world. Thus, after so many trials, the Church has given to the world a calendar which enables all nations to have a fixed time from which to date events.

The followers of Mahommed count their days according to the twelve changes of the moon, making their year of 354 days, which not agreeing with the motions of the earth around the sun, sometimes their seasons change from year to year. They count their years from the flight of Mahommed, July 16, 622.

---

[1] Greg. xiii., Bull Inter gravissimas. [2] England adopted the new style by Act of Parliament, in 1752. [3] O'Brien, Hist. of the Mass, p. 351, note.

The calendar regulates the public offices of the Church. The age of the moon, which is counted from the moment of the new moon, is known by the epact and the golden number. The Dominical letter shows the Sundays. The age of the moon is the number of days from its beginning, or the new moon. The epact is the age of the moon on the first of January each year. Each year, then, has its epact. When the epact of the year is known, it is easy to find out the days of the new moon during the whole year. The solar year, marked by the sun, has 365 days; while the lunar year, marked by the moon, has only 354 days, being 11 days shorter than the other. If both the solar and lunar years begin on the first of January, there will be no difference in days that year; but the next year the lunar year will be 11 days behind the solar year, and 11 will be the epact. The following year the epact will be 22, and the third 33; but as there are 30 days in the month, the epact will be 3. Meton saw that after a period of 19 years the new moons would come again to agree with the times marked by the sun, and the Greeks, admiring that discovery, marked these dates with letters of gold. From that came the golden numbers. The golden numbers were very useful to the people of Athens, for they regulated their feasts by the changes of the moon.[1] One of the columns of the calendar has the seven first letters of the alphabet repeated a great number of times. They show the days of the week, and the Dominical letter tells the Sundays, for the days of the week do not always fall on the same day of the month. The Church also uses the letters of the alphabet to show the age of the moon in reading the Martyrology, and in the calendar to show the Sundays.

After 28 years the Dominical letters will succeed one another in the same way as before, and the days of the week will fall on the same dates. That is called the solar cycle. There is also another cycle used in Rome, called the cycle of indiction. These three cycles, the solar, lunar, and the cycle of indiction, form a period of 7,980 years, called the Julian period. Going back, they consider it to begin in 4,713 before Christ. No two years in that whole time can have the same numbers in the solar

---

[1] Cosmographie par L'Abbe Menuge, n. 181.

cycle, the lunar cycle, or the cycle of indiction; consequently, when we know the rank of any year in each of these three cycles, we know its place in the Julian period. There is a little book printed each year called the Ordo, which tells the clergy what offices and masses they are to say each day in the year; so it is not necessary for each one to arrange the feasts for himself.

V.—THE BIBLE AND THE YEAR.

During the year the Offices and the Masses are filled with parts of the Holy Bible. The word Bible comes from the Greek, and means a book, for it is the Book of all Books, because it contains the revelation made by God to man. In the fourth century, when St. Chrysostom, the Greek for golden tongued, was preaching his wonderful sermons and explaining the Word of God contained in the Holy Book to the people of the Byzantine empire, he called it The Book, in Greek, Bible. From that comes its name. Before that time it was called the Scriptures, that is, from the Latin, meaning the Writings, for of all writings it is the highest and the most sublime. It is called the Holy Bible, or Scriptures, for it contains the holy things revealed by God to the human race. It is called the Bible, not the Bibles, for, although there are many books in it written by many different persons, yet they all relate to one and the same thing—the salvation of the human race, and they were written by one and the same Person, the Holy Spirit. It is divided into two parts: the Old and New Testaments. The word Testament comes from the Latin,[1] and means the last will and testament of the dying, by which he leaves his goods and property to his heirs.[2] Thus, Moses, before his death upon the Mount, left the five books he wrote to the Hebrews as to his heirs, and our Lord, of whom Moses was but a shadowy figure, before his death made us the heirs of his kingdom by the New Testament. Again, Testament, in the old Hebrew tongue, signifies an agreement, for in these two Holy Testaments are found the agreement formed between God and man, so that we know that if we serve Him here on earth we will by his promise enjoy Him in heaven, for that is what He

---

[1] See S. Aug. Locut, De Gen. l. 1, n. 46.   [2] S. Aug. En. in Ps. lxxxii, n. vi.

promises us in his Testaments in the Bible. Thus, God told Moses to "anoint the tabernacle of the testimony and the ark of the testament,"[1] and our Saviour, the night before his death, said, "This is the blood of the new testament which shall be shed for many unto the remission of sins."[2] Therefore, the writings of the Old Testament are called the Old Testament, while the writings of the New Testament are called the New Testament.[3] As when a man is about to make his last will and testament he names his heirs, makes his will, calls the witnesses and signs the paper. Thus did God when He made the Hebrews the heirs of the promised land. He made his will, that is, the five first books of the Old Testament. He pointed out his heirs, the children of Israel; He called his witnesses, Moses and Aaron. Thus was the Old Testament made by God in the days of the miracles worked by the hand of God in the calling of his chosen people from the land of Egypt.[4] Thus did Christ when He made the Gentiles the heirs of heaven. He made his will the four Gospels; He pointed out his heirs, all the Gentiles of the world; He called his witnesses, the Apostles.[5] Thus was the New Testament made in the days of the miracles of the Son of God, in the calling of the human race from this world to our home beyond the skies. It is again called the Old Testament, because in it was promised the old land of Canaan, for the Lord spoke, and said, "I am come down to deliver them out of the hands of the Egyptians, and to bring them . . . . into a land that floweth with milk and honey."[6] That land was but a figure of that other land, that other home in heaven, "that eye hath not seen, nor ear heard, neither hath it entered into the heart of man, what things God hath prepared for them that love him."[7] It is called the Old Testament, for it was given to purge the old man[8] of sin into the new man of innocence. It was given to the old man born of Adam to prepare him to be the new man born of Christ. "To put off . . . the old man who is corrupted . . . . and put on the new man who, according to God, is created in justice and holiness of truth."[9] It is called

---

[1] Exod. xxx. 26. [2] Matt. xxvi. 28. [3] De consec. dist. 4. *sicut in sacras.* [4] S. Aug. L. De Sp. et List, n. 40. [5] S. Aug. De Gestis Pelag, n. xiv. [6] Exod. iii. 8. [7] 1 Cor. ii. 9. [8] S. Aug. Contra ii., Epist. Pelag., n. 13. [9] Eph. iv. 22-24.

the Old as compared to the New,[1] for the Old was to pass away and the New to take its place; "the old things are passed away, behold all things are made new."[2]

It is called the New Testament, for in it we are told of the new things in heaven promised to the servants of God.[3] It is called the New, for since it was made by our Lord, man becomes, as it were, a new creature by his grace. It is called the New, for when man makes a will or his last testament, and then makes another, the last is the new will and the old is useless; the last remains and is confirmed by his death.[4] Thus the Old Testament is gone and the New is confirmed by the death of our Lord. As the Old was confirmed and fulfilled by his coming, the new was made to last forever; for that it is called "the new and everlasting testament,"[5] for it is the last to the end of time. All this is given in the words of the Apostles, "and therefore he is the mediator of the New Testament, that by the means of his death for the redemption of those transgressions, which were under the former testament, they that are called may receive the promise of eternal inheritance, for where there is a testament the death of the testator must of necessity come in, for a testament is of force after men are dead."[6] But there is but one Testament, and the Old was but a figure and a preparation for the New, for "all happened to them in figures."[7]

In the services and the Offices of the Church during the year, from the very beginning of our religion, from the days of the Apostles, they took many parts of the Bible and composed the Masses and the Offices with portions of that holy Book. In the first ages there were many translations of the Bible into the various languages of that early time, but of all these none was more celebrated or more widely known than the Septuagint. It was translated from the Hebrew into Greek by the seventy-two elders[8] under Ptolemy Philadelphus, King of Egypt, the foster father of the learning of ancient Alexandria, 277 years before Christ. Under him and in his kingdom, lived the most distinguished and learned men of that early age. That translation of the Old Testament, made for

---

[1] S. Aug. c. 11, Ep. Pelag. l. iii., n. 13. [2] 2 Cor. v. 17. [3] S. Aug. L. De Sp. et List, n. 39. [4] Extrn De Celeb. Mis. *Cum Marthae*, S. Cae. [5] Can. Mis. Verb. Con. [6] Heb. ix. 15, 16, 17. [7] 1 Cor. x. 6. [8] S. Aug. De Civitate Dei, l., xviii., n. xliii. et lviii., c. xi.

the Jews of Egypt in the days of the rising republic of
Rome, was made by a pagan king ; it was translated into
Greek, as it were, by the hand of God, that that Greek
tongue, the language then of the learned of these days—
that the Bible might be spread through the Gentile
nations—might become a way of preparing them for the
gospel of Christ, who used this version when he preached
on the hills[1] of Judea, and soon after the time[2] of our
Lord[3] it was scattered through the world by the preaching of the Apostles. The word Gospel comes from two
old Saxon words, good spell, the good tidings, and signifies the good tidings of our redemption.[4]

From the time when St. Peter brought the Latin rite
to Rome, they used the Latin version in the services of
the Church, but by the work of those who copied it, toward the beginning of the fourth century, it had changed
a little. St. Jerome, under the direction of Pope Damasus, corrected the old Latin Bible and made it agree with
the Septuagint.[5] Soon it became so popular among the
people as to be called the Vulgate, the Latin for common.
It was approved by Pope Damasus. It was ordered to
be sung in the Church by Pope Gregory, and since that
time it has been the authorized version of the Bible.
The Old Testament was translated into English at Rheims
(1582), and the New at Douay (1609–10). This has since
been known as the English version of the Vulgate. Thus
the Latin Vulgate, revised by St. Jerome, is the Bible of
the Church, while a translation of it is used by the people who speak the English language.

During Advent we read at mass the Epistle of St. Paul
to the Romans, where he speaks of the coming of our
Lord; where he tells them of their salvation, and that
their hour has come;[6] where he speaks of the calling of
the nations of the earth to the Church of God;[7] where he
writes to them to rejoice on the Lord for their redemption,[8] and where he lays down before them the mysteries
of the priesthood, as the ministers of the Lord, dispensing
to the people the sacraments of the Church.[9]

During Advent we read in the broviary the prophecy of
the great Isaias, who, of all the men of the ancient world

---

[1] O'Brien, Hist of the Mass. p. 203. [2] Dixon, Introduc. to the Scriptures, p. 98. [3] Valt. Prolog. c. 11. [4] Cath. Friends, vol. III., p. 470. [5] S. Aug. De Civ. Dei, l. xviii., n. xliii. [6] Rom. xii. [7] Rom. xiv. [8] Rom. iv. [9] Rom. iv.

which the hand of God raised up to foretell the coming of
the Son of God, foretold in clearest language the life of
our Saviour. We begin with the vision of Isaias, the son
of Amos, where he calls the heavens and the earth to witness that the Lord hath spoken. He reproves the Jews
for their sins.[1] He tells them of the time to come when
the rod shall go forth from the root of Jesse, when the
flower from his root shall ascend, when the sevenfold
power of the Holy Spirit shall dwell upon him, and of
the power and of the greatness of his coming kingdom.[2]
He speaks to the Jews of the future kingdom of the Lord,
of His holy Church guarding truth and keeping peace, of
the synagogue rejected and the Gentile nations chosen in
its place, and of the Holy Spirit, through the pastors of
the Church, granting peace, justice and mercy to the people of the earth.[3] He speaks of the deserts and of the
solitudes blooming and blossoming like the rose. He
foretells the beauties and the grandeurs of that holy
Church of God spread through the earth, and under the
figures of the wild beasts of the forest, he tells of the
taming of the wild passions of men by the grace of the
Saviour, poured into the hearts of men by the sacraments.[4]

During the Christmas holidays we read still the prophecy of Isaias, telling of the birth of our Saviour,[5]
telling the people of God to be consoled, for their Lord
will come to them, foretelling the words of the Baptist
in the wilderness, crying out to "prepare the way of the
Lord,"[6] telling the soul of man under the figure of Sion
and of Jerusalem, to rise from sin and sorrow, and to put
on the garments of joy, for the Saviour was to come.
From the Christmas holidays to Septuagesima Sunday,
we read the epistles of St. Paul, where the Apostle lays
down the doctrine of the salvation of the race by the
death of the Redeemer, for by the Church this time is
set apart to the mysteries of the birth of our Lord. From
Septuagesima Sunday to Lent we read the book of Genesis, because during this time of the year the Church
celebrates and brings before the minds of men the creation of the world from nothing by the almighty hand of
God. To bring before the minds of the people the work
of the creation, we read that part of the Bible where the

---

[1] Isa. i.   [2] Isa. ii.   [3] Isa. xxvi.   [4] Isa. xxxv.   [5] Isa. ix.   [6] Isa. xl. 3.

creation is told, and where the story of the fall of our first parents is given. In Lent we read those parts of the Old Testament where it speaks of that remarkable way in which God prepared the Jews for the coming of His Son. As we come toward the end of Lent, the saddest and the most heartrending parts of the prophet Jeremias are given, where he prophesies of the sufferings and of the death of our Lord. We take those parts of the Holy Scriptures where penance and fasting are given, so that they may be an example to us in order to prepare us by fasting, for the coming joys of the Easter time. During the Paschal time, from Easter to Pentecost, the Church celebrates the glories of the risen Son of God, and she takes the most joyful parts of the Bible, and in her services and in her rites and ceremonies, she tells of the everlasting and transcendent splendors of the Crucified, passing from the tomb to the happiness of the other world, and of his ascending from earth to heaven. The early history of the Catholic Church is read each year,[1] as given in the Acts of the Apostles. The glories of heaven awaiting us beyond the skies are given as seen by St. John in the Apocalypse, while from Pentecost to Advent we read the Books of Kings, the Parables of Solomon, the Books of Ecclesiastes and of Ecclesiasticus, and the Books of the Maccabees, so that the whole or part of every book in the Bible is read in the Office of the Breviary during the Ecclesiastical year.

In the catacombs, where the persecutions of the pagans drove the first Christians from the light of heaven to the bowels of the earth, they held their services from day to day over the different tombs of the Apostles or the martyrs. With solemn procession they marched from their hiding places to the crypt, where rested the remains of those who gave their lives for the love of their Lord, and on the martyrs' tombs they offered up the sacrifice of the Mass. When by the edict of Constantine the Catholics were freed from the persecutions of paganism, they kept that custom, and each Sunday, each feast, each fast, and on days of penance they walked to the Church, where the Mass was to be said. By the lapse of time that ancient habit was dying out, till restored by command

---

[1] S. Ang., vol. xlv., 474.

of Gregory the Great.[1]　Now when the Church is free, when her head is not hindered by the tools of the gates of darkness, these processions are carried out with great pomp and solemnity, in the 365 churches of Rome.　Most of them have a station, where the mass of the different days are offered, while on the principal feasts of the cycle of the year the services are celebrated in the great Basilicas of the Eternal City.　Such is the meaning of the stations of the masses during the year, as named in the Missal, or mass book.

Let us then see how the Church, founded by Christ and guided by the Spirit of God, took the year and set apart its times, its seasons, and its days to the worship of the Lord.　The year is divided into four seasons : winter, in which nature sleeps and life appears to have gone from the earth ;[2] spring, in which the seeds are sown and new life springs forth ; summer, in which all things are in the strength and vigor of their growth; and fall, in which the harvest is gathered and the treasures of earth are laid away.　Thus, the year which comes and goes tells us of the great year of this world, beginning at the creation and measured by four seasons, lasting till the end of time.

Winter recalls to us the time when grace was lost to the human race; of the epoch from Adam to Moses, when the peoples and the nations of the earth were given to idolatry; when there was "none that doeth good ; no, not one."[3]　Spring recalls the era of old, when the seeds of the revelation of God were sown in the human heart; of the time from Moses to the birth of Christ, when man was taught by the mouths of the inspired prophets, who came to scatter the seeds of prophecy in the spring time of our holy religion, when the God of the Old Testament told the children of Israel, "Hear, O Israel,　.　.　.　.
thou shalt love the Lord thy God with thy whole heart, and with thy whole soul, and with thy whole strength,"[4] to the time when all had been prepared for the coming of the Lord.　The summer figures the present age from the coming of the Saviour to the end of the world, when the grace of God reigns in the heart of man in all its strength ; when the Church, like summer beauties, covers the earth;

---

[1] Gueranger l'Avent, p. 118, note.　[2] S. Aug. Sermo. xxxvi in Prov. n. iv.　[3] Psalm xlii. 8.　[4] Deut. vi. 4, 5.

when the deserts and the wilderness bloom and blossom
like the rose ; when the souls of men are led on to God
by the teachings of the Church. Fall recalls to our
minds the last days of the world, when the great harvest
of souls will be gathered into the granaries of God, and
the treasuries emptied by the fall of the angels will be
filled, and at last the beings made to praise him will
stand before his throne and sing forever the glories of
our God in the endless ages of eternity.

In the winter time of the human race, by the sin of
Adam, the blooming flowers of faith, hope and charity
were frozen up by the coldness of infidelity; in the spring
time of the race the prophets sowed the seeds of the
revelation ; in the summer time the Church obtains her
highest and her fullest growth ; in the fall, the fruits of
holy souls will be gathered into the heavens of the Lord.
Thus, in the times of the Apostles, they took the seasons
of the year to teach, by figures, symbols and ceremonies,
the work of the Saviour and the salvation of the race.

The winter of the human race, when man turned from
God, from the fall of Adam to the call of Moses, is represented by the rites and the ceremonies of the Church ;
from Septuagesima Sunday to Easter, when the altars,
the clergy and the sanctuary put on their violet colors,
the sign of penance ; when the gladsome hymns of the
"Glory be to God in the highest," and the "Thee, O
God, we praise," give place to tones of sorrow, to tell of
the time of sorrow for our sins. Then all is hushed but
the solemn tones of the Masses calling down forgiveness
for our sins, and for the sins of our race in the days of the
winter of the world. During the Paschal Season, from
Easter to Trinity Sunday, the Church is clothed in all
the gorgeous grandeurs the mind of man conceives, the
organ peals forth its joyful tones, the hymns and songs
of praise are multiplied and alleluias are oft repeated ;
the clergy clothe themselves with vestments of gold ; the
altars pour forth their perfumes of flowers ; the sanctuaries are brilliant with the lights of the candles ; the
building breathes of joyousness and happiness ; hymns
and canticles re-echo from the vaulted roofs and recesses
of our great cathedrals. The Church rejoices. We are
celebrating and recalling to the minds of men the time
when the Saviour came and lived upon our earth, when

he redeemed us, and when he taught us the way to heaven. From Trinity Sunday to Advent, the Church celebrates the summer of the race, when the Christian religion, in all its strength, beauty, vigor and power is spread throughout the world, calling the nations to her saving bosom.[1] From Advent to Christmas, we recall the signs and the wonders foretold to come to pass at the end of the world; when the moon shall be darkened and the sun refuse to shed its light; when the heavens will be rolled up and the stars shall fall from heaven, and when the last scene of the death of the world will tell all men of the coming of the Son of God, foretold by the prophets spoken of by our Lord.[2]

The vestments worn by the clergy tell their story to the people,[3] and by their shape and by their color teach their lessons.[4] White has always been the color of innocence and of purity.[5] For that reason it is used on all the feasts of our Lord, for who was purer or more innocent than he?[6] It is worn on all the feasts of the Virgin, for who was purer or more beautiful than she? It is seen in the vestments of the clergy on all feasts of the saints and virgins, to teach the people to practice their innocence and their purity, and these lessons taught the people by the Church is so strong, that rarely was any other color used but white before the sixth century.[7] Red is the color of fortitude and of martyrdom.[8] For that reason it is used at Pentecost to recall the red fiery tongues in which the Holy Ghost came down upon the Apostles. It is worn on the feasts of the Passion of our Lord, for he was the greatest martyr, and on feasts of the Apostles and of the martyrs in remembrance of the way they died martyrs for our holy religion.[9] Green is the color of hope[10] and of youth. For that reason it is used from the octave of Epiphany to Septuagesima Sunday,[11] as a symbol of the hope of the redemption soon to be celebrated in Holy Week. Black is the color of darkness and of death. For that reason the Church and the clergy are clothed in black in the services of Good Friday,[12]

<hr>

[1] Is. xi. [2] Is. xxxiv.; Matth. xxiv.; Mark xiii.; Luke xxi. [3] See Bish. Moran, Discipline of the Early Irish Church. [4] El Porqué de Todas las Céremonias de la Iglesia, Cap xii. [5] O'Brien. Hist. of the Mass, p. 63. [6] El Porque de las Ceremonias, c. xii., Blanco. [7] Kozma, 78. [8] O'Brien, Hist. of the Mass, p. 63. [9] Ibiden. [10] El Porque de las Ceremonias, c. xii. [11] El Porque, Ibiden. [12] El Porque de las Ceremonias, c. xii., Negro.

in memory of the darkness which covered the earth at the death of our Lord.[1] It is used also at funerals, as a figure of the Church mourning for the dead. From the Church, in ages past, the people learned to put on black, when mourning for their dead. Violet is the color of fasting and of penance.[2] For that reason it is used in the Advent, Septuagesima and Lenten seasons, and at the Quater Tenses, at all processions, except that of the Blessed Sacrament. It is used on the feast of the Holy Innocents,[3] on account of the lamentations of sorrow heard in Bethlehem, when the little children were put to death by Herod.[4] When their feast falls on Sunday the vestments are red, and on the octave of the feast, for now the lamentations have ceased and the octave signifies the glory of Heaven,[5] and the red symbolizes their martyrdom.

As violet is the color of fasting and of penance, it is the color of the dalmatic and of the tunic of the deacon and sub-deacon, in Advent and Lent, on days of fasting, except the eves of the saints' days, on the third Sunday of Advent, the fourth Sunday of Lent, Christmas Eve, Holy Saturday, and the blessing of the Paschal candle. Violet is used also at masses of the Quater Tenses of Pentecost at the blessing of the candles, during the procession at the feast of the Purification of the Blessed Virgin; at the blessing of the ashes on Ash Wednesday, and of the palms on Palm Sunday.[6]

As the dalmatic and the tunic are vestments of solemnity and of joy, the deacon and sub-deacon should not use them on days of fasting and of penance,[7] except on the days given above. But they may be used on Holy Thursday and on the eve of Pentecost, because folded vestments are not used, except violet and black. In cathedrals and in large churches, as colleges, monasteries and important parish churches, on the days when the dalmatic and tunic are not allowed, the deacon and sub-deacon use the folded vestments, which are of the same form and color of those of the celebrant, but they are folded or rolled up in front before the breast and fastened

---

[1] O'Brien, Hist. of the Mass, p. 63. [2] El Porque de las Ceremonias, c. xii, Morado. [3] El Porque de las Ceremonias, Morado. [4] Math. ii. [5] De Hert, S. Lit. Prax. i., p. 190 ; Bouvry, Rub. ii. 199. [6] Rub. Mis. XIX De Qual. Par. n. 6. [7] See El Porque de as Ceremonias, c. xiv., Dalmatica.

with pins. They are thus fastened because of the customs of olden times, when the vestments covered the
whole body, they tied them up so as not to be in the way
of their hands when ministering at the altar, and we tie
them up as the remains of these old customs. The deacon
and subdeacon laid aside their folded vestments, when
singing the Epistle and the Gospel, to show that to them
does not belong, by right of their order, the power of
preaching the Word of God, but to the celebrant.[1] Formerly the chasuble was worn by all the clergy, and was
their common dress. The deacon and the subdeacon, in
the cathedrals and other large churches, have continued
that habit during Advent, Lent, and times of penance.
In its first form, covering the whole body, the chasuble
hindered the free use of the arms, and for that reason
they tied it up in front on their breasts while serving at
the altar. The deacon, being the most active during
Mass, used to take off his chasuble, and folding it in the
form of a sash, placed it on his left shoulder, as soldiers
sometimes do with their cloaks. Thus, little by little the
deacons became accustomed to use large stoles in place
of their chasubles, folded across their left shoulders.[2]
Formerly the deacon folded his chasuble, and placing it
on his left shoulder, tied it under his right arm, like a
diaconal stole. Now, according to the rules, the deacon
does not do so, but laying it aside, he takes in its place a
stole longer than the one commonly used, and places it
over the one he has on. That large stole takes the place
of the chasuble folded and tied across his shoulder. It
has, therefore, no crosses or fringes, and is not enlarged
at the ends. Such are the explanations of the meanings
and the histories of the folded dalmatic and tunic of the
deacon and subdeacon.

---

[1] De Herdt S. Lityrgias Prax. t. I., p. I., tit. xix., n. 50, De Qual, Par. [2] De Conny,
Ceremon. de l'Eglise, p. 71.

The Holy Chapel of the Palace, Paris.

REASONS RELATING TO THE ADVENT SEASON.

The word Advent comes from the Latin and means the coming, and well, for it tells of the time set apart by the church to prepare for the coming of our Lord.[1] We know not when Advent was established.[2] It goes back till its history is lost[3] in the silence of the Apostolic times. Some writers say[4] that it was instituted by St. Peter himself,[5] others by Pope Gregory the Great.[6] It appears to have been celebrated in Rome from the beginning of the Church. As the Jews were taught by John Baptist in the desert, "Prepare ye the way of the Lord, make straight His paths," "preaching the baptism of penance unto the remission of sins,"[7] thus Advent is to prepare the world for his coming at Christmas. Advent began in the western church, for it appears that the time of holding it was laid down only after Christmas was fixed for the 25th of December. That it was held in the church from the earliest ages all monuments of antiquity teach. In the fifth century it was customary to assemble the people, and by sermons and services prepare them for Christmas, as can be seen by the sermons of SS., Maxim of Toul, Ambrose of Milan, Augustin of Hippo, and Cæsar of Arls, besides of many of the early saints, while the bishops of the Carlovingian kingdom told Charles the Bald that he must not take the people from the churches during the time of Advent or Lent, under the excuse of State matters or the necessity of war." St. Gregory of Tours says that S. Perpetuus, one of his predecessors,[9] ordered that the faithful of his diocese should fast three times a week, from St. Martin's day till Christmas.[10] An ancient council[11] commanded the people and the

---

[1] Praec. Eccl. Fest., § 1. [2] Durandus, Rationale Div. L. vi. n. 10. [3] Gueranger, L'Aannee Lit. L'Avent. p. 7. [4] El Porque de las Ceremonias, c. xxx., Del Adviento, etc. [5] Benedic. XIV. Inst. 11, n. 7. [6] Durand . Rational. Div. L. vi. c. 11, n. 2, [7] Mark i., 3, 4. [8] Capit. of Charles the Bald. [9] About 480. [10] Hist. des Francs. [11] Concil Macon. in 582.

clergy to fast mondays, wednesdays and fridays, from St. Martin's day till Christmas, and that the Holy Sacrifice should be celebrated with the same solemnity as during Lent. Another council[1] made a law that monks should fast from the first of December to Christmas, while Rhaban Mur,[2] and many writers of that early age leave no doubt that the custom of keeping Advent comes down from the most ancient times. The people first kept an Advent of forty days, till in after years they shortened it to four weeks. Thus, we read of its being kept in England,[3] in Italy,[4] in Germany, Spain, etc.[5] The first official act of a Pope shortening Advent to four weeks is found in the letters of Nicholas I.[6] Although St. Peter of Damien and St. Louis of France, in after years, kept it for forty days, they did it only through devotion.

In the beginning of the Church they were to fast both from food and to fast from meat during Advent. But the people, by the lapse of ages, losing their fervor, the Church released them from the obligation of fasting from food, but continued to command the fast from meat, while she relaxed in nothing regarding the clergy.[7] From the beginning of the church, as in our day, every bishop being free to make rules regulating these matters in his diocese, the discipline was not the same everywhere regarding Advent, but we know from the olden monuments of that time that it was kept with severe rigor by the whole Papal Court,[8] and by the people of France,[9] even to the thirteenth century. Laxer and more relax became the people, so that Urban V.[10] to prevent the custom of keeping Advent being completely lost, commanded the clergy of his Court to fast from meat, saying nothing of fasting from food. In after ages St. Charles of Borromeo tried to renew the old custom among the people of the diocese of Milan, directing the parish priests to exhort their people to receive Holy Communion, at least on the Sundays of Advent and of Lent.[11] Benedict XIV., when archbishop of Bologna, taught the people of his diocese the high idea they should have of the holy time of Advent, and telling them that it was not only a time for penance

---

[1] Concil. VI Tour. held in 567. [2] L. De Inst. Cler. [3] Venerable Bede. [4] Astophus, king of the Lombards in 753. [5] Dom. Martine De Ant. Rit. Eccl. [6] Lit. ad Bulg. [7] Concilia Seling. 1122; Avr. 1172; Salisbury 1281, etc. [8] Innocent III, Lit. ad Epis. Bra. [9] Durand., Rationale Div. 1. vi. c. 11. [10] In 1362. [11] Concil. IV.

among the clergy and in the monasteries, but also for the people,[1] that they might prepare themselves for the coming of their Lord in the feasts of Christmas.

In the Greek Church they keep Advent for forty days, from the 14th of November, the feast of St. Philip, to Christmas, all that time eating neither meat, butter, eggs or milk, which they never eat in Lent. They fast from food seven days during the course of their Advent, which they call St. Philip's Lent. Following their own rules, they say no Mass of the pre-sanctified, as in Lent, but from the 14th of November to the nearest Sunday to Christmas in their masses and in their offices there are many words and prayers relating to the birth of Christ, to the Maternity of Mary, to the stable of Bethlehem and to the coming of our Lord; showing that although they separated from us in the remote ages, still they have kept their services formed by the Apostles and known by the name of the Greek Rite, and that they prepare their people for the coming of our Lord by the special ceremonies and rites of their church.

The Franco-Roman Missal gives a Latin hymn, composed in the eleventh century, relating to the birth of Christ, while the Ambrosial Missal has a special prayer for the second Sunday of Advent. The same may be seen[2] in the hymn book of Tomasi,[3] and in the Mozarabic Missal with its beautiful hymns and prayers, in the Gallican Missal with its sweetly sounding collects,[4] in the Gallican Sacramentary with its prayers for Christmas, in the Anthology of the Greeks with its beautiful hymns, in the Ambrosian Liturgy with the prayers for the weeks of Advent, in the Mozarabic Breviary with its offices of Advent, in Cluny's Missal with its hymns to the Virgin,[5] in the hymns and the prayers composed by Peter of Damien, in all the monuments of these ancient times, in these books of Liturgy, old and venerable, we find the Offices and the Masses of Advent to be preparations for the coming of our Lord in the holidays of Christmas.

In the following pages, we will not go into the other Rites of the Church, or treat of these services of other churches, or of these ceremonies which have come down from the

---

[1] Inst. Eccl.   [2] In Ad. Dom.   [3] Composed in the ninth century.   [4] In Ad. Dom.
[5] Ed. of 1528.

times of the remote ages, but we will give the people the meaning of the grand and striking Liturgies of the Latin Rite, such as have been used by the western branch of the Catholic Church.

The ceremonies and the services of our Church, such as we have them to-day, appear to have been reformed by Pope Gregory the Great,[1] who pointed out the form to be used by those who followed the Latin Rite. He sanctioned the custom of fasting during Advent, but left to the bishops the manner of putting the law in practice. We see by the writers of the ninth and tenth centuries[2] that where the Latin Rite was carried out they had four weeks of Advent, and in the fourth came the happy day of Christmas, except when it falls on Sunday.[3] St. Peter, the first Pope, therefore marked out three weeks before Christmas in which to prepare for the coming of our Lord, and the fourth week is never ended, for the happy day of Christ's birth falls within the last week. All this to signify the fourfold coming of the Saviour of the world when he was born at Bethlehem,[4] when he comes in Holy Communion,[5] when he comes at each one's death, and when he will come at last to judge the world. The first three weeks are to prepare for his first three comings,[6] but the fourth week is never ended, for his fourth coming is to bring to the good and to the holy the glory of heaven, which for them will never end. First, he came in the form of man and took our flesh, as the Apostle says: "And the Word was made flesh and dwelt among us."[7] Secondly, he comes into the heart of man, as the Gospel says: "If any one love me he will keep my word, and my Father will love him, and we will come to him and will make our abode with him."[8] Thirdly, he comes at our death, of which he says: "Blessed are those servants whom the Lord when he cometh shall find watching."[9] Fourthly, he will come at the last day[10] to judge the world, of which he says: "They shall see the son of man coming in the clouds of heaven with much power and majesty."[11] The first time he came with the sweetness of a

---

[1] Sacra. St. Greg., El Porque de las Ceremonias, c. xxx. [2] Pope Nicholas I. Bernon Tathier, etc. [3] L'Anne Liturgique par D. P. Gueranger L'Avent, Hist. de L'Av. [4] 441, etc. [5] S. Aug. vol. vii., 197. [6] El Porque de las Ceremonias, c. xxx. [7] John i., 14. [8] John xiv., 23. [9] Luke xii., 37. [10] S. Thomas, P. iii., q. 1, 6 ad 3, etc. [11] Math. xxiv., 30.

child, the second with the love of a God, the third with rewards for each, and the fourth time with the awful majesty of an eternal Judge. His first coming was to deliver the world from the slavery of the devil, the second is to strengthen the soul of man with his Body and his Blood, his third is to take his servants to heaven, while his fourth will be to judge the good and bad, and to show the everlasting justice which appears not now. Thus from the very beginning that holy Church, founded by the Son of God and scattered through the world by the preaching of the Apostles, took the four weeks before the time of Christmas and set them apart to prepare the people for these four comings of the Lord.

For four thousand years the world waited for the coming of the Son of God, and to keep before the minds of men those times of waiting, the Church set apart these four weeks before Christmas to typify these four great periods of time, when God, in heaven, prepared mankind for the coming of his Son. There were four kinds of men who prepared the world for the coming of our Lord. The first were those who lived from Adam to Moses ; the patriarchs who, guided by the law of reason, kept the faith revealed to the race in the garden of Paradise ; the second were those who lived from Moses to David, who, guided by the law given to the Hebrews, in the ceremonies and the services of the temple, prefigured the coming of our Lord ; the third were the prophets, who, living in the days of the Old Testament, were inspired by the Holy Spirit to foretell the times, the days and the manner of his coming ;[1] the fourth were those who, living in the times of Christ, were guided by the words of our Lord himself to receive him as their Saviour, and spread his holy Church throughout the world. The first week, therefore, relates to the Patriarchs, the second to the Priests, the third to the Prophets, and the fourth to the Apostles. As God in the beginning of the world prepared the human race for the coming of his Son, thus the Church prepares the people to receive him; and for ever to keep before the mind of man his coming, she formed the rites and the services of the holy time of Advent to renew each year his coming and his birth.

---

[1] El Porque de las Ceremonias, c. xxx.

Alas! look at the world to-day and see how it needs the coming of the Lord : no Christian government on the earth ; God banished from the laws ; honor no more the best policy ; old age not honored ; youth given up to pleasures ; the sayings of the saints forgotten ; the love of money the god of man ;[1] the banks the great temples where Mammon is adored ; the mind of man turned from the Saviour, and his coming and his works forgotten. Behold how the Church renews each year by the ceremonies and the services of Advent the coming of the Lord![2]

Thus to the end of time the Church renews the years of the waiting of the world for the coming of the Saviour, when the just and the holy ones of the Old Testament waited and prayed for the Advent and the coming of the Desired of the everlasting hills.

Thus in her offices and in her prayers there are no remembrances or suffrages of the saints', for the saints of the Old Testament were not in heaven: they went to that place of happiness and of joy only at the going there of our Lord, on Ascension Thursday, when he opened heaven for them. Her clergy are clothed in violet, the color of fasting and of penance for sin; her altars and her temples wear a sombre hue, for she is waiting for her Lord. The chants and the music sounds no more of joy and of gladness, for she sits in mourning and in sadness. The joyful song of the angelic host, the "Glory be to God in the Highest" is stopped till the midnight Mass of Christmas. The exultant hymn of SS. Augustin and of Ambrose, "Thee, O God, we praise," is no more said in the office.[3] In her ceremonies and her services the Church breathes only of sorrow, of penance, of affliction and of repentance, all to renew in the mind of men the state of the world before the coming of Christ and to prepare the soul for his coming at Christmas. The "Go, the dismissal is at hand" is not said, but in its place "Let us bless the Lord," the remains of the ancient custom when the people waited after the services for the prayers of sorrow and of penance said in Advent when the Masses were ended. The people are

---

[1] Fabri Conciones, vol. 1, Con. 11. p. 111.   [2] M. Le Vicomte Walsh, Tab. Poet. des Fet. Chret., p. 55.   [3] C. de palu. sacra largi L. *Scrinei*, in prin. L. 12.   [4] El Porque de las Ceremonias,c. xxx.

forbidden to marry, for the time of penance, of fasting and of prayer are not to be interfered with or broken by marriage feasts. The people are instructed in the churches and prepared for the holidays by frequently receiving the sacraments. Thus by the inspired hand of the Church in the days of old that time of Advent was taken and set apart as a time of preparation for the coming of our Lord.

The holy Church, our mother, with tears of sorrow, and with works of penance awaits the coming of her founder and her Lord in the first week of Advent, and for that reason the Mass is filled with passages taken from the Prophets and from the Old Testament, who sent up their supplications to the throne of grace, for the coming of their Saviour, and to them the Church adds her desires, and sends her prayers to the ear of God the Eternal Father, who sent his Son to redeem the world, that he may send him again to continue that work of the redemption and save the individuals of the race of Adam. In the second week we wait for the coming of the Lord into the hearts of men in the Holy Eucharist, that he may visit his people, the hierarchy who rule the Church, the people who make the Church, the people who do not practice their religion, the persons who do not belong to the Church, the enemies who oppose her, the pagans and the infidels, and all, that coming he may come, and give to them a new heart and a new mind to know and to serve their Lord and their Redeemer. In the third week the Church looks to the coming of the Lord at the death of each one, when our work is done which he has given to each to do; when at the death-bed scene the dying Christian says to the Lord, "Come, Lord Jesus,"[1] when with the spirits of the blessed saints, the "spirit and the bride say, Come, and she that heareth him say Come."[2] The third week we celebrate the fourth coming of the Lord, when that "day of calamity, that great and awful bitter day" shall end the world, "when God will come to judge the world by fire."[3]

If thus the holy Church passes the time of Advent in preparing for the coming of the Lord in his four-fold visit to his creatures, we must unite ourselves to her and be filled with the same spirit. For the Church is not made

---

[1] Apoc. xxii. 20.   [2] Apoc. xxii. 17.   [3] De Exequiis.

up of the wood and bricks and the stones, which make
the building, but of the bodies and the souls of the
people, for we are the "temple of the Holy Spirit,"[1]
and like living stones and bricks we make the Church,
scattered throughout the world, and each one of us is the
object of the love of God, forming the Church bought by
his blood.

Let us then join our hearts to our Church during the
four weeks of Advent, going back in memory to the four
thousand years of the ancient world before the time of
Christ.   We see they were times when the darkness of
paganism covered the minds of men, the times when
the law of God was far from the children of Adam, the
times when the false gods of the Assyrians were worshipped on the banks of the Euphrates, when the rows of
the winged bulls lined the avenues leading up to the
vast temples of the heathen worshippers of Babylon;
when the grandeurs of ancient Thebes reared its tombs
and its temples on the shores of the Nile, when the ancient
dynasties of the Pharaohs ruled the land of Egypt, when
their dead were embalmed and laid away in the massive
sepulchres and in the pyramids now standing on the
Nile, to the times of the mythology of Athens and Rome,
to the time when the religion of Buddha first rose on
the banks of the Ganges, when they invented the fables
of the Vedas and corrupted the first revelation made to
man in the garden of paradise; when the Druid priests of
the north of Europe were deceiving our forefathers by
the pagan rites of Woden and of Friga, when all nations
were corrupted from the law of God, when the race so
much needed the teachings of the Saviour.   Let us go
back to that olden time and see if there was one who
worshipped God in spirit and in truth, and history will say
no, not one, but those of the Hebrew race who were kept
from falling like their neighboring nations by the rites
and the services of the tabernacle and the temple, built
by Moses and by Solomon, that by these quaint services
and grand ceremonies of the church of the Israelites the
people of God might keep before their eyes the coming
and the death of their Messiah and their Lord.   Thus we
see how man must keep before his mind in the services of
our Church, the first coming of the Saviour.

---

[1] 1 Cor. vi. 19.

Again let us join our hearts to our Church during the four weeks of Advent, going into the hearts of men and seeing how they need the coming of their Lord in Holy Communion. We see the mind of man turned from God, the life of the soul dead by sin, the Holy Spirit fled from the heart, man made for God worshipping the world, his blood like a poisonous stream flowing in his veins, temptations dwelling in his members, his mind poisoned with error, his will rebelling against the restraint of his superiors, the people and their rulers rejecting the church, heresies multiplying, infidelity gaining every day, and those nations of the north of Europe, once the fairest parts of the Church, torn from her motherly bosom and lashed with the storms of every doctrine. We see the members of the Church grown cold in their religion, their children growing up without instruction and families falling away, all because the people do not live up to their Church and go frequently to the sacraments. Behold how the world wants the Lord to come in Holy Communion and fill the hearts and the souls of his people with the life of himself, and live in them the life which is beyond the strength of nature.

Yet again let us unite ourselves to the Church in this holy time of Advent, and let us see how men die. We see what millions of men never heard of the Gospel, what nations unconverted, what races lost, what numbers of people upon their bed of death depart from this world like so many animals, no fear of the future, no thought of eternity, no dread of hell, no sorrow for the past, no repentance for wickedness, no faith in the rewards of heaven, no desire to escape the future punishments; they die like beasts. Thus as the waters of the rivers rolling on to be buried in the ocean, we are drifting onward on the waves of time, to be buried in the fathomless abyss of eternity, from which we will never return to take our place again upon the earth, and when the Son of God will come to each one at the moment of his death, how many will he find ready and waiting for his coming; how many will have their house in order and the account of their stewardship? Thus the Church prays that when the Lord comes at the moment of the death of her children he may find them ready to receive the rewards awaiting with his glory in the mansions of his bliss.

Still again let us enter into the spirit of the Church, and guided by the prophets of old, inspired by the Spirit of the Lord, and taught by the words of Christ in the Gospels of the Evangelists, let us look to the future, to that time at the death of the world, when in power and in majesty for the fourth time the Lord will come to judge mankind, when he will take his place on Calvary's top and all the races of men will come before his face, when from the burned world as from a mighty tomb the dead shall rise to judgment, when the angels will separate the good from the bad and place them on the right and on the left, and the just will ascend to heaven to enjoy the sight of God forever, and the bad shall be driven into the fire which will never quench, there to burn with everlasting torments as long as God will be God for the sins they committed in the flesh. Such are the thoughts the holy Church places before her children during the time of Advent.

I.—The First Sunday of Advent.

The first Sunday of Advent is the fourth before we celebrate the birth of Christ, and always falls on the nearest Sunday to the feast of St. Andrew.[1] The Church, waiting for the coming of her founder and her Lord, during the whole of this holy Season, says in her services and in her offices, "Come, let us adore the Lord, the coming King."[2] Again we cry out continually, "Drop down dew, ye heavens, from above, let the clouds rain the just: let the earth be opened and bud forth a Saviour,"[3] foretelling the words of the Angel Gabriel to Mary: "The Holy Ghost shall come upon thee, and the power of the most High shall overshadow thee. And therefore also the Holy which shall be born of thee shall be called the Son of God."[4] In the deep figurative language of the Hebrews the work of the Holy Ghost in the mystery of the Incarnation is likened to the shadows cast by the clouds upon the earth. It was the same Holy Ghost, who, in the figure of the cloud upon the mount of Tabor, overshadowed our Lord in the wonders of the Transfigur-

[1] Nov. 30. O'Brien Hist. of the Mass, p. 138, note. [2] Brev. Roman, I.. Dom. Adv. [3] Is. xlv., 8. [4] Luke i., 35.

ation, and he was the cloud which Moses entered on the mount of Sinai at the giving of the law.

The earth which is asked to bud forth the Saviour is the Blessed Virgin, who brought forth the Lord while remaining a Virgin. The earth which is asked to put forth the Saviour is the heart of man, which is asked to open by love and to bring forth the Lord at the Christmas time.

To-day the Station is at the great Church of St. Mary Major, where they guarded from the fourth century the manger in which our Lord was laid when he was wrapped in swaddling clothes at his birth. For that reason this venerable church is sometimes called St. Mary at the Manger. We see the wisdom of choosing this church in which to salute from afar the coming of the Lord in the Divine Birth at Christmas.

In the Offices of the Breviary the Church begins the Prophecy of the great Isaias, who was the greatest of all the men of old, raised up by the Lord to do his mighty works. Of all the prophets, Isaias most clearly foretold the coming of the Lord. From this time till Christmas the words of Isaias, the greatest of Israel's inspired prophets are read. The Offices of the clergy, such as we read in Advent, appears to have been arranged by Pope Gregory the Great,[1] but his was only a work of revision of the Advent part which came down from the most early times, the first revision having been made by St. Jerome in the fourth century.

The whole service of the Church on this Sunday breathes our desires for the coming of our Lord. Every word is like a strong desire of the heart of man, looking for his coming. The last year has closed with the sad history of the destruction of the world, and with the scene of the general judgment as foretold by the prophets and given by our Lord. This Sunday opens the Year. It is the beginning of the year according to the Church, while the civil year begins on the 1st of January. As the time of Christmas draws nearer and nearer our joy and happiness increases. The Church our mother wishes not to disturb our joy towards Christmas by the sad thoughts of the fourth coming of our Lord at the last and general judgment. For that reason we read the

---

[1] Durandus Rationale Div. L. vi., c. iii., n. 2.

Gospel[1] of the destruction of the world on the first Sunday of Advent. Another reason is that as it is the first day of the religious year we should all remember our last end and the last end of the world.

II.—THE IMMACULATE CONCEPTION.

The Immaculate[2] Conception of the Virgin took place when God united to her body an immortal soul.[3] Joakim and Anna were her parents, and some of the old Apocryphal writings give many reasons why she was related to some of the Apostles, by which they were called the brethren of our Lord through Mary, a younger sister of the Holy Virgin, for according to the customs of the Jews, cousins were called brothers.

Joakim and Anna had no children, but by the power of the Lord, Mary, their first child, was born to them. Before God foreshadowed her conception by the birth of Isaac,[4] of Samuel,[5] and later the birth of Christ by the miraculous sanctification of St. John the Baptist.[6]

In the beginning God made our mother Eve immaculate and without sin. When she fell God, speaking of her fall, said to the devil: "I will put enmities between thee and the woman, and thy seed and her seed: she shall crush thy head, and thou shalt lie in wait for her heel."[7] By these words the Lord meant that from the seed of the fallen race would rise another Eve, created as beautiful and as perfect as our fallen mother and one who would resist the serpent's guile. God from eternity had chosen Mary to become his Mother. "I was set up from eternity, and of old before the earth was made."[8] He chose her to be as an impregnable rampart against the wiles of the demons. "Who is she that cometh forth as the morning rising, fair as the moon, bright as the sun, terrible as an army set in array."[9] She was conceived without sin, as the Holy Ghost says of her: "Thou art all fair, O, my love, and there is not a spot in thee."[10] The whole of Solomon's song called the Canticle of Canticles is but the inspired words of Israel's greatest

---

[1] Luke xxi. [2] The word immaculate comes from the Latin and means pure and without spot. [3] Benedictus XIV., De Festis B. Mariae Virginis, c. xv., n. 1. [4] Gen. xviii., xxi. [5] 1 Kings, i. [6] Luke 1. [7] Gen. iii., 15. [8] Prov. viii., 23. [9] Cant. of Cant. vi., 9. [10] Cant. of Cant. iv., 7.

king[1] in the name of the Holy Ghost speaking of the beauties and of the graces of Mary.

The most early writers speak of the wonders of the Immaculate Conception of the Mother of God. They preached some of their most sublime sermons in her praises, telling us that as the breaking light of the early morning comes to remind us of the rising of the sun, thus Mary came into this world of sin as the forerunner of the Son of justice, her divine child. We cannot give all the reasons of Mary's greatness here, as it would be out of place in matters relating to the feasts of the year.[2] God could have created her so that she was never under original sin. He could have created her so that she would have been for a time in sin, or in the first instant of her creation she might be free from sin.[3] The Blessed Virgin, the Mother of our Lord, was never an enemy of God, neither by reason of actual sin nor by reason of original sin; but she would have been born with the sin of Adam had she not been preserved.[4] The subtle doctor Scotus held and proved this truth before the whole faculty of the great University of Paris in the presence of the most learned men of the world, in a solemn convention presided over by the legates of the Holy See.

The feast of the Immaculate Conception is not new in the Church. Its commencement is lost in the earliest times. The Greeks, keeping to the traditions of the Apostles, celebrated that feast from the earliest ages, even beyond the sixth century, as we can see by their Ceremonials and Liturgical works.[5] The Gothic Church of Spain celebrated the feast in the eighth century,[6] and we see that Paul, the Deacon, who was at first secretary to Charlemagne, when he became a monk at Mont-Casin he composed a beautiful hymn in honor of the Immaculate Conception. After a miracle in favor of the pious Helsin in 1066, the feast was celebrated in England for the first time. After that, by the labors of the great St. Anselm, Archbishop of Canterbury, it was spread throughout the British Isles,[7] from where it passed into Normandy, and was celebrated by the whole French nation. In 1049 we

---

[1] Solomon. [2] Les Tresors de Cornelius A. Lapide, Marie. [3] Scotus L. iii., Sent. Dist. 3, q. i. n. 1. [4] Scotus Dist. 18, n. 13. [5] Cer. S. Sab. [6] El Porque de las Ceremonias Nat. Cuar., Cap. Prim. [7] El Porque de las Ceremonias, Ibidem.

Notre Dame of Paris.

find it in Germany, for it is mentioned by a council presided over by the great Pope St. Leo X.[1] We find it again in Belgium, at Liege, in 1142. After that time we find that it was spoken of in all parts of Europe.

In 1476, Sixtus IV., stating that it was always, and from the beginning, celebrated in the Church, granted a decree by which the feast was celebrated with great pomp and ceremony in the eternal city, and the capital of the world vied with the other churches, peoples and nations in honoring the glories of the Immaculate Conception. In the following century[2] Pope Pius V. published his edition of the Breviary, by which all the Breviaries which for the two hundred years before that time had been published, and had been changing, were then forbidden, and the old Breviary was restored to the whole Church. There we find the feast of the Immaculate Conception in its place as one of the chief feasts of the year.

The three great Catholic nations of Europe, France, Germany and Spain, each showed their love of the Virgin, Mother of God. By the request of the great Louis XIV., France obtained from Pope Clement IX. the favor of celebrating the feast with an Octave, a favor which was extended to the whole Church by Innocent XII. Long before that time the faculty of the University of Paris directed the professors to preach on the wonders of the Mother of God conceived immaculate. Ferdinand III., the Emperor of Germany, in 1647, erected in the grand square of Vienna a beautiful column adorned with emblems and figures, typical of the victory gained by Mary over the old serpent. That column was crowned with a statue of the Immaculate Mother of God. Spain has always been celebrated for her love of Mary. In 1393, John I., King of Aragon, by a royal decree, placed himself and his kingdom under the protection of Mary conceived without sin. Afterwards King Philip III. and Philip IV. of Spain, sent their ambassadors to Rome, asking that her Immaculate Conception be proclaimed, but it was put off till our time. Charles III.[3] obtained from Clement XIII. the favor of celebrating the feast of the Immaculate Conception as the patron festival of the Spanish kingdom. The good and pious people used to write on the doors

---

[1] Concil Navar. [2] 1568. [3] El Porque de las Ceremonias Trad. Cuar. C. P., n. 1.

and in the fronts of their houses the praises and the glories of Mary, Jesus' mother. The Mother Superior of the convent of the Immaculate Conception, wrote a book[1] from which the great painter, Murillo, the pride of Spain, drew his inspiration in painting those masterpieces which even in our day excite the wonder of the world.[2]

From the earliest of the histories of the Armenians, of the Copts and of the Alexandrians,[3] we learn that they celebrated from their very beginning the feast of the Immaculate Conception. Matthew Parisius says, that when the Archbishop of Armenia came to England, he was asked by one of the monks if they celebrated the feast of the Immaculate Conception in his country, and he replied: "It is celebrated; and this is the reason, because, when Joachim was sorrowful in the desert, an angel told him that the conception had taken place. In the same way the conception of St. John the Baptist, and for the same reason. Regarding the conception of the Lord which was announced to Mary by the angel, whom she conceived by the Holy Ghost, there is no doubt among the Faithful."[4] The Basilion Council decreed, that she was conceived without sin. The Council of Trent, when speaking of the sin of Adam having been transmitted to all his children, stated that they did not wish to say that Mary was under that penalty, but made an exception for her.[5] Many councils have spoken the same regarding the privileges of Mary.[6] Many Popes have, from the chair of Peter, taught the world of the spotless conception of the Mother of God.[7] It remained for our day to declare to the world the Apostolic tradition of the wonders of Mary. The great Pontiff, Pius IX., on the 8th of December, 1854, in the presence of fifty-four cardinals, forty-two archbishops and ninety-two bishops, surrounded with thousands of clergymen and numberless people from all parts of the world, in St. Peter's, the cathedral of the world, proclaimed that the truth of the Immaculate Conception was revealed by God. From every part of the world prayers had gone up before the throne of God for the light and the help of the Holy Ghost, and

---

[1] Mystic City of God. [2] Gueranger L'Avent, p. 414. [3] El Porqne Trat. 4. [4] Benedictus XIV., De Festis B. Mariae Virginis, c. xv, n. 17 in fine. [5] Concil. Trident S. v. n. 5, in fine. [6] See Concil. Trident S. vi., can. xxiii. [7] Sixtus IV., c. 1, 2, Extrav. Com. iii., etc.

the Pontiff had joined his voice to the universal cry to God. The oracle of God spoke the truth waited for so long. The Holy Sacrifice was offered on the Confession1 of St. Peter. The hand of the Pope had placed the diadem on the head of the statue of the Virgin. The Vicar of Christ is carried on his brazen throne, the tiara. the triple crown, decks the head of the successor of Peter, the fisherman, and the procession comes to the door of the great Basilica. There, on bended knees, he meets the two followers of the Seraphic St. Francis, one the General of the Minor Observances, the other the General of the Minor Conventuals. One presented to him a beautiful golden rose, the other a brilliant silver lily. The lily and the rose, the most beautiful of the flowers of the field, represent the purity and the burning love of Mary.[1]

That was the day when the spotless conception of Mary was proclaimed as having been revealed to man, but hidden in an obscure manner in the holy Scriptures.

III.—THE SECOND SUNDAY OF ADVENT.

The Second Sunday of Advent relates to the second coming of our Lord, when he comes to his beloved in Holy Communion, to strengthen our faith in this his second coming. Many words and parts of the services of this day allude to his first coming as a little child, that those who believe he came and took the form of man at his birth, may be strengthened in the faith of the Blessed Eucharist. The mystery of the Incarnation has such a close relationship with the mystery of the Eucharist, that they are often mentioned together in the ceremonies and the rites of the Church.

Jerusalem has many meanings in the Scriptures and the services of the Church. Josephus says that in the Book of Genesis it was named Salem, the city of the high priest Melchesadeck, who offered bread and wine, a figure of the priests of the new law.[2] The word Jerusalem in ancient Hebrew means " the possession of peace," for it signifies the heavenly city, our home beyond the skies. Many are the meanings of the word in the Holy Bible. To-day, in the services of the Church, it signi-

---

[1] Gueranger L'Avent, p. 415.   [2] Bib. S. Concordantia, nota Jerusalem.

fies the soul of the Christian preparing for the coming of our Lord in the Sacrament of the altar.

What wonders, what love, what consolation for the soul of man, and what stupendous humiliations for the Son of God to come down, and day by day to renew forever the mystery of the Incarnation by the mystery of the Eucharist, by becoming the food of man. But how few receive him often. How few receive the Bread of Life, which makes them strong to resist the temptations which are everywhere around the path of the Christian.

The whole office of this Sunday is filled with hope and joy for the good souls of those who are waiting for the coming of our Lord,[1] the spouse of the Christian soul.

The Station, according to the Mass Book, is held in Rome, in the Basilica of the Holy Cross in Jerusalem, the venerable church in which Constantine placed the part of the true Cross his mother Helena sent him from Jerusalem. At the same time there they placed the title written by Pilate, "Jesus the Nazarine, King of the Jews." These precious relics are guarded there in that holy church,[2] which in the Latin rite is considered as Jerusalem itself, as we see by the many allusions to it in the services of the Church during the year, there many Masses are celebrated within its sacred walls.

At the Matin office we read the magnificent words of Isaias, where he foretells the time when the root of Jesse will bring forth the flower,[3] "That branch of Jesse," says St. Jerome, "is the Virgin Mary, while the flower is the Saviour himself, who says in the Canticle of Canticle, 'I am the flower of the field and the lily of the valleys.'"[4] All ages have celebrated the beauties of that wonderful flower. "The Son of the Virgin is the flower, the flower white and purple, chosen among all others— a flower, the sight of which fills the angels with joy, and the odor of which gives life to men," says St. Bernard. Thus the flower of the root of Jesse, the father of David, was to be our Lord the Saviour of the world, foretold by the Prophets, foreseen by the Sibyl of the pagan nations. For as a dim shadow the revelation of the coming Saviour came down through the mists of idolatry till it found its

---

[1] Gueranger L'Avent, p. 157. [2] L'An Lit. par Gueranger L'Avent, p. 157. [3] Is xi., 1. [4] Cant. of Cant. ii. 1.

expression in the words of the prince of the poets of ancient times.[1]

IV.—THE THIRD SUNDAY OF ADVENT.

The Mass said on this Sunday is called the Station at St. Peters, that is, in St. Peter's Church at Rome, the great Church of the Vatican, the Cathedral of the world, the building covering the relics of the Apostle St. Peter, certainly the grandest temple ever raised by the hand of man to the worship of the true God.

On the third Sunday of Advent the Church celebrates the third coming of the Lord, when he will come to each of us at the moment of our death. Although the hour when we leave this world may be a time of sorrow for our friends, the Church looks upon it as the moment of gladness, when we enter the everlasting happiness of heaven. For that reason on the third Sunday the tones of the organ, hushed since Advent began, are heard again resounding throughout the vaulted ceilings of our temples, the flowers of the valleys bloom upon our altars, the deacon and the sub deacon take their dalmatic and their tunic, in the cathedrals the bishops are clothed in gorgeous vestments, the magnificent poetry of the ceremonies are resumed, the Church rejoices, for she is celebrating the taking of her children from this exile of sorrow to the world of bliss beyond the skies.

For that reason, from the most ancient times the sorrow and the gloom of Advent is broken by the joyful services of this Sunday. From the first word with which the Mass begins "Gaudete," rejoice, to-day is called Gaudete Sunday,[2] for the Church rejoices at the ending of the trials of her children here below. In the same way the fourth Sunday of Lent is called Laetare Sunday, from the first word of the services, "Laetare," rejoice. Thus it shows the spirit of the Church, that the soul of man may not be exposed to the sin of despair during the two great seasons of fasting and of penance, of Advent and of Lent, and for that reason she relaxes somewhat in the rigors of penance on the third Sunday of Advent, and on the fourth Sunday of Lent.

---

[1] Virgil, "Jam rediit et virgo." [2] O'Brien Hist. of the Mass, p. 65.

The week following the third Sunday of Advent is devoted to the quater tenses or Ember days. The quater tenses come down to us from the customs of the Jews, and in the Church the fast of Wednesday, Friday and Saturday of the quater tenses of the four seasons of the year goes back to the time of the Apostles. Such is the testimony of St. Leo, of St. Isidore of Seville of Rhaban Maur, and of many of the most ancient and venerable of the writers of antiquity. In the first ages of the Church the fast of the quater tenses were fixed at the time of the year when we observe them at present. By some of the Fathers they are called the Three Times of Fasting, because the quater tense of the Spring, falling the first week of Lent, add nothing to the fast, for, by the law of Lent, all were then obliged to fast. The object of the fast for the quater tenses, both among the Jews and in the Church, is to sanctify the four seasons of the year by prayer and fasting.

In ancient times the quater tenses of Advent were callled the Fast of the Sixth Month. St. Leo tells us that the quater tenses were fixed at this time of the year because all the fruits of the earth having been gathered, it is only right that we should return thanks to the Lord for his bounty towards us.

Besides the consecration of the four seasons of the year, the quater tenses are times of fasting and of prayer, because on the saturday of the week closing those fasts, the clergy are ordained, and the ordination of the clergy does not usually take place at any other time except there be some sufficient reason. According to the Latin rite the ordination of the month of December at the quater tenses, is very ancient and goes back to the time of the Apostles. It was but natural that they would choose this time of prayer and of fasting, when the people by their self-denial and their prayers would call down the blessings of Heaven on the newly ordained clergy of the Church. We find in the short lives of the Popes in the Breviary, that many of them ordained the clergy in the month of December, following the Apostolic time.

The Station of Wednesday is in the Church of St. Mary Major, in Rome, because the Gospel gives at the Mass

¹ St. Leo Sermo II., de Jejun. decem. men. et Coll.

the history of the Angel Gabriel coming to announce to
Mary the mystery of the Incarnation. We fast on wed-
nesdays of the quater tenses, because on wednesday the
Jews conspired to put our Lord to death. On Friday the
Station is held in the Church of the Twelve Apostles.
We cannot find out why the services are held here,
except that it is one of the churches built by the Emperor
Constantine, who first gave liberty to the Church, spread ·
throughout the world by the preaching of the Apostles.
According to St. Augustine, the Christians of Rome were
accustomed to fast on wednesdays, fridays and saturdays, from their very conversion.[1] It appears that the
Romans learned to fast on saturday from the example of
St. Peter, who fasted on saturday before he began his
celebrated discussion with Simon Magus.[2] Saturday,
the Station is held in the great Church of St. Peter,
because there the ordinations take place and great crowds
of people come to see the ordination rites, which according to the custom and the canons of the Church are held
on the Saturday before Christmas.

V.—THE FOURTH SUNDAY OF ADVENT.

If the fourth Sunday of Advent falls on the 24th of
December, it is omitted, then the Vigil takes its place
when Christmas falls on monday.[3] We have now come
to the last Sunday before we celebrate the coming of our
Lord ; the day differs each year. The anniversary of the
birth of the Saviour may come on monday or any other
day of the week. The Church waiting for His coming
clothes her ceremonies with greater splendors since the
17th of December. As the days pass she varies the
Antiphons. At Lauds and Vespers, she expresses the
joyful tenderness of her wishes for his coming, while at
the Masses she takes from the Prophets the most brilliant
language, to show the people her joy at the birth of her
Spouse. She strikes the last stroke to wake her children
from their sleep in worldly things, and calls them to the
knowledge of the glorious birth of their Saviour. She
leads them into the desert, she shows them John the
Baptist preaching penance, whose voice reaches even to

---

[1] S. Aug. Ep, xxxvi., n. 9   [2] S. Aug. Epist. xxxvi., 21.   [3] Gueranger Adv., 243.

our day, and teaches us to prepare for the coming of our Lord.

The fourth Sunday of Advent is called "Rorate," rain down, because by this word the Mass begins, or "Canite tuba," the first words of the first response of Matins. Thus, to-day, the Church sounds for the last time the trumpet of the Lord, to wake her children from their slumbers of forgetfulness of God, and to receive his only Son. We read the stirring words of St. John the Baptist preparing the way before the Lord. The voice of the holy and austere forerunner of Christ prepares the Christians for the coming of their Saviour. He preaches penance for the remission of sin. He warns the hardened hearts of the reprobate Pharisees. To-day his trumpet tones are sounded through the length and breadth of Christendom, and in every church his warning words tell the Christians to come and receive their Lord.

The station where the services are held, is at the tomb of the Twelve Apostles, where are guarded the relics of the twelve followers of our Lord.

From the earliest days of the Church they prepared for the feast of Christmas by celebrating the Vigil or Eve. They spent the night in the churches singing Psalms and reading parts of the Holy Bible. From that holy Book, from the writings of the great Saints, they formed the Office of Christmas Eve. This Office of the Breviary, in the monasteries and the houses of the religious orders, took up the greater part of the night. The people in the Middle Ages gathered in great crowds in the churches to pray, to hear the Offices sung, and to be present at the midnight mass of Christmas.

Among these night Offices of the Church, Christmas Eve from the preaching of the Apostles was of great devotion and of solemnity because the Lord was born at the midnight hour. Of all times of the year this is the only night we can say Mass at midnight, to celebrate the hour when Christ was born. We find it mentioned by many writers of antiquity that the people were accustomed to spend the whole night in the church in prayer. At Rome for many ages they had two Offices of Matins, the first in the Basilica of St. Mary Major, followed by the midnight Mass of Christmas, celebrated by the Pope himself. Then all the people went in procession to the

Church of St. Anastasia, where as the morning was breaking he said the second Mass. Having finished, they all gathered in the great Church of St. Peter's, where they began the second Nocturn, and at the end the Pope celebrated the third Mass at nine in the morning.[1] Those Offices of Christmas Eve began in the great Church of St. Mary Major, because there is preserved the Manger of Bethlehem, where our Lord was laid when wrapped in swaddling clothes.

Three places in the world are holy from their relations to the birth of our Lord. The first of these is Bethlehem, where is seen the grotto where Christ was brought into the world. What pious and holy thoughts rise in the mind of the Christian in visiting really or in thought that holy place where the Man-God first left the footprints of his coming in the mystery of the Incarnation. The second place is Rome, from where the God-Man speaks to the world by the mouth of his the Supreme Pontiff, where in the Basilica of St. Mary Major are kept with care the Manger wherein our Lord was laid the night of his birth, where is still to be seen the picture of the Mother of God, painted by St. Luke ; and that Church standing on the Esquiline hill, brilliant in marble, gold and precious stones, proclaims itself the most magnificent temple raised by man to the honor and to the memory of the Mother of God. As from her the Son of God took human nature, by her began the mystery of the Incarnation. How appropriate then to begin the ceremonies of the Christmas time in the great church built in Mary's honor. The third holy place is the tomb of the Apostle St. Peter himself, the spot where rest the bones of the greatest follower of the Lord. These relics rest on the Vatican Hill, where on the same day he was put to death. The Pope, when his strength allows, says the third Mass of Christmas in the Cathedral of the world, in St. Peter's magnificent Church, near the tomb of the great Apostle, the last Mass of Christmas is offered up to the throne of God by the Vicar of Christ.[2] The fourth holy place is the heart of man, which the Redeemer born on Christmas night comes to purify, and the feasts of

---

[1] Amalarius, and other Liturgists of the XII. century. Antiphon, of the Roman Church, etc. [2] Gueranger Le Temps De Noel, p. 172 to 175.

this holy time with all their sweetness will not be celebrated by us rightly, unless Christ comes to us and takes up his abode with us[1] in the sacrament of his love the Holy Communion.

As the Infant born to us is God, the Mighty, the Prince of Peace with the government on his shoulder[2]; to honor that power of the Son of God, since the two great Princes of antiquity, Clovis and Charlemagne, came to Rome at the Christmas time, the Eve before the Vicar of that same Lord, in the name of God, blesses a sword and a helmet to be given to some Christian Prince, that like Don Juan at Lepanto,[3] he may overcome the enemies of God. That sword is sent to one whom the Pope wishes to honor, in the name Christ himself, who is the King of kings, and the Lord of lords, of whom the angel said to Mary: "The Lord God shall give unto him the throne of David, his father."[4] From him alone comes the power of the sword, and as by a sword in the hands of an angel the Lord "slew a hundred and eighty-five thousand" of the Asyrians,[5] as he said to Cyrus, "I girded thee,"[6] to do his work among the ancient nations of the earth, as he says to Christ by his prophets, "Gird the sword upon thy thigh, O thou most mighty,"[7] thus the Christian Prince is to draw the sword only in a just war. For that reason these symbols of war, the sword and the helmet, are blessed in the church, the temple of justice, on Christmas Eve. On the helmet is an image of the Holy Spirit formed of pearls, telling that not according to passion, or according to his own caprice, must the Christian king go forth to war, but in a just cause led by the wisdom of the Spirit of God.[8] How wonderful is Rome in her ceremonies, and long is the list of the Heroes, the Generals, the Princes, the Kings and the Emperors she has blessed and crowned since the most remote ages in the ceremonies of Christmas Eve, when in the Middle Ages she was their mother, and the nations of Europe were like children under her maternal care.

Where the Latin rite is carried out entirely, the people having gathered in the Church, the clergy sing matins on Christmas Eve. It is divided into three Nocturns or watches. The first signifies and recalls the first age of

---

[1] John xiv., 23. [2] Is. ix., 6. [3] 1571. [4] Luke i., 32. [5] 4 Kings, xix., 35. [6] Is. xlv., 5.
[7] Ps. xliv., 4. [8] Cardinal Polus in Letter to Philip II. and his Queen Mary.

the human race, the time of the Patriarchs, and in the Middle Ages, while they were singing the first watch the altar was covered with a black veil, to signify the curse of God upon the earth, and on man for his sin in the garden.   The second Nocturn signifies the time of the ceremonies of the law of Moses, and the altar was covered with a white veil, to tell of the light of God revealed to man in the ceremonies of the temple and the tabernacle, and in the prophesies of the old law. The third Nocturn typifies the time of the Christian Church, and the altar was veiled in purple to bring to our minds the love of Christ for his Spouse the Church, in the ineffable union of our Lord with those who receive him in Holy Communion.[1] With sorrow we say that we cannot give these Offices of the Breviary, as they would make many books like this.

At Rome the Prince or King, to whom the sword and helmet blessed before Matins are to be given, takes part in the ceremonies.   He reads the fifth Lesson, for it tells of the great fight against the demon and of the mystery of the Incarnation, while the choir are singing the response "O Great Mystery," the master of ceremonies leads him to the Pope, before whom he draws his sword. Touching the earth with the point three times he brandishes it three times in a warlike manner, and then lets it rest on his left arm.   He is then led to the rostrum, where taking off his helmet and clothed in cope he reads the Lesson. Such were some of the ceremonies of the Church in Rome in the Middle Ages, when the Christian warriors fought the Pagans before the Church taught them to turn their swords into plowshares.[2]

At the third Nocturn three parts of the three Gospels are read, which form parts of the three Masses of Christmas.[3] The Gospel read tells of the numbering of the people by Augustus Cæsar. According to the Roman ceremonial it should be read by the Emperor himself, if he be at Rome, so as by that to honor the governments of the world ; for by the providence of God one of the most remarkable of the Emperors of old, Augustus, ruler of the Roman Empire, by that decree proved that Christ

---

[1] Gueranger, Le Temps De Noel, p. 183. [2] Gueranger, Le Temps De Noel, v. 1.,
p. 208. [3] Luke c. ii., 1 ; Luke ii., 15 ; Luke iii., 5, and John i., 1.

was born of the tribe of Judea, and of the family of David, as foretold by the prophets. The Emperor is led before the Pope, where he is robed with the cope. Then with a Cardinal-Deacon on each side, he ascends the rostrum, and there reads the passage of the Gospel. He then returns again to the feet of the Pope, he kisses his foot to honor the Vicar of Him who was born at Bethlehem, and returns to his place. We find that ceremony was carried out by the Emperor Frederic III. in the presence of Pope Paul II. as late as Christmas Eve in 1468.

The text of the Gospels given are explained by St. Gregory the Great, St. Ambrose and St. Augustin, the three greatest Doctors of the Church, and who wrote the finest commentaries on the Gospels. The three watches of the night are now ended. The prophesies and the figures foretelling his coming have been read. The midnight hour draws near. All has been prepared to celebrate the birth of the Lord and Saviour of the world, and the Church is filled with people waiting for the midnight Mass of Christmas.

St. Stephen's at Vienna.

REASONS FOR CELEBRATING CHRISTMAS TIME.

The Christmas season begins on the 25th of December and lasts till the 2d of February. In the cycle of the year, it is a special season like Advent, Lent, and Paschal Time, a time of joy, second only to the glorious days of the Easter times. It ends the days of fasting and of penance during Advent.

The custom of celebrating for forty days the joyful time of Christmas dates from the most ancient times, for the early Christians learned from the Gospel that, according to the law of Moses,[1] when the days of her purification were accomplished, Mary carried her Son to the temple, and there, like the mothers of Israel, she presented him to the Lord.[2]

It came to pass by the overruling hand of Providence, that Cæsar Augustus,[3] the first Emperor of Rome, commanded a census of the world to be taken, that he might know how many people lived under him in each of the provinces over which his empire extended, and the amount of tax he could levy on each.[4] That numbering of the people took place under Cyrinus, the Governor of Syria.[5] Only the men were called to give an account of their families, the women and children could stay at home.[6] But the Holy Virgin came because she was the only child and heir of her father's house.[7] Mary and Joseph therefore came from Nazareth to Bethlehem, to the city of their tribe, Juda, that Mary might represent her father's home, that in the records of the Roman Empire their names might be found,[8] and thus prove to the world, that Jesus was born at Bethlehem, of the tribe of Juda, and of the family of David, as the prophets foretold

---

[1] Levit. xii. [2] Luke ii., 22. [3] Caius Julius Caesar Octavianus. [4] Benedict XIV., De Festis D. N. Jesu Christi II., Ambrose, Bede Euth. and Meldonatus in Cap. ii., Lucae. [5] Luke ii., 2. [6] Calmet in ii., Lucae n. 4. [7] Benedict XIV., Ibidem :0 [8] Tertullian against Marcion, book iv., c. vii.

more than seven hundred years before.[1] The Roman law relating to these things, says, that when the census was taken they should come from their own cities.[2] Thus Jesus was born at Bethlehem and not at Nazareth.

We can imagine the children of the different tribes of Israel setting out for the towns and the cities of their fathers.

The time foretold by the prophets had come. The Roman Empire had seen its highest power, as Balaam prophesied. The sceptre had departed from Juda as Jacob said, Herod the King of the Jews was but a crowned slave in the hands of the Romans,[3] when the Governor of Syria, beginning with Phœnecia and Celocyria, commenced the numbering of the people, so that three years after the decree went forth they came to Bethlehem.

Fall was drawing to its close. The half tropical torrents were rushing down the valleys of Palestine. The cold wind moaned through the olive trees and the sky showed the signs of the coming winter on the morning of the 20th of December, 748, from the founding of Rome, and 4,004 from the creation, when a man and a woman might be seen in one of the poorest houses of Nazareth preparing for a journey.[4] They were Mary and Joseph. They were going to Bethlehem to be enrolled. The distance was 72 miles, and the tradition is that they walked the whole distance,[5] for they were too poor to ride.[6] At length, when five days had passed, they came in sight of the turrets and flat roofed houses of Bethlehem, the city of their fathers, situated on a rising ground surrounded with green hills, smiling with vineyards, groves of olives, and forests of oak.[7] Crowds of people were coming from various parts of Palestine to be enrolled, and the hotels were full. There was no place for the poor old man and his young wife. Even in the city of David his descendants could not find a house to shelter them from the chilly air of that winter day. Before the gates of the city were closed for the night, they went outside the walls, and southward, a short walk from the city, they found a cave

---

[1] Lamy, Concord. Evang. l. 1., c. 9, n. 1.   [2] Ulpianus L. lll., Dig. de Censibus.
[3] Orsini's Life of the B. Virgin, c. xi.   [4] Orsini's Life of the B. Virgin, c. xi.   [5] Benedict XIV, De Festis D. N., J. C., cap. xvii. n. 14.   [6] Orsini says, Mary rode on an ass, ibidem.   [7] El Porque de las Ceremonias, Trat. Cuarto c. xiii.

in the rocks used as a stable,[1] or as a place of shelter for the shepherds, when watching their sheep on stormy nights.[2] There, on the 25th of December, at the midnight hour; "while all things were in quiet silence, and the night was in the midst of her course, thy almighty word leaped down from Heaven from thy royal throne,"[3] when the brilliant constellation Virgin was rising in the eastern sky,[4] then the Virgin brought forth the Son of God.

There are in Christ two natures, one Divine, the other human, and therefore to him alone belongs two births; one in eternity from his Father, the other in time from his Mother.[5] His human nature came not from Heaven as Valentin the heretic said, but was formed from the purest blood of his Mother like all our bodies are made, and therefore she is his Mother.[6] "The temporal birth of Christ took place like ours, because he was born for our salvation, and for that reason he was born of a woman in the regular time, but not like other children, but by the Holy Ghost and of a holy Virgin."[7] There was no human person in Christ, but in the place of the human person which is in each of us, was the Second Person of the Trinity. As all we do, or everything relating to us is attributed, not to the body or to the soul, but to you or to me, that is, to the person, thus everything relating to Christ is attributed not to his body or to his soul, but to his Person. That Person being Divine, it follows that he was born God. God was then born of Mary. Thus Mary is the Mother of God.[8] If human nature alone, or a man only, had been born of her, she would have been the mother of a man, or of that human nature; but she was the Mother of the whole Being born of her, and as that Being was God, she was the Mother of God.[9] "As among men the soul is considered to be one with the body and born with it, if any one would say that the mother of the body is not the mother of the soul, he would talk foolishly. We see the same thing in the birth of Christ, for the word was born of the substance of God the Father,

[1] St. Jerome, Epist. 17; Eusebius, Vita Const., l. ii.; Origen, l. i., con. Celsum. [2] Orsini, Life of the B. Virgin, c. xi. [3] Wisdom, xviii., 14, 15. [4] Dupin in note in Orsini, ibidem. [5] St. Thomas, P. 3, q. xxxv., a. ii., et Syn. vi, act. ii. [6] St. Thomas, 3 P., q. xxxv., a. iii. [7] St. Damascen, Orth. Fid., l. iii. c. 7. [8] Concil. Ephes. Can. I., contra Nestrium. Concil. Chalcedon., A. vii., Sy. Via. II Concil. Lat. c. iii., St. Cyrillus Alex. St. Athanasius, St. Irenæus, etc. [9] St. Thomas, 3 P., q. xxxv., a. iv.

but because he took flesh we must confess that according to flesh he was born of a woman."[1]

He was born in Bethlehem, because he wished to show all men that he was of the tribe and of the family of David.[2] As David was born in Bethlehem and chose Jerusalem to be the city of his throne, that there he might prepare to build the great temple of the Lord for the sacrifices of the law, thus Christ was born in Bethlehem, and died in Jerusalem. The sacrifice of his life for man's salvation was offered at Jerusalem. To give a lesson of humility, he was born in the little city of Bethlehem, that men might see the lowness of his birth; he was crucified at Jerusalem, that men might see the awful disgrace of his death, while he was brought up at Nazareth, the lowest of all Judea, so that men might see nothing in him to attract the world to his teachings.[3] The whole life of the Saviour speaks the same wonderful providence. If he had chosen the great city of Rome, men would say he changed the world by the power and authority of its great people. If he was the son of an Emperor, men would say he got his power from his father's throne; but that men might learn that by the grace of God alone the world was converted to the Gospel, he chose a poor mother;[4] he was born of the race of Juda, the most despised of all the ancient nations; he descended from the family of David, when they had lost the kingly power; he was born in a stable, he was laid in a manger, and he was wrapped in swaddling clothes, that all the world might see that his power came not from the world but from God. And that he might still in a further manner show his guiding hand over his Church he was not born in Rome, lest men might think that the Church got her power and her authority from the Cæsars. But when he had gone up into heaven, Peter, the first Pope, the rough, vulgar fisherman of Galilee—Peter changed the papacy to Rome, and amid the ten frightful persecutions of the following ages, when all the power of pagan Rome was hurled against that Church to crush her to the earth and wipe the name of Christ from the world, the Church came out in triumph, to show that she was of God. Truly, "the weak things of

---

[1] St. Cyrillus, in Epist. contra Nestorium, P. I., c. 2, n. 12. [2] Rom. 1., 3. [3] St. Thomas, 3, P. q. xxxv., A. vii., ad 2. [4] Theodore, Ancyr.. iii., c. 9.

the world hath God chosen that he may confound the strong."[1]

Other children are born when God sees fit. Christ chose his own time.[2] He came into the world at the time when Cæsar commanded all his subjects to be enrolled. The Roman Empire bears witness of his royal birth, and Cæsar without knowing it carried out the designs of God.[3]

At that time the whole world bowed down under the power of the Roman Emperor. All was peace, "for he is our peace."[4] If we examine the ancient histories," says St. Jerome, "we will find that up to the 28th year of Cæsar Augustus there were wars in the whole world, but at the birth of the Lord all wars ceased."[5]

Let the proud of the earth learn from the birth of their Saviour a lesson of humility. Who would want to have it known that they were born in a cabin, but who would like his neighbors to hear that he was born in a stable? He was not born in the imperial city, Rome. He was not born in the capital of Palestine, Jerusalem. He did not first see light in the city of Galilee, Nazareth. He was not born in the home of his fathers, Bethlehem. He was born in a stable, to destroy in the mind of man the pride of his birth and to teach us a lesson of humility.[6]

Mary knew her time was soon to come. She remembered that on the 25th of March, before the angel told her, she would conceive and bring forth a son.[7]

She knew that her nine months were up on the 25th of December. She had provided cloths for her Divine Son. She wrapped him in swaddling clothes, and laid him in a manger.[8]

Thus the greatest fact of history came to pass, God had prepared the world for four thousand years before, for that miraculous birth of his only begotten Son. In the groves of Paradise, when our first parents in fear and trembling heard the voice of God in condemnation of their sin, they learned to hope in a Redeemer, for in the same words was the promise given, that of the race one would rise and to crush the serpent's head.[9] The sacrifices of the Patriarchs foretold his coming. Isaac, brought

---

[1] 1 Cor. i., 27. [2] St. Thomas, 3 P., q xxxv., A. viii. [3] Bossuet, Elevation, xvi., sem. elev. v. [4] Ephes. ii., 14. [5] Super Isaias, c. ii., "Non levabit gens," etc. [6] St. Thomas, iii., q. 66, etq., 46, 10, ad. 1. [7] Luke i., 31. [8] Luke ii., 7. [9] Gen. iii. 15.

forth in the decline of his mother's life, when she was ninety years of age, prepared for the bringing forth of the child of Bethlehem. Anna, the barren woman of the tribe of Ephraim, by the hand of God gave birth to Samuel, the leader of God's people. Elizabeth gave birth to John the Baptist, in her old age, and Joachim and Anna gave birth to Mary by the power of God. Thus all these miracles of the Lord were to prepare the world for the birth of Christ by the operation of the Holy Ghost, from a Virgin, who before, and in, and after his birth, always remained a Virgin. The calling of the three shepherds[1] to adore the new born babe, the Angels' singing of "Glory to God in the highest," are related by the Evangelist.[2]

Clement of Alexander[3] writes against those in ancient times who pretended that Christ was born either on the 20th of April, or in May. St. Epiphanius[4] and Casianus[5] say some of the early Christians of Egypt believed that he was born on the 6th of January, and for that reason they celebrated Christmas, Circumcision and Epiphany on the sixth of January. But the whole tradition of the Church, the writings of the Fathers and all monuments of the early ages say he was born on the 25th of December. It is proved by the Homilies of St. Chrysostom,[6] the writings of St. Gregory, of Nyasen,[7] by the works of St. Augustin,[8] and by all the great writers of antiquity. After summing up all said on that subject, Baronius writes,[9] "All these assertions relating to the birth of our Lord, the belief of both the Latins and the Greeks, is, that he was born on the twenty-fifth of the month of December." There is no doubt on this question, for the Roman Senators had the right to examine the records of the census, taken by command of Cæsar, and the knowledge of the birth of our Lord on Christmas day was carried to Constantinople, at the time when St. Chrysostom sat there upon his throne as archbishop, after having been changed from the see of Antioch.[10]

The people of the East began to celebrate Christmas on the 25th of December, about the beginning of the fourth century. Before that time they kept the birth-

<hr>

[1] V. Bede, L. de Locis Sanctis. [2] Luke ii., 14. [3] Lib. i., Stromat. [4] Haeres, 51. [5] Coll. 10. [6] Hom. 33. [7] Orat. in S. Lumena. [8] L. iv., de Trin., c. i., et Epist. 119. [9] Ap. ad Annales n. 121. [10] Benedict XIV., De Festis D. N., Jesu Christi, c. xvii., n. 45.

day of the Lord sometimes on the 6th of January, sometimes on the 20th of April, and sometimes on the 15th
of May, and St. Chrysostom says in a sermon preached by
him in 386, that at Antioch for six years the people had
followed the custom of the Romans in keeping Christmas
on the 25th of December. It appears that they changed
because the knowledge of the exact time of the birth of
the Saviour was intimated to them by the supreme
authority of the Pope, who, in Rome, had examined the
records of the census, or by the commands of the Emperors Theodosius and Valentine, who decreed that Christmas and Epiphany should no longer be celebrated on
the same day.[1] The Armenians still continue to celebrate
Christmas and Epiphany together, on the 6th of January,
because from the most ancient times they were separated
from the centre of authority, Rome.

Christmas time begins on the day when our Lord was
born, and ends on the day when Jesus was presented in
the temple, and Mary was purified. That feast of the
Purification of the Virgin appears to go back to the most
ancient times, and we find no mention of when it began,
all writers agreeing that it is the most ancient of all the
feasts of the Blessed Virgin. Having its history given in
the Gospel,[2] it is no more than natural that they celebrate it from the earliest days of the Christian religion.
Where the Latin rite had spread, it was held on the 2d of
February, but some of the Christians of the East kept
the feast at different times, till the sixth century, during
the reign of the Emperor Justinian, when they changed to
the day kept by the Latins.

The Christmas time in the Latin rite is a time of happiness and of pleasure celebrated by the whole of the
Christian world in memory of the Son of God made man.[3]
For that reason all are filled with joy and happiness.
Among us, the children's stockings are filled by Santa
Claus,[4] the Christmas tree bends under its load of sweets
for the little ones, the poor, who at other times have
scarcely enough, try and provide a feast that day, the
rich invite their friends to their Christmas dinner, all

[1] Gueranger, Le Temps de Noel, p. 11. [2] Luke ii, 22, 23. [3] Gueranger, Le Temps
de Noel, v. 1, p. 12. [4] The name Santa Claus is a corruption of St. Nicholas, which
was celebrated by the Dutch in the times of the colonies, and from that it has been
changed to Christmas.

salute their friends and acquaintances with "a happy
Christmas." The trials and troubles of the past are forgotten, injuries are overlooked, presents are made, and the
members of society try to pass the holidays in social
pleasures, even those whose fathers left the Church in
ages past, by tradition, have still kept the customs im-
planted so deeply by our ceremonies in the heart of the
people of the Christian world.

While the Church celebrates the mystery of the Incarnation, she cannot forget at the same time the Maternity
of Mary, for they are so closely united one to the other,
that the thought of one brings with it the idea of the
other. For that reason, during the Sundays and the feasts
of Christmas Time, which are not of the double class,
we mention Mary in the prayers and Offices.[1] We resume
again her suffrages not said in Advent, and the prayer
with the beautiful anthem composed by Herman Contract.[2] Such are the ways the Church honors the Son of
God in the praises of his Mother during the Christmas
time of the cycle of the years. From the most ancient
times the people were accustomed to honor Mary. The
French dedicated to her their great Metropolitan Churches
of Paris, Notre Dame,[3] and of Chartre. The people of
Rome named after her St. Mary Major,[4] while every
church of any fame or name has one of its altars dedicated
to the Mother of God.

In the course of the year there are six Sundays after
Epiphany, so that when the Christmas time of 40 days
has its full length before the movable feasts come in, the
Christmas season takes four, three, two, or only one week,
depending on the time when Easter falls, which being
on the first Sunday following the first full moon after the
14th moon of March, varies each year. But nothing changes
the joy and gladness of the ceremonies of the Church
during these 40 days of Christmas time but the violet
color of the vestments and the silence of the Angelic
Hymn when the Christmas season extends beyond Septuagesima Sunday.[5] When any of the Sundays after
Epiphany cannot be celebrated after Septuagesima Sun-

---

[1] Dens qui salutis aeternae beatae Mariae virginitate fecunda, etc., and V. Post par-
tum Virgo, etc. [2] Alma Redemptoris Mater, etc. [3] Our Lady. [4] St. Mary the
Great. [5] The Gloria in Excelcis Deo.

day, because Easter comes sooner than usual, they are put back to the last of the year before the following Advent. Although the Church celebrates the mysteries of the holy Childhood of our Lord during the Christmas season, when Easter comes towards the last of March we read many parts of his public life, because there is no other time in the year for this part of the Gospel.

The Greeks during this holy time celebrate the Maternity of Mary, but they have a special veneration for the twelve days from Christmas to Epiphany.[1] They eat no meat during these days, and in old times the Emperors of the East decreed that no work was to be done or courts held from Christmas till after Epiphany.[2]

No time of the year is so filled with mystery as the Christmas holidays, when the Church celebrates the birth of the Saviour of the world, born of his Father in eternity, and born of his Mother in time. The Son of God, the wisdom of the Father, the Divine Word, the Plan of creation, the Creator of all the source of all light and grace flowing into angels and men[3] takes to himself, raises to the throne of the Deity that nature of man which contains all the perfections of the beings made by God. He raises all and defies all by uniting all to himself, and thus, he lifts all creatures to the throne of the God-head. The Mystery of the Incarnation breathes through the Masses and the Offices of the Church. "The Word was made flesh, and God became man," resounds through the whole of the grand Liturgy of the Latin rite during the holy season of Christmas. The great Fathers of the Church preached their finest sermons on the birth of our Lord.[4] St. Augustine[5] and St. Isidore says, that according to the traditions of the early Christians, man was created on Friday, and on that day Christ died to satisfy for his sin, while he rose from the dead the third day after, which was Sunday, the day God said, "let there be light." The ancient writers say Christmas is celebrated as the years roll by on each of the days of the week, to sanctify each one of them, and take from them the curse of Heaven for the sin of Adam,

---

[1] They call them Dodecameron. [2] Gueranger, Le Temps de Noel, v. i, p. 14. [3] St. Thomas, III. P. q. 8. 1, etc. [4] St. Augustin has thirty-two sermons on Christmas which he calls Natalis Domini. [5] Epis. ad Jan.

while Christ rose from the dead with the splendors of
the sun on Sunday, and for that reason Easter is celebrated only on Sunday.

He was born in the winter of the world, when the
nations had lost the revelations given by God to their
father Adam, when the poets of Greece and Rome had
poisoned the minds of the ancients by their gods and
godesses,[1] and the daily decreasing light of the sun in
the fall of the year before the winter solstice, is a picture of the light of God's revelation decreasing as the
years of the olden times rolled by, before the birth of
Christ.

The great writers of the early ages of the Church[2] stand
astonished at the thought of the Lord having been born
during the darkest part of the year, and during the darkest
period of the pagan world ; that God would thus make
the natural decline of the light of the sun to be a figure
of the decline of the light of the revelation made to man
in the garden, and that just as the sun began to return to
the northern hemisphere, the Son of justice would come
to enlighten the world. "On the day when the Lord
commenced to diminish the shades of darkness and the
light increases, night is driven from the earth. Certainly,
brethren, that did not come to pass by chance on the day
when shone forth he, who is the human and the Divine.
Nature, under that symbol reveals a secret to those whose
eyes are penetrating, and who are able to understand the
surroundings of the Saviour's coming."[3]   "Rejoice,
brethren, for this day is holy, not because of the visible
sun, but because of the birth of the invisible Creator of
the sun.   The Son of God chose the day of his birth as
he chose his Mother, but he is the Creator, at the same
time, of the day and of the Mother.   When the light
begins to increase, that day was apt to signify the work
of Christ, by his grace ever renewing our inner man.
The Eternal Creator having wished to be born in time,
it was right that his birth was in harmony with creation."[4]

In another sermon on Christmas, the great bishop of

---

[1] Tebault, The Church and the Gentile World.   [2] St. Maxim of Turin, St. Leo, St.
Bernard, etc.   [3] Greg. Naz. Hom. in Nat. Dom.   [4] St. Augustin Sermo in Natali,
Dom. Lil.

Hippo[1] explains to us the mysterious words of St. John the Baptist: "He must increase but I must decrease."[2] He says these are prophetic words, which in the literal sense mean that John's mission had come to an end when he had shown the Messiah in the person of Christ. But there is a deeper meaning. The holy Baptist came into the world, when at the summer solstice the days began to grow shorter, while Christ was born when the days commenced to grow longer.[3] The infidels of the old world tried to prove that religion and science do not agree; but the deeper we dive into science and religion the more we are struck with their agreement. We must confess that while we are in love with our age, while we have read the wonderful discoveries of our times, while we count as our friends the great inventors, yet we must confess that day by day we are obliged to admit that God made the world but for Christ, for the Church, and for the salvation of the race; and while the mind of man goes on daily grasping the secrets of nature, and using them for the happiness of man, still the truths revealed by God can neither increase nor diminish, but ever be the same as fulfilled by the Son of God born at Bethlehem.

He was born in Bethlehem, as the prophet foretold. "AND THOU, BETHLEHEM EPHRATA, out of thee shall he come forth unto me that is to be the ruler in Israel."[4] The prophets knew it, the people of Israel expected it, and the wise ones of Judea told Herod of it.[5] God chose the race of Abraham before all the nations of the earth, that he might prefigure the ceremonies of the Mass by the ceremonies of their temple. He chose the fairest maiden of the race of Juda for a Mother for His Son, he wished to be born at Bethlehem (in Hebrew, "The house of bread"),[6] because he was to become "the living bread which came down from heaven,[7] and there, in the city of "the house of bread," he was first seen by man. "Your fathers did eat manna in the desert and are dead," but the Saviour came to be "the bread which cometh down from heaven, that if any man eat of it he

---

[1] St. Augustin. [2] John iii, 30. [3] St. Augustin, Sermo in Natali Domini, xi. [4] Mich. v, 2. [5] Matth. ii., 5. [6] Gregorie Mag. Hom. viii., in Evang.; El Porque de las Ceremonias, Trat. Cuarto, c. xiii. [7] John vi., 41.

may not die."[1]   Thus the greatest act of God was the
birth of his Son at Bethlehem, the mystery of the Incarnation.   The greatest act of God now is Communion,
the mystery of the Eucharist.   One is a series of miracles by which the Lord united with his creatures, the
other is a series of miracles by which the Lord unites
with his Christians, and these two wonders of the works
of God are so closely related, that when celebrating the
solemnities of the Blessed Eucharist we say the Preface
of Christmas.   The Incarnation is the uniting of that
soul and body of Christ to the Divinity of the Second
Person of the Trinity, while Communion is the uniting
of the same Christ to each one who receives him.   Thus
while we have with the Church waited and prepared
during the weeks of Advent to receive Him, that preparation would be useless if we let this holy time pass without going to Communion, for whoever receives him he
has given to become the sons of God by adoption.[2]

In the cycle of the year, during the holy time of the
Christmas holidays, the Church surrounds the manger of
the Infant-God with the names of her most illustrious
Saints.   Like the twinkling planets circling around the
sun, we celebrate the memory of the most celebrated
Saints during these happy days of the birth of our Lord.
St. Stephen who, first among the followers of the Saviour,
gave his life in martyrdom;[3] St. John, the beloved Apos-
tle;[4] the Holy Innocents, put to death by Herod;[5] and
St. Thomas of Canterbury, the great Saint of the Eng-
lish race.[6]   No other season of the year shows such
noble names as those we mentioned.   The Apostolic
College gives us the names of its greatest stars: St.
Peter, the first Pope on the throne of his supremacy at
Rome,[7] and St. Paul in his conversion on the road to
Damascus.[8]   The army of the millions of martyrs send
us the names of Timothy, the companion of St. Paul;[9]
St. Ignatius, the third after St. Peter to sit on his throne
as Bishop of Antioch;[10] St. Polycarp, the disciple of John
the Evangelist and Bishop of Smyrna;[11] St. Vincent and
Anastasius, one a Spaniard, the other a Persian; one
put to death under Dioclesian and Maximin, the other

---

[1] John vi., 50.   [2] John i., 12.   [3] Dec. 26.   [4] Dec. 27.   [5] Dec. 28.   [6] Dec. 29.
[7] Jan. 18.   [8] Jan. 25.   [9] Jan. 24.   [10] Feb. 1.   [11] Jan. 26.

by Chosroa. The line of the Popes gives us four of their most noble names: Sylvester, the great Pope who led Constantine the Emperor to become a Christian;[1] St. Telesphor, who kept to the Apostolic traditions and ordained the seven weeks of Lent to be kept before Easter, and that Mass should be said at nine in the morning;[2] St. Hyginus, who condemned the dangerous errors of the Gnostics, and upheld the Divinity of Christ;[3] St. Marcellinus, the first martyr of the last of the ten great persecutions of the Church.[4] The sublime school of the doctors of the Church gives us the names of St. Hilary,[5] who by his writings against the Arians, and his resolute opposition to the Emperor, saved the Church, and St. Chrysostom, who, as Archbishop of Antioch and Constantinople, left us the grandest homilies on the Bible. The Pastors of the people have St. Francis of Sales, the great Bishop and Prince of Geneva. The ascetics give us St. Paul, the first Hermit;[6] St. Maurus, the Patron of the Cloister; St. Peter, the redeemer of captives;[7] St. Raymond of Pennafort, the teacher of justice and the regulator of consciences.[8] The defenders of the Church have St. Canutus, King of the Danes, who, to help the English against William the Conqueror, sent his brother to fight for the cause of religion, but the holy king was killed at the altar by his brother.[9] The holy Choir of Virgins is represented by the sweet St. Agnes,[10] the noble Roman Lady,[11] and by the heroic St. Martina,[12] while the poor are there in the person of St. Paul, the humble lover of the manger. Behold what a bright galaxy of Saints circle around the cradle of the born God when we celebrate his feast. But the Church celebrates the day of the death of the Saints, and not of their birth, for they were born sinners. They came into this world with the sin of Adam on their souls; while they lived they might have sinned, and it is not reasonable to rejoice at the birth of a poor exile like man when born into this world. For these reasons the Church celebrates the birthdays of our Lord and of his holy forerunner St. John the Baptist,[13] for these came into the world without sin. The

---

[1] Dec. 31; Brev. Roman. [2] Jan. 5; Darras, Hist. of the Church, v. 1., p. 103. [3] Jan. 11. [4] Jan. 16. [5] Jan. 14. [6] Jan 15. [7] Jan. 31. [8] Jan. 23. [9] Brev. Roman. Of. S. Canuti, Jan. 19. [10] Jan. 28. [11] Jan. 30. [12] Jan. 30. [13] S. Aug. Ser. ccxxxvii. n. 1.

birth of both was told by angels. One was born of a
sterile woman, the other without a father; both had disciples, both baptised; both were the greatest men born
of women.[1] We celebrate the death of the patriarchs,
the prophets, the apostles, the martyrs and the millions
of her Saints. The birthdays of Christ and of St. John
the Baptist the Church holds sacred, and St. Augustine
says he has received this doctrine from the most ancient
traditions of the early ages, showing how the Church
never changes in her rites and ceremonies.[2]

Guided by the hand of the Holy Spirit, the Church in
ages past formed her rites and ceremonies to teach her
children the truths revealed by God to man. And to tell
the joy with which she celebrates the happy time of the
Christmas holidays, the vestments are always white
during the twenty days following the great feast of
Christmas. Only on the feasts of the holy martyrs, and
on the Octave of the Holy Innocents, the clergy are
clothed in red in memory of their blood, while on the
feast of the Holy Innocents we use the violet vestments,
the color of sorrow to recall the weeping of the mothers
of Bethlehem, for the death of their little ones.[3] The
pure whiteness of the sacerdotal robes tells the people of
the shining angels, of the pure Mother, of the chaste
Joseph, and of the holy shepherds around the manger of
the transcendent Son of God, born to be the Redeemer
of our race.[4]

During the last twenty days of the Christmas time the
many feasts of the Saints require that the vestments of
the clergy are in harmony, sometimes with the roses of
the martyrs, with the immortals which crown the heads
of the Popes, the bishops and the priests, and with the
lilies of the valley, the types of the virgins. If there be
no feast of the double class on the Sundays of this time
calling for red, or if the Septuagesima time does not require violet, the vestments will be green, signifying by
the white and the green that our Lord is the "flower of
the field and the lily of the valleys."[5] As green is the
color of hope, the green vestments tell us that the Lord
is born to give us the hope of salvation, and after the

---

[1] Matth. xi., 11 ; see St. Augustin., Sermo cclxxxvii., de Nat. Joan Baptst. [2] St.
Augustin, Sermo ccxcii., de Nat. Joan Baptst., vi. [3] Matth. ii., 18. [4] Gueranger,
Le Tempt de Noel, p. 25. [5] Cant. of Cant., ii., 1.

winter of the human race, the winter of the Pagans and of the Jews, the blooming springtime of green plants and of white flowers has come to us in the grace of Christianity.[1]

Such are some of the meanings of the Christmas time, when God becomes so familiar with the children of men. But the mystery of the wonderful birth of our Lord asks something on our part. for he took that human nature of ours that we might adore him, love him and receive him. We must adore him, for he is God, and to adore anything but God is idolatry. For that reason we never adore the Saints, the Apostles, or the Virgin Mary. But as we celebrate the feast of our birth, as we renew the centennial of the foundation of our great nation, as we love to honor the names of the great and the honored dead, we keep the days of the great and honored ones of the Christian religion. That is the reason why the Feasts of the Saints are celebrated. We must adore only God. But we must not only adore him, we must also love him. And in all the world what is there which excites our love like the face and the form of a little child? For that he came and took the form of a little babe, to win our love. Thus to renew forever the memory of that God-child born at Bethlehem, the people of each church lay the image of a little child in a manger each Christmas night, when the people, seeing the beautiful form of the infant, remember the Babe of Bethlehem born to them so long ago, of the Virgin Mother, on the first Christmas night, when Immanuel became man. Not only should we love him, but we must receive him. In mystic teachings Advent is called the Cleansing Life, for by the self-denial and the penance of that holy time, the soul is prepared for the coming of the Lord, while the Christmas time is called the Enlightening Life, for then the Lord comes to enlighten the souls of his people.[2] Light here is used as a figure of grace, and the way God sends grace into the heart of man is by the Sacraments; therefore, for man to be enlightened he must go to the Sacraments—he must receive the bread of life, the Holy Eucharist, "as many as received him he gave them power to be made the sons

---

[1] Gueranger, Le Temps. de Noel, p. 26.   [2] Theologia Mystica.

of God."[1] By the decrees of God he was born in Bethlehem, "The City of Bread," that we might receive him, "The Bread of Life."[2] The custom of going to Holy Communion has been continued in the Church since its very beginning. In old times it was made a solemn duty to approach the altar at this holy season,[3] as well as at Easter and at Pentecost. Such has been the ideas always preached to the people by the Popes, the bishops and the clergy.[4]

Christmas Eve has come. One day more to Christmas. In the most ancient times the children of the Church fasted till the evening, to prepare themselves for the coming of their Lord, but now, by the motherly indulgence of the Church, they are allowed to take a meal and a collation.[5] In the afternoon the clergy say their Office and end with the first Vespers of Christmas. According to the most venerable traditions of our holy Church this Eve of Christmas is a solemn day, and the great Fathers of the Church preached their finest sermons in honor of the Word became man on Christmas night. St. Gregory of Nazianzen,[6] of the Greek Church, St. Bernard of the Latin Church,[7] and St. Ephraim of the Syrian Church, appear to exhaust their poetry and their eloquence in their sermons to their people, preparing them on Christmas Eve for the coming of their Saviour.

Ancient Europe, that part of the globe beloved of God, saw the principal events take place this day. France came forth from the darkness of paganism at the baptism of Clovis, converted by St. Remus, and the fierce warrior became the docile christian. A hundred years rolled by, and St. Augustin was sent by Pope Gregory the Great to convert the half savage English. He brought their king Ethelbert into the Church on Christmas Eve. He went onward toward York[8] preaching the Gospel, and the crowds of converts asked to be baptised. He fixed the great day of Christmas Eve as the time for the solemn rite, and ten thousand men, not mentioning women and children, were washed in the waters of baptism. From that day till the time of Henry VIII. the English people were

---

[1] John i., 12. [2] John vi., 48. [3] Concil. Ag. c. 15, held in 506. [4] See Leo. ser., in Nat. Dom., vi. Ven. Bede Com in Luke, St. Bonaventure Rhaban Maur, Ser. xi., in Nat. Dom., etc. [5] Gueranger, Le Temps de Noel, p. 151. [6] Ser. xxxviii. ad Theophn. [7] Ser. vi. in Vigil. Nat. Dom. [8] An Cyclop. Augustin.

fervent Catholics. In Rome on Christmas Day, in the year 800, St. Leo III. placed the Imperial crown on the head of the great Charlemagne, and his empire from that time became the means of spreading the Gospel among the peoples of the north of Europe. The nations of the west of Europe, struck with wonder at the great feast of Christmas, began to count their years by beginning on that day, and it is the first day of the year in some of the most ancient calendars, martyrologies, in the bulls of Popes, in the letters of embassies, in the decrees of kings, and in one of the Councils of Cologne.

When Christmas falls on Friday or Saturday, there is no fast from food or from meat, for a dispensation was given by Pope Honorius III.[1] Even before, in the ninth century, Pope St. Nicholas I.[2] had given a dispensation of the same kind for the feasts of Christmas, of St. John the Evangelist, of the Epiphany, of the Assumption of Our Lady of St. Lawrence, of St. John the Baptist, and of St. Peter and Paul when they fell on Friday or Saturday. But these exceptions were but for those to whom they were sent, and not for the whole Church. Now the only time we can eat meat on Friday is when Christmas falls on that day. Even the laws of the nations of the Middle Ages allowed the people the freedom of not paying their debts during the time of the week following Christmas, called for that reason the Remission Week.

I.—CHRISTMAS DAY.

We now come to the time of the great ceremony of Christmas, to the sacrifice of the Mass, when our Lord who came into the world by the Virgin, comes again by the words of the priest, and upon our altars as from the manger he showers down his blessings on us all. At other times of the year the clergy can say but one Mass on the same day, or two when it is necessary for all the people to assist, and that by the permission of the bishop.

The word Mass comes from an old Hebrew word Massah, a debt, or from the Greek Myesis, or from the

---

[1] In 1216.   [2] Resp. ad. con. Bulgar.

ancient word of Northern Europe, Mess or Messe, a feast, or from the Latin words sending away the people at the end "Ete Messa est." Go the Dismissal is at hand. The latter appears to be the origin of the word. Christmas, comes from Christ's Mass, shortened into Christmas, or from Christ's Feast, feast being Mass,[1] from that comes also Michaelmas Day, Candlemas Day, and other English names of the feasts of the Church during the year.

Such is the greatness of the mystery of this day, that the clergy say three Masses; these three Masses are to honor the three Persons of the Most Holy Trinity. The first is to give glory to the Father for sending his Son to be born into the world, the second is to glorify the Holy Ghost because he formed the body and soul of our Lord in the breast of the Virgin, while the third is to praise the Son for becoming man.[2]

Pope Telesphorus[3] ordered these three Masses to be said to show that by the birth of Christ that three classes of Saints were, save those of the patriarchs, guided by the law of nature, those of the Israelites led by the law of Moses, and those of the Church directed by her laws.[4] The first Mass is said in the middle of the night, to tell of the darkness on the mind of man when he fell by the sin in the garden; the second is said at the dawn of day, to show the light of revelation dawning by the prophecies of the Old Testament, and the third Mass is offered up in the brightness of the day to teach us of the time when Christ illuminated the world by his heavenly Gospel.[5] The first Mass is offered up in memory of his birth as a man, and for that reason we read the Gospel which tells us of the edict of Augustus, that all the inhabitants of the Roman Empire should be numbered,[6] proving to us that he was born of the family of David. The second Mass is said in remembrance of his birth in the hearts of his followers,[7] and for that reason we read the Gospel giving the history of the calling the pastors to adore him.[8] The third Mass commemorates his eternal birth from the bosom of his Father[9] before all ages, and

---

[1] See O'Brien, Hist. of the Mass, etc., p. 1. [2] An. Liturg. du Predicat. par M. L'Abb. J. p. 24. [3] 127 to 142; Durandus Rationale Div. I. n. 17; El Porque de las Ceremonias, Trat. Cuarto. c., xlii. [4] Durand., Rationale Div., L. vi. c. xiii. n. 17. [5] El Porque de las Ceremonias, Trat. Cuarto., c. xiii. [6] Luke ii. [7] O'Brien, Hist. of the Mass, p. 169. [8] Luke ii. [9] Fabri con. in Fest. Nat. Christi, con. iii.

for that reason its Gospel tells of the time when the word was, "In the beginning was the word, and the word was with God and the word was God."[1]

The first Mass celebrates his birth as a man, for as a man he was born that night; as a man we love to call him, as we cannot understand him as God. He was born of Mary, but the Gospels give the parentage of Joseph, and not of Mary,[2] for the Evangelists wrote for the early Christians, among whom were many Jews, and the custom of the Jews was never to give the ancestors of women. The writers of the Gospels being Jews, wanting to convert their brethren, followed their customs, and give the genealogy of Joseph, who, according to the law of Moses, married Mary, his cousin. The parentage then of Joseph is the same as that of Mary. The one who gives us the account of the three births of our Lord are St. Luke and St. John; for "in the mouth of two or three witnesses every word shall stand."[3] The first Mass is said at midnight, for tradition tells us it was the hour of his birth, the second is said at the twilight hour, for then the shepherds came to adore him, while the third is said in the day that its brightness may figure the glories of the Godhead.

The three Masses of Christmas are found in the Sacramentaries of Popes Gelasius and Gregory, and the custom of saying these three Masses were introduced into France at the time when the Catholic religion began to flourish under the reign of Charlemagne.[4]

At the second Mass a remembrance is made of Anastasia, a Roman lady, who, converted on Christmas day, excited the wrath of Publius, her husband, because of her kindness to the poor and the imprisoned Christians. At last she was burned alive under the reign of Dioclesian. The church dedicated to her name was built on the ruins of her house, and that is where the second Mass of Christmas is said in Rome. On the same day a virgin, Eugenia, suffered martyrdom in the persecution of Gallienus,[5] nevertheless the widow Anastasia was preferred before her, to show that although virginity is a higher state than the

---

[1] John i. ; An. Lit. du Pred. par. M. L'Abbe, J. p. 24. [2] Math. i. [3] Deut. xix. 15. [4] L'An Lit, par L' Ab. J. p. 25. [5] Publius Licinius Egnatius Gallienus, born 233, died 203.

married life, yet the married are holy and are blessed in their children as Mary was at Bethlehem.[1]

The Preface of Christmas is said on the day of the feast, at the three Masses, and on all the feasts of this time, except on the Octave of St. John the Evangelist, also on all feasts of the Blessed Sacrament, because the mystery of the Eucharist is so like that of the Incarnation. During the three Masses of to-day we pray that he who is born the Saviour of the world as he is the author of our divine birth, he may be also the giver of our everlasting birth in Heaven.

Such are some ideas taken from the great writers and Fathers of the Church relating to the holy day of Christmas, but we cannot close without giving the history of Christmas Day in 303. Dioclesian had published a decree throughout the Roman Empire, which brought a most frightful persecution on the Church. The edict was nailed up in Nicomedia, where the Emperor then lived. It was quickly torn down by a Christian, who paid for his courage with his life. The faithful on every side prepared themselves for death for the love of Christ and of his Church. Christmas Day came and they gathered in their churches. Thousands crowded the great cathedral of Nicomedia for the Christmas Mass, for they thought that, perhaps, it would be their last Christmas on earth. Dioclesian heard of the meeting and sent his soldiers to surround the church, with orders to fire the building at the four corners. The people, devoutly hearing Mass, suddenly were startled by the sound of the trumpet and by the voice of a crier telling them, that those who wished could save themselves by coming out and offering sacrifices to the image of Jupiter, standing before the door of the church, otherwise they would be roasted alive. In the name of the people one cried out: "We are all Christians ; we honor Christ as the only God and the only King ; we are ready to offer our lives as a sacrifice this day." At that reply the church was set on fire, and the flames rose heavenward like a holocaust of burning flesh to the Son of God, the 303d Christmas after he was born, to found the Catholic Church, which alone gives such examples of heroism.

---

[1] See St. Augustin in Natal. Dom. ix.

II.—New Year's Day.

Among all civilized nations New Year's Day begins the year. Few know how much they are indebted to Pope Gregory XIII. for fixing the calendar so as to know the date of events.[1] In ancient times there was no fixed era from which to date the years. Some people counted from their birth; monarchs from their coronation; the Romans, from the foundation of Rome; the Greeks, from their Olympic games; the Babylonians, from the reign of Nabonassar; the Mohammedans, from the flight of Mohammed; the Persians, from the beginning of the reign of Yezdegird; and the Armenians from the Council of Tiben.[2] The Hindoos have three eras to count from, the Chinese date from the beginning of the reign of their Emperors, the Jews count from the creation; the Russians, in Church matters, using the Septuagint version of the Bible, dated from the creation,[3] but in civil affairs they date from the birth of Christ,[4] like the other civilized nations of the world. We can understand from these different ways of counting time, the difficulty of fixing the dates of ancient times and the wisdom of the Church in adapting the method of counting from the birth of Christ.

The Romans dedicated the first of January to the god Janus, offering sacrifice to him on twelve altars, and they took the events of that day as signs of the coming year. They met each other with kindly greetings and sent presents to their friends. From that comes our "Happy New Year," and the custom of sending presents to our friends. From the time of the Apostles the Church celebrated New Year's Day,[5] in memory of our Lord's circumcision, eight days after his birth, as given in the Gospel.[6] They condemned the idolatrous rites of the pagans on that day, for not only the Romans, but the Druids and the Saxons sent gifts and carried out their superstitious ceremonies.[7] The presents of the people and of the nobles became sources of revenue to the kings in ancient times and to the aristocracy in feudal days. In New York and many cities of this country, gentlemen make social calls on New Year's, a custom coming from

---

[1] Am. Cyclo. A. Chron. [2] Held in 552. [3] 5508 years B. C. [4] Last year they changed to the Georgian style. [5] Concil. Turon, c. xvii., in an. 567, El Porque, Trat. Cuarto c. xx. [6] Luke ii. 21. [7] See Fabri Conciones, Dom. Quinq., con. iv. n. iii.

CATHEDRAL OF SEVILLE.

the Dutch settlers of this state. The creation would be the natural time to date from, but with the exception of the Hebrews, all other nations go back till they are lost in fable. In the sacred writings of the Hebrews there are two periods, one of the Jews, stating that the creation took place 4,004 years before Christ, the other of the Septuagint, putting his birth 5,508 from the creation. The Church knowing that dates and exact times have nothing to do with salvation and faith, and wishing to honor the two great Versions of the Bible, uses the Septuagint manner of counting the years from creation in the martyrology and the Hebrew in all other computations.

When God called Abraham from the land of the Chaldeans[1] and from his father's home, and when he promised to make him the father of many peoples, he commanded him to circumcise himself and all his house.[2] Every baby boy was to undergo that operation the eighth day after his birth. It was the way the children of Abraham were to be known from the gentiles.[3] Under the law of Moses we see that the same command was given.[4] From the Hebrews the Egyptians learned to circumcise their children, for we find by the oldest histories that they practiced that rite.[5] The Jews, from whom Christ was to be born, descended from Abraham, to him was promised that from him would descend the Redeemer. As many ages elapsed from the time of Abraham to that of Christ, it was necessary to have some sign by which to know the children of Abraham, so as to be sure he was the promised Christ. That sign was circumcision.

Christ was circumcised to show that he was of the race of Abraham;[6] to prove that he took human flesh against the Manitchians, who said his body was of thin air; against the Apollinarians, who taught that his body was the same as his Divinity; against the Valentians, who thought his body came from Heaven, and to give the Jews no reason for not receiving him as one of their race. He was circumcised to give us an example in being obedient to the law of Moses,[7] that coming in the likeness of sinful flesh he did not reject what purified the flesh, as the

---

[1] S. Aug. vol. 309, 310. [2] Gen. xvii. [3] Benedict xiv. de Fest., D. N. J. C. L. I., C. I. n. 1, 2, 3. [4] Levit xii. 3, Exod. xii. 44. [5] Diod. Sicul. Bib. 1 i., Cap. 17; Herodotus. L ii. Cap. 10. Jerem. iv. 8, Natalis Alexander, Hist. Vet. Test. T. I. d. 6, etc. [6] El Porque de las Ceremonias, Trat. Cuarto, c. xv. [7] Calmet. sup. Lucam, l. ii. n. 41.

Apostle says : " God sent his Son, made of a woman, made under the law."[1]   " Thus it was meet that he take the mark in sin, as he was born to wipe out sin."[2]   Circumcision was the figure of the old man of sin in Abraham, the first father of the faithful being renewed[3] in the new man free from sin in the second Father, Christ,[4] and therefore it was right for him, a child of Abraham, to be circumcised.[5] He was circumcised in the stable,[6] for not in the temple, or in the synagogues, but in their houses were the Jews accustomed to perform that operation.[7] He was circumcised the eighth day,[8] as the law of Moses required, and as the Gospel says ; " And after eight days were accomplished that the child should be circumcised, his name was called Jesus, which was called by the angel before he was conceived in the womb."[9]

From the beginning of the Church the early Christians celebrated the eighth day after the birth of our Lord, in the Codex of the Church called sometimes the Gelasian Sacramentary, because of the prayers added by that Pope,[10] this feast is called the Octave of Christmas, and thus it appears to have been known in ancient times.[11] As it falls on the eighth day after Christmas, it can be called either the feast of the Octave of Christmas or the Feast of the Circumcision.[12] For that reason it is named in the Missal " The feast of the Circumcision of our Lord and the Octave of his birth," and, in some of the oldest Missals, there is a remembrance of the birth of Christ on New Year's day.[13]

The pagans used to celebrate the day[14] by sacrifices to the god Janus and to the goddess Strenia.   The men dressed themselves in women's clothes and the women in men's garments, and during the ceremonies they spent their time in feasting, debauchery and badness. To warn the Christians St. Augustin preached a sermon against these pagan rites.[15] The Council of Tours condemned them,[16] opening with the words, " Our fathers commanded

[1] Gal. iv. 4. [2] Bossuet xvii., Semaine Elevat. I. [3] See Fabri Conciones in Test. Circum. Dom. con. iii. [4] Concil. Tredent L. vi. c. iv. [5] St. Thomas, p. iii. q. xxxvii. a. 1. [6] Apocryphal Gospels, Arabic Gospel of the Saviour's Infancy, n. 5. [7] Benedict xiv. de Fest. D. N. J. Christi. c. n. 14. [8] S. Aug. Sermo xv. in Oct. Nat. Dom. n. 1. [9] Luke ii. 21. [10] Benedict XIV. says Pope Leo is its author. De F. D. N. J. Christi, C. I. n. 17. [11] Can. Pron. de Consecrat. dist. i. [12] Ivonis Carnot. in Sermone de Circumcis. Dom. and Thomassinus Tract de Die. Fest. Cel. L. II., C. 8, n. 12. [13] Baronius Not. ad Martyr. Rom. Ia. Jan. [14] See S. Aug. Ser. xv. in Octav. Nat. Dom. n. 1. [15] Sermo ccxviii. [16] Held in 567, Can 17.

the Litanies to be said on the Kalends of January, the bells to be tolled at the eighth hour, and the Mass of the Circumcision of our Lord to be properly celebrated." As far as we are able to go back we cannot find when this feast was commenced to be celebrated. All histories prove that it came from the Apostles. Formerly they said two Masses on New Year's, one in remembrance of the circumcision, and the other in honor of the Blessed Virgin,[1] but after the XIIIth century the latter Mass fell into disuse.[2]

The Catholic Church has no prayers relating to the beginning of the civil year, as the ecclesiastical year begins on the first Sunday of Advent, but we ask the people to thank God for his graces showered down on us during the last twelve months, and we ask them to beseech the Lord to continue his blessings for the coming year. To give all an example, the Pope goes to the Church of Jesu, there to sing the "Thee, O God, we praise," to the Lord, and finishes with the Benediction of the Blessed Sacrament.[3] The same sentiments are found carried out in the ancient Gothic Church of Spain.[4]

The Greek Church celebrates the Feast of the Circumcision of our Lord on the 26th of December, under the title of the Synaxis of the Mother of God. Thus the Eastern and the Western churches delight in honoring the Mother of our Lord. The Greeks call her "Theotocos," and the Latins "Deipara," both meaning Mother of God, customs going back to the Council of Ephesus, when, according to the Apostolic traditions, they commended all to remember Mary in the feasts of the Christmas time. The days when her honor is celebrated are different in the Latin and Greek Rites, but the teaching of the two churches is the same. Pope Sixtus III. beautified the great Church of Mary Major with magnificent mosaics, and that monument of the faith of the fifth century comes down to us with the inscription placed upon it by the saintly Pontiff, "Sixtus, bishop of the people of God."[5]

The Mass for New Year's is entitled "At St. Mary's across the Tiber," for there in that Church, the oldest

---

[1] El Porque de las Cerem., Trat. ca., c. xv. [2] Benedict XIV. de Festis D. N. Jesu Christi C. I. n. 25 et Durandus Rationale Div. l. v. c. xv n. 16. [3] Gueranger, Le temps de Noel vol. ii. p. 464. [4] Missal Mozarabic. [5] Xiatus Episcopus Plebis dei. Les Plus Bel. Eglises du Monde Par Bourasse, p. 103.

and most venerable of the temples built in Rome to the honor of the Virgin, the New Year's Mass is said. It was built on the celebrated spot, where, according to the legend, a well of oil flowed from the ground the night the Lord was born, bursting forth and flowing even to the Tiber. The early Christians saw in it a figure of the Christ that is the Anointed, for that is the meaning of Christ in the ancient Hebrew. That Church was built in the third century and consecrated by Pope Calistus. To-day it is known by the name of the Fountain of Oil.

The Feast of Christmas is ended. The four Octaves of Christmas, of St. Stephen, of St. John, and of the Holy Innocents, have gone their course, and now we come to the Eve of the Epiphany. The word Epiphany comes from the Greek and means to manifest or to show forth, for on the twelfth day from his birth he was known to the Gentiles in the person of the three Kings.

The Eve or Vigil of Epiphany is not a fasting day like the Eve of Christmas, when we waited for the coming of our Lord, because now he has come ; and to show our joy we wear at Mass the white vestments and not the violet as at the Eve of Christmas. When this Eve falls on Sunday, it has with the Eve of Christmas the honor of not being anticipated the day before, having all the privileges of the Lord's day, and then the Mass will be that of the Sunday within the Octave of Christmas.

The Greeks keep a fast this day in remembrance of their baptism, which in former times was administered on the Eve of Epiphany. During the night they bless the baptismal water with great ceremonies, and then baptise their converts.

To-day we have a remembrance at Lauds and in the Mass of Pope Telesphorus, who was the eighth Pope from St. Peter, who was crowned in the year 127, and put to death in 142.[1] To honor the birth of our Lord he ordered three Masses to be said on Christmas, and the " Glory be to God in the Highest " sung at Mass, but we do not know whether he only renewed these customs which were falling away from Apostolic traditions or instituted them.

---

[1] St. Ireneus says he was martyred in 138.

III.—THE EPIPHANY.

To-day we celebrate the feast of Epiphany, that is[1] the manifestation of our Lord to the gentile nations in the person of the three kings of the East, who came to adore him.[2]

After his birth it was necessary for the salvation of man for Christ to manifest himself to some, but not to all. If he was known to all, the Jews would not have crucified him, for, "if they had known it, they would never have crucified the Lord of glory."[3] If all had known him they would not have had any merit for their faith, which is the belief of things which appear not.[4] Again, if they had known him as the Son of God, they would have doubted that he was at the same time a man.[5] But it was in the designs of God, that his birth should be known to some, and by these shown to others. For that reason he was "made manifest, not to all the people, but to witnesses pre-ordained by God,"[6] who by their words preached him to others, and thus the knowledge of his life and wonders came to us. Mary and Joseph only knew him before his birth, but that his birth might become known to all of different conditions of life, he made himself known to persons of every station in life.[7] "The shepherds were Israelites, the Magi gentiles; these were near to him, those far from him, nevertheless all came to the corner stone." The Magi were wise men. They knew the course of the stars.[8] They were men of power, for they ruled kingdoms, while the shepherds were of the lowest ranks of society. Simeon and Anna were just and innocent, the Magi sinners; Joseph and Simeon men, Mary and Anna women; thus he made himself known to persons of all conditions of life.[9] He came first of all to the Jews, and for that reason he was made known first to the Jews in the person of the shepherds. He came in the second place to the gentiles, and for that reason he was manifest to the gentiles in the persons of the Magi.[10]

The Magi came from the East, for there the light begins; they were the first to be called to the faith, for

---

[1] S. Aug. Ser. ii. in Ep. Dom. n. 1. [2] Math. II. [3] 1 Cor. ii. 8. [4] Heb. xi. 1. [5] St. Augustin Epist. ad Voluslanum, 136 Al. 101. [6] Acts x., 40, 41. [7] St. Augustin, ser. de Epiphania xxxii., et de Temp., c. i. [8] St. Anselm. Ven Bede, Rupertus in ii. Matt., St. Chrysostom. Hom. St. Leo Ser. ii. de Epih., etc. [9] St. Thomas, iii. P. q. xxxvi. a. iii. [10] St. Augustin, Ser. xxx. de Temp.

faith is the light of the soul.[1] We know not from what part of the East they came; some writers say from Chaldea, others from Persia, while others again think that they came from Arabia Felix. But it is enough to know that they came from the land of ignorance, from the midst of the gentiles, where God was not known, nor the Messiah expected or promised.[2] But, perhaps, the prophecy of Balaam had been handed down by tradition to the Magi,[3] or some knowledge of the birth of our Lord was given to the gentiles, as the Fountain of Oil bursting forth across the Tiber, at Rome, or as the three suns appeared in Spain,[4] or they learned it from the writings of Zoroaster. When the Angel came to tell the birth of our Lord he went not to the Scribes, or to the Pharisees, for they were corrupted with jealousy, but he called the shepherds, for they were upright and simple, keeping the law of Moses, and thinking of the prophecies relating to the coming of the Saviour.[5]

Christ was born for man's salvation, the foundation of which is faith in his divinity and in his humanity, he was then to be known in such a way that he would be believed to be both God and man. If he had shown by miracles in his infancy that he was God, they would not believe that he was man. Therefore, he showed himself in his childhood, as a child born like other men, that they might first believe that he was man, while he reserved the wonders of his power till his public life, when he showed that he was God. For that reason we read that he lived and grew, and waxed strong, gaining in wisdom before God and man just like other children.[6] How wonderfully God showed his wisdom in making known to the world the birth of his Son!

The Jews were accustomed to receive truth from heaven by the ministry of Angels, for they "received the law by the disposition of angels,"[7] while the gentiles, and especially the Chaldeans, were highly versed in the science of the stars. To the holy ones of the Jews, to Simeon and to Anna, the birth of the God-man was shown

---

[1] St. Chrysostom Hom. II., Op. Im. [2] Bossuet Elevat., 17 e Sem. elev. iv. [3] St. Basil Hom. de hum. nat. Christi; St. Christ. Hom. vi. In Math. S. S. Hieron, et Anselm in cap. ii. Math. et Origen, Sep. Num. Arabic Gospel of the Saviour's Nativity, n. 7: See Smith's Dic. of the Bible, Art. Magi. [4] Eusebius in Chron. In August, 3 years before his birth, Olymp. 184, Innocent III. Ser de Nativ. [5] St. Chrysostom, Sup. ii. In Lucam. [6] Luke 11, 52. [7] Acts vii. 53.

by the interior illumination of the Holy Ghost. The shepherds were men given to sensible things, and to them his birth was made known by a vision of angels, as often before the heavenly Spirits appeared to the Jews; while to the Magi, learned in the knowledge of the stars, a star appeared and led them to the manger of the Infant God.[1] He was preached to the Jews, who reasoned by a reasonable being, that is by an Angel; but the gentiles, who knew not how to use reason so as to lead them to the Lord, they were led by signs."[2] This manifestation of the Lord was not regarding his flesh and his human nature, which could be seen by all, but it was the showing forth of him to be the Son of God. No one can control a star. Of all the old astrologers, no one ever said that a star left its course and led a man to the place of a new born babe. No birth but that of Christ was pointed out by a star.[3] St. Chrysostom says that there is a tradition in the East, that a people on the borders of the ocean had kept a book written by Seth, the son of Noe, in which was the legend that a star would appear and tell them the time of the birth of God. Carefully they watched for the appearance of that star, till at length it came. They ascended a mountain when they saw it coming. When it came near, it had the form of a little child stretched out upon a cross. We give the legend as it is given, but we know that a star alone would not lead the Magi to the manger. Perhaps Angels told them of the heavenly birth,[4] or rather, as St. Leo says, God enlightened their minds by his grace,[5] for a star alone, which appears only to the eye, could not bring them to the new born King. The light of the star enlightened their eyes, but the light of God was in their minds, and when they saw the star the Lord touched their hearts to come and see Jesus, who says, "No man can come to me except the Father, who hath sent me, draw him."[6] An ancient tradition says, an Angel appeared to them in the form of a star.[7]

The night of his birth the shepherds were called to adore him; on the twelfth day the Magi offered him their gifts; forty days after his birth Simeon and Anna wor-

---

[1] S. Aug. Sermo. XIX. de Ep. Dom. n. 1 ; St. Thomas III. P. q. xxxvi. a. v. [2] Greg. Hom. x., in Evang. [3] St. Augustin. con. Faustum, l. II., c. 5. [4] St. Augustin Ser. de Epiphania. [5] Ser. in Epiphania, 4. c. 3. [6] John vi., 44. Bossuet. [7] Arabic Gospel of the Saviour's Infancy, n. 7.

shipped him in the temple, thus his coming was announced. If the angels had not told the pastors, they
would not be in that place ; if the kings of the East had
not come the twelfth day, they would not see him in
Bethlehem, for after Mary offered him in the temple the
Holy Family departed from Jerusalem.[1] If Simeon and
Anna had not seen him in the temple, they would never
have the honor of taking him in their arms, for he fled
from the face of Herod into Egypt, and for seven years
dwelled at Heliopolis.[2] The pastors called to worship
him signified the Apostles, called from the fold of Israel;
the Magi called to offer him their gifts typified the gentile nations called to the faith.[3] The common tradition
of the remote ages tells us that the star appeared two
years before his birth. so that the kings travelling from
their homes came to the manger on the twelfth day after
the Nativity. For that reason the impious Herod gave orders to kill all the children from two years old and under.[4]
Others say that they came from a country to the east of
Judea, not far away, and that the star appeared to them
the night of his birth, so that travelling as fast as they
could, they arrived at Bethlehem on the twelfth day.[5] According to St. Chrysostom that star which appeared to
them was not one of the stars of Heaven, because none of
the heavenly bodies change their course from east to
west, while the one which led the Magi moved from the
north to the south, and, because it was seen, not only in
the night, but led them also during the day. Again sometimes it vanished, then suddenly appeared again ; when
they stopped it stopped, and when they travelled it went
before them, like the column of cloud by day and the
pillar of fire by night, leading the Israelites towards the
promised land.[6] Considering all these traditions, some
think it was the Holy Spirit, who in the form of a dove
came down on Christ at his baptism ; thus the same Spirit
appeared to the Magi in the form of a star. Others think
the star was an angel, but the most probable opinion is
that it was a star, created by God for the purpose of

[1] Luke. ii. 39. [2] St. Bonaventura, Vita Christi. [3] St. Thomas. p. ii., q. xxxvi.,
a. vi. [4] Math , ii., 16. ; SS. Chrysostom, Hom. ii. in Math., Augustin, Sermo vii.
in Epiphania. Cano de Lec Theo. 1 li. c. 5. [5] See St. Thomas, p. iii., q. xxxvi.
a. vi ad., 3; El Porque de las Ceremonias, Trat. Cuarto, c. xvi. [6] Exod. xiii . 21 :
Math. ii., 9 ; El Porque de las Ceremonias, Trat. Cuarto, c. xvi.

leading the Magi to the manger.[1] The Magi then enlightened by the Holy Ghost[2] came to adore the Lord, that the testimony of the gentiles as well as the prophecy of the Jews might prove him the desired of the nations.[3]

To-day the Church celebrates three remarkable events in the life of our Lord,[4] the adoring of the Magi, his baptism by John the Baptist and the changing of the water into wine;[5] while some of the ancient writers say that on the sixth of January our Lord also fed the thousands of the people in the miracle of the loaves and fishes.[6] At Bethlehem the Magi found him a little child; at his baptism the Jews found him the Son of God; in the Jordan John's followers found him the true God.[7] In the Bible the number of the Magi is not given, but the tradition of the Church says that there were three,[8] and that their names were Melchior, Balthassar and Caspar,[9] three kings of the eastern nations.[10] Their skulls are still preserved in the Cathedral of Cologne.[11] When they came to the manger, "falling down, they adored him, and opening their treasures they offered him gifts, gold, frankincense and myrrh."[12] As the sons of Jacob offered their brother gifts when they came to the land of Egypt,[13] as the queen of Saba[14] offered presents to king Solomon, thus the wise kings brought their offerings to the Lord when they came to adore him. They gave him gold as a present to a king, for that was the custom of the eastern nations; they presented him frankincense, for that is offered only to God; and they presented him with myrrh as to a man, knowing he was to die, for that was to be rolled in the bandages around his body when dead and laid in the tomb.[15] From this it appears that they were inspired by the Holy Spirit, and before they started on their way, they prepared these gifts as presents to the Divine Infant.[16]

From the very days of the Apostles Epiphany has[17]

____

[1] St. Thomas III., p. q. xxxvi. a. vii., St. Leo Ser. in Epiph. i. c. i. [2] St. Thomas III. p. q. xxxvii. [3] St. Leo Ser. iv. de Epiph c. ii. [4] S. Aug. Sermo. de Ep. Dom. iv. n. 1; et Sermo. iii. de Ep. Dom. [5] Matth. 11, Mark 1, John 11: El Porque de las Ceremonias, Trat. Cuarto, c. xvi. [6] John vi.; St Bernard Ser. iii. de Epiphan. [7] S. Bernard, Ser i. in Epiphan. [8] S. Leo Ser. xxx in Epiph. S. Caesarius Ser. 139, etc. [9] Bolland 1st Jan. p. 8. [10] O'Brien's History of the Mass, p. 282. [11] O'Brien's History of the Mass, p. 282, note: El Porque, Trat Cuarto, c. xvi. [12] Math. ii. 11. [13] Gen. xliii, 26. [14] 3 Kings x. [15] Origen, SS. Basil, Ambrose, Augustin, Jerome, Hilary, Bernard and all in Math ii. [16] Same authors. [17] Saurez, Tom. i., de Relig. l. ii. c. v. n. 9: Martine de Antiq. Rit. Eccl. dis. 14 n. 14: El Porque de las Ceremonias Trat. Cuarto, c. xvi.

been celebrated as one of the chief feasts of the Church.
In the writings of the Greek Fathers and of the early
ages it is called the Theophania, from the Greek, meaning God appearing to man.[1] Among the nations of the
East it is called the Feast of the Holy Lights, because
they baptize their converts on that day in memory of the
baptism of our Lord, and because then they are enlightened by the faith they receive at their baptism. Like
Christmas, Easter, Ascension and Pentecost, Epiphany is
honored in the Canon of the Mass by having a special
part belonging to it, and being called a most holy day.[2]

Being one of the chief feasts of the year, the Sundays
following Epiphany are called the Sundays after Epiphany. Epiphany is always celebrated on the sixth of
January, except in France. For when after the great
revolution the French were disposed to pay for the property of the Church stolen from her, in arranging the
feasts of the year, Epiphany, which before was held on
the 6th, even when it fell during the week, they agreed to
put it off till the following Sunday.[3] In the Latin rite
from the earliest times Epiphany has been celebrated on
the 6th of January.[4]

Among the Romans the 6th of January was dedicated
to the three triumphs of the Emperor Augustus ; but when
they had been converted to the religion of Christ, the
celebration of this triple glory of the Emperor was
changed to the triple triumph of Jesus Christ, the Lord
of lords and the King of kings. For that reason,
although the baptism of our Lord, and his miracle at
Cana are mentioned in the Office, yet the Church celebrates chiefly to-day the calling of the Gentiles figured
by the calling of the three kings of the Gentiles.[5] His
baptism in the Jordan is celebrated on the Octave of the
Epiphany, and the miracle of the loaves and fishes on
the second Sunday after Epiphany.

In the services of the Greek Church, there is no mention of the Magi on the Epiphany, as on that day they
celebrate the birth of the Saviour, while the Ambrosian
and Mozarabic Missals speak in their services to-day of
the changing of the water into wine, and of the multipli-

---

[1] Eusebius, SS. Greg. Naz., Augustin, Ser. 203 or 64 Isodore, etc. [2] See Pref. Mis.
Infra Actionem. [3] Concord. granted by Pius VII. to the French. [4] Apostolical Constitutions, Book v. sec. iii., n. xiii. [5] Gueranger le Temp de Noel, v. ii., p. 155.

cation of the loaves and fishes, as so many manifestations of the Divinity of our Lord.

Two remarkable events happened in the first ages of the Church, on the feast of Epiphany. On the 6th of January, 361, Julian, a Christian by outward profession, had advanced in the ranks of the Clergy to the Order of Reader, but at heart he was an apostate. He desired the aid of the Catholic Church to gain the throne of the Cæsars, soon to be left vacant by the death of Constantine. He was at Vienna. He went and consulted the impious pagan priests to gain their favor. He then entered the church and was seen in the midst of the people pretending to adore the Saviour, to gain the good will of the Christians, whom he was soon to put to death by a frightful persecution, when he became Emperor of Rome. All this time his heart burned with hatred against the Christ and against the Church he founded, and from which, like the impious Voltaire, he received his education. Like the latter, he died saying Christ had at length conquered. Eleven years had passed away. In 372 another Roman Emperor came to the church while the Christians were celebrating Epiphany. He was Valens,[1] a Christian by profession, and by baptism like Julian. Both were apostates. One persecuted their mother, the Church, in the name of his cold pagan philosophy, the other, in the name of the false teachings of the Arians. Valens came to Cesarea, where the great St. Basil, in the crowded cathedral, was celebrating Epiphany. What he intended we know not; perhaps to put them all to death. He enters the church. The people, like a sea of heads, are before him. The soul-inspiring hymns of praise, the grandeur of the ceremonies, the golden vestments of the clergy, but above all, the holiness and magnetic grace of the great archbishop, St. Basil, on his throne, strike fear and terror into the heart of the emperor. His head reels, his eyesight fails, his heart grows faint, and he falls like a dead man.[2] God touched his heart. At the moment of the Offertory he came to the railing, and, according to the ancient custom, he gave his gifts to the Lord. Soon he forgot the lesson God taught him that day; and became a persecutor of the

---

[1] Flavius Valens, born 328, killed 378.   [2] St. Gregory of Naz.

Church. But in after ages a new race of emperors rose to rule the people of God, and Theodosius, Charlemagne, Alfred the Great, Lawrence of Hungary, Edward the Confessor, Henry II., Ferdinand of Castile, Louis IX., and all the great rulers, kings and emperors of the past. came on the 6th of January, like the kings of the East, to offer their gifts unto the Lord. Even down to 1378, the Christian kings offered gold, frankincense and myrrh, as their gift to the Infant God. Not only the kings of the middle ages, but the people and the nobles brought these three offerings on the Epiphany, and we see that custom continued to-day in some of the dioceses of Germany, where the beautiful Christian customs have not been blotted out by the persecution of Bismarck. The form of blessing these gifts was found in all the Rituals before the time of Pope Paul V. Again, during these ages of faith, each family chose one of its members to be the king of the feast of Epiphany, in remembrance of the feast of Cana. They had a wedding cake, which they broke into three parts, one for the Infant Jesus, another for the family, while the third was given to the poor, who, with the neighbors, gathered to the feast given in honor of the adoration of the Magi. Thus was celebrated the day of the adoration of the Magi, the day of the Baptism of our Lord, the day of the marriage feast at Cana during the thousand years[1] when the devil was bound from poisoning the souls of men, in the middle ages—when the Saints lived—before the errors of modern times began to turn the nations and the people back to the errors of paganism or to the infidelity of the present times.

As the Archbishops of Alexandria, from the time of the Council of Nice, used to compute the time of Easter and the movable feasts for the whole Church, the feast of the resurrection was announced to the people from the ambo, the pulpit, from which the Gospel and Epistle were read.[2]

On Epiphany, also, in former times, in all parts of the world, the date of the following Easter and movable feasts were announced, which is seen to-day in the Pontifical; also the date of the holding of the Diocesan Synod was given on Epiphany, which should be held each year, if practicable.[3] It is not usual now to announce those feasts,

---

[1] Apoc. xx.   [2] O'Brien, Hist. of the Mass, p. 220.   [3] Pontif. Roman.

because the people can find them in many almanacs and books of that kind.

IV.—FEAST OF THE HOLY NAME OF JESUS.

Among the Jews, it was the custom to name the child on the day of his circumcision, as among the Christians, on the day of baptism. On the 6th of January, then, our Lord was called Jesus,[1] but as the Church that day celebrates his circumcision, the feast of his Holy Name was postponed till the second Sunday after Epiphany.

The Christians of all ages loved the holy name of Jesus, which, in Hebrew, means "The Saviour." The name was brought from heaven by the angel, "and thou shalt call his name Jesus."[2] The promoter of the devotion to the holy name of Jesus, in the fifteenth century, was St. Bernardin, of Sienna, who, taking its first letters in the Greek, IHS, formed them into a monogram surrounded with rays of light.[3] That devotion, encouraged by St. John, of Capistran, spread throughout Italy and the south of Europe, till at length it was solemnly approved by the Holy See. Some time afterwards, in the beginning of the Pontificate of Pope Clement VII., the Franciscans obtained the privilege of celebrating a feast in honor of the name of the Saviour of the world.

In the Bible the name of God is often taken for his power; for that reason, when Christ sent his Apostles to preach the Gospel, he said : "Going therefore, teach ye all nations, baptizing them in the *name* of the Father, and of the Son, and of the Holy Ghost."[4] When Sts. Peter and John came into the temple, they said to the man lame from his birth, "In the *name* of JESUS CHRIST of Nazareth, arise and walk;"[5] saying that there is no "salvation in any other *name* ;"[6] while St. Paul tells us, "that in the *name* of Jesus every knee should bow, of those that are in heaven, on the earth, and under the earth."[7] The whole of the New Testament is filled with reverence and devotion to the most holy name of Jesus, and it is found 143 times in the Epistles of St. Paul.

In the Old Testament the name of God was surrounded

---

[1] Luke ii., 21. [2] Luke i., 31. [3] El Porque de las Ceremonias, Trat. Cuarto, c. xvii. [4] Matth. xxviii., 19. [5] Acts iii., 6. [6] Acts iv., 12. [7] Philip. ii., 10.

with fear and trembling. God had not yet come to earth ; God had not become a man. The Saviour had not been called by the sweet name Jesus, by which we love to know him. St. Matthew, the Evangelist, of his human nature, had not written of him ; St. Mark, the Evangelist, of the sacrifices of the law of Moses, had not yet appeared to instruct us. St. Luke, the Evangelist of the priesthood, St. John, the Evangelist of the Divinity, all speak of the most holy name of Jesus. The Holy Spirit says of our Lord: "Thy name is as oil poured out,"[1] and St. Bernard, explaining these words says: "Oil gives light, nourishes and heals. It feeds light, it nourishes the body, and it decreases pain ; it is light, food and medicine. See the name of the Spouse. Do you think there is in the whole world such a light of faith as the name of Jesus? Is it not in the light of this name that God called us into his wonderful light, by which you are enlightened, and in this light you see the light? Well, St. Paul says: "For you were heretofore darkness, but now light in the Lord."[2] The same Apostle was commanded to carry this name before kings, nations and the children of Israel, and he carried that name as a light, and he enlightened his country, and everywhere cried out: "The night is past and the day is at hand. Let us, therefore, cast off the works of darkness and put on the armor of light."[3] And he showed to all the candle upon the candlestick, preaching in every place Jesus, and him crucified. How that light shone forth and enlightened the eyes of all looking upon it, went forth from the mouth of his Father, as the lightning flashing forth, he cured the wounds of one and illuminated the eyes of many spiritually blind.

Did he not show forth the fire when he said: "In the name of Jesus Christ of Nazareth, rise and walk?"[4] Not alone the name of Jesus is light, but it is our food. Are you not comforted whenever you think of it? What so strikes the mind of the one thinking of it? What so helps the tired senses, strengthens the virtues, aids good and honest morals, fosters chaste thoughts? Every food of the soul is dry if not mixed with this oil ; it is insipid, if not cured with this salt. If you write, I am not pleased

---

[1] Cant. of Cant., 1. 2 ; El Porque de las Ceremonias, Trat. iv., c. xvii. [2] Eph. v., 7. [3] Rom. xiii. 12. [4] Acts iii., 6.

if I do not there read Jesus. If you speak or talk, I am not pleased if I do not there hear the word Jesus. Jesus is honey in my mouth, music in my ears and joy in my heart. But it is also a remedy. Is any one of us sorrowful? Let Jesus come into his heart and he is heard in his mouth. And behold, at the rising light of that name, the fog disappears and the sky becomes serene. Does any one fall into sin? Is he in despair? Does he fall into the snares of death? Is it not true that if he invokes that name of life he will revive and live?[1] Before Christ was born he was called Jesus by men, as he was called by the Angel before he was conceived in the womb. For indeed he is the Saviour of angels and of men, but of men only since the Incarnation. His name was called Jesus as he was called by the Angel. "In the mouth of two or three every word shall stand,"[2] and what was foreshadowed in the prophets, more clearly in the Gospel is read, "and the Word was made flesh!"[3]

Well, then, whilst the child born for us was circumcised, he was called the Saviour, because from that moment he began our salvation, shedding for us that sacred blood. Nor is there any reason for Christians to ask why the Lord Christ was circumcised. He was circumcised because he was born, because he was to suffer. None of these he did for himself, but all for the chosen ones. He was not born in sin, nor circumcised in sin, nor did he die for his own sin, but rather for our wickedness. What he was called the Evangelist says, "he was called by the Angel before he was conceived in the womb." He was called—the name was not given. For this name was from eternity. It belongs to him from nature that he is the Saviour.[4]

Great and wonderful is the mystery. The child was circumcised and called Jesus. Where is the connection between these two? Circumcision belonged rather to those to be saved than to the Saviour; and it belonged to the Saviour to circumcise rather than to be circumcised; but understand, the Saviour was between God and man, who from the beginning of his birth raised the human to the highest of the Divine. He was born of a

---

[1] St. Bernard, Sermo 15 Sup. Cant. of Cant. [2] Deut. xix., 15. [3] John i., 14. [4] St. Bernard, Sermo I., de Circumcis.

woman, to whom the fruit of her fecundity came so as not to destroy the flower of her virginity. He was rolled in swaddling clothes, but the clothes themselves were honored by the praises of the angels. He was laid in the manger, but the brilliant star shone down upon him from Heaven. This and the rite of circumcision proved the truth of his humanity, and his Name, which is above all names, showed forth the glory of his majesty. He was circumcised as the true son of Abraham; he was called Jesus as the true Son of God. But for me this name of Jesus is not an empty or useless name, like those of old. There is not in it a shadow, but the truth of a great name. The name came from Heaven as the Evangelist[1] says, as "he was called by the angel before he was conceived in the womb."[2]

V.—CANDLEMAS DAY.

The forty days of the Christmas season end on the feast of the Purification, or Candlemas Day, thus called from the custom of blessing the candles brought to the church by the people.

According to the law of Moses,[3] a woman who brought forth a man child was to be separated from the rest, and remain for forty days like in a retreat, and then go to the tabernacle or temple, and offer a sacrifice for her purification. The sacrifice was a lamb to be wholly consumed with fire, and a turtle dove and a pigeon as sacrifices for sin.[4] When they were too poor to offer a lamb, they were to bring two doves or two pigeons in its place.[5] There was another commandment given by God that the first born was to be offered to the Lord, but the parents could redeem the child by giving five shekels, according to the weight of the sanctuary. That sum is a little more than five dollars. Mary was not obliged to fulfil that law, for she conceived and brought forth her Son by the power of the Holy Ghost, and not by the ordinary laws of nature.[6] What relation was there between the brides of men and the spouse of the Holy Ghost, between com-

----

[1] Luke I. 31. [2] Luke ii., 21. [3] Levit. xii., 4; Exod. xiii., 12. [4] Levit. xii., 6. [5] Levit. xii., 8. [6] Durandus. Epist. Mont. Feltri, t. ii. ; Bernard, etc. ; St. Thomas, p iii., q. xxxvii., A. 4; Benedict XIV., De Fest. Pur. B. Virginis.

mon women and she who was a Virgin in her conception, in her bringing forth and always remaining a Virgin?[1] The most chaste of all, she brought forth the God of chastity. Nevertheless the Holy Spirit, who dwelt within her, revealed to her that she was to fulfil the law of Moses, and we see the august Mother of God coming with the common crowd, and mingling with the mothers of Israel.

It was in the designs of God that his Son would be made known to the world slowly and by degrees; that he would spend his infant days at Bethlehem, Nazareth and in Egypt; that he would grow up like other children, and be the supposed son of Joseph; that a great prophet would prepare the Jews for his coming by preaching penance on the banks of the Jordan. Till then the world knew not that it possessed its Saviour and its Lord. The shepherds of Bethlehem had not proclaimed what they saw, the Magi had not yet told of the infant—God, the fishermen of Galilee had not preached to the ends of the earth, and the Church he founded had not spread throughout the world; nevertheless, "after the days of her purification, according to the law of Moses, were accomplished, they carried him to Jerusalem to present him to the Lord. As it is written in the law of the Lord, "Every male opening the womb shall be called holy to the Lord,"[2] and to "offer a sacrifice, according as it is written in the law of the Lord, a pair of turtle doves or two young pigeons."[3] What deep and wonderful humility moved the most holy Virgin to obey a law she was not obliged to follow.[4] She was not obliged to fulfil that law, but she willingly obeyed. St. Thomas says, "and therefore Christ, although not subject to the law, wished to be circumcised, and to be subject to the other duties of the law, to show us an example of humility, that he might approve the law, that he might take away from the Jews all occasion of calumny." For the same reasons his mother fulfilled the observances of the law, although she was not subject to it.[5]

Among the lowly and the poor came the lowest and the poorest, Jesus, carried by his Mother to the temple, be-

---

[1] Gueranger, Le Temps de Noel, vol. ii. p. 621. [2] Exod. xiii., 2. [3] Luke ii., 22, 23, 24. [4] Benedict XIV., De Fest., B. M. V., c. ii., n 3. [5] St. Thomas, p. iii, q. xxxvii., A. 4; Fabri, Con. In Fest. Purif., B. M. V., Con. 1.

cause for us he became poor and was born in a stable.[1]
He came to the temple to show that he was obedient to
the law of Moses. He did that to give us an example to
be obedient to all laws which are just. Although there
is no mention in the Gospel of the giving of the five shekels
of silver, nevertheless we must conclude that they were
offered, for Mary and Joseph fulfilled the whole letter of
the law.[2]

Our Lord did not come to the temple built by Solomon,
for that was burned by the Assyrians, when they carried
the children of Israel into captivity; it was the temple
built by command of Darius on, the site of the one destroyed by Nabuchodonosor,[3] when, according to the prophecy of the Lord, a stone was not left upon a stone. He
was presented in the temple built by the Jews after their
return from their captivity in Babylon. He was brought
to the temple built by command of God by the prophet
Aggeus in the second year of the reign of King Darius,
when filled with the Holy Ghost, the prophet cried out,
"thus saith the Lord of Hosts: Yet a little while and I
will move the heaven and the earth, and the sea and the
dry land. And I will move all nations, AND THE DESIRED
OF ALL NATIONS SHALL COME, and I will fill this house
with glory. . . . Great shall be the glory of this last house
more than that of the first, saith the Lord of hosts, and
in this place I will give peace, saith the Lord of hosts."[4]
Such was the temple as it stood beautified and restored
by Herod the Great, when our Lord, carried in his
Mother's arms, came to be presented in it to his Father
on the day of the purification of his Mother. Emmanuel
comes forth from his repose at Bethlehem. He takes
possession of the temple wherein the bloody sacrifices
and the grand ceremonies of the law of Moses prefigured
his coming, his life and his death. By his coming the
glory of that temple sat with a brighter halo on its pinnacle than on the edifice raised by his forefather Solomon.
The shadows of its grand and mystic rites were soon to
vanish before the Son of Justice, but it was meet that for
a little time the blood of the victims should crimson the
horns of the altar, and that day while the priests of the

[1] St. Thomas, p. III., q. xxxvii., a. 3. [2] Calmet. in c. II. Luke, et xiii., Exod. Suarez
in III. D. ; Th. t. ii, q. 37, dis. 16, sec. 1. [3] IV. Kings xxv. [4] Aggeus ii. 7, 8, 9, 10.

old law were preparing the victims for the sacrifices, the victim of the world, the Lamb of God, carried in his sacred veins the blood which was to wipe away the sins of mankind.[1] Among the crowds which pressed around the smoking altars, were many who waited for the coming of the promised Redeemer. All had been prepared, foreseen by an overruling Providence. Simeon was just, holy, and feared the Lord. The Holy Ghost revealed to him that he would not die till he had seen the Saviour.[2] Led by the Spirit of God, he came into the temple ; he knew his Redeemer in the child of the lowly Mary. He took the babe in his venerable hands, and the inspired poetic Canticle broke from his lips :

> " Now thou dost dismiss thy servant, O Lord,
> According to thy word in peace,
> Because mine eyes have seen thy salvation
> Which thou hast prepared before the face of all peoples,
> A light to the revelation of the Gentiles,
> And the glory of thy people Israel."

And Simeon blessed them and said to Mary his Mother, " Behold this *child* is set for the fall and for the resurrection of many in Israel, and for a sign which shall be contradicted. And thy own soul a sword shall pierce,"[3] foretelling of the sorrows of the Virgin Mother when partaking of the sufferings of her Son.[4] At the same time there was in the temple a holy woman, Anna, a prophetess filled with the Holy Ghost. "She was far advanced in years, and had lived with her husband seven years from her virginity.....Now, she at the same time coming in confessed to the Lord and spoke of him to all that looked for the redemption of Israel."[5]

Thus the Divine Infant was presented in the temple. Thus was he shown to all the people by these holy ones waiting for his coming. In the feast of the third of February, as kept by the Greeks, we find it given that Simeon and Anna died on the day following the presentation of our Lord.[6] Some of the ancient writers think Simeon was one of the priests of the temple,[7] while others say he was one of the common people.[8] The feast of the Purifi-

---

[1] Gueranger, Le Temps de Noel, v. ii., p. 626. [2] Luke ii. 26. [3] Luke ii. 29 to 35. [4] Benedict XIV., De Fest, B. M. Virgi., c. ii., n. 5. [5] Luke ii. 36, 38. [6] Menol., Graecorum, 3 Feb. [7] El Porque de las Ceremonias, Trat. Cuarto, c. viii. [8] SS. Athanasius, Epiphanius, Cyrilus, etc.

cation of the Virgin, and the Presentation of our Lord, took place forty days after his birth, because in the law of Moses, this was the time when women were to be purified and to offer their first born to the Lord.

To commemorate these, the Church instituted this feast in the most remote ages.[1] In the Greek and the Ambrosian Rites, this feast is considered among the festivals of our Lord,[2] while in the Latin Rite it is one of the feasts of the Virgin, when we celebrate her purification.[3] We celebrate the purification of the Virgin in place of the presentation of our Lord this day ; for the Gospel says, "after the days of her purification according to the law of Moses were accomplished."[4] That it is the oldest of the feasts of the Mother of God all monuments of the early age of Christianity testify.[5] The mothers of families, from the preaching of the Apostles, used to come to the Church to receive the blessings of the priests, after childbirth, a custom they learned from the Jewish mothers and from the Virgin Mother of our Lord, and the ceremony is called the churching of women.[6]

Before Mass the people have always brought candles to be blessed by the priest. Then with the lighted candles in their hands, they marched in procession around the Church or through the open air in Catholic countries. A writer of the XIth century gives us the meaning of that ceremony coming down from the Apostolic times.[7] The light of the candles recalls to our minds the words of the holy Simeon, "a light to the revelation of the gentiles."[8] That is, Christ is "the light of the world,"[9] who by the light of his teachings enlightens the minds of all men by his doctrines, which came from his Divinity.[10] The people, to show that they carry as it were Christ in their hands,[11] take the blessed candles in their hands.[12] The wax of the candles is made from the fairest flowers of earth, and recalls the body of our Lord formed by the Holy Ghost, from the blood of the Virgin, the fairest flower of the

---

[1] El Porque de las Ceremonias, c. viii. ; Raban. Mauri de Inst., Cler. L. li., c. 33.
[2] The Greeks call it the Hypante. [3] Suarez, t. 1. de Rell , l. ii., c. v., n. 10 ; Gales Not. ad Martyr. 2 Feb. Azorius, Inst. Moral. p. ii., l. i., c. 18. [4] Luke ii. 22. [5] Florentinius, N. ad Martyr, 2 Feb. [6] Benedict XIV., De Fest. B. V., Mariae, c. ii., n. 7. [7] Yvo. Epis. Carnot. de Purif., B. V. Sermo 11. [8] Luke ii. 32. [9] John i. 9 ; El Porque de las Ceremonias, c. xx., De las luces, de Cira, etc. [10] Virtus Explic. Caerem. Eccl., t. ii., p. 17. [11] Fabri, Conciones in Fest. Purif., B. M. V. Con. vii. [12] El Porque de las Ceremonias, Trat. Cuarto, c. viii.

human race. The wax comes from the bodies of the bees which are the virgins of the hive, and signify the Virgin, the Mother of our Lord. As the wax comes forth from the bees without injuring them,[1] thus the Lord came from his Mother without destroying her virginity. The wick of the candle tells of the soul of Christ in his virgin body, while the flame of the candle recalls to us the glories of his Divinity[2] the source of all light to men and angels. by this telling us of the transcendent splendors of the Divinity, which shone on Tabor's Mount in the mystery of the transfiguration.[3] On the 11th of February the pagans carried candles in honor of one of their goddesses. The Apostles changed that ceremony from the pagan rites to the honor of our Lord in his presentation in the temple, and in the purification of his Mother.[4]

When this feast falls on one of the Sundays of the Septuagesima time the candles are blessed as usual, and the Mass of the day is said, while the Mass of the feast is changed to the following day, unless the next day is a feast of a higher class.[5] The candles must be blessed before the Mass by the celebrant vested in purple stole and cope, signifying penance and sorrow for our sins, which the Lord presented to-day in the temple came to take away by his death, while the vestments are of white at Mass to recall the holiness and the sanctity of the Son of God presented to-day in the temple, and the virginity of his Mother in bringing him forth. As the candle signifies our Lord, each one takes a candle as Simeon took the Saviour. All the people march in procession, recalling the journey of Mary and Joseph to the temple carrying our Lord in their arms.[6]

All authors agree in saying that this feast was first held by the people of the East. Baronius[7] says it goes back to 496. Labbeana,[8] speaking of a great plague having broke out in Constantinople in the last years of Justinian the Emperor, says that long before that time this feast was celebrated in all the churches of the East.[9] In an old martyrology of the Western church which the venerable Bede,

---

[1] El Porque, Ibidem. [2] Fabri, Conciones, in Fest. Praesent. B. M V. Con. vii., n. 11. [3] Matth. xvii. [4] Joan. Gerson, t. iii., p. 474. [5] Rub. In Fest. Purif. B. M. V. [6] Catech. Montis., p. 814; Baronius Thomasinus De Die. Fest. Celebr. l. ii., c. 2, etc. [7] Aunal. [8] Concilior um Coll., p. 1234. [9] Saxius In Dis. Apol. de Corp. SS. Gervas. et Protasii, n. 14.

Casiodorus and Walfred say was composed by St. Jerome, and therefore going beyond the time of Pope Gelasus, the 2d of February is called " The Purification of Holy Mary the Mother of our Lord Jesus Christ."   St. Theodosius, the abbot, says the feast was celebrated at Jerusalem in the fifth century, and that then it was an old custom.   The Bollandists say it was kept in Phœnicia, Syria, Cyprus, and by the Copts from times going back to the days of the Apostles.   We can then say with the great St. Augustin, " what the whole Church holds, or was not instituted by the councils, but was always held, most correctly is believed to have come only from the Apostles.'   We say then from deep research, that the feast of the 2d of February comes from the days of the Apostles.

---

[1] L. iv. de Bapt., c. 24, t. 9.

Cathedral of Salisbury.

Chapter V.—The Septuagesima Season.

REASONS RELATING TO SEPTUAGESIMA TIME.

The number of Sundays coming after Epiphany depends
on Easter, as the day of the resurrection of our Lord regulates all the movable feasts of the year. There can
never be more than six nor less than one Sunday falling
between Epiphany and Septuagesima Sunday. But these
two extremes happen so seldom, that in old times there
was no Mass for the sixth Sunday after Epiphany, and
when it came they said the Mass of the fifth, as may be
seen in the Missals before the time of Pope Pius V., who
arranged the Mass for the sixth Sunday after Epiphany.

White is the color of the vestments these Sundays, for we
are celebrating the feasts of our Lord. The Second Sunday after Epiphany is dedicated to the memory of the
miracle of the water changed into wine;[1] the Third
Sunday to the healing of the leper by our Lord;[2] the
Fourth Sunday we celebrate the miracle of the stilling of
the tempest, when our Lord slept in the boat on the Sea
of Galilee;[3] the Fifth Sunday we recall the parable of the
sower, who went forth to sow;[4] the Sixth Sunday we remember the parable of the grain of mustard seed which
filled the whole earth.[5]

As Easter, which rules the movable feasts, seasons and
fasts of the year, is itself ruled by the changes of the moon,
Septuagesima Sunday cannot come sooner than the 18th
of January, when Easter comes on the 22d of March, nor
later than the 22d of February, when Easter falls on the
25th of April.

Septuagesima means in Latin the seventieth, that is the
seventh day, Sexagesima the sixtieth day, Quinquagesima
the fiftieth, and Quadragesima the fortieth day before Easter. Septuagesima Time, then, is the seventy days of preparation for the great feast of Easter. In the most ancient

---

[1] John ii.   [2] Matth. viii.   [3] Matth viii.   [4] Matth. viii.   [5] Matth. xiii.

times, it was kept as a strict time of fasting and of penance, as now we keep Lent. This was the meaning of the words of the Emperor Charlemagne,[1] which he learned from a large number of bishops and others learned in church matters, whom he called to his palace to teach him the meaning of those things. In many churches of antiquity the people, as well as the clergy, began Lent on Quinquagesima Sunday, which, in the Mosarabic Missal is called "The Sunday before meat is forbidden." By Mathew of Paris, it is called "The day of abstinence from flesh." Long before the twelfth century the clergy began the fast of Lent on Sexagesima Sunday, and for that reason it was called the "Beginning of the Priests' Lent."[2]

The Greeks call Septuagesima the "Sunday of the Prodigal Son," because they read that parable that day. Again, they call it the "Proclamation," because they proclaim the fast of Lent that day, and the week after Sexagesima is named "No Meat," for it is the last day they eat meat before Easter. During the week they eat cheese, milk and other foods called white meats, but on Monday following Quinquagesima Sunday they begin their Lent, to which the foregoing days are but a preparation. Among the Greeks Lent is very severe. They use no cheese, eggs, milk or other white foods, but they have three meals each day, and keep Saturdays and Sundays in honor of the creation, and sometimes Thursday in honor of the Holy Eucharist. They begin so early their fast in order to complete the full forty days of Lent. In the reign of Charles the Bald,[3] when they reproached the Latins for not fasting forty days like our Lord, the reply was, that on account of their many feasts held during Lent they fasted only forty days like those of the Latin Rite.[4] In order to have the same custom everywhere, a Council forbade the laity to begin Lent on Quinquagesima Sunday. The Second Council of Orange made the same law for the people relating to both Quinquagesima and Sexagesima Sundays, while the custom of the clergy, beginning Lent on Monday after Quinquagesima, and the monks on Monday following Septuagesima Sundays, was continued.[5] Peter of Blois says :[6] "All religious begin

---

[1] In Lit. ad Alcuin.   [2] Guliel. Neubrig. l. v. c. 10, Math. Paris, L. v. c. 10, Stat. Syn. Nich. Episcopi Andegavensis, etc.   [3] In the year 875.   [4] Ratramnus L. c. Graec. Errores, Thomassin Des Junes, II.. p. c. i.   [5] Vita S. Ulrick, Episc. Augsb.   [6] Ser. xiii. de Quad.

the Fast of Lent from Septuagesima, the Greeks from Sexagesima, ecclesiastics from Quinquagesima, the whole army of Christians for the term of forty days." The Council of Orleans[1] says, that many pious persons of the early days of the Church used to fast for seventy days before Easter, and for that reason, the first Sunday when they began their fast, was called Septuagesima Sunday.[2] It is said by some writers that the captivity of the Jews in Babylon for seventy years first gave the Christians, in the days of the Apostles, the idea of fasting for seventy days.[3] The Council of Clermont[4] commanded the clergy to fast from meat from Quinquagesima Sunday. The Council of Angers[5] commanded all priests, under pain of suspension, to begin their fast on Monday after Quinquagesima Sunday. The Council of Salzburg[6] ordered the religious orders to do the same. These were matters relating to different provinces and dioceses, and these laws relate to discipline, which may be changed. Fasting does not relate to faith. These Councils, then, made these laws for the people under their authority, and not for the whole Church. The regulations for keeping the fast of Lent belongs to the bishops of the dioceses into which the whole world is divided. In this country it is the custom of the bishops to have the regulations for Lent read in the churches, by the pastors, the first Sunday of Lent. That is why we see these different changes made in the ancient times.

Septuagesima Time lasts three weeks. The first week is called Septuagesima Week, the second Sexagesima Week, and the third Quinquagesima Week ; names taken from the Sundays beginning each week. This season of the year was formed long after Lent. The Mozarabic Missal in Spain, from the times of Isidore of Seville, has eight or nine Sundays from Epiphany to the beginning of Lent, and the last of these was called the Sunday before the fast. The whole breathes a deep spirit of penance and of self-denial before the holy season of Lent, showing that in these early times Spain had not lost the discipline preached to her by the Apostle St. James.

Easter Time is so holy that it requires a long time for

---

[1] Held in 545. [2] Goffin Devout Instruction, p. 141. [3] Goffin Ibidem, p. 142.
[4] Held in 1035 under Pope Urban II. [5] Held in 1270. [6] Held in 1291.

the world to receive worthily and well its risen Redeemer. That time of preparation is Lent, but Lent itself is so important that it requires a preparation for it, and that preparation is Septuagesima time. This season of the three weeks of the Septuagesima time does not come down to us from the Apostles. It first began among the Greeks in the early days of the Church, for they did not fast on Saturdays like the people of the Latin Rite during Lent, and to complete the full forty days of the fast of our Lord, they began on Septuagesima Sunday. Towards the end of the sixth century St. Gregory[1] says, "There are six weeks from the first Sunday to Easter; that makes forty-two days. As we do not fast on these six Sundays, there are only thirty-six fasting days; thus we dedicate the tenth of the year unto God." It was after the pontificate of that great Pope that the four days beginning with Ash Wednesday were added to Lent, so as to make the Lent of forty days of fast like the forty days of our Lord's fasting in the desert.[2] We cannot find out the exact time when this season was introduced into the Liturgy.

All the writings of the early ages, the fathers of the Church before the ninth century and the Gregorian Sacramentary, speak of Ash Wednesday as the beginning of Lent. Amalarius, who gives with great minuteness the ceremonies of the ninth century, tells us that the fast began on the fourth day before the first Sunday of Lent, while the Councils of Meaux and Soissons confirm the same. By this we see that the Church never went far from the customs established by St. Gregory the Great, when regulating these things so many centuries ago. In the XIIth century, Peter of Blois says of the customs of his times, "All religious begin the fast of Lent at Septuagesima Sunday, the Greeks at Sexagesima Sunday, and the clergy at Quinquagesima."

The Gallican Rite preserves many of the ways of the people in the middle ages; and we see by many of the writers of this time that from the XVth century, the clergy began to put off fasting during Lent till Ash Wednesday, like the people.

The Gallican Liturgy continued many of the usages and the customs they learned from the people of the Eastern

---

[1] In Hom. xvi. in Evang.   [2] Gueranger, Le Temps de la Septuagesima, p. 8.

Church, and in the early days it was with some trouble that they were brought to fast on Saturday, like those who followed the Latin Rite. Before that time the Council of Orleans commanded them to begin the fast of Lent at Quinquagesima Sunday, and not at Sexagesima Sunday, in the words of the council, "so as to be like the rest of the Church." That was in the VIth century. Toward the end of the same century, the IVth Council of Orleans gave the same directions, and explained the reason for commanding the fast on Saturday. Already the second Councils of Orange[1] condemned the same abuse, and told the people to begin the fast at Quinquagesima Sunday. The Latin Rite was brought into France by the Emperors Pepin and Charlemagne,[2] and from that time, following its customs, they began to fast on Saturday, and the fast of Lent was put off till Ash Wednesday, while the clergy still continued to fast from the Monday following Quinquagesima Sunday.[3] From that time all the churches of the West began to keep the fast like the churches of Rome. Poland alone continued the ancient custom of beginning on Monday after Septuagesima Sunday, which they learned in the most remote times from the Greeks. But it was finally ended by command of Innocent IV.[4]

Following the Latin Rite the Western church fully fills the term of the forty days fast, according to the example of our Lord, by beginning Lent on Ash Wednesday. We fast each day except Sunday, and willingly the Church allows the Greeks to follow their customs of beginning earlier. During the Septuagesima time, from the XIth century, we say no more the "Alleluia,"[5] or the "Glory be to God in the highest."[6] The rule of St. Benedict was not the same regarding these hymns of gladness till Alexander II., in the middle of the IXth century, commanded them not to be said at the Masses of this season. But he only renewed the old custom sanctioned before by Pope Leo IX.[7] in the beginning of the IXth century. Thus, this important time, this part of the cycle of the ecclesiastical year, this Septuagesima time of the Latin Rite, was at length established throughout the world more than a

---

[1] In 511 and 541. [2] In viiith century. [3] Gueranger, Le Temps de la Septuagesima, p. 6. [4] In 1218. [5] Fabri, Con. Dom. Quing., Con. iv. [6] O'Brien, Hist. of the Mass, p. 207. [7] Cap. Hi. Duo De Con., Dist. I.

thousand years ago, but it became common among the nations of Europe only after many trials and attempts on the part of the authorities of the Church. We say that Septuagesima Sunday is the seventieth day before Easter, but really it is the sixty-third. There is a mystery here, for this time of the year is filled with mysteries; not only the three weeks of the Septuagesima Season are mysteries, but the whole time of Septuagesima and of Lent to Easter Sunday is filled with the deepest mysticism.[1]

The number seven is found in numberless places in the Bible, and here the holy Church invites us to stop and ponder on this number, and on these seasons of the year. Let us go back to the olden times of the fathers of the Church. St. Augustine[2] says "there are two seasons, one the time of our trials and of our temptation during this life, the other the time of our happiness and of our glories in the other life. We celebrate these times, the first before Easter, the second after Easter. The season before Easter represents the trials of the present life, the season after Easter signifies the happiness we will have in heaven. Such is the reason we pass the first of these seasons in fasting and in prayer, while the second season is consecrated to canticles of joy, and then fasting is not allowed."

The Church, the guardian and the interpreter of the Holy Bible, tells us that there are two places relating to the two seasons spoken of by St. Augustine.[3] They are Babylon and Jerusalem. Babylon is the symbol of this world of sin and of temptation, in the midst of which the Christian must pass his time of trial;[4] Jerusalem is the heavenly country where the good Christian rests after his trials and his labors of this life.[5] Of these two cities, the one worldly, the other heavenly, St. Augustine writes in his immortal work, "The City of God." The people of Israel, whose history in the Bible is but a grand figure of the history of the human race, were exiled from Jerusalem and were held as captives in Babylon.[6] Their captivity in Babylon lasted for sixty-six years, and according to the great writers on the Liturgy of the Church,[7]

---

[1] Gueranger, Le Temps de la Septuagesima, p. 8. [2] Enar. in Psalm cxlviii. [3] Vol. lx., 194. [4] S. Aug. vol. 524. [5] S. Aug. Enar. in Psal. lxiv., n. 2. [6] IV. Kings xxv. Jerem. Lament. [7] Alcuin Amalaire Yves of Chartres, etc.

the seventy days of fasting and of prayer, from Septuagesima Sunday to Easter, recall the captivity of the Jews
in Babylon.[1]

Seven is a mystic number.[2] In six days God made the
world and he rested on the seventh day.[3] The most
ancient traditions of Christianity tell us, that seven times
ten is the age of the world, and that the race of man
upon the earth is divided into seven great epochs. The
first dated from the creation of Adam to the Flood, the
second from Noah to the calling of Abraham, the third
from Abraham to Moses, the fourth from Moses to David,
the fifth from David to the captivity in Babylon, the sixth
from the captivity to the coming of the Saviour, and the
seventh from the time of our Lord to the end of the
world. Thus the age of man on the earth is measured
by these great epochs. During these different times
the Lord prepared the race to receive their Redeemer,
and to come into the Church he established for their
salvation. In the first epoch, from Adam to Abraham,
all justice, all goodness, all godliness, which look down
from heaven and was planted in the heart of man, was
driven out by sin. In the second, from Abraham to
Moses, God called the people of Israel and made of them
his chosen race, to receive the prophecies relating to his
Son. In the third, from Moses to David, God commanded the tabernacle to be made, the Rites and
Services of the Jewish law to be carried out, to prefigure
the Services of our Church. In the fourth, from David
to the Captivity in Babylon, the nation of the Jews were
ruled by kings, the temple of Solomon stood grand and
gorgeous, and the world saw the greatest glories of the
people of God. In the sixth, from the captivity to the
days of our Lord, the Jewish people were the prey of
conquering nations; the Maccabees alone could restore
in part their departed splendors. In the seventh, from
Christ to the end of the world, the Church, founded and
established by our Lord, shines out before the nations
called to the faith. Its glories are far greater than those
of the tabernacle of Moses. The cathedrals of Christendom exceed in splendor Solomon's temple. The cere-

____

[1] See S. Aug., vol. xii., 91. [2] See S. Aug. Quest. Evang., Q. vi. [3] See S. Aug., vol.
xxvii., 442.

monies in our sanctuaries are more sublime than the most gifted imagination of the Jewish priests could fancy.

Deeper still we find the number seven. When we dig deep into the earth, when we study the remains of the ancient world, when we seek the foot-prints of the ages which have gone before the time of man's coming on this earth, we find in the crust of the earth seven great epochs. The first is found in the solid granite forming the crust of the earth, in the crystallized rocks of the mighty mountains as they rear their heads amid the regions of everlasting storms. The second epoch is found in the sandstones and the limestone rocks found lying on the everlasting granite, called the lower Silurian Era. The third epoch is found in the trap rocks and the salt formation, with their remains of shells and forms of the lowest life, called the Upper Silurian Era. The fourth epoch is found in the red sandstones of various kinds, filled with the remains of fishes peopling the waters of the world before the creation of man. The fifth epoch is found in the coal measures, where, by the hand of a guiding Providence, were stored up the countless tons of black diamonds to work our arts and warm our homes. The sixth epoch is found in the chalk rocks and the formations showing the prints and the remains of the reptiles of gigantic forms, which walked the earth or sported in the waters of those early days. The sixth epoch is found in the rocks and in the stones in which are found the remains of the gigantic animals of the kind whose race is run, which approached in form and habits near to man. The seventh epoch is found in the sands, the gravels and the remains left by the flood in the days of man's appearance on our earth.[1]

The wonders of the spectroscope show the seven primary colors into which all shades and colors are divided, and the musical scale is composed of seven principal notes.

Thus the number seven is deeply planted in the works of the Creator of the universe. Thus for seven weeks we bow our heads in prayer and fasting before the coming of

---

[1] Molloy, Geology and Revelation ; Lyell, Elements of Geology ; Figuer, The World before the Deluge, etc.

the glorious day of Easter, and in joy and praise we raise
our heads for seven weeks during the glorious Paschal
time following Easter.   The seven weeks of sadness for
our sins before the passion of our Lord, are followed by
the seven weeks of happiness following his resurrection.
Thus after having fasted and prayed like the Saviour in
the desert, we rejoice with him as we rise from the sackcloth and ashes of Lent.   We rise with our souls filled
with the seven gifts of the Holy Spirit imprinted in our
souls.   This is what the mystic writers on the ceremonies of the Church tell us.   They say that the seven weeks
before Easter, and the seven weeks following Easter, are
according to the mystic number seven, revealed to man
from heaven.[1]

The seven weeks from Septuagesima to Easter yearly
come and go, while the years of our lives, like the waters
of the rivers, flow onward to be lost in the vastness of the
ocean; thus our years pass rapidly on toward the boundless ocean of eternity.   The Church, our mother, tells us
each year to stop and to think of the Babylon of this
world in which we live as strangers, exiled from our home.
She tells us to hang our harps on the willows growing on
the banks of the Euphrates,[2] like the Jews of old held
captives in Babylon, and to prepare for our call to our
heavenly Jerusalem above,[3] which is our home beyond
the skies, and whose glories we celebrate during the joyful time which follows Easter.   She wishes us to sing
the canticles of joy in her services, and that while we
live here, far from our home in heaven, yet to keep our
thoughts on God while in this world, lest attached to
earthly things we may be exiled for ever from everlasting
bliss with him, for our unfaithfulness while here below,
yet, "How shall we sing the song of the Lord in a strange
land?"[4]   Following thus the inspired Book, the songs
and hymns of gladness are hushed in the Church Services
during this time of penance, signifying our exile here below.   At other times of the year the heavenly Alleluias
are often repeated, now they are heard no more,[5] for exiles in the Babylon of this world of sin, we are travelling

[1] Gueranger, Le la Septuagesima, p. 10.   [2] Psal. cxxxvi. 1, 2.   [3] Psal. cxxvi.   [4] Psal.
cxxxvi. 4.   [5] Council of Toledo, held in 633 ; St. Liguori, De Caerem. Mis. c. vi, n. 1,
ad. 3.

onward toward the Jerusalem which is above, for " we are travellers far from the Lord."[1]

The angelical hymn, "Glory be to God in the highest," is sung no more.[2] Each Sunday of the year its glorious tones are heard at the High Masses in our churches. Its joyous strains are heard no more in the Septuagesima Season, for this is the time of sorrow and of penance for our sins. We sing it only when we celebrate the feast of some saint, to show our joy, when we remember the heroic victory gained by that servant of God over the world, the flesh and the devil. The grand Canticle of St. Ambrose and of St. Augustine, the "Thee, O God, we praise," is not said at Matins[3] except on the feasts of the Saints. The Masses end now no more with the customary "Go, the Dismissal is at hand," but in its place the celebrant or the deacon or a High Mass says, "Let us bless the Lord," for in olden times the people remained in the church, while the clergy, after having taken off their sacred vestments, entered the sanctuary and read the long prayers and Litanies for the people.

At the Masses, in the place of the Alleluia, before we came to the words of our Lord himself in the Gospel, we read the Tract;[4] from the long, slow way it is sung.[5] That our eyes may see, and that our minds may remember the sack-cloth and the ashes of the prophets, and the great men doing penance in the Old Testament during this holy time of prayer and of sorrow for sin, except when celebrating a feast of a saint, the color of the vestments are violet, signifying grief, prayer and sorrow for our sins. Till Ash Wednesday, in the cathedrals and chief churches, the deacon and subdeacon wear their dalmatics and tunics, but when Lent begins they lay them by, or fold them up before the remains of ancient customs. Thus, the Church, inspired by the Holy Ghost, teaches her members by these signs, symbols and ceremonies, to prepare for the austerity of the Lenten Season by suppressing all pomp and all grandeur which are carried out during the other seasons of the year.

The joyful forty days of the Christmas season have passed. With happiness have we celebrated the birth of

[1] The Angelic Hymn "Glory be to God in the highest." [2] By order of Popes Alexander II. and Leo VII. [3] By order of Popes Alexander II. and Leo VII. [4] Tractatus. [5] Amalarius, L. III., c. 12 ; Card. Bona, L. II., c. 7.

God on earth. Now the Church enters the sad and
solemn time when we prepare for the mysteries of the
suffering and the dying Saviour. All around us in the
Church are the sombre signs of penance. We are entering in amid the three weeks of our baptism of penance,
that we may well and worthily celebrate the Lord's
baptism of blood in his sufferings for us on Calvary's
cross. We are leaving Bethlehem and going to Calvary.
We are leaving the infant God in his mother's arms, and
following his steps to see him fasting in the desert. We
are leaving him in the manger, and looking for him in
Gethsemane. The *Illuminating Life* of the Christmas
time has passed, and the *Preparing Life* of the Septuagesima
time has come. We have seen him in his sweetness as a
child; we are going to see him in his weakness as a man,
fasting in the desert. But we must pray God for his
light, in order to see his Son as each year the Church
shows him to us. We must ask for grace to look first
into ourselves, and see the sins which dim the brightness
of our souls and keep us from seeing the truths of religion.
We must ask the light of God to clearly understand how
the human race had fallen when our parents sinned by
eating in the garden, and to realize the deep wickedness
of our sins and the deeper mercy of God in becoming
man to save us from being lost forever.

The Septuagesima Season, then, is the time of the year
for the deepest thought. In the words of a great
writer of the eleventh century,[1] the Apostle says, "We
know that every creature groaneth and travaileth in pain,
even till now; and not only it, but ourselves, also, who
have the first fruits of the spirit, even we ourselves
groan within ourselves, waiting for the adoption of
the sons of God, the redemption of our body."[2] That
creature which groans is the soul looking at the corruption of sin which weeps to be still subject to the vanities
of this world in this exile of tears. It is the cry of the
Royal Prophet, "Woe is me that my sojourning is pro-
longed."[3] Thus holy David desired the end of his
exile in this vale of tears. The Apostle who was wrapped
up to the third heaven says, "I am straightened between
two, having a desire to be dissolved and to be with

---

¹ Yves of Chartres.   ² Rom. viii. 22, 23.   ³ Ps. cxix. 5.

Christ." St. Paul wishes to be taken from this world of sorrow and to be with Christ. We must then pray during these days more than at any other time, giving ourselves up to sighs and to tears, so as to merit by the bitterness of our repentance, to return to the innocence we lost in our first parents. Let us weep then on the way, so as to rejoice at its end. Let us pass along the arena of this life so as to merit the awards awaiting us at its end. Let us not be like foolish travellers, who, forgetting their country, get attached to their place of exile and remain loitering on the way to their home. Let us not be like the senseless people who look not for the medicine which will cure their deadly sickness. Let us run to the healer of our diseases, saying to him, "Have mercy on me, O Lord, for I am weak; heal me, O Lord, for my bones are troubled."[1] Then our Physician will forgive us our sins. He will cure our sickness. He will shower down on us his choicest blessings.

Such are the thoughts which the Church brings before her children during this holy time of Septuagesima, that all may be prepared to celebrate well and worthily the holy Season of Lent.

I.—Septuagesima Sunday.

The Jews lived for seventy years captives in Babylon, where, as a penance imposed on them by God, they served the Chaldean king. In the same way we serve this world, which in the Bible is called Babylon. Now, the time for us to do penance has come. The Septuagesima Season is the Babylonian captivity of the Christian. During this time of penance, we read the first five books of the Holy Scriptures.[2] Genesis tells us of faith and of hope, the foundations of true penance as practiced by the Patriarchs, for unless we have faith we can do nothing for our salvation. "Without faith it is impossible to please God."[3] Without hope in a reward awaiting us in heaven, we would not practice self denial.

The Book of Genesis tells us that "In the beginning God created heaven and earth,"[4] that is, the unseen world of holy Spirits and the visible world around us. "In

---

[1] Ps. vi. 3. [2] Fabri, Conclon., vol. i., Dom. in Sep. Con. IX. [3] Heb. xi. 6. [4] Gen. i. 1.

the beginning," that is, in the beginning of time, before, all was the eternity of God. "In the beginning," that is by the Son of God the Father created all things.[1] As the Son is the Wisdom of the Father, in the Son of God are the plans according to which all creatures were made. "And the Spirit of God moved over the waters,"[2] that is, the Holy Spirit ruled and now rules all things. Here we have in the beginning of the revelation made to man a dim foreshadow of the three Persons in God,[3] at last clearly told by our Lord to the Apostles, "Teach ye all nations, baptizing them in the name of the Father, and of the Son, and of the Holy Ghost."[4] Genesis teaches us to have faith in the Incarnation, suffering, death and resurrection of our Lord, who died as man, but not as God. Isaac was not sacrificed, but a ram was offered in his place,[5] typifying that Christ was given to be our Redeemer, not from our own merits, but chosen by God, as Jacob was freely chosen, and not his brother.[6] This holy book of the Bible, Genesis, by the example of Joseph sold into Egypt, which he saved from famine, tells us of our Lord saving the whole world by being sold by his brethren for our salvation. It teaches us to fast from food by the example of the awful misery caused by our father Adam eating the forbidden fruit, and that we, like him, are under the curse of God upon the world: "Cursed is the earth in thy work; with labor and toil shalt thou eat thereof all the days of thy life."[7] To bring more vividly before our minds the miseries into which we have fallen by the sin of our first parents, we read first of the dignity of man, and how he was created in justice, in innocence, and made to the likeness of God.[8]

The Introit[9] is like the cry of the penitent sinner opening out his heart to his God. It is the Church groaning in her miseries brought on by sin. It is the human race in hunger, cold, sickness, sufferings and death itself, which fell on the whole world for the sin of Adam. But lest all these evils might drive men to despair, hope rises in the heart of man, when hearing these inspiring words of the Introit. Again this Mass gives us the

---

[1] S. Aug., S. Thomas, S Chryst., Haydock's Bible, etc. [2] Gen. I. 2. [3] S. Aug. [4] Math. xxviii. 19. [5] Gen xxii. 13 [6] Rom ix. 13. [7] Gen. iii. 17. [8] Durandus, Rationale Div., L. vi. c. xxv. n. 2, 3. [9] Ps. xvii. 5, 6.

words of the Church of the Patriarchs of old, weeping over the death of the first martyr of the Old Testament, the holy Abel, whose blood cried to heaven from the earth,[1] who prefigured St. Lawrence the first martyr of the New Testament, killed by his brothers the Jews. Thus to bring these things out before the people the Mass of to-day is entitled : The Station at the church of St. Lawrence, outside the walls of Rome, where the Services of to-day are held.[2]

Lest the church militant upon the earth should be inclined to despair of salvation, in the midst of all these trials and miseries so vividly brought before them during this time of penance, in the Epistle of this Sunday, three rewards are offered to the good,[3] the prize, the mastery and the incorruptible crown. The Apostle, in order to obtain heaven, says : "I chastise my body and bring it into subjection, lest perhaps when I have preached to others I myself should become a cast-away."[4] Thus St. Paul did penance and practiced self denial ; and to bring before our minds his penance on this the first Sunday of the great season of penance, the Church gives him to us as an example of penance.

The gradual speaks of the Lord being "a helper in due time in tribulation."[5]

The Gospel speaks of the Kingdom of Heaven being like to a vineyard.[6] That vineyard of the Lord is his holy Church going back to the beginning of the world. The third, sixth, ninth, and eleventh hours are according to the manner of counting the hours of the day among the Jews. The householder is the Lord, who made the world and the Church. The laborers are those whom God called into his Church by his grace—all the just and holy ones from Abel to the last of all the saved. The morning.hour of the world was from Adam to Noah, the third from Noah to Abraham, the sixth from Abraham to Moses, the ninth from Moses to the coming of our Lord,while the eleventh is from the time of Christ to the end of the world,[7] wherein he called and sent his Apostles and their successors to labor in his vineyard and gather in the great harvest of souls. Thus those called in the beginning of the world

---

[1] Gen. iv. 10. [2] Durandus, Rationale Div. L. vi. c. xxv. n. 4. [3] 1 Cor. ix. 24 to end and x. 1 to 5. [4] 1 Cor. ix. 27. [5] Ps. ix. 10, 11, 19, 20. [6] Math. xx. [7] Gregorias, Mag. Hom. XIX. in Evang.

had no cause to murmur, if those who were called at the last hour to the labor of the Lord received as great a reward as those who were called in the beginning of the world.[1]

Renewed by the Body and the Blood of the Lord like saints, the members of the Church rejoice in singing to the Lord.[2]

The Mass ends, like all the Masses during times of fasting and of penance, by the words : "Let us bless the Lord."

Thus as we closely study the prayers of the Church in the Mass of Septuagesima Sunday, we see the spirit of affliction. In the Introit fasting, in the Prayers battle, in the Epistle help, while in the Gradual and in the Gospel we are called to work for God, and then to rejoice with him forever in Heaven.[3]

II.—SEXAGESIMA SUNDAY.

The word Sexagesima means the sixtieth, for it is the sixtieth day before Easter. It was thus called because Lent in the Quadragesima Time, that is the forty days before Easter, and the first Sunday before Lent is the Sunday of Quinquagesima, the Sunday before that Sexagesima, and the one before that Septuagesima.[4]

The Sunday following Septuagesima is Sexagesima. On Sexagesima Sunday the Church recalls the deliverance of the Jews from their captivity in Babylon. To celebrate the deliverance of the Christians from the captivity of sin by the penance of this holy time, the Church is represented as a widow, weeping for the absence of her spouse. Who is the widow but our holy Church, and who is the spouse but our Lord? For although the Lord is with the Church according to his Divinity, as he says, "Behold I am with you always, even to the consummation of the world,"[5] yet he has gone from us, gone up into Heaven, where he always "makes intercession for us,"[6] and during this time of penance the Church, his spouse, weeps for the absence of her beloved.[7]

---

[1] Annee Lit. de Predicateur, p. 60. [2] Annee Lit. du Pred., p. 60. [3] Durandus, Rationale Div., L. vi. c. xxv. n. 11. [4] De Herdt. S. Liturgiae, Prax. t. iii. n. 12. [5] Math. xxviii. 20. [6] Heb. vii. 25. [7] Durandus, Rationale Div., L. vi. c. xxvi. n. 1.

As the word Sexagesima means the sixtieth day before
Easter, it means that we must keep the ten commandments and six principal virtues, for these are the foundations of the Christian lives of those who form the Church,
the bride of the Lamb. And to bring more clearly before our minds that holy Church, we read to-day of Noah
and of the ark.[1] For Noah was a figure of the human
race lost by the deluge of sin. The ark was a figure of
the Church, which is the only ark of salvation for the
fallen race of Adam.[2] Thus of old, God wiped out the
sins of the world by the baptism of the earth by the
waters of the flood. From the three sons of Noah came
the three great races of men which now people the earth,
the Europeans, the Asiatics, and the Africans.[3]

All is mystery in the services of the Church during
this week. The sins of the ancient world were wiped
out by the destruction and the drowning of the sinners.
A new race of men, fearing and serving God, came forth
from the little band saved in that ark, made by command
of the Lord. They were a figure of the few saved from
the world in the Church by the word of the Lord in the
Gospel. The race to-day is steeped in sin, as deeply as
were those of the race of Adam before the flood. A few
are saved by entering into the ark, the Church built upon
the Apostles, built by the true Noah, our Lord himself.
Those are saved "who are born not of blood nor of the
will of the flesh, nor of the will of man, but of God."[4]

By the Greeks this Sunday is called the Apocreos, because from this day they date their fast from meat till
Easter Sunday.

The title of the Mass is: The Station of St. Paul, for
the Services on this day are carried out in the great
church of St. Paul, beyond the walls of Rome. Thus
around the tomb of St. Paul, the Apostle of the nations,
the Catholic Church founded by him and St. Peter, first
Pope, calls the nations of the world to celebrate her holy
mysteries on this Sunday of the year.

The Introit of this Mass is one of the finest pieces of
the Latin Rite, both as to its composition and to the
musical tones according to which it is sung. It is the pour-

[1] Of. Mat. in Brev. [2] Gueranger, Le Temps de la Septuagesima, p. 172. [3] Gueranger, Ibidem, p. 173. [4] John i. 13.

. CATHEDRAL OF CORDOVA.

ing forth of the Christian soul, in sorrow humbled to the ground. It is the cry to God for the help of the Saviour foretold by our fathers coming to save us.[1]

The Epistle is taken from the writings of St. Paul,[2] where the Apostle speaks of his trials, his troubles, his combats, his victories, his sufferings, his afflictions, and of the obstacles placed in his way by men and devils while he was spreading the faith. Such trials are before any one who, like St. Paul, tries to save souls.[3]

The Gospel[4] speaks of the time "when a very great multitude was gathered together out of the cities unto him; he spoke by a similitude" of the sower who went forth to sow. Some of the seed fell by the wayside, and was trodden down or eaten by the fowls of the air; some fell upon a rock and withered away; some fell among thorns and was choked, while some fell on good ground and brought forth a hundred-fold. Our Lord himself explains the meaning of the parable. But what we must carefully consider in the explanation of the Lord is that the seed is the word of God, the field is the world, the fowls of the air the devils, the thorns the false riches of this world.[5] What is more striking than the likeness of the seed sown on the ground to the word of the Lord sown in the hearts of the people by the clergy? But there is a difference between the seed sown in the ground and the spiritual seed of the word of God sown from the mouth of the preacher. For while the seed injures not the ground if it does not grow, the word of God never falls in vain, but always for good or evil to the hearers, according as they hear it with good or with bad dispositions.[6]

In order that the word of the Lord may take deep root and bear fruit in our souls, we here pray at the Offertory for the grace of God to aid us in our path through this life.[7]

It is in our churches before the altar that the word of the Lord is heard, and it is in our youth that it takes the deepest roots.[8]

III.—Quinquagesima Sunday.

The word Quinquagesima means the fiftieth, for it is the fiftieth day before Easter. During the year there are

---

[1] Annee Lit. du Pred., p. 64. [2] II. Cor. xi. 19 to xii. 10. [3] An. Lit., pp. 64, 65.
[4] Luke viii. [5] St. Gregory the Great, Hom. 15 in Evang. [6] Annee Lit., p. 66.
[7] Annee Lit., p. 66. [8] Annee Lit., p. 67.

three periods of fifty days, one from to-day to Easter, another from Easter to Pentecost, and the third from Low-Sunday to the Saturday after Pentecost.[1] The first is the time of fasting and of penance for our sins, the second is the time of rejoicing for the resurrection of our Lord, the third is the time for us to rejoice for having risen from our sins by fasting and by penance.[2]

The number fifty was written, deeply written in the customs of the people of God by the law of Moses and by the prophets, prefiguring our services. Among the Jews, each fifty years they had their year of jubilee which fell on the fiftieth year, when all their slaves were liberated,[3] while, when any one wished to remain in slavery, his ears were pierced and he was kept a slave forever. Their land was not ploughed or cultivated that year, and their fruits and the products of their fields were gathered in common, to prefigure our religious orders where all their goods and all their property are held in common. That year all debts were cancelled and injuries forgiven, for it was their great year of jubilee and of rest from labor, a figure of our rest in the never ending jubilees and happiness of heaven. Thus the word jubilee comes from the Hebrew, and means forgiving or initiating into, for they were forgiven all their debts, and they were initiated into the figures of the everlasting jubilee of heaven. Now from time to time the great head of the Church grants a jubilee to the whole world, when by fasting, and by works of penance, the sins of the people are forgiven them in the reception of the sacraments.

Thus Quinquagesima is the time for forgiveness, the time of penance and remission of sin by fasting and self-denial. For that reason Popes Telesphorus and Gregory commanded that all the clergy should begin their fast of fifty days from Quinquagesima Sunday to Easter.[4] They ordered the fast to begin at this time so as to supply the days necessary to make up the forty days of Lent, for on Sunday we never fast, because it is a day of rejoicing for the resurrection of our Lord, who delivered us from the slavery of the devil, as the Jewish slaves were liberated from their bondage on the fiftieth year, as on the fiftieth

---

[1] Concil. Aurelian, De Consecr. dist. 4 Sacerdotibus.   [2] Durandus, Rationale Div. L. vi. c. xxvii. n. 1.   [3] Levit. xxv.   [4] 4. Dist. Statuimus.

day the law of the paschal lamb was given, as on the
fiftieth day from our Lord's resurrection the Holy Ghost
was poured out upon the world.[1] By the Spirit of God
the world and all the people go on day by day in perfection and in virtue. Thus was foreshadowed these perfections and these virtues of the Christian Church by the
Psalms, which were divided into three series of fifty in
each series. As the Israelites went up to their great
temple, built in all the splendor of the inspired Solomon,
they ascended by fifteen steps,[2] and sang the holy
Psalms of David as they ascended towards the sanctuary
of the Lord.

To-day the Church invites us to ponder on the calling
of Abraham, the father of the faithful, how he was commanded by the Lord to leave his father's house in the land
of Chaldea to become the father of the Israelites.

When the waters of the flood had left the earth and the
race had again peopled the world, evil morals had corrupted the children of Noah. All became worshippers of
idols. The great nation of the Chaldeans and of the
Babylonians had raised their wonderful monuments on
the banks of the Tigris and the Euphrates. They en-
graved their histories in cuniform characters on the stones
and the bricks of their buildings. They left the remembrance of the flood, received from the traditions of
their fathers, on buildings now in ruins. They first
studied the movements of the stars and became the
fathers of astronomy. Their remains are now being
brought to light by the labors of Layard and of Rawlinson;
their legends, their religions and their histories are read
by the learned. But they were all adorers of idols. From
them God commanded Abraham to go out and become
the father of his people. Wonderful was his providence.
He foresaw that from age to age man would become more
and more corrupt, and that the revelations made to Adam
and to the holy ones of old, little by little, would be lost,
and he chose Abraham to preserve the faith to mankind.
As the race began and descended from one man, Adam,
so the new race was to descend from one man, Abraham.
Such was the origin of the race of all the children of
God, of all those serving the Lord to the end of the world.[3]

---

[1] Acts ii. [2] Apocryphal Gospels; Gosp. of the Nativ. of Mary, c. 6. [3] Gueranger, Le Temps de la Septuagesima, p. 210.

Let us imitate the father of the faithful. His life contains such a model of submission to the divine will, obedience to God's commands and self-sacrifice. "Abraham was a great man, wonderful in works. The faith in truth was greater than the lie of the ambitious eloquence which no philosophy could equal, ... That virtue comes first which is the foundation of the others, and, therefore, God first asked this faith from him, saying : " Go forth out of thy country and from thy kindred, and out of thy father's house, and come into the land which I will show thee,"[1] . . . . . But because there was another land before him, that is the land of the Chaldeans, from whence his father, Thare, came and settled in Charran, and because he brought his nephew with him, it was said to him, go from thy kindred. Let us consider that this is to go from this world, to go from the society of this body to that other, of which Paul says: " But our conversation is in heaven."[2]

The Church, then, during this time of the year, sets before her children the example of Abraham, called to the promised land, which God gave to him and to his children. But that land of milk and honey was but a figure of that other land beyond the grave, to which we are all called. A land not flowing with honey, but filled with joy for ever. Well does the Apostle say of him : "By faith, he that is called Abraham obeyed to go out into a place which he was to receive for an inheritance, and he went out, not knowing whither he went. By faith he dwelt in the land of promise as in a strange country, dwelling in cottages with Isaac and Jacob, the heirs with him of the same promise. For he looked for a city that hath foundations, whose builder and maker is God. . . . . All these died according to faith, not having the promises, but beholding them afar off . . . . but now they desire a better, that is to say, a heavenly country."[3] Thus the Patriarchs desired to see the Church, the city whose foundations are the Apostles, whose builder and maker is God.[4] They looked for the land of heaven promised to the race of Adam.

We are then, as the children of Abraham, exiles on this

---

[1] Gen. xii. 1. [2] Phil. iii. 20 ; St. Ambrose L. de Abram. Patriarch, l. ii. c. 2. [3] Heb. xi. 8, 9, 10, 13, 16. [4] Ibidem.

earth, and during this time of Septuagesima we are to always have before our minds the thought that this world will pass away and the concupiscence thereof. "For we have not here a lasting city, but we seek one that is to come."[1]   Thus as Abraham came forth from Babylon, a figure of this world of sin, into the promised land a figure of heaven, thus must we come forth from this world of temptations into the true promised land of heaven on the earth, thus must we come from the bad ones around us to the Church, the true land of promise, where all are saved who live within her holy laws.   May God and his holy angels look down on us from their heavenly abode, while the times and the years flow on and death comes rapidly towards us.[2]   When our Saviour calls us, may he find us waiting and prepared.

In some of the oldest Liturgies they read that part of the Gospel, where the history of the blind man of Jericho, who was healed by our Lord, is given—a figure of the blindness of the people of our days, when the coldness of infidelity is blinding the hearts of men.   Among the Greeks this Sunday is called Tyrophagi, because it is the last day they can use white meats, such as cheese, eggs and milk, for, according to their ancient customs, these were allowed the preceding week.   From Monday following Quinquagesima Sunday their Lent begins.

The Title of the Mass of to-day is the Station at St. Peter's, that is, the Mass and the Services of the Church for this Sunday are held in the great church of St. Peter's in Rome, built on the Vatican Hill.   This church was chosen for the Services of to-day in the most ancient times, when they were accustomed to read the portions of the Bible, giving the history of the law of God coming from Mount Sinai, because the early Christians looked on Moses as a figure of their first Pope Peter.   Moses on Mount Sinai was a type of Peter on the Vatican Hill. Moses dying on the mount foreshadowed Peter dying on the Vatican, and when the Church put off the reading of the account of the giving of the law of God to the Fourth Sunday of Lent and began to read on Quinquagesima Sunday, the calling of Abraham, still St. Peter's church on the Vatican Hill remained as the place of the Services.[3]

---

[1] Heb. xiii. 14.   [2] Introduc. a la vie devote IIL c. xxxiii.   [3] Tract. de Offic. Div., Rupert.

God and his Sacraments are the true sources of our sanctification. For that reason we begin the Mass of to-day by these words of the Introit, so full of confidence in God.[1]

To work out our salvation we ask, in the prayer of to-day, three things, for God to hear our prayers, to break the bonds of our sins, and to deliver us from all evil.[2]

The Epistle is taken from St. Paul to the Corinthians,[3] where he speaks of the charity which should be in all Christians. That charity of which St. Paul speaks is freedom from mortal sin, for when we are in sin our good works are not rewarded by God, but they only merit the grace of disposing us to obtain forgiveness by confession.

The Gospel is taken from St. Luke,[4] and tells of the prophecy of our Lord, how he was to go up to Jerusalem and be taken by the Gentiles, be mocked, scourged and put to death, and on the third day he would rise from the dead. Such is one of the most celebrated prophecies of our Lord, who, in this Gospel, foretells the chief part of his passion. No one but God could have so clearly told before the manner of his death and how he would rise on the third day.[5] We are coming nearer and nearer to the sufferings of our Lord, and in the grand Liturgy of the Church, we are recalled from the things of earth to meditate on the sufferings of our divine Master. Our Redeemer foreseeing that at his death his disciples' minds would be disturbed, long before he predicted the sufferings of his passion and the glory of his resurrection.[6] This Gospel also speaks of the blind man of Jericho having received his sight by a miracle of our Lord. "The blind man is the human race, which, in our first parent, was driven from the happiness of heaven. Human nature ignoring the brightness of the heavenly light, suffers the darkness of its loss. Nevertheless, it is enlightened by the presence of its Redeemer. . . . . You will notice that when Jesus came near to Jericho the blind received his sight, for Jericho means the moon, but in the holy Bible the moon means a defect of the flesh, while it changes during the month ; the moon typifies the weakness of human nature. When our Creator comes near to Jericho, the blind receives his

[1] Annee Lit., du Predicat., p. 69. [2] Annee Lit., du Predicat., p. 69. [3] I. Cor. xii.
[4] Luke xviii. [5] Annee Lit., du Predicat., p. 71. [6] Gregorius, Mag. Hom. II. in Evang.

sight, because the Divine took the defects of our flesh, and human nature received what it had lost, whence God suffered in his human nature. Thence man was raised to the Divine nature."[1]

To celebrate the miracle of giving sight to the blind man of Jericho, the Church thanks the Lord, and asks to be taught in the services of to-day his justifications.[2]

The chief gift the Church asks of God, in this time of penance, is the forgiveness of our sins, and for that the priest offers the sacrifices of the Mass.[3]

IV.—SHROVETIDE.

The three days following Quinquagesima Sunday are called Shrovetide. The word comes from the old Saxon, shrive, which means to go to confession, for in the days of old when all England was Catholic, they were accustomed to prepare on Monday and to go to confession on Tuesday to their own parish priest.[4] Our English ancestors following the customs of their fathers taught by St. Augustine, redoubled their fervor on these days. All who fell under the censures of the Church received forgiveness from the hands of their bishop or from the clergyman named to act in his place. Public penance was practiced in every church. All who injured their neighbors, were obliged to restore.[5] That was the custom of the Christians of Alexandria in the second and third centuries. "Look about very diligently to whom you ought to confess your sins . . . . that if he has shown himself a skilful and tender physician and shall give you any advice, you carefully follow it."[6] The Christians of all ages began the fast of Lent by first going to confession, as shown by the Fathers and the Councils of the Church. In ancient times, St. Chrysostom says, "The Fathers being aware of the dangers and of the mischief of rashly approaching the holy table, appointed these forty days to be spent in fasting, prayer, hearing the word of God, and meeting together in public prayers, that in those holy days, by devotion, alms-deeds, fasting, watching, tears, confession, and all other means, every

---

[1] Greg. Mag., Ibidem. [2] Annee Lit. p. 61. [3] Annee Lit., p. 72. [4] P. Cyc., Brande. [5] Butler's Mov. Feasts and Fasts, pp. 121, 122. [6] Origen, Hom. II., in Psalm xxxvii.

one may carefully cleanse his soul in order to partake of it with a pure conscience."[1] Alcuinus tells all Christians to confess their sins on the "Head of the Fast," that is, on these days before Lent.[2] Theodulph, bishop of Orleans, requests the people, as a preparation for Lent, to make their confessions and reconcile their differences.[3] Burchard, bishop of Worms, says the same.[4] The council of Paris[5] commanded that no one should be allowed to go to Communion on Easter who had not been to confession about the beginning of Lent. The third Council of Ravenna[6] ordered all priests to explain to their people the IVth Lateran Council, which obliges all of both sexes, from the age of seven years old and upward, to go once to confession at least each year, under pain of being driven from the Church while living, and deprived of Christian burial when they die.[7] Another council, held in Spain, commanded, under pain of excommunication, Rectors of churches to publish the Decree of the IVth Lateran Council.[8] From these Fathers and Councils, it will appear how clear is the spirit of the Church in exhorting the people to prepare for the Lenten season by going to confession and receiving the grace of God, and to be in the state of grace in order that their fasting may have merit before God, for penance and fasting in the state of sin has no reward before God. "If I have not charity, I am nothing."[9] On the care with which we make this confession depends the fruit of our penance and fast during Lent. If any one has the misfortune to be in a state of mortal sin, their works are only a means of obtaining a perfect conversion; but when they are not in a state of grace, or of charity, as the Apostle says, their fasting and their works of penance are neither satisfactory nor merit everlasting life.[10] Confession also prepares the penitent to spend Lent in a Christian manner, to apply the right remedies to the wounds made in his soul by sin.

This has been the practice of the most holy and the most venerable of the great Saints and Pastors of the Church. St. Charles Borromeo wrote many of his pas-

---

[1] Or. in eos qui Pascha jejunant con. Judeos. [2] L. de Div. Offic. c. 13. [3] Capl. c. xxxvi. [4] Decret. l. xv. [5] Held in 1420. [6] Concil. Raven. iii. sub. Clemente V., 1311. [7] Concil. iv. Lat. sub. Innocent III. c. xxi. [8] Concil. Sabiensi sub. Joanne XXI., an. 1322. [9] I. Cor. xiii. 2. [10] Butler's Feasts and Fasts, p. 124.

toral letters against the excesses and the profanations of Shrovetide.[1] In one place he says, "God calls upon us to mourn, but despising his voice, we run to banqueting."[2] This holy pastor each year exhorted the people of his diocese to spend well these three days before Lent.

Cardinal Archbishop Palæota, when he sat on the archiepiscopal throne of Bologna, was the second great light after St. Charles in keeping up the devotion of the people during Shrovetide. He began at Bologna the thirty hours' devotion in the monasteries and in the parish churches during the three days of Shrovetide, having each day a sermon with indulgences. Afterward the wonderfully learned Cardinal Lambertini, who became Pope Benedict XIV., at Bologna began the prayers of the Forty Hours' Devotion to the Blessed Sacrament, in remembrance and in honor of the forty hours of our Lord in the tomb. He commanded the Devotion to be carried out with sermons, processions and the Benediction of the Most Holy Sacrament.[3] When he became Pope he granted many privileges to all the clergy, who would confess, communicate and visit any church in which the Blessed Sacrament is exposed on three days each in the weeks of Septuagesima, Sexagesima and Quinquagesima. His successor, Pope Clement XIII., extended this privilege to the whole Church.[4] Now it has become spread throughout the whole world, and the devotion is known by the name of The Forty Hours' Devotion. This devotion to our Lord in the Blessed Sacrament is held in every diocese of the world in such a way that it is opened in each church on a certain day of the year, by direction of the bishop, so that our Lord is worshipped every day in some part of the diocese where there are churches enough to have it three days in each. The people come, and all receive the sacraments and gain the indulgences. The clergy, nuns and the people spend their time before the altar on bended knees, in adoration of their Lord.

Fr. Angel, of Joyeuse, once a duke, a peer and a marshal of France, renounced all worldly honors to serve God as a Capuchin friar. He preached eloquent sermons against the disorders of the people at Shrovetide.

---

[1] St. Charles Acta Concil. Mediolan. t. ii. p. 920. [2] T. ii. p. 922. [3] Benedict XIV. Inst. xiv. [4] Brief, July, 1765.

Felix, bishop of Ipres, charged the clergy of his diocese to keep from all banquets, meetings and places of pleasure during this holy time.[1] Thus should we pass the days of Shrovetide.

Another part of this preparation for Lent consists in increasing our self denial, making frequent acts of sorrow for sin, doing good to others, overlooking the faults of our neighbors, and mortifying ourselves. When in this time of penance the Church clothes her altars and her clergy in mourning, and sings no more her joyful songs of praises to the Lord—when she sits amid the signs of penance and of sorrow, if we enter not into her spirit of penance, the prayers of her services are but mockery and hypocrisy in our mouths. By her sermons and her grand Liturgy she now invites us with her to sanctify our fastings and to prepare for Lent. "As wrestlers exercise themselves before the combat, so must Christians practice self denial, so as to prepare themselves for fasting."[2] "As doctors before they give medicine prescribe fasting, so as to prepare the body for carrying off the morbid humors, so fasting, that it may be made wholesome for the soul, must be preceded by the practice of temperance."[3] In another place he says, "Who can be so extravagantly mad as to pretend to prepare himself to live chastely by wallowing in the filth of impurities?"[4] This was the way the monks and hermits of old prepared themselves for their long and austere fasts, by which they became great saints; and to follow them to heaven we must follow them in their penance and self denial. Two passions are strongest in us—the sense of taste and the sense of immodesty. They are both good, and were given to man by God for a good purpose. One is to preserve the individual, and the other to preserve the race. When we give ourselves up to the first we become gluttons or drunkards; when we give ourselves up to the other, we become immodest or libertines. These two passions are so closely united, that unless we control our tastes we cannot control our lower passions. Thus with the wisdom of the Lord does the Church tell us to fast at first, that we may be able to keep our passions under con-

---

[1] Instruc. Past, I. 18, 1768. [2] St. Basil. Hom. I. de Jejun., n. x. p. 9. [3] St. Chrysostom, Hom. IV. in Gen. t. 4, Ed. Ben. [4] Hom. V. de Penet., n. 5, t. ii. p. 316.

trol. The most celebrated doctors in the world say that nearly one third of the race die by diseases brought on by over eating, and as a rule, those who are temperate in eating and drinking enjoy good health till ripe old age.

When that arch enemy of the Christian religion, Mahomet, stole parts of the Bible, and wrote his book, the Koran, he took the practices of the first ages of Christianity relating to fasting, and his followers have preserved them till to-day. For some time before their Lent, which lasts a month, they fast on herbs, seasoned with salt and vinegar, drinking nothing but water.[1]

The seasons of Septuagesima and of Lent were commenced by the Christians of the Apostolic time to turn their followers from the heathen customs of the pagans.

From the customs of past ages we see that all people prepared for Lent by going to confession. From the spirit of the Church in keeping the time of Septuagesima as a season of fasting and as a preparation for Lent, we see that the people should not spend the time in pleasures, in parties and dancing, as they are accustomed to do in our days, but in a spirit of penance and fasting as a preparation for Lent.

V.—Ash Wednesday.

The fast of Lent begins on Ash Wednesday and lasts till Easter Sunday. During this time there are forty-six days, but as we do not fast on the six Sundays falling in this time, the fast lasts for forty days. For that reason it is called the forty days of Lent. In the Latin language of the Church it is called the Quadragesima, that is, forty. St. Peter, the first Pope, instituted the forty days of Lent.[2] During the forty-six days from Ash Wednesday to Easter, we are to spend the time in fasting and in penance for our sins, building up the temple of the Lord within our hearts, after having come forth from the Babylon of this world by the rites and the services of the Septuagesima season. And as of old we read that the Jews, after having been delivered from their captivity in Babylon, spent forty-six years in building their temple

[1] Auger. Ghislin. Bus. Legat. Turcicae, Ep. iii. [2] Durandus, Rationale Div., L. vi. c. xxviii. n. 2.

in place of the grand edifice raised by Solomon and destroyed by the Babylonians, thus must we rebuild the temple of the Holy Ghost, built by God at the moment of our baptism, but destroyed by the sins of the past year. Again in the Old Testament the tenth part of all the substance of the Jews was given to the Lord.[1] Thus we must give him the tenth part of our time while on this earth. For forty days we fast, but taking out the Sundays of Lent, when there is no fast, it leaves thirty-six days, nearly the tenth part of the three hundred and sixty-five days of the year. According to Pope Gregory,[2] from the first Sunday of Lent to Easter, there are six weeks, making forty-two days, and when we take from Lent the six Sundays during which we do not fast, we have left thirty-six days, about the tenth part of the three hundred and sixty-five days of the year.

The forty days of fasting comes down to us from the Old Testament, for we read that Moses fasted forty days on the mount.[3] We are told that Elias fasted for forty days,[4] and again we see that our Lord fasted forty days in the desert.[5] We are to follow the example of these great men of the old law. But in order to make up the full fast of forty days of Moses, of Elias and of our Lord, Pope Gregory commanded the fast of Lent to begin on Ash Wednesday before the first Sunday of the Lenten season. Christ began his fast of forty days after his baptism in the Jordan, on Epiphany, the twelfth of January, when he went forth into the desert. But we do not begin the Lent after Epiphany, because there are other feasts and seasons in which to celebrate the mysteries of the childhood of our Lord before we come to his fasting, and because during these forty days of Lent we celebrate the forty years of the Jews in the desert, who, when their wanderings were ended, they celebrated their Easter, while we hold ours after the days of Lent are finished. Again, during Lent, we celebrate the passion of our Lord, and as after his passion came his resurrection, thus we celebrate the glories of his resurrection at Easter.

During the services of Lent we read so often the words :

---

[1] Exod. xxii. 29 ; Levit. xxvii. 89. [2] De Consecr. dist. 5 Quadragesima. [3] Exod. xxiv. et xxxiv. 28. [4] III. Kings xix. 8. [5] Math. iv. ; Luke ix. ; St. August. in Epist. 119.

"Humble your heads before the Lord," and "let us bend our knees," because it is the time when we should humble ourselves before God and bend our knees in prayers. After the words, "Let us bend our knees," comes the word, "Arise." These words are never said on Sunday, but only on week days, for Sunday is dedicated to the resurrection of our Lord. Pope Gregory says: "Who bends the knee on Sunday denies God to have risen." We bend our knees and prostrate ourselves to the earth in prayer, to show the weakness of our bodies, which are made of earth; to show the weakness of our minds and imagination, which we cannot control; to show our shame for sin, for we cannot lift our eyes to heaven; to follow the example of our Lord, who came down from heaven and prostrated himself on the ground in the garden when in prayer;[1] to show that we were driven from Paradise and that we are prone towards earthly things; to show that we follow the example of our father in the faith, Abraham, who, falling upon the earth, adored the Lord.[2] This was the custom from the beginning of the Christian Church, as Origen says: "The holy prophets when they were surrounded with trials fell upon their faces, that their sins might be purged by the affliction of their bodies."[3] Thus following the words of St. Paul: "I bow my knees to the Father of our Lord Jesus Christ,"[4] we prostrate ourselves and bend our knees in prayer. From Ash Wednesday to Passion Sunday the Preface of Lent is said every day, unless there comes a feast with a Preface of its own.[5] That custom was in vogue as far back as the twelfth century.[6]

At other times of the year, the clergy say the Office of Vespers after noon, but an ancient Council[7] allowed Vespers to be commenced after Mass. This is when the Office is said altogether by the clergy in the choir. The same may be done by each clergyman when reciting privately his Office. This cannot be done on the Sundays of Lent,[8] as they are not fasting days. The "Go, the dismissal is at hand," is not said, but in its place, "Let us bless the Lord," for, from the earliest times the clergy and the people remained in the church to sing the

---

[1] Math. xxvi. 89. [2] Gen. xviii. 2. [3] Origen, Hom. in Verba; Erant Joseph et Maria mirantes. [4] Ephes. iii. 14. [5] Rub. Mis. Fer. IV. Cin. Prae. [6] Durandus, Rationale Div., l. vi, c. xxviii, n. 11. [7] Concil. Cabilonens. De Con. Dist. I. Solent. [8] Rub. Sab. I. in Quadrag. Brev. P. Verna.

Vesper Office and to pray during this time of fasting and of penance.

We begin the fast of Lent on Wednesday, for the most ancient traditions of the Church tell us that while our Lord was born on Sunday, he was baptized on Tuesday, and began his fast in the desert on Wednesday.[1] Again, Solomon began the building of his great temple on Wednesday, and we are to prepare our bodies by fasting, to become the temples of the Holy Ghost, as the Apostle says, "Know you not that you are the temple of God, and that the Spirit of God dwelleth in you?"[2] To begin well the Lent, one of the old Councils directed all the people with the clergy to come to the church on Ash Wednesday to assist at the Mass and the Vesper Offices and to give help to the poor, then they were allowed to go and break their fast.[3]

The name Ash Wednesday comes from the ceremony of putting ashes on the heads of the clergy and the people on this day. Let us understand the meaning of this rite. When man sinned by eating in the garden the forbidden fruit, God drove him from Paradise with the words: "For dust thou art, and unto dust thou shalt return."[4] Before his sin, Adam was not to die, but to be carried into heaven after a certain time of trial here upon this earth. But he sinned, and by that sin he brought upon himself and us, his children, death. Our bodies, then, are to return to the dust from which God made them, to which they are condemned by the sin of Adam. What wisdom the Church shows us when she invites us by these ceremonies to bring before our minds the dust and the corruption of the grave by putting ashes on our heads. We see the great men of old doing penance in sackcloth and ashes.[5] Job did penance in dust and ashes.[6] By the mouth of his prophet the Lord commanded the Jews "in the house of the dust sprinkle yourselves with dust."[7] Abraham said, "I will speak to the Lord, for I am dust and ashes."[8] Joshua and all the ancients of Israel fell on their faces before the Lord and put dust upon their heads.[9] When the ark of the covenant

---

[1] Durandus, Rationale Div., l. xxviii. n. 13. [2] I. Cor. iii. 16. [3] Concil. Cabilonen. De Consecr. Dist. 1 Solet. [4] Gen. iii. 19. [5] El Porque de las Ceremonias, c. xxx. Cuaresma. [6] Job ii. 12. [7] Mich. i. 10. [8] Gen xviii. 27. [9] Joshua vii. 6.

was taken by the Philistines, the soldier came to tell the sad story with his head covered with dust.[1] When Job's three friends came and found him in such affliction, "they sprinkled dust upon their heads toward heaven."[2] "The sorrows of the daughters of Israel are seen in the dust upon their heads."[3] Daniel said his prayers to the Lord his God in fasting, sackcloth and ashes.[4] Our Lord tells us that if in Tyre and Sidon had been done the miracles seen in Judea, that they had long ago done penance in sackcloth and ashes.[5] When the great city will be destroyed, its people will cry out with grief, putting dust upon their heads.[6] From these parts of the Bible, the reader will see that dust and ashes were used by the people of old as a sign of deep sorrow for sin,[7] and that when they fasted they covered their heads with ashes. From them the Church copied these ceremonies which have come down to us. And on this day, when we begin our fast, we put ashes on our heads with the words, "Remember, man, that thou art dust, and into dust thou shalt return."[8]

In the beginning of the Church the ceremony of putting the ashes on the heads of the people was only for those who were guilty of sin, and who were to spend the season of Lent in public penance. Before Mass they came to the church, confessed their sins, and received from the hands of the clergy the ashes on their heads. Then the clergy and all the people prostrated themselves upon the earth and there recited the seven penitential psalms. Rising, they formed into a procession with the penitents walking barefooted. When they came back the penitents were sent out of the church by the bishop, saying : "We drive you from the bosom of the Church on account of your sins and for your crimes, as Adam, the first man was driven from Paradise because of his sin." While the clergy were singing those parts of Genesis, where we read that God condemned our first parents to be driven from the garden and condemned to earn their bread by the sweat of their brow, the porters fastened the doors of the church on the penitents, who were not allowed to enter the temple of the Lord again till they

---

[1] I Kings iv. 12. [2] Job ii. 12. [3] Lam. ii. 10. [4] Dan. ix. 3. [5] Math. xi. 21 ; Luke x. 13. [6] Apoc. xviii. 19. [7] S. Aug. vol. xi. 34. [8] Gen. iii. 19.

finished their penance and came to be absolved on Holy Thursday.[1]   After the eleventh century public penance began to be laid aside, but the custom of putting ashes on the heads of the clergy became more and more common, till at length it became part of the Latin Rite. Formerly they used to come up to the altar railing in their bare feet to receive the ashes, and that solemn notice of their death and of the nothingness of man.   In the twelfth century the Pope and all his court came to the Church of St. Sabina, in Rome, walking all the way in his bare feet, from whence the title of the Mass said on Ash Wednesday is the Station at St. Sabina.

---

[1] Gueranger, Le Temps de la Septuagesima, p. 242.

CATHEDRAL OF LINCOLN.

Chapter VI.—The Lenten Season.

REASONS RELATING TO THE LENTEN SEASON.

The word Lent, in the ancient languages of northern
Europe, means the Spring fast, to distinguish it from Advent, the Fall or Winter fast.   The Latin and Greek
names of Lent mean forty days, and from these come the
names of Lent in the French, Italian, Spanish, and the
tongues of southern Europe, which are formed from the
Latin and Greek.   Lent is the solemn fast of forty days
held yearly by the Church before the feast of Easter.
This season is commanded to be observed by the laws of
the Church, and is most venerable for its ancient origin,
its holiness and its spiritual fruit.   Going back through
the ages past, we trace its history through every generation and age up to the times of the Apostles.   All histories, all monuments, all writers, all the Fathers of the
Church, and all records which speak of these things, even
to the times of the successors of our Lord's disciples, all
who have written on these subjects, speak of Lent as a
time of fasting and of penance.   It is mentioned so often[1]
and in words so clear in the works of the bygone centuries, in the sermons of the pastors, in the letters of the
bishops, in the homilies of the Saints, in the decrees of
the councils, and in the letters of the popes, that no one
ever doubted that it began at the Apostolic ages.   Pope
St. Telesphorus commanded it to be kept as an Apostolic
tradition.[2]   Scarcely a hundred years had gone from the
death of St. John, the last of the Apostles, when a misun-
derstanding arose among the early Christians about the
time when the yearly fast of Lent should be kept and the
feast of Easter celebrated.[3]   The Christians of Asia celebrated the ceremonies of our Lord's resurrection on the
fourteenth moon of the month of March, the day the Jews

[1] S. Aug. speaks of Lent in 52 places in his works.   [2] Brev. Rom. Of. S. Telesphori.
[3] Eusebius l. v., Hist. c. 23.

celebrated their Easter, while the converts of Europe, following the Latin Rite, kept Easter on the first Sunday following the fourteenth moon of March. St. Polycarp, the disciple of St. John the Evangelist, when bishop of Smyrna, came to Rome to get instructions on the matter from the Pope Anicletus.[1] Again, St. Irenæus wrote to Pope Victor, asking him to tolerate the custom of the Asiatics in celebrating Easter on the same day as the Jews. In the year 200 all Christians throughout the world kept the fast of the forty days of Lent.[2] Not being thoroughly instructed, there were many customs then among the early Christians. "They measured their day by counting the hours both of the night and of the day. And this variety among those who observe the fast did not begin in our age, but long before us, among our ancestors, many of whom, probably, not being very exact in their observances, handed down to posterity the custom as it had been through simplicity or private fancy introduced among them. . . . . For the difference in observing the fast does only so much more commend the common unity of faith in which all are agreed." By these words, St. Irenæus tells us, that this "observance was handed down to posterity," and, consequently, as he wrote before the end of the second century, it must carry us back at least a hundred years to the time of the Apostles.[3] The Apostolic Constitutions say Lent "is to be observed by you as containing a memorial of our Lord's mode of life."[4] They also give instructions to begin the solemnity of Lent before the Passover. Tertullian speaks of fasting in eighteen places in one of his works.[5] St. Epiphanius says three classes of persons kept the fast of Lent in his time. Some took nothing till the evening, and then only dried meats or bread and water during the whole Lent; others eat a full meal each day, while others continued this severe fast to Holy Week.[6] St. Dionysius of Alexandria, in the third century, speaks of these different ways of fasting on Holy Week, saying that some passed the whole week without taking any food at all, others went only four, and others but two days of the week before Easter without eating. The name "forty days' fast"

---

[1] In 158. [2] St. Irenæus Frag. Ep. ad Victor ap. Eus. l. v, Hist. c. 24. [3] Bishop Beveridge. Ip. Cod. Can. Vind. I. iii. c. vii. [4] Book V, Sec. iii. n. xiii. [5] Tertullian, vol. iii. Clark's Edition. [6] Epiphanius de Expos. Fidei.

is spoken of by Origen.[1]   Montanus, a hermit of the second century, who claimed that the Holy Ghost dwelled in him for the reformation of Christians, and those who followed him, kept three Lenten fasts during the year.[2] Some think that the name, "Forty Days' Fast," must have been given to Lent in the early days of the Apostles,[3] and to have been called from the forty days of our Lord's fasting in the desert. St. Jerome, speaking of the error of the Montanists says : "We fast one Lent of forty days in the year, the whole world agreeing with us. They fast three Lents, as if three Saviours had suffered."[4] Tertullian, who fell into these errors, tries to defend the observance of these three Lents which were condemned by the Church.[5] There is no doubt that the Apostles commanded the last days of Lent to be kept as fasting days, as all writers of those early times teach, and it is almost certain that they taught that the whole forty days should be observed, although we cannot find it in any of their writings or in the works of their disciples, for many of their books were destroyed.[6] St. Irenæus, who lived before Tertullian, tells us that of the fast of forty days, that he and the Fathers knew Lent to be an Apostolic tradition. St. Jerome says : "Lent, as well as the keeping of Sundays, comes from the Apostles."[7] Pope Leo calls it an Apostolic institution.[8] St. Chrysostom thinks it came not from man, but from God.[9] Theophilus, Bishop of Alexandria, and his nephew and successor, St. Cyril, declare Lent to have come down from the Apostles. St. Isidore, of Seville, writes : "Lent is kept over the whole world by an Apostolic institution."[10] Dorotheus teaches that "The holy Apostles consecrated the fast of Lent as a tithing of the year to penance and to the purging away of sin."[11] St. Augustine says : " Whatever days we keep not from any written law but from tradition, and which are observed over the whole world, are understood to be recommended and established either by the Apostles, or by Plenary Councils, such as the yearly solemnities of Christ's passion."[12] "What the whole Church holds, and what was not instituted by councils but always observed,

---

[1] Hom X. in Levit., t. i. [2] St. Hier. Ep. ad Marcel. [3] Rig. l. t. i. [4] Ep. xxvii. ad Marcellum, t. iv. [5] Tertul. de Jejunio, c. xiii. [6] Tertul. L. de Orat. c. xiv. et L. Adv. Pych., c. xiv. [7] L. ii. in Galat. c. 4. [8] Sermo iv., v. et ix. de Quadragesima [9] Sermo xl. et clxvi. [10] Orig., l. vi. c. 19. [11] Doctrina 15. [12] Ep. cxviii. ad Jan. t. ii

is justly looked upon as being derived from the authority
of the Apostles."[1]   The Apostolic Canons command
clergymen to be deprived of their office, and lay persons
to be suspended from the Church for not fasting during
the forty days of Lent.[2]

No writer has ever dared to doubt that Lent goes back
to the beginning of the Church and to come down to us
from the time of the Apostles and their disciples.   We
are obliged to fast, not by the law of nature, but by the
example of the great and holy ones of the Old Testament,
and especially by the example of our Lord in his fast of
forty days in the desert.   All Christians of the early ages
considered that they were obliged to fast as a strict obligation.   St. Basil declares that those who are able to
fast, and yet do not, will be called to account by him who
is the lawmaker of the fast, God himself.[3] St. Irenæus
tells us that: "Not to fast in Lent is a sin."[4]   St. Gregory of Nazianzen wrote to a judge who did not fast in
Lent, "O judge, you commit a crime by not fasting."[5]
St. Ambrose left seven sermons on Lent.   St. Augustine
speaks in his works in sixty-seven places of the fast of
Lent.   Among other things, he says, that "Lent is a holy
time throughout the whole world," that "it is held each
year," that "it is the chief fast," that "it is observed by
abstaining from wine and meat," that "it is held not by
superstition, but by the law of God," that "the Christians
of his time eat no meat or certain kinds of fruit or deli-
cacies of the table,"[6] that "those who kept it are happy,"
that "it is the way to take up our cross and crucify the
body, give to the poor, forgive our enemies, keep from
plays, do good to all, and that we fast before Easter and
before baptism, because Christ fasted forty days after his
baptism," and many beautiful things besides he gives relating to the fast of Lent, as held by the Christians of his
time.[7]

The councils of the Church command the fast of Lent.
The Council of Laodicea uses a Greek word which expresses the strictest obligation of fasting the forty days
of Lent.[8]   Another forbade breaking the fast[9] on Thurs-

---

[1] St. Aug., l. iv. de Bapt., c. xxiv. n. 81. [2] Can. 69. [3] Hom. II. de Jejun. [4] Aurel.
Hom. II. [5] Epist. lxxiv. ad Celus. [6] S. Aug. Contra Fourt, l. xxx. n. v. [7] St.
Augustine, Bishop of Hippo, Opera Omnia Pariis Apud. Meller. [8] C. xix. [9] Concil.
Laodiceeum. An. 820, under Silvester I.

days of Lent. Later the fathers of a council ordered Lent to be observed before Easter.[1] Again, "Let Lent be kept by all churches."[2] The old custom of fasting will be continued by the monks from Quinquagesima to Easter.[3] All priests were obliged to preach to the people about the fast of Lent before Epiphany,[4] and those who were weak for any reason were not bound to keep the fast in Lent,[5] but those who were able had to fast with devotion and prayer in this holy time.[6] At one time cheese and eggs were not allowed in Lent.[7] The same with butter were forbidden by a later council.[8] From these and many other councils of the Church, which could be given, the reader can see how old and how widespread is the obligation of fasting during Lent.

The Nestorians, the Eutychians, the Armenians and the other heretics of the East, who separated from the Catholic Church in the fifth century, agree with us in celebrating the forty days of the fast of our Lord by keeping Lent,[9] and to-day they cannot believe any one a Christian who does not fast in this holy time. In the fourth century, Aerius, a follower of the false teachings of Arius, taught new doctrines, that there is no difference between bishops and priests by divine law; that it is useless to pray for the dead, and that it is not necessary to keep feasts and fasts. His teachings are to-day held by the Presbyterians.[10] Aerius was living when St. Epiphanius and St. Augustine wrote against him.[11] He was condemned by the Arians as well as by the Catholics. Lent was so well known in the days of St. Basil that he says : "There is no island, no continent, no city, no nation, no corner of the earth ever so remote, in which this fast is not proclaimed. Armies, travellers, sailors, merchants, though far from home, everywhere hear the solemn promulgation and receive it with joy."[12] Thus was the fast of Lent held in the days of the Byzantine empire, when the learning of the great St. Basil was heard in Asia Minor, and when the golden tongued St. Chrysostom was preaching his grand

---

[1] Concil. Aurelian I., An. 507, under Pope Symmachus. [2] Concil. Aurelian IV., An. 545, under Pope Vigilius. [3] Concil. Turonen. An. 570, under Pope John III. [4] Concil. Antisiodorens, An. 590, under Pope Gregory I. [5] Concil. Toletan. XII., An. 659, under Pope Martin I. [6] Concil. Tribur., An. 985, under Pope Formosus. [7] Concil. Quintilin. C. 8, An. 1093, under Gregory VII. [8] Concil. Mediolan. C. 7, An. 1565, under Pope Pius IV. [9] O'Brien, Hist. of the Mass, p. 171, note. [10] Heylin's History of Presbyterians. [11] An. 376, 428. [12] Hom. Jejun.. p. 11, Ed. Ben.

and eloquent sermons in Constantinople, the capital founded by Constantine the Great, when he moved his empire from Rome to the banks of the Bosphorus.

From the days of the Apostles the members of the Church always fasted during Lent, a custom which they learned from the Jews. The people of Nineve by their sins had provoked the anger of God; but, at the preaching of Jonas, the prophet, they observed a strict fast, and crying to the Lord for pardon, they were forgiven.[1] The Jews fasted when they asked God pardon for their sins.[2] God spoke to them by the mouth of his inspired prophet, "Be converted to me with all your heart in fasting and in weeping and in mourning."[3] The Rechabites, the descendants of Jonadab, in the reign of Jehu, never drank wine, and were afterwards porters in the temple of the Lord.[4]

Many of the Jews dedicated themselves to God under the name of Assideans, and kept a continual fast.[5] The Nazarites did the same.[6] The Pharisees were noted for their fasting. "I fast twice in a week," says one of them.[7] By direction of Samuel, the people of Israel kept a fast after they were defeated by the Philistines.[8] King David fasts at the death of his child,[9] and when defeated, "till[10] his knees are weakened through fasting."[11] In the time of danger, King Josaphat prayed with fasting.[12] Esdras, the rebuilder of the temple, fasted. The bad Achab, by fasting, turned away the anger of God.[13] Ninemias, by fasting, hastened the return of the Jews from their captivity in Babylon.[14] Judith and the people of Bethulia, by fasting and prayer, were delivered from the army of Holofernes.[15] Mordecai, and Esther with her maids, fasted, and by that means were given strength to deliver their people, the Jews, from destruction.[16] Tobias, by fasting, was cured of blindness, and received great comfort from the Lord, whence the Archangel said to his son, "Prayer is good, with fasting and alms, more than to lay up treasures of gold."[17] The lives of the Apostles, of the disciples and of the early Christians were like a continual

---

[1] Jonas iii. [2] I. Kings vii. 6; II. Kings xii. 16; Ps. xxxiv. 13; lxviii. 11; cviii. 24; II. Esdras i. 4. etc. [3] Joel ii. 12. [4] Jer. xxxv. 8; Calmet Com in Jer., t. viii. p. 70. [5] I. Mac. ii. 42; vii. 18, and II. Mac. xiv. 6. [6] Numb. vi. 2; Jud xiii. 7, 16; Amos ii. 12; Acts xviii. 18. [7] Luke xviii. 12. [8] I. Kings vii. 6. [9] II. Kings xii. 16. [10] Ps. xxxiv. 13. [11] Ps. cviii. 24. [12] II. Par. xx. 3, 6. [13] 1. Esdras viii. 21, 23. [14] II. Esdras i. 4. [15] Judith iv. 7, 11. [16] Esth. iv. 16; Esth. xiv. 2. [17] Tob. xii. 8.

fast,[1] for they followed the example of the Jews ; but especially in Lent they followed the severe example of Moses, of Elias and of our Lord in their fast of forty days. All Christians keep Lent, besides the fasts of Wednesdays and Fridays of the year, established by the Apostles, as tradition tells us.[2]

The example of our Lord, in his fast of forty days in the desert, has been the origin of the Christian Lent. All his disciples followed his footsteps, as he says, " But the days will come when the bridegroom will be taken away from them, and then they shall fast.[3] Speaking of a certain devil, he says : " This kind is not cast out but by prayer and fasting."[4] Anna, in the temple, fasted day and night. [5] The Lord told his followers, " When you fast, be not as the hypocrites, sad.''[6]

After their Lord went up into heaven, we find that his followers fasted, for we read that, as they were ministering to the Lord and fasting, the Holy Ghost commanded them to ordain Saul and Barnabas, "Then, they, fasting and praying, and imposing their hands upon them and sent them away."[7] Again we read, that sailing " was dangerous, because the fast was now past ; Paul comforted them."[8] St. Paul himself, the Apostle of the nations, telling us of his sufferings, speaks of fasting " in prisons, in seditions, in labors, in watchings, in fastings."[9] Again, " in much watchings, in hunger and thirst, in fastings often."[10] He tells us how to live so as to be saved. " I chastise my body and bring it into subjection, lest, perhaps, when I have preached to others, I myself should become a castaway."[11]

Not only the Jews, but all the nations of the ancient world fasted, which they held as one of their religious ceremonies. The priests of Isis and of Osiris fasted from meat, eggs, milk and wine, eating only rice seasoned with oil.[12] The magicians of Persia eat only meal and pulse. The Gymnosophists of India lived on fruits plucked from the trees on the banks of the Ganges. The prophets of Jupiter, in Crete, would take no meat or anything cooked by fire. The pagan priests never offered sacrifice to their

---

[1] Clemens Alex., l. ii. Paedag. c. 1.   [2] Butler's Feasts and Fasts, pp. 156, 157 ; Gueranger, Le Careme, p. 10, etc.   [3] Math. ix. 15.   [4] Math. xvii. 20 ; Mark ix. 29. [5] Luke ii. 37. [6] Math. vi. 16.   [7] Acts xiii. 2, 3.   [8] Acts xxvii. 9.   [9] II. Cor. vi. 5.   [10] II. Cor. xi. 27.   [11] I. Cor. ix. 27.   [12] Jerome, Adv. Jovin., l. ii. t. 4.

gods without first preparing themselves by fasting.[1] The
heathens prepared themselves by fasting before they
consulted their oracles.[2] When taking part in the ceremonies of the goddess Ceres, they fasted till the evening.[3]
The ladies of Egypt and of Athens had their feasts and
fasts, when they slept on the bare ground.[4] All the
members of the seven sects into which the Mohomedans
are divided in the countries of Asia and of Africa, keep
the fast of their month of Ramazan, which, because they
count the year by the changes of the moon, runs through
all the seasons. At this season, no one is excused from
fasting; the high and the low, even the Sultan himself
abstains from eating. When they are too sick to fast in
this time, they make it up by fasting when they get well.[5]
The Jews to-day, as well as in olden times, practice fasting as a religious ceremony. Pythagoras and Aristotle
recommend abstinence from flesh meat. Thus, all nations of antiquity had their days and their times for
fasting, showing us that such a widespread custom came
from the origin of the race, and that they had preserved
a tradition of the fall of man by eating in the garden of
Paradise.[6]

Three things were forbidden to the Christians in the
different ages of the Church during Lent : wine, meat and
food. In the first ages, wine was not allowed.[7] Abstinence from wine was never very common among the people of the Western Church, but it is yet a law among the
Eastern Christians. Abstaining from meat in Lent is not
different from the abstinence commanded on other days
of the year like Friday, the eves of the great feasts, and
the Quater Tenses. Meat is forbidden because it is the
food nearest like our flesh, and we can easier do without
it. Fasting from food means that we are to practice
self-denial by mortifying ourselves. To the Church our
Lord left the power of imposing and of arranging the
feasts each year. For that reason as the peoples, customs and ways of the world change, to them the Church
accommodates the law of fasting. For if the Lord had

---

[1] Alexander ab Alex., l. iv., c. 17. [2] Tertullian, L. de Anima, c. 48. [3] Cyr. Alex.
Adv. Jul., l. vi., c. xix. [4] Joseph Laurent. de Prand. et Cen. Vet., c. 22. [5] Voyage
de Perse par Chardin, t. vii. [6] Butler's Feasts and Fasts, p. 160, note. [7] St. Cyril of
Jerusalem, Catech. iv.; St. Basil, Hom. I, de Jejun. ; St. Chrysostom, Hom. IV., ad
Pop. Antioch. ; St. Theophilus, Lit. Pasch. iii.

made it a strict law, when he was on earth, as no power
can change the law of God, it might have become a great
burden on mankind to keep a rigorous fast. For these
reasons the bishops of the different dioceses into which
the world is divided send forth their instructions to be
read in the churches before Lent, and the way of keeping
Lent may change from year to year and from century to
century.

In the early ages, the Christians used to fast till the
evening, and that continued to be the way of keeping
Lent till the ninth century. Then they began to break
their fast at the hour of noon, corresponding to our three
in the afternoon, as we see some of the bishops preached
against the habit.[1] But the fervor of the people gradually grew less. The saints were few. Rathier, bishop of
Verona, gave the people liberty to break their fast at three
in the afternoon.[2] We find that the bishops of the Council of Rouen forbade the fast to be broken till Vespers
were begun in the church after the Office of None,[3] and
Vespers were said at that hour, to give the people a chance
to eat. Before that, on fasting days, they used to sing
the Offices of the Breviary in the church, and None was
begun at three in the afternoon, followed by Mass,[4] and
Vespers about sundown. The people gradually began to
break their fast before these hours, and the Offices and
the Masses were begun earlier, so as to have Vespers at
about noon, when the people were allowed to break their
fast at midday. In the XIIth century the custom of breaking the fast after None had become general throughout
the world.[5] A hundred years after, that was the rule
laid down by the great scholastic writers.[6] Still the
people became more relax, and toward the end of the
XIIIth century they broke their fast at the hour for the
Office of None, that is, at noon, and in the XIVth century
that custom became universal in the Church,[7] and was
followed by the Pope, the Cardinals and Religious of
both sexes.[8] Such were the ways and the manner of keeping Lent in the XVth century, as we see in the writings of
the great masters of that age.[9] In vain St. Thomas and

---

[1] Theodulphus Capitul. 39 Lab. c. t. vii. [2] Ser. I. de Quad. [3] Oderie Vital, Hist.,
l. iv. [4] Gueranger, Le Careme, p. 15. [5] Hugo de S. Victor, in Reg. S. Augustine, c.
iii. [6] St. Thomas, in IV. Dist. xv. A. 3. Quest. 8 [7] Richard of Middleton, Durand of
Saint-Pourcain, Bp. of Meaux. [8] Durand., in IV., Dist. xv. q. ix. A. 7. [9] Card. Caje-
tanus, Lawrence Poncher, Antoninus, etc.

others tried to stem the downward tide of discipline among the people. They became still more relax, and the discipline of our days became established. They partook of only one meal each day. The constitution of man appeared to have become weakened. The clergy then allowed the people to take a little lunch in the evening.

The origin of the lunch seems to be very old, and comes from the monasteries. The Rule of St. Benedict allowed it during a great many of the fasting days at other times of the year besides Lent. Among the Benedictines it was taken at three in the afternoon. With that custom the fast was not so severe, either among the religious or the people, who, in the days of that great Saint, fasted till sundown.[1] As the monks worked hard in the fields, their superiors, from the fourteenth of September, allowed them to take a little wine when the bell rung in the evening for the Office of Complin. When they came together for their wine the Abbot or the Prior said a few words to them, and that gathering was called the Collatio, from the Latin, meaning to meet together. From that comes our English word Collation, meaning a part of a meal taken on fast days. Before the IXth century the monks ate only one meal during Lent, but at that time an assembly of Religious allowed the monks to take a little wine during Lent.[2] In the XIVth and XVth centuries they were allowed a small piece of bread with their wine. That weakening of the rigorous fast of the primitive ages of Christianity, thus beginning in the monasteries and in the cloisters, spread among the people, and it was so common in the XIIIth century that St. Thomas, examining the question if it breaks the fast, says that it does not;[3] on the contrary, he says that we can take a little solid food at that time. In his day they took that little collation at three in the afternoon. Toward the end of the XIIIth and the beginning of the XIVth centuries they began to break the fast at noon, in place of at three, and in the evening they began to take a few fruits or fish, but in such a way that it never became a second meal. During all these ages meat was not taken on fast days, only fish was allowed because of its cold nature, and because of many deep and mysterious reasons founded on

[1] Gueranger, Le Careme, p. 17. [2] Convent. Aquisgran., c. xii., Lab. c. t. vii. [3] In Quest., cxlvii. A. 6.

the Holy Bible. Milk, eggs, cheese and all such food called "white meats," were not allowed, and even in our days butter and cheese are not used in Rome during Lent on the days when meat is not eaten.[1] From the IXth century these "white meats" were used in Germany and many parts of the north of Europe. In the XIth century the Council of Kedlimbourgh tried to dissuade the people from using these kinds of food, but afterwards the Popes granted their use from time to time. Even to the XVIth century, the Christians of France continued the old customs of the early ages in observing Lent, changing only about the XVIIth century. As a reparation for the loss of the ancient discipline of the apostolic age, all the people of the parishes of Paris, with the Dominicans, the Carmelites, the Augustinians, and the other Religious Orders, marched in procession to the Cathedral of Notre Dame on Quinquagesima Sunday, and the Canons forming the chapter of the Cathedral, with the four parishes under them, went to the palace of the kings and sung an Anthem before the royal Court in the Sainte Chapelle, where a relic of the true Cross was exposed. Those ceremonies of the ancient church of France were broken up by the furies of the French Revolution.

The permission to use "white meats" does not allow the eating of eggs, according to the old discipline of the Church, and in Rome they are not eaten except when meat is allowed, but a dispensation to eat them on certain days is granted. All this is for the spiritual good of the members of the Church, and when Pope Benedict XIV. saw the ease with which the people excused themselves from fasting in every part of the world, he renewed the ancient customs of the Church by forbidding meat and fish at the same meal when meat was allowed in Lent.[2] Before that time, in the first years of his Pontificate, he addressed an Encyclical Letter to all the bishops of the world, expressing his sorrow at seeing Lent no more kept as in the early ages. "Lent is the place of our warfare, by it we are able to know the enemies of the cross of Jesus Christ, by it we turn aside the anger of the divine wrath, by it we are protected by heavenly aid, and during the day we are helped against the princes of darkness."[3]

---

[1] Gueranger, Le Careme, p. 19.   [2] Const. Benedict XIV., June 10, 1745.   [3] Const. Non Ambigimus.

Another century went by after that solemn warning of the head of the Church, but still the people became more and more relax in keeping Lent.   In the XIIIth century the bishop of Prague informed the great Pope Innocent III. that the people of his diocese were obliged to eat meat during Lent, because a kind of famine deprived them of other kinds of food, asking of the Pope to be allowed the use of meat, and besides inquiring what he was to do regarding those who, when sick, asked to be allowed to eat meat.   The reply of the Pontiff is full of moderation, but it shows us that the general law of Lent was then carried out.[1]   Wenceslas, king of Bohemia, a little after, considered himself by sickness unable to keep the Lenten fast, and he asked to be allowed to eat meat. His case was examined by two abbots appointed by the Pope, and finding that no vows had been taken by him, Rome granted his request to use meat, except on Fridays, Saturdays, and the eve of St. Mathias, but he was to eat alone and with moderation.[2] In the fourteenth century Pope Clement VI. allowed John, king of France, to eat meat in Lent, because in the wars he was then engaged in, he could not always find fish.   In another case the same Pope granted a like indulgence to the queen.[3] A few years past, and Gregory XI. gave a new brief to Charles V. and to his queen, in which he delegated to their confessor, with the advice of their physician, the liberty of eating eggs and cheese in Lent.   In the fifteenth century Sixtus IV. allowed James III., king of Scotland, the use of meat on fasting days, but with the advice of his confessor.[4]   In the sixteenth century Julius II. granted the same to John, the king of Denmark, and to Christina, his queen;[5] a few years after Clement VII. gave the same privilege to the Emperor Charles V.[6] and afterwards to Henry II. of France and Spain, as well as to his Queen Margaret.[7]   Such was the care with which the Church proceeded to grant to even kings and emperors leave to break the law of the fast in Lent. Still the people became more relax in keeping the fast, and it was no wonder that they became ripe for the Reformation, which soon followed, and plunged the north of Europe into the storms

---

[1] Decret. l. III. c. Con. ; de Jejun. tit. xlvi. [2] 1297. [3] Raynaldi, Ad. An., 1297. [4] D'Achery, Spicil., t. iv. [5] In 1505. [6] In 1524. [7] In 1538 ; Raynaldi.

of division and of error in which it is laboring at present.

We are tracing the history of Lent in different respects. Soon after the times of the Apostles, when the Roman empire was converted to the faith, all theatres and meetings of pleasure were forbidden by the law of the land, wherever the Roman power had extended.[1]   In 380, Gratian[2] and Theodosius ordered the courts of law not to open during the time of Lent.[3]   Many councils of France commanded the Carlovingian kings to close their law courts during this holy time.[4]   Many nations of the west of Europe keep no more that custom of closing the courts, but the Turks continue to close their tribunals during their yearly fasts.

In the Middle Ages the larger part of Europe was covered with great forests, and hunting was a pleasure for the people.   Hawks were trained to take the game.   But the noise and excitement were judged contrary to the spirit of penance and of fasting.   For that reason, in the ninth century Pope Nicholas I. forbade hunting during Lent among the Bulgarians who had recently been converted to the faith.[5]   That was not surprising, for, from the fourth century all military exercises were forbidden by Constantine on Sundays and Fridays, in honor of Christ's death and resurrection from the dead on these days, so as not to disturb the devotion of the people, for the early Christians devoted these days to our Lord.[6] During the ninth century war was forbidden by the Church throughout the greater part of Europe during Lent.[7]   Nothing equals the horrors of war, and for that reason we read in the letters of Pope Nicholas I. to the Bulgarians, of Gregory VII. to Didier, the Abbot, in many of the ancient monuments of the Church, in the Councils of Meaux, of Aix-la-Chapelle, and in the acts of the ancient Church of England, that war was forbidden during the whole time of Lent.   War was the chief business of the nobles of Europe before the Church put a stop to the shedding of blood.

When the barbarians of the north of Europe and from

---

[1] Nono canon. tit. vii:, c. 1. [2] Augustus Gratianus. [3] Cod. Theodos., l. ix. tit. xxxv. l. 4. [4] Council of Meaux in 845 ; Council of Tibur, in 895. [5] Ad Consultat. Bulgar. Labb., Con. t. viii. [6] Eusebius, Const. Vita, l. iv. c. xviii. et xix. [7] Lab. Council, t. vii.

the west of Asia came down and destroyed the Roman
Empire, when no more peoples remained to be overcome,
each chief rested in the valleys and in the fertile plains
which they subdued, and there they built their castles.
The soldiers became their vassals, while they and their
children became the lords and the aristocrats of Europe.
From that came the nobility and the common people of
ancient times. From that comes the landlords and the
tenants of our days. Each lord and nobleman in his
castle was at war with his neighbors. For that reason
each castle was built like a fort. Great was the work of
the Church to keep peace between them and to put a stop
to the widows' woe, to the orphans' wail, to the cry of
the wounded and to the groan of the dying. At length
she succeeded in the eleventh century, by the celebrated
" Truce of God,"[1] in stopping all battles for four days of
the week, from Wednesday evening till Monday morning,
during the whole year. That agreement among the people
of the Middle Ages was sanctioned by many Councils
and Popes. It was but an extension of the rule laid
down generations before by the Church, forbidding fighting during Lent. St. Edward the Confessor, king of
England, made a law which was confirmed by William the
Conqueror, and by which the Truce of God was extended
so that war was never carried on from the beginning of
Advent to the Octave of Easter, from Ascension Thursday
to the Octave of Pentecost, nor during the four Quater
Tenses of the year.[2]

In 1095, Pope Urban II., with wisdom laid down the
rules relating to the Crusade for the recovery of the Holy
Sepulchre, to break the power of the Turks and the false
religion of Mohammed, which was threatening Europe
with war and carnage. He used his authority to extend
the " Truce of God " by forbidding fighting during Lent.
One of his decrees was confirmed a year later by the
Council of Rouen. It was that all acts of war must stop
from Ash Wednesday till the Monday following the Octave of Pentecost, on all feasts of the Blessed Virgin, of
the Apostles[3] and during the latter part of the week as
given before.[4] Thus all Christian nations showed their

---

[1] Cardinal Wiseman's Holy Week, p. 174.   [2] Lab. Concil., t. ix.   [3] Gueranger, Le
Careme, p. 29.   [4] Orderic Vital Hist. Eccl., l. ix.

respect for the holy time of Lent during the Middle Ages.

Among the Greeks and the nations of the west of Asia, on Septuagesima Sunday they published the rules and regulations of Lent. From the following Monday they use no meat, but eat what they call "White Meats," as eggs, cheese, butter and things of that kind, while on the Monday before Ash Wednesday, their Lent begins with all its rigors. From that time they eat neither meat, eggs, cheese or even fish. The only things allowed are bread, fruits, honey, and for those who live near the sea, shell-fish. Wine, for a long time forbidden, is drank no more among them.

Besides their great Lent, as among us, their preparation for the grand solemnities of the Easter Time, they keep three other Lents during the year. One, called the Apostles' Lent, begins at the Octave of Pentecost and lasts till the feast of Sts. Peter and Paul, the other, called the Virgin Mary's Lent, begins on the first of August and ends on the eve of the Assumption,[1] and the third begins forty days before Christmas, and lasts till the birth of our Lord. The fasting, penance and self-denial of the people of the East, during these three seasons of penance, are like those of Lent—severe and rigorous, and are kept by them like the times of fasting and of prayer kept by the early Christians in the days of the Apostles.[2]

Lent is filled with mystery. During the Septuagesima Time the number seventy recalls to our minds the seventy years of the captivity of the Jews in Babylon, where, after having purified themselves from their sins by penance, they returned again to their country and to their city of Jerusalem, then they celebrated their Easter. Now the holy Church, our Mother, brings before our minds the severe and mysterious number forty, that number which, as St. Jerome says, is always filled with self-denial and with penance.[3]

When the race became corrupt, God wiped out the sin of man by the rain of forty days and forty nights upon the world, but after forty days Noah opened a window in the ark and found the water gone from the earth. When the Hebrews were called from the land of Egypt for forty

---

[1] 14th of August.   [2] Gueranger, Le Careme, p. 32.   [3] In Ezech., c. xxix.

years they fasted on manna, wandering in the desert, before they came to the promised land. When Moses went up the Mount of Sinai, for forty days and nights he fasted from food before he received the law graven on tablets of stone. When Elias came near to God, on Horeb, for forty days and nights he fasted.[1] Thus these two, the greatest men of old, whom the hand of the Lord hath raised up to do his mighty will, Moses on Mount Sinai, Elias on Mount Horeb, what do they figure but the law and the prophecy of the Old Testament pointing to the fast of forty days and nights of our Lord in the desert? Like shadowy forms they prefigured the Son of God, who first established Lent when the Christians, his disciples, fast, following the example of our Master, when they keep the Lenten Services of the Church.

Let us follow our Lord in his Lent in the desert. "At that time,"[2] says the Gospel. When? The moment after his baptism, to show that the Christian after baptism must prepare for a life of self denial. When? Thirty years before, on the same day, the three Magi adored him, a little child in the manger. When? One year from that day, at his mother's request, he changed the water into wine. At that time, by contact with his most holy body, the waters of the earth received the power of washing the souls of men from sin in baptism. St. John the Baptist had preached penance from the banks of the Jordan. Now Christ was to preach penance from the sands of the desert. John had lived in fasting on locusts and wild honey from his twelfth year.[3] He alone was worthy of baptizing our Lord. Now Christ is led by the Spirit into the desert. By what spirit? By the Holy Spirit, to show that those who fast and do penance during Lent are led by the Holy Ghost. To show that the Church was led by the Holy Ghost in commanding all her children to fast during Lent. Into the desert he is led by the Holy Spirit, with the burning sun of Judea above his head by day, and the parched sands beneath his limbs by night; into the desert he is led, where the hot air burns his hallowed cheek, and the burning sands give way beneath his feet; into the desert he is led, where below him stretches the Dead Sea, beneath whose stagnant,

---

[1] S. Aug. Sermo CCX. in Quadragesima, n. 9. [2] Ev. 1. D. q. in Missale. [3] Math. iii. 4.

slimy waters lie the remains of Sodom, Gomorrah, Salem
and the cities of the plains destroyed by God for their
sins.   Here comes our Lord to do penance and to fast for
the sins of mankind.   Here comes our Saviour to keep
the first Lent.

Not far from the banks of the Jordan rises a mountain
harsh and savage in its outlines, which tradition calls the
Lenten mountain.[1] From its rugged heights flow down
the streams which water the plains of Jericho.   From its
rocky sides is seen the valley of the Dead Sea.   From its
inhospitable crags stretches out the gloomy expanse of that
spot where once the five smiling cities of the plains sat
amid the fertile land, but now, of all places of the earth,
marked with the curse of God for the sins of Sodom and
Gomorrah.   There came the Son of God to establish
Lent.   There came the Saviour to show by penance how
to gain our everlasting crown by fasting for our sins.
There, deep amid the desert fastness, in a cave formed
by the ancient upheaval of the mountain, there he found
a home.   There he fasted forty days and forty nights.
No water cooled his burning tongue, no food repaired his
weakening strength.   The wild beasts of the wilderness
were his companions.   The heat of the simoon from the
burning desert poisoned the air he breathed.   The hot
sands burned his feet.   The rocks became his bed.   Such
was the beginning of the Christian Lent.

"After he had fasted forty days and forty nights, afterwards he was hungry;" for his nature was human, like ours.
"And the tempter came."   He prepared himself for temptation by fasting, to show us that we must prepare ourselves by fasting for the temptations of this life, to show
that by fasting and by penance we are to overcome
the enemies of our salvation.   He was not hungry till at
the end of his forty days of fasting, to show that he was God,
for no one can fast for that time without being hungry.
At the end of forty days he was hungry, to show that he
was man, with all the weakness of our nature.   Our
nature had been badly hurt by Adam eating the forbidden fruit.   Christ came to restore our nature to its lost
inheritance in heaven, and he begins his public life by
fasting.   And now, at the end of that fast, the devil, who

---

[1] Gueranger, Le Careme, p. 46.

was the cause of our fall, found him weak and hungry.
He came to tempt him in the desert, as he came to tempt
our first parents in the garden. Let us draw near and
see the temptation of our Lord.

The devil had seen him baptize in the Jordan, he had
heard the words of the holy Baptist point him out as the
"Lamb of God." He had heard the words of the Father
in heaven call him his beloved Son. He had seen the
Holy Spirit in the form of a dove, with outspread wings
overshadow him. He says to himself, "Can this be the
Son of God, this weak and hungry man?" The demon is
in doubt. He comes near to the person of Jesus Christ.
He could not enter into his members as he can in ours,
and tempt him. He could only tempt him from without,
as he tempted our first parents from without. Coming near, he says, "If thou be the Son of God, command
these stones to be made bread." Mark well the words.
It is a temptation of pride. "If thou be the Son of God,"
here is a chance to show your power. Long before the
same demon came to our Mother Eve, and said, "In what
day soever you shall eat thereof . . . . you shall be as
gods." The temptation of pride. Thus he was tempted
by being asked to eat, like our parents in the garden.
Thus he was tempted by pride, as our mother Eve was
tempted of old.[1]

This life is a continual battle against temptation, and
the Church, made up of the clergy and of the people, is
like a great and powerful army in ceaseless battle array
against our enemies. For that reason Lent is called the
fighting time of the Church. For that reason, in the offices
of the breviary we say the psalms, wherein is recalled
that battle of the Christian against his old enemies, the
powers of hell.

We are coming near to the sad sight of the death of
our Lord. We are to see that rage of the Jews against
him which ended by his death on the cross. The Church
prepares us beforehand, by celebrating certain feasts on
each of the Fridays of Lent, which are like so many
preparations for the tragedy of Good Friday. The Friday following the first Sunday of Lent we celebrate the
memory of the holy Lance and Nails which pierced his

----

[1] Fabri, Conciones, I. 1. Dom. I. Quad. con. XL.

sacred flesh ; or, in some cases, the feast of the Crown of
Thorns he wore upon his head. The Friday of the second
week we say the office of the Linens, which Joseph and
Nicodemus wrapped around his body when dead and laid
in the tomb. On the third Friday we commemorate the
memory of the five Wounds of our Lord ; while the offices
of the fourth Friday are devoted to the memory of the
most precious Blood shed for our redemption.[1]

During the early ages of the Church, Lent was the
time when the catechumens, that is, the newly converted
Christians, prepared for baptism by fasting and by penance, before they were washed from their sins by the
waters of regeneration on Holy Saturday. For many
months they had been instructed for that holy rite by the
saints of old, and in the Lenten Season they redoubled
their penance and their prayers.

Again, Lent was the time when the public penitents,
those who were guilty of great sins, purged themselves
from their crimes by public penance. From Ash Wednesday, when they were driven from the church, like Adam
from Paradise, in sackcloth and in ashes, in tears and in
fasting, they wept at the doors of the churches, till received again into the bosom of their mother, the Church,
by confession and Communion on Holy Thursday. Because the people are no more saints like those of the
early ages, although the Church in her motherly indulgence has changed these laws, still their traces are found
in the ceremonies and the services of the Latin Rite.

To forever keep to the traditions of the Apostles, and
to preserve Lent as a time of penance and of sorrow for
sin, the Church has never easily allowed the feasts of the
saints to be celebrated during this holy time. In our
days, but a few months ago, Pope Leo XIII. changed
many of the offices of the saints during Lent, so that
from the year 1884 Lent will have more ferial offices than
before.[2] That is but coming back to the ancient times,
when most of the offices of the year were simple ferials,
before there were so many saints to celebrate their feasts.
In the fourth century the council of Laodicea would not
allow any feast to be celebrated or the remembrance of a
saint to be made in the offices, except on Saturdays and

---

[1] Brev. Rom. Of. pro Aliq. Locis.   [2] Brief of Leo XIII., July, 1882.

Sundays.[1] The Greek Church, for many ages, kept the same rule, and it was only after the lapse of time that they celebrated the feast of the Annunciation on the 25th of March. The members of the Latin Rite kept that custom for a long time, but finally allowed the feast of the Annunciation to be held on the 25th of March, and at length the feast of St. Matthew, on the 24th of February. In later times, some saints' feasts were allowed in Lent, but always with great care, because a feast is a day of joy and of gladness, which would break in upon the solemn, penitential time of Lent. For that reason the Greeks and the followers of the Eastern rites believe that no feast can be rightly held during a time of fasting and of penance, while the followers of the Latin Rite think the contrary, and allow certain feasts of great importance to be celebrated. For these reasons, Saturday among the Greeks is never a fasting day, nor do they fast the day of the Annunciation, as they celebrate it as a great feast.

These customs of the East gave rise, in the seventh century, in the Western Church, to the ceremony of the Mass of the Presanctified. Each Sunday during Lent, a priest of the Eastern Rites consecrated six Hosts, only one of which was consumed by him at the Sunday Mass; the five others were kept for the five following days of the week, when they went through the ceremonies of the Mass without consecrating again till the next Sunday, taking the Host during the week days as a simple Communion. In the Latin Rite, we have that ceremony once each year, on Good Friday,[2] which will be explained in its proper place. That manner of saying Mass by the Greeks during Lent appears to have come from the Council of Laodicea,[3] which commanded the holy sacrifice not to be offered in Lent, except on Saturdays and Sundays. In the following ages the Greeks concluded that Mass breaks the fast, as we see from their dispute with the Legate Humbert.[4] In the evening after Vespers they celebrate that Rite, and then the priest who celebrates alone receives the Holy Communion as among us on Good Friday. The only exception they have is on the

---

[1] Concil. Laod., Cant. ll.   [2] O'Brien, Hist. of the Mass, p. 13.   [3] C. xlix., held in 314.
[4] Con. Nicetam., t. iv.

day of the Annunciation, when all the people may receive.

The rule of the Council of Laodicea was never received in the Western Church where the Latin Rite prevails, following Rome where it is carried out in all its purity, except in the early ages, on Holy Thursday. In the eighth century Pope Gregory II., wishing to complete the Roman Sacramentary, added the Masses said during the first five weeks of Lent.[1] It is hard to give a reason why they did not say Mass in the first ages after the Apostles on Holy Thursday, or why in the churches of Milan, where they follow the Ambrosian Rite, they say no Mass on the Fridays of Lent. The best reason appears to be because our Lord said the first Mass at the last supper on Thursday and died on Friday, and out of respect for him they would not offer the august sacrifice on these days.

In the middle ages, from the most early times they used to draw a veil before the altar during the most solemn parts of the Mass. That custom ceased long ago; but during Lent, in Notre Dame, of Paris, and in many Churches of Europe, they veil the altar from the view of the clergy and the people, no one but the celebrant and the servers seeing the ceremonies taking place behind that violet veil. The violet color signifies penance, into which the whole Church is plunged during this holy time. It typifies the penance and the fasting of sorrowful souls, by self-denial, satisfying God for sin; it recalls the deep humiliations of our Lord in his passion, which like a veil was drawn aside when he rose glorious and immortal from the grave; it represents the veil of the temple shutting off the Holy of Holies, of the temple of Jerusalem rent by the hands of angels when the Redeemer died on Calvary's cross for our salvation.[2] Also in the early ages they used to form into great processions during Lent, and to march from one church to the others, especially on Wednesdays and Fridays, walking in their bare feet in the monasteries and convents, thus imitating the processions of Rome, which were daily seen for many centuries, and which gave rise to the Stations of the Titles of the Missal. They increased their prayers during this time of

---

[1] Anastas. in Greg. II.   [2] Honorius, Gem. Animae, l. III., c. lxvi.

CATHEDRAL OF MAYENCE.

penance, and for that reason they added to the usual prayers of the Breviary on Mondays the Offices of the dead, on Wednesdays the Gradual Psalms, and on Fridays the Penitential Psalms. In the churches of France during the week they added the whole 150 psalms to the ordinary Office.[1]

L—THE FIRST SUNDAY OF LENT.

We have now come to the first Sunday of Lent, the most solemn of all the Sundays of the year.[2] Like on Passion Sunday and on Palm Sunday, no other feast can be celebrated on this day; not even the feast of the Patron Saint of the church, or the Office of its Dedication. It is called the Fifth Sunday[3] because it is the fifth Sunday before Easter. It is called Brand Sunday, because in the middle ages the youths who had given themselves up to the dissipations of the carnivals, used to come on this Sunday to the doors of the churches with lighted tapers in their hands, as a sign of public penance for their sins.[4] It is called "Invocabit," from the first word of the Introit.

From to-day to Easter there are 42 days, but our Lent of 40 days, beginning on Ash Wednesday, ends on the evening of Holy Saturday; and taking out the Sundays, which are not fasting days, we fast for forty days which make up the Lent, which brings us to the glories of the Easter Season. These 40 days of Lent were prefigured by the Children of Israel wandering in the desert, fasting on manna, and resting at forty stations. As they were led by Josue into the promised land, so we are led by Jesus into heaven—by that Lord who came to us by the forty generations descending from our father, Adam.[5] We fast then for forty days, as St. Augustine says, because St. Matthew gives the forty generations of our Lord that by the number forty we might go up to him[6] who for forty days remained with his disciples after his resurrection from the dead.

Although the Greeks are against celebrating any feast during Lent, yet on the first Sunday of Lent they have

---

[1] Martine, De Antiq. Eccl. Rit., t. iii., c. xviii.   [2] Gueranger le Careme, p. 145.
[3] Durand. Rationale. Div. L. vi., c. xxxii., n. 1.   [4] Gueranger le Careme, p. 145.
[5] Durand. Rationale, Div. L. vi., c. xxx., n. 1.   [6] De Consecrat. Dist., v. Jejun.

one of their greatest solemnities, when they hold their services in memory of the restoring of the holy images in Constantinople and in all the Empire of the East, by the Empress Theodora and the great Archbishop Methodius in 842, after they had been destroyed by the rage of the image breakers, during the religious persecutions which had taken place some time before.

The title of the Mass is "The Station at St. John Lateran," the Basilica of the Saviour, the ancient residence of the Roman Emperors, the old Church of Pope Silvester, "The Lateran Church the Mother and the Mistress of all the churches of Rome and of the world."[1] There the Mass of the first Sunday of Lent is said. There the people of Rome gather at the divine services. There the public penitents were reconciled on Holy Thursday. There, in Constantine's Baptistery, the catechumens were baptized on Holy Saturday. There the fast of Lent was announced so many times by the great Popes SS. Gregory the Great and Leo the Great.

The Introit is taken from the XC. Psalm, which alone forms the parts sung during the Mass. Its sacred words breathe faith and hope for the Christian soul.

The Epistle is taken from St. Paul to the Corinthians,[2] and contains the most beautiful advice directing us how to keep the Lent.

The Gradual and the Tract are taken entirely from Psalm XC., and would be too long to give here.

The Gospel comes from St. Matthew,[3] and tells us how our Lord was led by the Holy Spirit[4] into the desert to spend his Lent, and how he was there tempted.

Each Sunday of the year offers us a subject taken from the life of our Lord, on which we are to meditate, but the Sundays of Lent above all set before us the most vivid scenes from his life. The first Sunday of Lent we are called to contemplate him tempted by the devil. We are all tempted, and our Lord, who came to save us, came also to show us how to resist temptation,[5] for he was "one tempted in all -things like as we are, without sin."[6] The ineffable mystery of the Incarnation had been kept secret from the devil. For that reason Mary

---

[1] Inscription on the Church of St. John Lateran. [2] II. Cor. vi. [3] Matt. iv. 1. [4] Fabri Conciones, Dom. 1, Quad. cxl., n. 112. [5] Fabri Con., Dom. 1, Quad. c. 1, n. 111. [6] Heb. iv. 15.

was espoused to Joseph[1] to conceal the birth from the devil. The tempter approaches the Lord and tempts him to change the stones into bread, so as to satisfy his hunger. With the simplicity and the majesty of the Saint of Saints, he resists the temptation. It was a temptation to satisfy the appetites of our nature. The demon then took him in his foul hands, and placed him on the highest pinnacle of the holy temple in Jerusalem, and told him to throw himself down and let the people see him borne up by angels' hands. With the words of holy Moses he resisted.[2] It was a temptation of pride. Again the Leader of the fallen Angels carries him to the top of a high mountain, and showed him all the kingdoms of the earth and the glories of this world, and says he will give him all these if, "falling on his knees, he would adore him." Again with the words of Moses, "The Lord thy God thou shalt adore,"[3] he repels the arch tempter.[4] Finding that he cannot lead our Lord into sin, he leaves him.

Mark well these three kinds of temptations. The first attack was like the one the devil made upon our first parents in the garden. The second was like the temptations of all the race of Adam. The third was like the temptation of all those in high places and in power. The first was a temptation of our lower appetites, the pleasures of the senses; the second was a temptation of the soul, the sin of pride; while the third was a temptation to be great. The love of the things of this world, carnal pleasures, worldly pride, ambition—these are the poisoned sources from which spring forth all the sins of mankind, the temptations of our fallen nature, as the Apostle says, "All that is in the world is the concupiscence of the flesh and the concupiscence of the eyes and the pride of life."[5] The world, the devil and the flesh, these are the fountains of all the sins of man, and in the Gospel of this, the first Sunday of Lent, we read this part of the Gospel to warn the people against temptation.

Each week day during Lent there is a special Mass of the day, for the days of this holy time are of such importance, that, like the feasts of the year, they have their

---

[1] St. Ignatius cited by St. Jerome.   [2] Deut. vi. 16.   [3] Matt. iv. 10.   [4] Deut. vi. 13.   [5] I. John ii. 16.

Masses, and in the Office we always make a remembrance of them when we celebrate any other feast.

The title of the Mass of the Monday following the first Sunday in Lent is, "The Station at St. Peter in Chains." That is, in Rome, the services are held in the church built in the fifth century by the Empress Eudoxia, wife of Valentinian[1] III. There are guarded with jealous care the chains with which St. Peter was bound, first in Jerusalem and again in Rome.

The title of the Mass said on Tuesday is "The Station at St. Anastasia." It is the church where the Mass at the aurora hour is offered upon Christmas morning.

To the Lenten fast comes now the fast of the Quater Tenses of spring. On Wednesday, Friday and Saturday of this week we will have a double reason to fast, because of the law of Lent and of the law of the Ember days or Quater Tenses. In the early ages, till the eleventh century, the Ember days were celebrated the first week of March, and those of summer on the second week of June. But by a decree of Gregory VII. they were fixed at the times of the year we celebrate them now; that is, the Ember days of spring during the first week of Lent, the Ember days of summer during the week following Pentecost Sunday, the Ember days of autumn following the 14th of September, and the Ember days of Winter in the third week of Advent. The title of the Mass on Wednesday of this week is, "The Station at St. Mary Major, the august temple built in ancient times to the honor of the Mother of God. In the Offices of the Breviary to-day, the Church offers us the example of Moses and Elias fasting for forty days in order to signify the Christian Lent, and to show the law and the prophecy of the Old Testament, represented by these great men of old, who fasted, and that we must follow them, our fathers, in the faith. To-day the Greeks chant a grand and beautiful hymn in praise of fasting, called Triodion.

The title of the Mass on Thursday is "The Station at St. Lawrence in Paneperna," one of these great churches raised by the piety of the people of Rome in ancient times to the honor of the great St. Lawrence. In the

---

[1] Placidius Valentinian, born in 419, assassinated in 455.

Offices of the Breviary to-day, we find the words of the
Lord to his prophet, Ezechiel,[1] foretelling the mercy of
God to the Gentiles throughout the world converted to
the church and doing penance after their baptism. The
Gothic Missal has some beautiful poetic pieces relating
to this time of the year.

The title of the Mass on Friday is "The Station at the
Holy Twelve Apostles," one of the most beautiful of the
grand Basilicas of Rome, where are preserved the bodies
of the Apostles, SS. Philip and James the Less. Again, to-
day we read the prophecy of Ezechiel,[2] where God speaks
of sin, saying that the one who commits any sin shall die
and shall not live, but if he do penance and cease from
sin he shall live. The death here spoken of is the death
of the soul by being deprived of the grace of God, which
is its life. In the services of the Greek church are found
some beautiful sentiments relating to prayer and self denial during this time.

The title of the Mass on Saturday is "The Station at
St. Peter's," that is, the services of this day are held in
the noblest building raised by the hand of man to the
worship of Almighty God, St. Peter's at Rome. The
lessons of the Breviary[3] tell us that the nation which will
be faithful in keeping the law of God will be blessed, and
we find that no nations of old left the worship of the Lord
but they perished. The old Missal of Cluny has a sweet
poetic piece to the Virgin Mary said on Saturday of the
first week of Lent.

II.—The Second Sunday of Lent.

In former times this Sunday was called the "Vacent,"
because it had no service which belonged to it. The
Quater Tenses or Ember days were celebrated the week
before, and as then the church from the earliest times
ordained her clergy, the people spent the week in prayer,
asking God to give them good and holy priests. The
ceremony of ordination began on Saturday and lasted
long into the small hours of the morning. Then they
celebrated the Mass of ordination, which became the
Sunday service,[4] or, as a writer of the twelfth century

---

[1] c. xviii. [2] c. xviii. [3] Dent. c. xxvi. [4] 75 Dist., *Quod a patribus*. Extra. de
Temp. Ord. *Literas*.

says, they used to repeat the services of the preceding Wednesday.[1] All was carried out in the church without the sound of the organ or other musical instruments, for as it is the fifth Sunday from Septuagesima, it represented the Jews on the banks of the rivers of Babylon hanging their harps on the willows and weeping to return to Jerusalem, a type of the children of the church sorrowing for their sins, and weeping to be taken to the Lord their God in heaven.

The second Sunday of Lent is called "Reminiscere," from the first word of the Introit. It is called the Sunday of the Transfiguration, because to-day we celebrate the glories of the Son of God, transfigured on the mount Tabor.[2]

Leaving Galilee to go up to Jerusalem for the last time to celebrate the Passover, Jesus came to a mountain midway between Nazareth and Tiberida. It was Tabor, a spur of Libanus. It was the night of the 6th of August, in the 33d year of his age, and the third of his public life, that Jesus, taking with him Peter, James and John, ascended the mountain to pray. He took with him three to be witnesses of the glories of his Divinity,[3] for, " in the mouth of two or three witnesses every word shall stand."[4] He took only three, as he wished to keep the mystery secret till after his death, as he said: " Tell the vision to no man till the Son of Man be risen."[5] He chose Peter, James and John, the three who witnessed the glories of his transfiguration on Tabor's heights, which proved him God, the three who witnessed the wretchedness of his sorrows in the garden of Gethsemene,[6] which showed him to be a man. These three fell asleep and woke to find Jesus surrounded by the majesty of heaven. Who are the witnesses of these glories? Peter, the Prince of the Apostles, the future Bishop of Rome, the first Pope who was to grasp the crown from the very brow of the Cæsars, and from the eternal city, Rome, to illuminate the world by their infallible doctrine. Peter was the first witness. James was the second, James, the brother of John, the model of mortification, the first Bishop of Jerusalem, the first of the Apostles who died

---

[1] Durand, Rationale Div., L. vi., c. xxxix., n. 1. [2] Annee Lit., p. 80. [3] S. Leonis, Hom. de Transfig. Dom. [4] Deut. xix. 15. [5] Matt. xvii. 9. [6] Matt. xxvi. 37.

a martyr's death, the first to follow his master to martyr-dom—James was the second witness. Behold the third. Isaias, looking dimly through the mists of coming ages, sees the glories of the Son of God generated from the Father before all ages, and knowing that to understand the generation of the Second Person of the Trinity is beyond the grasp of created minds, Isaias cries out : "Who shall declare his generation?"[1] Who can describe the generation of the Son of God, the Splendor of the Father, the Figure of his substance, the Glory of his majesty? O, yes! there is one holy prophet, John, enlightened by the Holy Ghost, who declares his generation when bursting forth in these sublime words : "In the beginning was the Word, and the Word was with God, and the Word was God."[2] Moses, illuminated by the same Inspiring Spirit, goes back to the commencement of time and declares the creation of the world. "In the beginning God created heaven and earth."[3] St. John goes beyond him, soars higher like the eagle, goes to the beginning of eternity, and gives the generation of the Word, of Jesus, Son of God, coming forth from the bosom of his Father. But that is not all; with the eyes of prophecy he penetrates the future and reveals to us the things which will come to pass hereafter in his revelations in the Book of the Apocalypse. Behold the third witness of the transfiguration, St. John, the first Bishop of Ephesus. The whole church is there represented. Her authority and supremacy in St. Peter, the constancy and fortitude of her martyrs in St. James, her charity and learning in St. John.

And while Jesus prayed, "his face did shine as the sun, and his garments became white as snow."[4] The glory of his Divinity within his human nature shone forth from his whole person, and lightened up his sacred form so as to far exceed the brightness of the noonday sun. And while this took place behold, there appeared Moses and Elias. Each fasted forty days to prefigure our Lent. Moses, who received the Law from the hands of God on Sinai's summit; Elias, who rode on the fire chariot of the Lord of hosts. Why are they there? Moses represents the Law of the Old Testament; Elias typifies the Prophecy of the Old Testament. The Law

---

and the Prophecy related to Christ. They prepared the way for his coming. They gave testimony that he was to be the Son of God. But they were like dead letters. They were not understood by the Jews. But because there is a charm in the living voice, there is a spell in the flash of the eye, when eloquent words are added to convince the soul of man. Thus it was that the two greatest men of old came to point out our Lord. Moses, whom no one saw die, Elias, who ascended into heaven—with eloquent tongues and heavenly forms they come to the side of Jesus. These two, without doubt the greatest ones of old, whom the strong hand of the Lord hath raised up to show forth his power—these come, and like shadowy forms they stand and proclaim the greater power and majesty of the Son of God on Tabor's heights. With living words they seem to say by their presence, that the Law and the Prophecy are now sealed up, and that all that they foretold are now to be fulfilled in Jesus of Nazareth.

But behold a cloud overshadows them. What is it ? No one can control a cloud. This cloud is bright and luminous. What does it signify? It is the Holy Ghost, who before overshadowed the Virgin[1] when she conceived and brought forth the Son of God, as foretold by the prophet. It is the Holy Ghost, who wrapped the mountain in its misty form when the law was given to Moses on Sinai's top. It is the Holy Spirit, who came in the form of a little cloud to Elias on the mount.[2] From out of the cloud came forth the words : "This is my beloved Son, in whom I am well pleased. Hear ye him."[3] It is the voice of the eternal Father in heaven, proclaiming the Divinity of his Son.[4]

Behold the greatest and the grandest meeting earth ever witnessed. Moses and Elias, the greatest men of the Old Testament; Peter, James and John, the three greatest men of the New Testament; The Father, Son and Holy Ghost, the three persons of the most holy Trinity—all these are there. What are they talking of ? Of the greatest scene ever witnessed on this earth—the death of Jesus on Calvary's cross for the salvation of mankind.[5] Such is the mystery the church celebrates to-day in her services and ceremonies.

---

[1] Luke i. 35. [2] III. Kings xviii. 44. [3] Math. xvii. 5. [4] Pope Leo, Hom. de Transfig. Dom. [5] Luke ix. 31.

But let us continue on and see how each year the church prepares the people to celebrate the awful death spoken of at the mystery of the transfiguration of our Lord.

The title of the Mass of the second Sunday of Lent is " The Station at St. Mary's in Dominica ; " that is, the services are held in the church of that name on the Cælian hill in Rome, where, as an ancient tradition tells us, St. Lawrence gave charity to the poor, and to tell the people that we must give to the poor as well as do penance during Lent.

The Epistle is taken from St. Paul to the Thessalonians,[1] where he tells them how to live so as to be good Christians.

Monday of the second week of Lent, the Station where the Mass is said, is in the Church of St. Clement, a Pope and martyr. Of all the churches of Rome it still preserves its peculiar character of antiquity. Under its altar reposes the body of its Patron St. Clement, with those of the holy martyr St. Ignatius of Antioch, and of the Consilar Flavius Clemens.

On Tuesday the Station where the services are held is at the Church of St. Balbina, a Roman virgin, the daughter of Quirinus the Tribune, who in the third century suffered martyrdom during the Pontificate of Pope Alexander.

The Station on Wednesday is in the great Church of St. Cecilia, one of the most venerable and august temples of Rome, built on the spot where once stood the house of the illustrious virgin and martyr, Cecilia, the Queen and the Patron of church music. Under its main altar rest the bodies of SS. Cecilia, Tibure, Maxim, and of the martyred Popes Urban and Lucius.

The services of Thursday are held in the celebrated Church St. Mary's, beyond the Tiber, the first church consecrated to the Mother of God in the second century, during the reign of Pope Calistus.

The Station of Friday is at the Church of St. Vital, a martyr, and the father of the illustrious martyred soldiers Gervas and Protas.

On Saturday the Station is in the Church of Peter and

---

[1] C. iv. 1 to 7.

Marcellin, martyrs, who suffered during the persecution
of Dioclesian, and whose names are found in the Canon
of the Mass.

III.—THE THIRD SUNDAY OF LENT.

This Sunday is called "My Eyes," from the first words
with which it begins. Again it is called "Ballot Sunday," because in old times they used to vote for those
whom they baptized on Holy Saturday, when all the
people gathered in the church in former times to see
them washed in the saving waters of redemption. The
Roman Sacramentary of Pope Gelasius[1] gives the words
by which they were called to the ceremony. The names
of those who were found worthy of being baptized were
written on tablets on the side of the altar.

To-day we celebrate the memory of our Lord with his
mighty power driving out the demons from the dumb
man.[2] Before the death of our Lord the devils had
great power. They overcame man in our first parents,
and as they conquered Adam, the king of the world,
they had the whole world, his kingdom, under their control. They took possession of the idols of the pagans,
and received the adorations of all ancient peoples. They
entered into man, and taking possession of his body and
soul, caused disease and plagues. They worked in every
way to destroy the beauties of God's works in this world
before their power was broken by our Lord and by his
church. Each clergyman in his ordination receives the
power to overcome them and to drive them out.[3] For
that reason all things used in the services of our holy
religion are blessed by the clergy, to drive away all
diabolical influence and to take away the curse which
God spoke to Adam after his sin.[4] The Old Testament
tells of the demon who tried to destroy Tobias,[5] and who
was bound by the Archangel in Upper Egypt. The
New Testament speaks of the devil bound by another
Archangel in the same place.[6] Many are the examples
given in holy writ of the evil works of these powerful
and loathsome spirits of darkness; and to-day we see

---

[1] Sac. Gel. [2] Luke ii. [3] See Hom. V. Bede, L. iv., c. 48. in cap. ix., Lucas. [4] Gen.
i. 17. [5] Tobias viii. 3. [6] Apoch., xx., 2.

their work in the doings of those who profess spiritual-
ism.

The Mass to-day is said in the Basilica of St. Lawrence,
beyond the walls of Rome, to recall to the minds of those
preparing for baptism the heroic virtues of this great
martyr preparing for baptism.

The Mass of the Monday of the third week of Lent is
said in the great Church of St. Mark's, built in the fourth
century in honor of St. Mark, the evangelist, by Pope
St. Mark, whose body rests there till this day.

The Station of Tuesday is held in the Church of St.
Pudentiana, the little daughter of Senator Pudens. She
lived in the second century and was noted for her
piety, her charity and her care in burying the bodies of
the martyrs. The church built in her honor stands on
the site of her house, where she lived with her father and
her sister, St. Praxeda, the same house which in the
time when her uncle lived in it was honored by the presence of St. Peter himself when he came to Rome.

On Tuesday the services are held in the Church of St.
Sixtus, in the Apennine way. It is called the old
Church of Sixtus, to distinguish it from another of the
same name built in honor of the same Pontiff saint and
martyr.

Thursday of the third week of Lent is the middle of
Lent, for that reason it is called "Mid-Lent" by many of
the authors who treat these matters. By the Greeks it
is called the "Middle of the Fast," although they sometimes give that name to the whole of this week, it being
the fourth of the seven weeks which make their Lent, and
Thursday is among them a solemn feast. Those who follow
the Latin Rite have always held Thursday of this week as
a time of gladness; but so as not to give any excuse for
dissipation, or for breaking the fast, its celebration is
put off till the following Sunday.[1]

The Station to-day is in the Church of SS. Cosmas
and Damien, two physicians of Rome, and the Church by
celebrating the Mass in the Church dedicated to their
honor, tells us that she looks not only to our spiritual,
but also to our bodily health, in asking the powerful patronage of these two celebrated doctors of Rome. The

---

[1] Gueranger le Careme, p. 339.

learned Gavantus treats at length that idea of the wisdom of the Church in choosing these saintly brothers as the patrons of this day, the middle of Lent, when our bodily strength is weakened by our fasting and our penance.

In the Gospel of to-day the Church celebrates the healing of Peter's wife's mother from the fever.[1] The woman is the human race, the fever is the many sins and bad inclinations toward sins that are in our fallen nature healed by our Lord.[2]

The Station where the Mass of Friday is said is held in the Church of St. Lawrence, built where once stood the temple of Lucina, the Goddess of Child-birth, where is now kept the gridiron on which St. Lawrence was roasted to death.

To-day the Church celebrates the history of Moses striking the rock in the desert, from which flowed the clear and limpid waters to quench the thirst of the dying children of Israel.[3] St. Paul and all the fathers of the Church tell us that the rock struck was a figure of Christ.[4] The rod in the hands of Moses typified the cross of Christ. Moses struck it twice, for the cross was of two pieces. The water which flowed was the water of baptism which flowed from the side of our dead Lord when the soldier opened it with a spear.[5] This has been the belief of all Christians from the very beginning.

In the gospel[6] we recall the conversation of our Lord with the woman of Samaria, where, under the figure of water, he speaks of grace and of everlasting life. The woman was a figure of the Gentile nation. In her simplicity and humility she was better than the Jews; although she had no husband, but had lived with five different men, she was easily converted by our Lord, confessing her shame. She became like an apostle, for, leaving her vase at the well, she ran into the city and called all the people to the feet of our Lord, where many of them were converted.[7]

On Saturday the Station is in the Church of St. Susanna, the virgin and martyr of Rome, because to-day the Church in her offices celebrates the history of the chaste Susanna, as given by the prophet Daniel.[8]

---

[1] Luke iv. [2] St. Ambrose, l. iv., in Luke c. 4. [3] Exod. xvii. 6. [4] I. Cor. x. 4.
[5] John xix. 34. [6] John iv. [7] John iv. 28, 29, 30. [8] Dan. xiii.

In the Gospel we celebrate the remembrance of the benignity of our Lord as shown forth in his treatment of the woman taken in adultery.[1]

IV.—THE FOURTH SUNDAY OF LENT.

This Sunday is called "Rejoice," from the first word with which the Introit begins,[2] and is one of the most celebrated Sundays of the year. Now the Church suspends her holy sorrows of the Lenten Season. The chants and canticles of her services breathe joy and consolation. The organ, silent for the three last Sundays, is played again. The deacon takes his dalmatic and the subdeacon his tunic. All proclaim joy and gladness, for to-day the Church celebrates the happiness of heaven.[3] These are the expressions of joy the Church has put off from the Thursday before till to-day, so that they can be carried out by all the people at the Sunday services. They are to encourage the children of the Church to continue their hard work of penance for the rest of Lent.

The Station is held in the Church of the Holy Cross of Jerusalem, one of the chief Basilicas of the Eternal City. In the IVth century it was built by Constantine the Great out of the villa of Sessorius, and it was enriched by the precious relics brought by the Empress Helena, Constantine's mother, who wished to raise another Jerusalem in Rome. With that idea she caused to be carried from Jerusalem great quantities of the holy earth of Calvary, the title,"Jesus, the Nazarene, King of the Jews," which Pilate wrote and placed over the head of our Lord on the cross, the nails and lance which pierced his sacred flesh, and the very cross on which he was crucified, and there in that Church they are kept to this day with jealous care. That holy Basilica from the most ancient times is called Jerusalem, a word which raises the highest thoughts in the soul of man, for it means the heavenly Jerusalem, wherein we are all to rejoice with God hereafter. For that reason the services of the Church to-day are filled with gladness, for they remind us of the celestial Jerusalem above, the home of all good Christians.

The blessing of the Golden Rose is one of the ceremo-

---

[1] John viii. [2] O'Brien, Hist. of the Mass, p. 65. [3] Durand. Rationale, Div. L., vi., c., iii., n. 1—2.

nies of to-day, from whence it is sometimes called Rose
Sunday. Writers tell us that it comes down from as
early as the time of Leo IX. The great Pope Innocent
III. leaves us one of the finest sermons which he preached
during this ceremony in the Basilica of the Holy Cross.
During the Middle Ages, when the Popes lived in the
Lateran Palace, after having blessed the rose, clothed in
gorgeous robes, with mitre of gold, and surrounded by
the whole College of Cardinals, clothed in pale rose colors,[1] they went in procession to the church where the
Station was held, the Pope holding the symbolic rose in
his hand. There one preached a sermon on the rose,
dwelling on its beauties and its perfections, as showing
forth the power of God. After having finished the Mass,
the Pontiff returned to his palace, where, when helped to
dismount by one of the kings of Europe, he presented
him with the rose as a sign of love and reward. To-day
this ceremony is carried out with much pomp, and
the rose is sent to some Prince or Princess, to a member of
a royal family, to a city or to whom the Pope wishes to
honor.[2] In mystic meaning the rose is our Lord; "the
flower of the field and the lily of the valley."[3] Or it
tells of the beauties of heaven awaiting us above.[4] Its
color signifies charity; its odor sweetness; its taste the
fullness of heavenly sweetness.

In the Offices of to-day we celebrate the calling of Moses
from the burning bush.[5] In the epistle of the Mass,[6] we
read that part of the epistle of St. Paul to the Galatians,
where he explains to us the rejection of Ismael and the
calling of Isaac.[7] In the Gospel we are given that part
where it tells of the feeding of the five thousand with the
five loaves and two fishes.[8] Under that figure we find
the blessed sacrament in which God feeds the souls of
thousands, and of which he began to speak and to explain
to them immediately after the miracle, telling them that
he was "the living bread which came down from heaven,"[9]
and promised them the Blessed Eucharist.

The first Christians gave that multiplication of the
loaves and fishes as a figure of Communion, and to-day

---

[1] O'Brien, Hist. of the Mass, p. 65. [2] Gueranger le Temp. du Careme, p. 376. [3] Cant.
of Cant., II. 1. [4] Durand. Rat. div. l., vi., c. 53, n. 8. [5] Exod. III. [6] See Scr. Basilii,
Hom. 1, de Jejun. [7] Gal. iv. [8] John vi. [9] John vi, 41.

it is often found in the pictures painted on the walls of the Catacombs, those wonderful Christian monuments of the early ages.

The Greeks celebrate to-day with great solemnity, with pomp and ceremony honoring the cross, and although it is Lent, they celebrate the feast of St. Climacus, an illustrious abbot of Mount Sinai, who lived in the VIth century.

The Station on Monday is at the Church of the Four Crowned Martyrs, Severus, Severian, Carpophorus and Victorinus, who suffered under the persecution of Dioclesian. There, in that church, repose their bodies with that of the great St. Sebastian. To-day the Church celebrates the wisdom of Solomon in deciding who was the true mother of the child brought to him when one agreed to have the baby cut in two, which the feelings of the true mother would not allow.[1] In the gospel we are given the history of our Lord driving from the temple the money changers and those who were turning the temple, that house of prayer, into a den of thieves.[2]

The Station on Tuesday is held in the Church of St. Lawrence, in Damaso, thus called because it was built in the fourth century in honor of this great Archdeacon by Pope Damasus, who directed St. Jerome to arrange the Offices of the Breviary and regulated many things in the Latin Rite. The body of this saintly Pope reposes in this church, for that reason it is called "In Damaso."

We are led by the services of to-day to think of the great sin of the children of Israel adoring the golden calf while Moses was upon the mountain, and how after that God told Moses and he made them the rites and ceremonies of the tabernacle, by which in typical meaning they would be reminded of the coming and of the death of their Lord and Saviour.[3] In the gospel we read the story of Jesus in the temple teaching them of the law of Moses, of circumcision, of how he came to do good, and how they tried to destroy him. But his time had not yet come.[4]

Wednesday in the Latin Rite is called the Ferial of the Great Elections, for, after many lessons and examinations, to-day the greater part of the Catechumens are ad-

---

[1] III. Kings iii. [2] John ii. [3] Exod. xxxii. [4] John vii.; See S. Aug., Tract 29 in Joan.

mitted to prepare for baptism. As the number is always very great, the station is held in the Basilica of St. Paul, outside the walls of Rome, because it is large enough for all, and in honor of the many converts the apostle of the nations made during his life.

The epistle of to-day is taken from the prophet Ezechiel, where he tells of the time when the Lord will gather together of all nations the elect, and will pour upon them the saving waters of baptism, and then they will be washed from all their wickedness.[1]

In the gospel we read the history of the man born blind to whom our Lord gave sight. The man, according to the writings of the fathers, is the whole human race,[2] which was deprived of grace by the sin of Adam, and by the waters of baptism all the children of Adam are enlightened with faith, hope and charity, the eyes of the soul. For that reason, this Sunday, when the Catechumens are baptized, is called "The Illumination," because they are then illuminated by these divine virtues which are infused into their souls.[3]

The Station of to-day is held in the Church of SS. Silvester and Martin at the Mountains, one of the most venerable of the churches of Rome, built in the early ages by St. Silvester, under whose patronage it has been placed.[4] It was dedicated to St. Martin, that great worker of miracles among the Gauls. In the VIIth century, with great pomp, the body of Pope Martin was carried and placed in this church. He suffered martyrdom but a short time before. It was the Titular Church of Cardinal St. Charles Borromeo, the great saint, and of Cardinal Tommasi, the great liturgical scholar, whose body is preserved there even to our days without corruption.

To-day the Church celebrates the miracle of Elias raising the dead boy to life.[5] Elias signified our Lord, who came and raised human nature to life by taking upon him our humanity, and infusing into us his life of grace by the seven sacraments.[6] In the gospel we read of our Lord raising from the dead the son of the widow of Nain.[7] The dead youth again is the human race, dead by all the sins that fell on us by the sin of Adam.

---

[1] Ech. xxxv. 1. [2] St. Aug., Tract 44 in Joan. [3] Gueranger le Careme, 425. [4] In the VIth century. [5] IV. Kings, c. iv. [6] Father Burke. [7] Luke vii.

The widow is the Church.[1] The Lord calls us daily
from the tomb of sin by the voice of his grace.[2]

Friday the Station is in the Church of St. Eusebius, a
priest of Rome who suffered martyrdom at the hands of
the Arians under the Emperor Constantius. To-day we
celebrate the miracle of Elias raising the widow's child
from the dead.[3] Three times he stretched himself out
upon the dead body before he arose, three times the
water touches us in baptism. This week is devoted to
the preparation of those preparing for baptism, for that
reason these figures of the holy Rite are given.

In the gospel we celebrate the raising of Lazarus from
the dead.[4] Lazarus was a figure of the sinner[5] raised
from the death of sin and the corruption of wickedness
by the voice of our Lord through his priests in the
tribunal of penance. Jesus cried, "Lazarus, come forth!"
and death heard his voice and the dead came forth from
the tomb. In the same way the voice of Jesus by his
minister calls the sinner, hell hears the call and loosens
its grasp on the soul of the wicked, and the sinner comes
forth, pardoned.

In the most ancient times Saturday of this week was
celebrated under the name of "Thirsting," because by
that word the Introit begins inviting those preparing for
baptism to come and drink the crystal streams of grace
flowing from the fountains of the Saviour.

The Station was first at Rome, in the Basilica of St.
Lawrence, beyond the walls, but it being too far, in latter
ages they changed it to the Church of St. Nicholas in
Prison. The lesson is taken from the prophet Isaias,
where he speaks of the joy of those preparing for baptism; how they shall come from the north and from
the sea and from afar off to the fountains of water,
where he tells of the beauties of the Church, where there
will be no storms, or fear, or thirst, for he shall be their
shepherd.[6] The gospel tells us of the time when our
Lord spoke to the crowd of Jews, and told them that he
was the son of God, and they would not believe him.[7]
Then he told them that he was the light of the world.[8]

---

[1] S. Ambrose, Com. in Lucæ, n, 7. [2] St. Ambrose, Coment. in Luc. c., vii., St. Aug.,
etc. [3] III. Kings xvii. [4] John xi. [5] Massillon Hom, sur. L'Ev. de Lazare. ; St. Augustine, Tract 19 in Joan, post In. etc. [6] Isaias xlix. [7] John viii. [8] St. Aug., Tract
34 in Joan.

V.—Passion Sunday.

Passion Sunday is thus named because on this day the Pharisees and the chief priests in council came to the conclusion to put our Lord to death, because on the Friday before he raised Lazarus from the grave and they came on Saturday and told it in the temple.[1] The Sabbath ended at sundown among the Jews. When the sun went down that day their Sabbath was finished. The day before Lazarus was raised from the dead. It was the first day of the month, toward evening, and they resolved to put our Lord to death. For that reason he hid himself, and to commemorate these things, toward evening, the Saturday before Passion Sunday, we veil the cross, the pictures and the images in our churches.[2]

Thus after the seven weeks of the Septuagesima season and of Lent, which typify the seven different ages of the world, we now come to the preparation for the death and funeral of our Lord. Two weeks are devoted to his passion, because he suffered for two peoples, the Jews and the gentiles ; because he was foretold to come in the two conditions of God's people, before the law of Moses and after the giving of the law. Again, there are two weeks as there are two Testaments, one before he came and one in which he suffered. Thus there are two weeks, one before he suffered and the other in which he was put to death.

From the Vesper time till the Mass of Holy Saturday, the words, "Glory be to the Father, and to the Son, and to the Holy Ghost,"[3] are not said, for they are to give glory to the Holy Trinity, to the Triune God, who was so dishonored in the sufferings of the Son. It is said at the end of the psalms and in other places, for the death of our Lord will be for our salvation, when we will glorify the Trinity in heaven. The Psalm, "Judge me, O Lord," is not said till Easter Sunday, as it is a joyous Psalm, which would be out of place in this time of sorrow.[4] In the three days of Holy Week all words of joy and gladness are heard no more. We make no remembrance of the Saints from now till Trinity Sunday, because we seek the suf-

---

frages of the saints for two reasons; to remember their great works and to ask their aid. But because now we are wholly taken up with the passion of our Lord, and after Easter we will celebrate his glorious resurrection and ascension, we must have nothing to take our minds from the sufferings of the dead Lord, or the glories of the risen Saviour. The Church makes a general remembrance of all the saints, because there are so many that it would be impossible to mention all their names.

The malice and the hatred of the Jews increases from day to day. The presence of the Lord in the temple irritates them, while his goodness, his sweetness and his miracles attract crowds of people to the holy place. He continues his wonderful works. His words become more energetic. His prophecies threaten the temple. He foretells the time to come prophesied by Daniel, when the Romans under Titus will come from the west and leave not a stone upon a stone of the holy city. But they could neither understand the prophecy of the destruction of the city nor the words of David, the royal prophet, nor the prediction of Isaias, Israel's greatest inspired prophet, relating to the sufferings and death of Jesus, the Lord's anointed. Obstinate in their errors, they would hear nothing. Blinded by their prejudices, they would not listen to him. Filled with pride, they would not have so lowly a man for their king. Ambitious for worldly gain, they looked for a Messiah who would conquer all nations and make them the ruling people of the world. Pushed on by all the worst passions of fallen human nature, they concluded to put him to death. They swore his life away, and brought upon themselves and upon their children that curse of his blood by which they are scattered into every part of the world, a living witness to all nations of the truth of the Gospel history of the sufferings and of the death of Christ.

The Passion of our Lord opens out many of the secret evils of the heart of man, but the Jews were no worse than the people of to-day, and the sinners who do evil and commit wickedness are as bad as the Jews, and in the words of St. Paul, they are guilty of again crucifying the Son of God.

Passion Sunday is thus named, because from this time

the Church is entirely taken up with the passion of our Lord. It is called "Judge Me," from the first words of the Introit. It is called the Sunday of the "Paschal Moon," because it begins at the new moon, while among the Greeks it is called the "Fifth Sunday of the Holy Fasts."

The Station of to-day is held in the great Basilica of St. Peter's Church, in Rome, because the feast of Passion Sunday is of such importance that no other service can be held on this day, and because there is such a large number of people present that they used to fill the largest churches of Rome. For that reason the Services are held in the great St. Peter's.

On Monday of Passion Week the Station is held in the Church of St. Chrysogonus, one of the most celebrated of the early martyrs of the Roman Church, and whose name is in the Canon of the Mass.

Tuesday, in ancient times, the Station was in the Church of the Holy Martyr, St. Cyriacus, and such is its title in the Missal; but that church having fallen into ruins and the body of the Saint having been carried and laid in the Church of St. Mary, in Vialata, there the Station is held in our days.

At Rome the Station of Wednesday is in the Church of St. Marcellus, a martyred Pope, to whom the noble Roman lady, Lucina, gave her house to be consecrated into a church.

The Station of Thursday, at Rome, is in the Church of St. Apollinaris, who was one of St. Peter's disciples, and the first Bishop of Ravenna, a martyr for his faith.

At St. Stephen's Church, on the Cælian Hill, the Station of Friday is held, and well are the services of that Friday, the last before Good Friday, held in that church, of one of the first of the martyrs who shed their blood for our Lord.

This whole time of the year is devoted to the sufferings of our Lord, but at the same time the people could not forget the mother, and for that reason they have always, while weeping at the untimely and atrocious murder of the Son, sympathized with his holy mother. Well it was then to choose a time in the year to devote to the memory of the desolate mother at the foot of the cross. Such has been from the beginning of the Church

the thought of the people.   But in 1423 the pious
Thierry, Archbishop of Cologne, in a diocesan Synod, commanded Saturday before Palm Sunday to be dedicated
throughout his archdiocese to the seven sufferings of
our lady.   That custom of celebrating the Feast of the
Seven Sorrows of the Virgin soon spread throughout the
whole Church, and was tolerated by the silent consent of
the Popes till the last century, when Benedict XIII.
solemnly placed it on the cycle of the Church, to be held
each year throughout the world[1] under the name of the
Seven Sorrows of the Blessed Virgin Mary.[2]

The Station of Saturday is at the Church of St. John,
before the Lateran Gate, in the Old Basilica, built on the
spot where tradition says the beloved disciple, by order
of Domitian, was plunged into a caldron of boiling oil,
from which he escaped unhurt.

---

[1] Decret. 22, August, 1727.   [2] Gueranger la Passion et la Semaine Sainte, p. 167.

CHURCH OF ST. GUDULE, BRUSSELS.

REASONS RELATING TO THE HOLY WEEK SEASON.

We are drawing nearer and nearer to the sufferings of our Lord. We have seen how the Septuagesima Time is a preparation for the Lenten Season. We have seen how Lent is like a vestibule leading us into Holy Week, when we celebrate the death of the Son of God. We here see how the week before Holy Week is like the holies leading us into the Holy of Holies, the great mystery of the sufferings and the death of our Lord for us and for our salvation, and how year by year the children of the Church renew in mystic Rites the sad scenes of Calvary's Cross.

The oldest liturgical works, the celebrated books of the ancient churches, the sermons of Saints, the works of the Fathers of the Church, the greatest histories of the past ages, the laws of fallen empires, the venerable traditions of the early ages, all proclaim and cry out with one voice, and the burden of their story is the sufferings and the death of Christ for the salvation of the race. And the Church into whose holy hands was given to guard the "deposit of faith,"[1] keeps forever bright before the nations the sad story of his death. By her ceremonies, her sacred Rites, her magic symbols and her holy ceremonies, she ever preaches the death of God for man. The primal thought of the Christian religion in her Liturgy is to keep before the minds of men his coming and his death; to celebrate each year, as the ages roll by, the grand and transcendent mystery of his death; to preach to the generations of men as they come and go upon the stage of this world, that the Saviour came, and that he died for our redemption.

During Lent, even to Palm Sunday, we sometimes celebrate, during the days of the week, the feasts of the

---

[1] 1 Tim. vi. 20.

Saints, when they are closely connected with the passion of our Lord, but no solemnity but that of the day itself must be held on Passion Sunday, on Palm Sunday, or on the days of holy week, for they are entirely set apart to the honor and to the remembrance of the sufferings and of the death of our Lord.

From the days of the Apostles the Christians celebrated with solemn rites and ceremonies the sufferings of their Lord.[1] In the dark and dismal days of persecution, when they fled to the catacombs, there they held their memorial services in remembrance of the death of our Saviour. Those sad and sombre rites were held in great veneration by the Christians of Alexandria[2] in the third century. A hundred years went by, and we find St. Chrysostom of Constantinople calling the days of these ceremonies the "Great Week."[3] We find it named the "Painful Week" by the early Saints, because of the sufferings of the Saviour. We find it spoken of as the "Week of Indulgence," because then the sinners were forgiven. We find its name as "The Greater Week" among the Greeks, because of the greatness of the mysteries.[4] We find it called by the Germans "The Week of Sorrows," or "The Week of Miseries," because the Church sits in sorrow for the sufferings and the death of her Spouse, our Lord, or they named it the "Week of Sufferings." We find it called by the early Christians of England, "Holy Week," and that is the name by which it is known wherever the English language is spoken.

The fast and self-denial increases as we draw nearer and nearer to the time of Holy Week. The people of the Latin Rite are allowed to use eggs, cheese and what are called "white meats," but the members of the Eastern Rites, keeping close to the traditions of the Apostles, observe a more rigorous fast, using only bread, water and salt, with sometimes fruits.

During the first ages of the Church fasting was carried as far as the power of man could bear it, many eating nothing during Holy Week, from Monday morning till the crow of the cock on Saturday night, before the break of Easter morning.[5] Few could fast so long, and the

---

[1] See St. Aug. Epist., lv., n. 24. [2] St. Denys Episcop.; Alexand. Epis. ad Basil, c. 1. [3] Hom. xxx. in Gen. [4] Cardinal Wiseman's Holy Week. p. 14. [5] St. Epiphanius Exp. Fidei Haer. xxii.

greater number took food each second day, eating noth-ing from Thursday till after the Matin hour of Easter morning.   Many are the wonderful examples of this rig-orous fast we find among the Eastern nations and among the Russians in the middle ages.

Long "Watches" during the night was one of the ways of celebrating the time of Holy Week in the early ages of the Church.   On Holy Thursday, after having offered up the Holy Sacrifice, in remembrance of the Last Sup-per, the people remained long into the night in the Church, listening to sermons, praying before the Blessed Sacrament, or bowed in humble praise, prayer and medi-tation before the altar.[1]   Good Friday and Holy Satur-day nights were spent entirely in the churches of the cities, in honor and in remembrance of the burial of Christ.   The most widespread and popular of all these "Watches" was the one of Holy Saturday night,[2] or the eve of Easter, which lasted till the morning. The churches were crowded with people.   The Catechumens received their last instructions.   The people redoubled their de-votions and their prayers.   All remained till the Mass began at the break of day, then they separated to go to their homes at the rising of the sun, there to prepare themselves for the great ceremonies of Easter, and for the joys of the Resurrection of our Lord.[3]

For a long time all servile work was forbidden during Holy Week, and the laws of the land united with those of the Church in making it a holy season, a time of vaca-tion from all kinds of labor, so that the people could bet-ter devote themselves to the celebration of the passion and death of our Lord.   The thought of the sad sacrifice of Calvary Cross was in every heart.[4]   The services of the Church took up all the time of pure souls.   Their watchings, prayers and fastings required all their strength, while the solemn, sombre services of the Church took such deep root in their minds as to last till the next spring came around, bringing with it again the same ceremonies.

In the days of the Roman Empire the laws of Gratian and of Theodosius[5] forbade all lawsuits during Holy

---

[1] St. Chrysostom Hom. XXX. in Gen. [2] S. Aug. Sermo., CCXIX. in Vig Paschæ. [3] St. Cyril, Hier. Catech. xviii. ; Const. Apost. l. i. c. xviii. [4] El Porque de las Cere-monias, c., xxx. Dom. I. Ramos [5] In 380 and 389.

Week and the week following Easter. We find in some
of the sermons of the Saints remarks relating to these
laws, and that during that fortnight the days were kept
like Sunday.[1]

The Christian emperors and rulers not only stopped
all law trials, but they held these days as days of mercy
to their subjects in honor of the mercy of God to the
world. These were the days when the Church opened
her doors to the public penitents and to the greatest
sinners, and the Catholic kings following their mother, the
Church, opened the prison doors to their prisoners jailed
for political reasons, to captives taken in war and to persons arrested for debts. The only exceptions were those
whose liberty would be dangerous to the public good, as
murderers or bad characters. According to St. Chrysostom, the Emperor Theodosius sent letters of pardon the
week before Easter to the cities and villages where the prisoners were kept when condemned to death, ordering them
to be set at liberty.[2] For a long time that was the custom among the emperors of Rome. That custom came
from the Jews, who liberated a prisoner each year at their
Easter,[3] as we see that they delivered Barabbas in place of
our Lord. From them it passed into the Roman laws
and became a part of the Theodosian code. It was found
in the laws of nearly all the nations of Europe during the
middle ages.[4] We find it in the chapters of Charlemagne that the bishops had the power of demanding the
deliverance of convicts from the judges on Holy Week,
and even that they could prevent the judges from entering the Church if they refused.[5] We find the same in
the life of Charles VI., when he had put down a rebel-
lion among the people of Rouen, and taken many of them
prisoners, on Holy Week he set them at liberty.[6] We
find the last remains of that truly charitable and Catholic
custom in the government and court of France before the
French revolution wiped out so many of the beautiful
Christian customs coming down from the earliest ages.
At first all work of the government was stopped from the
beginning of Lent till Low Sunday. Such was the way
in the middle ages. Then they began to take their

---

[1] Hom. St. Chrysostom, Ser. St. Augustine, etc. [2] St. Chryst. Hom. in Mag. Hebdom.,
xxx., in Gen. Hom. VI., ad Pop. Antioch. [3] St. Leo, Ser. XI., de Quadrages, II. [4] St.
Eligii, Ser. X. [5] Capit. i., vi. [6] Jean Juvenal des Ursin, in 1382.

vacations on Wednesday of Holy Week, but before ending, all the members of the government went to the prisons, where the chairman held a reception. Then they
questioned each prisoner relating to his case, and set at
liberty all those who were not great criminals. These
were the ages of faith, when the kings, the princes and the
members of the royal families of Christendom left their
thrones, their palaces and their abodes of wealth and
luxury and thronged the prisons to set the prisoners
free. Then they gathered in the hospitals to soothe the
sickness of the sufferers. They visited the asylums to
see the orphans. They called on the poor to give them
alms. They gladdened the home of the widow to give
her a ray of joy.

Those are remains of the olden times when God was
ever uppermost in the thoughts of men; when the letters
of kings were dated with the words, "Reigning our Lord
Jesus Christ."[1] Then the royal families were obedient
to the Church. Then there were no secret societies, no
Socialists, no Nihilists eating out the foundations of governments, for all were Catholics and all looked up to
their rulers as having their power and their authority
from God. From the converted nations of Europe sprang
the governments, and all worshipped the Lord their
God. But in this age of ours, they call progress that
onward tendency towards the denial of authority, towards
the rejection of the rule of the Church, towards the decay
of society, towards the dying out of the race itself by
sins against the sanctity of marriage, and that revolting
evil which we call divorce.

At the preaching of the apostles, slavery, that son of
sin, had spread throughout the world as a relic of the
pagan ages before the time of Christ. One of the first
acts of the Church, wherever she had spread, was to dis-
courage slavery, and in time it came to pass that there
was not a slave to be found in the whole of Europe.
They were delivered from their bondage by the preaching of the priests and by the still but prudent work of
the clergy, without war or bloodshed, as happened in
our own country during the late civil war. Although
law courts could not be held during Holy Week, still

---

[1] Gueranger la Passion et la Semaine Sainte, p. 9.

such was the lenient spirit of the Church that we find in the Justinian code, that "it will nevertheless be allowed to give slaves their liberty, and no act required for their delivery will be rejected by that law."[1] Justinian here but gives force to the laws made by his predecessor, Constantine, the morning after the triumph of the Church, when she came forth from the darkness of the catacombs. For a long time before Constantine gave liberty to the Christians, the Church, like a mother, had looked after the slaves, and had made laws obliging their masters to give them a fortnight to rest at Easter,[2] till in centuries after she set them at liberty, so that there has not been for many ages a slave in Europe.

In the same way the people have always been told to give to the poor during this holy time, to help them in their poverty and aid them in their distress, preaching that, "Who giveth to the poor lendeth to the Lord." This has always been the way the good Christians spend the time of Lent, but especially during Holy Week. St. Chrysostom praises the charity and liberality of the people of his day for their goodness to the poor.

The Liturgy of the Church is filled with mystery in these days, when she celebrates so many wonderful events in the life of our Lord; but we will leave the most of them till we come to the ceremonies which are carried out during the different days of this Sacred Season.

Septuagesima Time is a preparation for Lent. Lent is a preparation for Holy Week, but Holy Week is so holy that it must have for itself a preparation, and that is the week before it, or the week following Passion Sunday. Thus, as it were, by so many steps we rise to the most mysterious and to the most sacred time of the year, Holy Week.

Three things are in the mind of the Church during the time of Lent: the Passion of our Saviour, which from week to week draws nearer; the preparation of the newly converted, who are to be baptized on Holy Saturday, and the reconciling of sinners, who are to receive the Blessed Eucharist at Easter.

Our Lord had raised Lazarus from the rottenness of the grave, at Bethany, not far from the walls of Jerusa-

---

[1] Cod. lib. III., Tit., xii., leg. 2.   [2] Apostolic Constitutions, b. vii., c. 33.

lem, and that stupendous miracle excited to the highest
pitch the rage of the Jews against him. The people
were struck with astonishment to see Lazarus daily in
the streets whom they had seen dead, buried, and for four
days laid in the tomb. They wanted to make a king of
our Lord and to sing Hosannas to the Son of David.
The Pharisees of Jerusalem, the scribes of the temple,
the elders of the people, and the chief priests of the
holies, saw that they had not a moment to spare if they
would prevent him proclaimed the king of the Jews. We
are to be present at their wicked meetings where the
blood of the Saint of Saints was sworn away—where the
Divine Victim was sold for a few pieces of silver. We
are to hear the traitor kiss of Judas. We are to witness
the trial in the court of Pilate. We are to go on the sad
journey to Calvary. We are to be there, and to contemplate in mystic rites, in solemn liturgies and in grand
ceremonies, the majestic drama of the passion, the death
and the burial of the Son of God.

The catechumens or the newly converted draw nearer
and nearer each day to the fountains of living waters.
Their catechism and their instruction goes on. The figures of the Old Testament are explained to them ; the
mysteries of our holy religion are unfolded to them ; the
Apostles' Creed is given to them ; the wonderful humiliations of the Redeemer are shown them, and now with
the people they wait for the ceremonies of the Church,
typifying the sufferings and the resurrection of their
Lord and Saviour. On Holy Saturday they are to be
washed from their sins in the waters of regeneration.
They can be baptized at any time in the year, but Holy
Saturday has been from the beginning of the Church the
time when they are most solemnly baptized after the
blessing of the baptismal font.

The reconciling of sinners is the second work of the
Church in this time. From Ash Wednesday they have
carried the ashes on their heads as a sign of penance and
of sorrow for their sins. They fasted from food during
Lent ; they practiced self-denial all these weeks ; they
offered many acts of sorrow to the Lord ; and as the time
of the death of the Lamb of God, " Who taketh away the
sins of the world," draws nearer, they live in the hope of
being forgiven for their sins, and that like him they will

rise gloriously from the grave of sin to the glories of a better and a holier life.

The Church, like a widow weeping over the murder of her Spouse, sits in the deepest sadness. She covers the crosses, the pictures, the statues, the works of art, and the sculptures of the great masters in the churches with veils of violets, so that the people see but "Jesus and him crucified."[1] For a long time the heavenly "Alleluia" is heard no more; the "Glory be to God in the highest" is silent; the "Glory be to the Father," etc., ending each Psalm in the Office during the year, is said no more. The Psalm, "Judge me, O Lord,"[2] beginning Mass, is omitted. Her holy chants and sacred anthems breathe but woe. All the services, all the ceremonies,.all the rites of this time, from the evening before Passion Sunday, are of the most sad, solemn and sombre kind. Only when we celebrate the feast of some Saint does the Church relax a little in these rites and ceremonies, which wake the deepest sensibilities of the heart of man, making every sympathetic chord vibrate with affliction, with sadness, with sorrow, with woe and desolation, in remembrance of the death of the Saviour of the World.

Saturday eve before Passion Sunday the cross and the images are covered with a violet veil, because, say the great writers on these subjects. it signifies the humiliation of our Lord in his passion, when in his sufferings he veiled his Divinity, and because from this time, when the Jews tried to put him to death, he hid from them. The law of the Church relating to this veiling of the cross and the images is so strict, that even when the feast of the Annunciation comes in Passion Week they are not uncovered. From this time till Trinity Sunday we have no commemoration of the Saints, for the whole Church is completely taken up with the mysteries of our Lord.

During the year different parts of the Bible are read in the Offices and in the Masses, but during this time the sad words of the prophet of sorrows, Jeremiah, are read.

---

[1] I. Cor. ii. 2.   [2] Ps. xl.

I.—PALM SUNDAY.

Palm Sunday is also called the Sunday of the Boughs, because of the branches we carry in our hands; it is named Hosanna Sunday, because of the triumphant cry of the Jews ; it is called Flower Sunday because Easter, which is but eight days coming, is like the flower of the year. As a remembrance of this Sunday, the Spaniards, when they discovered the coast of Florida, on Palm Sunday, called it Florida, the Spanish for flowers, in honor of the feast of our Lord's entry into Jerusalem.[1]

Again, it is called the Sunday of washing the heads, because on this day in ancient times those preparing for baptism on Holy Saturday, washed their heads for the Holy Oils. It is called the Sunday of the Admitted, for on this day those who were prepared for baptism were admitted to the Mass till the Canon; while by the Greeks it is called by a word which means to carry palms.

Palm Sunday is thus named from the Jews taking branches of palm from the trees and strewing them in the way, and carrying them in their hands as they came with Jesus into the city, crying, "Hosanna, blessed is he that cometh in the name of the Lord."[2] As a remembrance of our Lord's triumphant entry into the holy city each year we celebrate Palm Sunday.   On the 20th of March,[3] when the Lord and his disciples were going up to Jerusalem to celebrate the feast of the Pasch, they came to Bethphage, a little village on the side of the Mount of Olives. From there he sent two of his disciples into the village, telling them to bring him an ass and her colt. Going they found them as he said, and brought them to him. Placing their garments on the colt, which was never rode before, the Saviour rode the animal into the city of Jerusalem,[4] as foretold by the prophet.[5] According to the custom of the Jews, great crowds had come to celebrate the feast. Spreading their garments in the way, and breaking boughs of palm, they spread them in the road, and all cried: "Hosanna to the son of David, blessed is he that cometh in the name of the Lord.[6] Blessed be the king-

---

[1] Gueranger le Demanche des Rameux, p. 228. [2] John xii. 13. [3] El Porque de las Ceremonias, CXXX., Domide Ramos. [4] John xii. 14. [5] Zach. ix. 9. [6] Math. xxi. 9.

dom of our Father David that cometh, Hosanna in the highest."[1]

From the oldest traditions we learn that the ass, the mother of the colt which had been used to being ridden, signified the Jewish people, who had been used to the law of God, who were, as it were, the mother of the Christian Church, and the colt which had not been broken typified the Gentiles, who had not received the law.[2] Our Lord, taking the colt in place of the mother, foretold the choosing of the Gentiles, who were to be called to the law of God in place of the Jews who were rejected. Hosanna is a Hebrew word signifying about the same as our English hurrah, and means an exclamation rather than a thing.[3] Such was the word used by the Israelites in honoring any of their public men.[4] "Hosanna to the Son of David," tells of his human nature. "Hosanna in the highest," proclaimed his divine nature; thus inspired by the Holy Spirit they honored him as God and man. They carried branches of palm, for that was the custom of the Jews as laid down in the law of Moses for the celebration of the Feast of the Tabernacles. "And you shall take to you on the first day the fruits of the fairest tree, and branches of palm trees, and boughs of thick trees, and willows of the brook; and you shall rejoice before the Lord your God."[5] The Mount of Olives, along which our Lord passed on his way to Jerusalem, was covered with palm trees.[6] Palm signifies peace[7] among all the people of the East,[8] and thus with palms of peace the Jews saluted the Prince of Peace coming to be offered up as a sacrifice to God for the peace of the world. The Jews celebrated the Feast of the Tabernacles with branches of palm, not only in memory of their deliverance from Egypt, but also to prefigure the coming of the future Messiah, who was to deliver them from all their enemies. Palm signifies victory, for that reason the martyrs are represented with palms in their hands. He rode upon an ass after the custom of princes and the nobles of the Jews,[9] for they did not use horses.[10]

---

[1] Mark xi. 9, 10. [2] S. Aug. En. in Ps. cxxvi. n. 11. [3] St. August. in Tract. L. in Joan. [4] Benedic. XIV. De Dom. Pal. n. 14 [5] Levit. xxiii. 40. [6] Benedict. XIV. De Dom. Palmarum, n. 12. [7] I. Mach. xiii. 37; Mach. x. 7. [8] Philo. Josephus de Alexandro, etc. [9] Judges x. 4, xii. 14. [10] Benedictus XIV. De Dom. Pal. n. 15.

In honor and in remembrance of this triumphant entry of our Lord into Jerusalem, in the last year of his life, and on the Sunday before his death, we celebrate each year the solemnities of Palm Sunday. We find that this custom of celebrating Palm Sunday comes down from the most ancient times—from the days of the apostles.[1] It is found in the calendars of the Church in the IVth century.[2] It is seen in the sacramentaries of Pope Gelasius and of Gregory the Great. It is mentioned in the most ancient Missals, in the oldest Ceremonials and Liturgical works which have remained to us since the times of the destruction of the Roman Empire, when so many books were destroyed by the barbarians of the North. They all speak of Palm Sunday.[3]

In former times those converts who had been prepared for baptism asked to be received into the Church, and they were all told to leave after the gospel, but on Palm Sunday they were allowed to remain during Mass till the celebrant began the Canon, while the others were sent away at the Offertory.[4] To-day also their heads were washed,[5] which was not done since receiving the ashes on Ash Wednesday.

Among the churches of the Oriental nations they bring a whole palm tree into the church, where it is blessed and carried in the procession. Then they all tear its branches off and carry them to their homes.[6]

The ceremonies of Palm Sunday are very ancient and go back to the most remote ages. In the IVth century, St. Cyril, bishop of Jerusalem, tells us that the palm tree from which the Jews in the time of our Lord broke the branches, was growing in his time in the valley of the Cedron.[7] That is not surprising when we know how long trees will live. In the following century we find that the ceremonies of Palm Sunday were carried out with great splendor in the churches of the East, and in the monasteries and the convents of Syria and of Egypt, with which the deserts of that time were peopled. At the beginning of Lent many of the holy monks were allowed by their superiors to pass the holy season of Lent amid the solitudes of the deserts, in fasting and in

---

[1] El Porque de las Ceremonias, cxxx. [2] Meratus T. I. p. 1004. [3] See Benedict XIV. De Dom. Palm. n. 20. [4] Benedict XIV. De Dom. Pal. n. 21. [5] St. Isidor L. I. Tit. 7, n. 1. [6] Gearius Not. ad Euch. Graecorum, p. 745. [7] Cateches x.

prayer, as in a deep and profound retreat. But they always came back to their monasteries on Palm Sunday.[1] We find Palm Sunday celebrated in all parts of Europe as soon as its nations were converted to the Gospel. In the VIIth century, when the missionaries from Rome and from Ireland had penetrated to the north of Europe, they found that the palm tree did not grow in these cold countries. Other branches then took the place of the palm, and the Church allowed cedar, box-wood, and laurel to be used in its stead, but the prayers were never changed, and to-day they are the same as in the most ancient times.

The ceremonies of Palm Sunday begin by the celebrant and ministers coming to the altar clothed in violet vestments, which they wore during the services of the Church since the beginning of Septuagesima Sunday, as a sign of fasting and of penance for their sins. At the corner of the altar the celebrant begins the services by the words of the Jews, when our Lord rode into Jerusalem, and a prayer for faith and hope in the Lord. He reads the Scriptures from the book of Exodus, which tells of the wonders of the Lord to the people of Israel at the fountains of waters and at the seventy palm trees,[2] followed by the history of our Lord entering Jerusalem in triumph, as given in the gospel.[3] The celebrant then blesses the palms with appropriate prayers, sprinkling them with holy water as a sign that they are washed from all bad influences, and become holy and clean for the services of the Church.[4] They are then incensed to show that they become like so many prayers of peace in the hands of all those who carry them. They are sprinkled with holy water three times incensed in honor of the three most holy persons of the Trinity.

The palms having been blessed with ceremonies, and with prayers and passages taken from the Bible relating to the triumphant entry of our Lord into Jerusalem, then the highest in dignity in the sanctuary gives a palm to the celebrant, who makes no genuflection nor kisses his hand, because the celebrant represents our Lord himself. Then the celebrant gives him a palm, who in taking

---

[1] Vita S. Eutnymius. [2] Exod. xv. xvi. [3] Math. xxi. [4] El Porque de las Ceremonias C. XXX. Dom. de Ramos.

it, kisses the hand of the celebrant. Then all come in
their turn, the highest in dignity first, who genuflecting on
their knees, receive the palm from the hands of the celebrant. During this time it is customary for one of the
servers of Mass to distribute the palms to the people in
the church. When all have received their palms the
celebrant prays over them, asking God to give them the
innocence of the children of Israel, who accompanied our
Lord in his entry into Jerusalem.

Then the procession takes place while the choir sings
of the triumphant entry of our Lord into the holy city.
All go outside the church except two or four chanters,
who sing a beautiful Latin hymn composed by Theodulphus,[1] the abbot, and which was sung by him in prison
when the Emperor Louis the Pius passed in the procession on Palm Sunday.[2] Hearing him singing it, he
restored to him his liberty.[3] Afterwards he became
Bishop of Orleans.

When the hymn is ended, the sub-deacon strikes the
door of the church with the staff of the cross, and the
doors of the church are opened to the procession, which
enters.

From the writers of the middle ages we learn the meaning of these rites and ceremonies. "The people of Jerusalem see an humble man riding on an ass and the colt of
an ass, and nevertheless they celebrate his glorious triumph by carrying palms and strewing the way with
their garments, singing to him their imperial praises,
because in spirit they see in him the Conqueror over the
devil and over death. This crowd, beloved brethren, by
the living boughs typify the triumphant standard of the
cross. And well they represent by the green branches
what they will always live up to in their morals, what
the winter cannot freeze, what the summer cannot
wither, what they can say with the Psalmist, 'I will bless
the Lord at all times, his praise shall ever be in my
mouth.'[4] The branches of palm signify the victory which
the Lord was to gain by his death conquering death, and
by the standard of the cross overcoming the devil, the
prince of death. The colt of the ass represented the

---

[1] Bishop England's Holy Week. [2] El Porque de la Ceremonias, c. xxx. Dom. de
Ramos. [3] Benedict. XIV. de Dom. Pal. n. 13. [4] Fabri Conciones, vol. I. p. 473 ; see
also El Porque de las Ceremonias, c. xxx.

simple hearts of the gentiles, who, by their conversion and obedience, came to the vision of peace in heaven.[1] " Thus since the dove brought the branch of olive, the olive and the palm have been signs of peace. The doors of the church are closed to tell us of paradise—closed to the human race by the sin of Adam. They are opened when struck by the cross in the hands of the sub-deacon, because heaven was opened to man by the cross[2] of Christ.[3]

Jerusalem in holy scriptures is but a picture of heaven, and our Lord entering into that holy city on Palm Sunday, surrounded by his disciples and by the children of Israel, was but a figure of his glorious entry into heaven the day of his ascension, surrounded by all the souls of the holy ones of the Old Testament.

In some churches in the middle ages they used to carry with great pomp the Book of the Gospels in the processions, because it contains the words of our Lord. At a place on the way called a "Station," the deacon opened the holy Book and sang that part giving the story of the triumphant entry of the Lord into Jerusalem. The cross which had been covered with a veil from the vesper time before Passion Sunday, was then uncovered, and all kissed the image of the Crucified, while each placed his branch at the foot of the cross as an offering to the Saviour. Then all marched into the church in the usual manner. In England and in Normandy, in the XIth century, after Berengarius had denied the Real Presence, they carried the Blessed Sacrament with great solemnity in the procession, as a lively protest against his errors, and that triumphant carrying of our Lord in the procession was but a foreshadowing of the procession of the feast of Corpus Christi and of the Forty Hours.

In the days of the crusades, Palm Sunday was celebrated with great ceremonies. The guardian of the holy land, with the religious orders and all the Catholics of Jerusalem, went in the morning to Bethphage, where taking palms in their hands, they entered the city in a great procession. Coming into the Church of the Holy Sepulchre, with the usual ceremonies there, they offered up the

---

[1] Isidore De Of. Eccl. L. I., c. 27. [2] El Porque de las Ceremonias, c. xxx. Dom. de Ramos. [3] Amati Pouget Inst. Cath. T. 1, p. 11, S. iv. c. 2, 9.

holy Sacrifice. For more than two centuries the Turks have forbidden these holy rites, which were carried out for so many ages, when Godfrey de Bouillon and his successors were the Kings of Jerusalem.[1]

The Station where the Mass is celebrated is in the great Basilica of St. John Lateran, the mother and the chief of all the churches of Rome and of the world. In former times, when the Popes resided at the palace beside this venerable Church, before St. Peter's was built, the papal ceremonies were here carried out with great splendors. But since Michael Angelo with those who followed him laid the plan of St. Peter's, the grandest building ever raised to the worship of the true and living God, the Pope celebrates Palm Sunday at the Vatican.

The Mass of this Sunday has none of the traits of joy and gladness we find in the ceremonies of the blessing and of the procession of the palms. The part of the Gospel read at this Mass is the history of the passion of our Lord as given by St. Matthew.[2] The passion, according to St. Mark,[3] is said on Tuesday, that of St. Luke on Wednesday,[4] and that of St. John on Friday.[5]

The manner in which these sad histories of the passion and death of our Lord are recited, is different from the other Gospels of the year. The lesson which the Church wishes to impress on her children by these sad histories is that the Author of Life was slain for our sins. To make a deep impression on our minds the ceremonies differ from those of the usual Gospel rites. The blessing is not asked, for the giver of all blessings is dead; no lights are carried before the book, for the light " of all men who cometh into the world "[6] is crucified; no smoke of incense ascends heavenward, for the piety and the faith of the Apostles are wavering; the salute, "The Lord be with you," is not sung, for by a salute the traitor Judas betrayed his master; the " Glory be to thee, O Lord," is omitted, for we are struck with grief at the sight of the Redeemer stripped of his glory. All is sadness.[7]

Among the Greeks and Romans, the way of reciting

---

[1] Darras Hist. of the Church, etc. [2] xxvi., xxvii.; by order of Pope Alexander, El Porque de las Ceremonias, c. xxx. [3] 14, 15. [4] Luke, 22, 23. [5] John xviii., xix.; el Porque de las Ceremonias, c. xxx. Dom. et Palmos. [6] John i. 9. [7] Bishop England, Cerem. of Holy Week.

tragedy was to have different persons take separate parts and recite them as they came in the piece, and the Church has preserved that way in the singing of the passion of our Lord during Holy Week.[1] We could have given a strong description of the passion and of the sufferings of the Saviour, but the most eloquent sermon is cold compared to strong and powerful dramatic tragedy, such as is carried out by the Church on these days.[2] It is beyond all description in its powerful effect, and it must be seen and heard by those who understand the Latin, to feel its beautiful sublimity, which moves the very depths of the soul, and leaves an impression which once heard is never forgotten.

In the principal churches, in seminaries, and wherever our rites and ceremonies are carried out, the passion is sung by three clergymen and the choir. The clergymen should be vested like deacons with stoles only. The historic part is sung by one in a manly tenor voice, what was spoken by a third person in a high key, and the words of our divine Lord are chanted in a deep, solemn bass; all producing a wonderful dramatic effect, each part having its own cadence, as in the dramas of the Greeks and Romans, each is suited to the character represented, and is well worthy of ancient tragedy. The singing of the narrator is clear, every word distinct and beautifully modulated. The words of any third person in the history of the passion come forth spritely, like the speech of a conversation, while the words of our blessed Lord are uttered in a slow, solemn, grave and dignified manner, beginning low and rising by full tones, then changing into rich, harmonious music, till they end in graceful cadences modulated into more beautiful tones, when the Saviour asks a question. This is the way they are sung in all parts of the world; but they are of wonderful beauty in the Pope's chapel, for there they are sung by members of the papal choir, who are chosen for their rich and musical voices, and trained for this purpose.[3]

The choruses are remarkable. When the Jews speak in the history of the passion, or when any crowd is made to cry out, the choir bursts out with its simple but mas-

---

[1] Cardinal Wiseman, Holy Week, p. 62 ; Bishop England, Holy Week, Palm Sunday; Canon Pope, Holy Week, etc. [2] Card. Wiseman, Holy Week, p. 62. [3] Card. Wiseman, Holy Week, pp. 67, 68.

sive music, and pours forth the ideas with an energy and a force which thrill the soul and overcome the feelings. These choruses were composed by Lewis de Victoria,[1] of Avila, who lived in the time of the great Palestrina, and the latter did not attempt to alter them, because he found them so beautiful and so suited to the Passion. When the Jews cry, "Crucify him," or, "Barrabas," the choir bursts forth with vehement energy, each syllable having a note, but the last word has a passage of key, simple yet strikingly impressive, while in most of the choruses the singing comes abruptly to an end by a quick termination, making the effect wonderfully powerful by the rapid stamping, marked manner, well suited to the noisy outcries of a furious mob.

In the third chorus of St. Matthew's Gospel, when the two false witnesses give testimony against him, it is a duet, one on a high key and the other a lower, with the words following one another in a stumbling way, as though one took his story from the other, one jarring with the other, or trying to imitate the other, aptly representing the words of the gospel that "Their witness did not agree."[2] The words, "Hail, King of the Jews,"[3] are sung in an exceeding soft and moving tone, inclining the soul to utter in earnest what the Jews said in mockery. In the Gospel of St. John, sung on Good Friday, one or two sentences are most exquisite in tone and modulation. They are the words, "If you let him go, you are no friend of Cæsar's;" but the most beautiful of all are the words of the soldiers, when dividing his garment, "Let us not divide it, but cast lots." The words follow each other in a falling cadence, becoming softer and softer, nearly dying away, till they burst forth into a mildly majestic swell of harmonious music.

Their effect is beyond description. The shortness of their length, the rapidity of their movements and their sudden breaking forth, produce a feeling of wonder, astonishment and admiration for their simplicity, beauty and overpowering effect. They are arranged according to the principle of a deep dramatic design, calculated to produce the most solemn and devout impressions on the soul. The stately rhythm, the triple chant and the

---

[1] In 1585.   [2] Mark xiv. 59.   [3] John xix. 8.

choruses, with their poetic feeling, each produces its effect. The strong voice in which the historic part is given, softens gradually as the catastrophe of the cruci-fixion approaches, dying away as the last breath of the Lord's life is given up on the cross. When all ends, a deep silence fills the church, and the clergy, with the whole congregation as one man, fall upon their knees in adoration of the Saviour's death. The same feeling fills every heart. Every thought goes back to the original scene, and every imagination brings before the heart the last moments of our Redeemer's life upon the cross, as though they were there on Calvary's top, when the world was redeemed by the blood of God.

The gospel is sung with incense after the Passion, which recalls the people from their sorrow and woe by giving a history of the sealing up of the sepulchre and of the resurrection.

During the four days before his passion, our Lord used to spend the nights at the home of Lazarus, Martha and Mary, in the village of Bethany, from which each morning he went into the city of Jerusalem, and in the temple he used to preach to the priests and people.[1] His words became more striking and more vigorous, denouncing them, with a vehemence that was unusual, for their wick-edness, foretelling the destruction of their city for the hardness of their hearts. He fasted each day. Once he came to a fig tree to find something to eat, and found but leaves. He cursed it, when it dried up—a figure of those who have good Christian intentions, but who do not put them in practice; they are cursed by God because of their infidelity to grace.

One day he came from the temple toward the evening hour and went along on the way to Bethany. Resting for a moment on the side of Mount Olives, his disciples gathered around him and asked him the time when the temple would be destroyed. Uniting in one prophetic picture the destruction of the temple, the city of Jerusa-lem and the world at the end of time, because one is but a figure of the other, in wonderful words he prophesied the time when the Romans under Titus would come, forty years from that time, and from the very place where he then

---

[1] Math. xxi., xxii., xxiii.

sat, threaten the holy city, surround it on every side, take
it, destroy it, level its walls, burn its temple, and not leaving a stone upon a stone, draw the plow over the spot
where the temple of Solomon once stood in all its glory.
From that he passed to the destruction of the world,
when the number of the saints would be completed;
when the world will have run its course; when the moon
will be darkened, and the sun refuse to shed its light;
when the stars would fall from the vault of heaven;
when all nature would groan in agony, and when the
death of the universe will take place as foretold by the
prophets.[1]

Monday the Station is held in the Church of St. Prax-
edes, the Church in which in the IXth century St.
Pascal, the holy Pope, placed the remains of the 2,300
martyrs taken from the catacombs, and erected the column to which our blessed Lord was bound when he was
scourged.   In the Mass the Gospel is taken from St.
John's narrative, where he speaks of Mary Magdalen
taking the box of precious ointment and anointing the
feet of Jesus in the house of Lazarus, her brother.[2]

Tuesday morning, as usual, he went to the temple to
teach the people, and passing on the way they came to
the fig tree which had withered away when he told his disciples to have faith.   Continuing on his way, he came to
the temple, when the scribes and elders, smarting under
his rebukes of the day before, asked him by what authority he did these things.   He confounded them by
asking them from whence came the baptism of John the
Baptist and its power,[3] and they were afraid to answer
him, for they feared the people.

The Station is held on Tuesday in the Church of St.
Prisca, which was once the house of the holy Acquila
and Prisca, to whom St. Paul in his epistle to the Romans sends his greetings.   In the third century, Pope
St. Eutychianus, because of having the same name, here
laid the body of St. Prisca, the Roman virgin and martyr.

The Passion, according to St. Mark, is said to-day in
place of the usual gospel; it is sung in the same way as
the Passion of St. Matthew on Palm Sunday.

---

[1] Math. xxiv.; Mark xiii.; Luke xxi.   [2] John xii. 63.   [3] Mark xi. 20. 24.

II.—HOLY WEDNESDAY.

On Wednesday the Chief Priests, with the elders of the people, gathered together in one of the principal halls of the Temple, to see for the last time what could be done to put Jesus to death. It was within a few days of their Easter festivities, and many strangers were in the city to celebrate the feast, and they saw that triumphant procession on Palm Sunday. Even some of the influential people of Jerusalem believed in him, and they did not know what to do, for they feared the people. Many projects were offered. While they were thus debating, one of the disciples came to the assembly and said : "What will you give, and I will deliver him to you?"[1] It was Judas the traitor. They offered him thirty pieces of silver, a little more than $18.00, smaller than the price of the lowest slave. They were filled with joy. They forgot the CVIII. Psalm, wherein holy David prophesied the selling of the Divine Victim. That day was spent by our Lord in the temple and in the holy city, teaching and preaching, according to his custom.

In honor and remembrance of this infamous betrayal of the Saviour by Judas, each Ember Season of the year, when the Church calls on us to fast, Wednesday is one of the fast days to recall Judas' treason.

The Station of to-day is held in Rome in the great church of St. Mary Major, to recall the sorrows of the suffering Mother, who saw her Son to-day betrayed by the accursed disciple. After the introit and prayers, the two lessons are taken from the Prophecy of Isaiah, foretelling the sufferings and the passion of our Lord.[2] In ancient times, the Catechumens were sent out of the Church as usual, but when Mass was ended, they returned. Then one of the priests said to them : "Next Saturday, the eve of Easter, you will at such an hour come to the Lateran Basilica for the seventh examination, there to recite the Creed, so that by the help of God, you may be washed in the waters of regeneration. Prepare yourselves with zeal and humility, in continual prayer and fasting, so that having been buried with Christ by that holy baptism, you may rise with him unto everlasting life. Amen."

---

[1] Math. xxvi. 15. [2] Isa. lxii., lxiii.

To-day the Passion of our Lord, according to St. Luke, is read in the same way as on Palm Sunday.[1]

We are now drawing near to the death of the Lord, and the Church celebrates that death by the most solemn, striking ceremonies of the year. All is sad, sombre, mournful. The rites and ceremonies breathe nothing but woe. From the most ancient times, the clergy have been accustomed to recite the Offices of the last of Holy Week on the evenings before. Because of this and because of the long ceremony of the blessing of the Holy Oils, Matins and Lauds of Holy Thursday are said on Wednesday evening, those of Friday on Thursday evening, and those of Holy Saturday on the evening of Good Friday. These Offices are taken from the Breviary, and are called the "Tenebræ," that is, darkness, for they used to be said in the darkness of the night, or in the darkness of the Catacombs in the first ages of the Church. They typify the darkness of the three hours hanging over the earth, while our Lord was dying on the cross.[2] Tenebræ are made up of three watches, for the darkness lasted for three hours ; from the sixth, that is, at noon, to the ninth hour, that is, at three in the afternoon.[3] The darkness of the sun was caused by a miracle, not by an eclipse, for the feast of Easter among the Jews was celebrated at the full moon, when the earth was between the sun and the moon, while an eclipse is caused by the moon coming between the earth and the sun, the shadow of the moon falling upon the earth. The sun was darkened then, for the "Son of justice" was dying for the human race.[4]

The Office of the "Tenebræ" opens on Wednesday evening, by the clergy assembling in the church, and saying in silence the Lord's Prayer and the Hail Mary, which belong to the New Testament, while the anthems, the psalms and the lessons are said aloud, because they belong to the Old Testament. The first prayers belonging to the New Testament are said in silence, for they were written by the Apostles, who ran away from our Lord and kept silence in his Passion, while the Prophets of the Old Testament proclaimed aloud his sufferings and his death. The saddest and the most solemn of the

---

[1] Luke xxii. [2] Math. xxvii. 45. [3] Mark xv. 33. [4] Durandus, Rationale Div. L v. c. lxxii. n. 2.

psalms are said, three for each watch. No hymn is said, no blessing asked, no chapter read, for there is no thought in the mind of the Church "but Jesus Christ, and him crucified.'"

The first lesson of Thursday, Friday and Saturday, is taken from the lamentations of Jeremiah, the prophet of sorrows.[2] Each verse of these sad lamentations is divided by one of the letters of the Hebrew alphabet, to show to the Jews that the history of the sufferings and the death of our Lord were as plain as the alphabet in the prophecies of the Old Testament,[3] and because each of the letters signify and told the Jews a truth which we will not stop now to explain.[4]

Jeremiah sits weeping over the holy city of Jerusalem, captured by the Assyrians.[5] In the Bible, Jerusalem means "The vision of peace,"[6] and in the strong figurative language of the Eastern nations, and in the mysticism of the Holy Scriptures, it means the Holy Church desolate, weeping over the death of her Founder and her Lord. Again, Jerusalem signifies heaven, and represents all heaven aghast at the sight of the Lord and Creator put to death by ungrateful men.

The music of the lamentations of Wednesday and Friday evenings was arranged by the great Palestrina. Nothing ever heard can compare with it in exquisite tenderness, rich pathos and indescribable woe. The music of this lamentation, sung on Thursday, was composed by Allegri, and it is even equal to that of Palestrina.[7] The lamentations are sung by one of the clergymen, chosen for his musical voice. In the middle of the sanctuary he sings, with his face turned toward the altar. Each lamentation ends with "Jerusalem, Jerusalem, be converted to the Lord thy God;" a sad and sorrowful appeal to the Jews to return again to their Lord whom they put to death.[8]

No words can tell the indescribable effect of these lamentations on the soul of the Christian. Sometimes tears flow down the cheeks of the people in the churches, listening to the sad and woful lamentations of Jeremiah,

[1] I. Cor. il. 2. [2] Jer. 1. 1. [3] Durandus, Rat. Div. l. vi. c. lxxii. n. 14. [4] See El Porque de las Ceremonias, c. xxx., Reg. gen. etc. [5] El Porque de las Ceremonias cxxx. ; Jueves Santo en post. [6] S. Aug. D. Civit. Dei. l. xix. c. xi. [7] Card. Wiseman's Holy Week, p. 95. [8] El Porque de las Ceremonias, c. xxx. Reg. gen. etc.

as the sorrowful tones of the great composers flow out
from the sanctuary, and are re-echoed from the vaulted
roofs of the churches, striking deep into the ears of the
clergy and the people, and bringing all minds back to the
sad tragedy of Calvary.

Before the Office begins, six candles of unbleached
beeswax are lighted on the altar, three on each side, and
on a triangle on the epistle side are fourteen more, with
one of bleached wax on the top. The Blessed Sacrament
before, has been taken to another altar prepared for it.[1]
The Church is now entering into the deepest mysticism.
Let us understand these ceremonies. In the ceremonies
of the Temple at Jerusalem they sang fifteen psalms as
they ascended the fifteen steps leading up to the holy
place,[2] signifying the fifteen grades of virtue, which make
man perfect. In the Office of to-day, we sing fifteen
psalms in honor and in remembrance of the perfect man
Jesus Christ, who was put to death. He is the light of
the world, and to signify the light of his heavenly teachings, which is perpect, the fifteen candles are lighted
on the triangle, which typify the Holy Trinity. A candle
is put out after each psalm, to typify the sufferings of
the perfect Man, our Lord. The fourteen of unbleached
wax tell us of his human nature. The one of white
bleached wax on top signifies his Divine nature. All
the unbleached candles are put out, to tell that his human nature died. The white candle on top is not
quenched, to show that his Divine nature did not die.
It is hidden behind the altar for a few moments, and
brought back and placed again on the triangular candlestick, to show that his Divine nature was hidden for a
time in his passion.[3] Light is a sign of joy.[4] They
are put out, to signify that there is no joy in the Church
celebrating the death of our Lord.

Some writers of the early times say that the putting out of the fourteen candles represents the Apostles, and the three holy women[5] leaving our Lord and hiding themselves during his passion,[6] while his holy Mother,
figured by the pure white candle,[7] never left him till,

[1] Cast. l. iii, S. vi. c. i. n. l. c. 2. Mer. S. vi. c. xiii. n. 1. [2] S. Aug. vol. xiii. 82. [3] El
Porque de las Ceremonias, c. xxx. Reg. gen. etc. [4] Claudius, Expenc. de Euthar.
Cult. c. ii. p. 16, 90. [5] El Porque de las Ceremonias, c. xxx. Reg. gen. etc. [6] Du-
randus, Rationale, Div. L. vi. c. lxxii. n. 18. [7] El Porque de las Ceremonias, c. xxx,
Reg. gen. para, etc.

overwhelmed with grief, she retired for a time, still hoping in him, till she met him filled with joy after the resurrection, signified by the hiding of the candle behind the altar.[1] There are seven candles on each side of the triangular candlestick, for the candlestick in the Holy of Holies in the temple had seven lights burning before the Lord. From it the Christians took the custom of the lights of the "Tenebræ." "Those candles then," says another writer, "recall the lights of the patriarchs and the prophets of the law of nature and of the law of Moses, prophesying the Messiah, before whose transcendent effulgence they paled and went out, or the prophets of the Old Testament put to death by the Jews."[2]

In the middle ages, before the Latin rite was carried out in all its purity, the number of candles on the triangle was not the same everywhere. In Canterbury, in England, they had twenty-five, to represent the twelve minor and the twelve major prophets of the Old Testament.[3] The candles were in some places put out with a wet sponge, to recall the sponge with which the vinegar and gall were given our Lord to drink. Again, they were in some places quenched with a wax hand, to symbolize the traitor hand of Judas, handing our Lord over to the Jews.[4] In other churches they had seventy-two candles, to typify the seventy-two disciples, who ran away from our Lord in his sufferings.[5] The seven candles, on each side of the triangle, represent the seven gifts of the Holy Ghost in the hearts of the Jews and the Apostles. The sanctuary is divided into two sides, the left and the right. The left typifies the Jews, and the right the Christians. Both the Jews and the Apostles doubted his Divinity during his passion.

The large white candle on the top of the triangle is Christ, made of bleached beeswax coming from virgin bees. It figures his body coming from his Virgin Mother. Made of bleached wax, it tells of his body glorified after his passion. The wick signifies his soul in that body. The burning flame tells of the glories of the Divinity,

---

[1] Card. Torre, Cremata de Eccl. c. 30, see Suarez de Fide, Spe. et Char. Disp. 96, 8; Canon Pope, Holy Week in the Vatican, p. 75. [2] Rupertus, iv. de Div. Of. c. 26, 28. [3] Lafranc. [4] El Porque de las Ceremonias, c. xxx. Reg. gen, etc.; Canon Pope, Ibidem, p. 76. [5] Durandus Rationale, Div. L. lxxii. n. 26.

such as appeared to Moses in the burning bush, and to
the three Apostles, during the transfiguration. Light in
the Bible, signifies wisdom and knowledge. The light of
that candle typifies the wisdom and the knowledge of
God which our Lord taught the world. The candle is
hidden, for he hid his Divinity in his passion. It comes
again from under the altar, for he came from the Sepulchre to enlighten the world with his wisdom.[1] In the
services of the church the altar represents the tomb of
our Lord, and the candle is hidden behind it to show in
mystic meaning his death and burial in the tomb. Only
the upper candle is of bleached wax, for neither the
prophets' nor the Apostles' bodies are yet glorified
in heaven, only our Lord and his mother have gone,
body and soul, into that abode of bliss.[2]

The candles are put out at the end of each of the
Psalms of Matins and of Lauds. The Lesson of the
Second Nocturn is taken from the writings of St. Augustine,[3] where he speaks of our Lord. The Passion Lesson
of the third Nocturn is taken from St. Paul to the Corinthians,[4] where he speaks of the institution of the Blessed
Eucharist. At Lauds, the Canticle of Moses takes the
place of the next to the last Psalm, where he sings so
gloriously of the delivery of the children of Israel from
the hosts of Pharoah, a figure of the Christians delivered
from the power of hell by our Lord, of whom Moses was a
figure. All rise and face the altar when they sing the Canticle of Zachary,[5] because the altar signifies Christ, to
whom the sacred words are addressed. This magnificent
piece of Hebrew poetry is composed of twelve verses.
At the beginning of the seventh verse, the last candle on
the right hand side of the altar is put out, and at the
next verse the last on the left is quenched, and so on till
at the last verse the last candle next the tabernacle is
put out, so that all the lights in the church are put out
except those burning before the Blessed Sacrament,[6] and
the bleached candle on the top of the triangle. While the
Anthem of the Canticle is sung, the white candle is taken
from the top of the triangle and placed upon the altar,
signifying Christ on Calvary, for the altar is like another

---

[1] Cardinal Bellarmin, t. 2, Cont. L. iii. de Eccl. Mil. c. 17, Abulensis Qu. 14. [2] Durandus Rationale Div. L. vi. c. lxxii. n. 26. [3] In Ps. liv. ad vi. [4] I. Cor. c. xi. [5] Luke
1. [6] Caerem. Epis. l. ii. c. xxii. n. 11.

St. John Lateran, Rome.

Calvary,[1] where he is sacrificed in a mystic manner every
day in the Mass. At the words, " Christ for us became
obedient unto death," the candle is hidden under the
altar to typify his death and burial. In a moment it is
brought forth to show that he came forth from the grave
in the glories of the resurrection. Before this, the candles on the altar were extinguished, to show that all faith
in him was gone from the hearts of both the Jews and
the Apostles, whom the Epistle and Gospel sides represent.

At the "Tenebræ" of Wednesday, the verse is as
above.[2] In the Friday Office it is " Christ for us became
obedient unto death, even to the death of the cross."
The Office of Saturday coming near to the resurrection, it
is, " Christ for us became obedient unto death, even to
the death of the cross, for that reason God exalted him
and gave him a name which is above every name." At
the beginning of these words, each day, all kneel to worship our Lord dying for us. In some churches, at these
words, they used to prostrate themselves on the ground.

Then begins the Psalm : "Have mercy on me, O God!"
etc.[3] It is sung in the most wonderfully sublime manner.
There are three ways of singing it, the productions of the
three great composers, Tomaso Baj, Giuseppe Baina and
Allegri. The one composed by Allegri[4] is surpassingly
beautiful, and is called a wonderful piece of music.[5] All
then say in silence the Lord's Prayer, and without the
usual " Let us pray," for all are struck with the thought
of our Lord praying on the cross. Tradition tells us that
while dying, he recited the seven penitential Psalms, till
he came to the words: " Into thy hands, O Lord, I commend my spirit," when bowing down his head, he gave
up the ghost. The chief among the clergy then says:
"Look down, we beseech thee, O Lord, on this thy family, for whom our Lord Jesus Christ wavered not to deliver himself into the hands of his enemies, and suffer
the torment of the Cross, who with thee liveth and
reigneth in the unity of the Holy Ghost, God, for ever
and ever, Amen." The last sentence is said in silence in
remembrance of the silence of our Lord in death on Cal-

---

[1] Gueranger, L'An. Liturg. Pas. et La Semaine S. p. 345. [2] Christ for us was, etc.
[3] Ps. l. [4] O'Brien, Hist. of the Mass, p. 99. [5] Canon Pope, Holy Week in the Vatican, p. 77.

vary when he died. All then strike the benches for a moment to recall the earthquake which shook the earth when our Lord died.[1]

Nothing ever seen or heard of the same nature, can equal the sad, doleful and woful effect of these rites and ceremonies, when we celebrate each year the funeral of our Lord. In order that no other ceremony may distract the minds of the people from the yearly funeral services of our Lord, from Holy Thursday till Monday after Easter, no funeral mass is allowed in the church, not even when the body is present.[2] We celebrate the Offices of the Tenebræ three days, for three days and nights our Lord lay in the tomb.

III.—HOLY THURSDAY.

Many rites and ceremonies are held in the Church on Holy Thursday. To-day the Oils used in conferring the sacraments[3] during the rest of the year are blessed. Mass is said in remembrance of the last supper.[4] The blessed Sacrament is carried to the altar, where it is kept for the adoration of the people in memory of our Lord's body laid in the tomb. The feet of thirteen are washed, following the example of the Saviour washing the feet of his Apostles. In former times the public penitents were received again into the Church.

We will see first, the ceremonies of the blessing of the Holy Oils. The size of this book will not allow us to go into detail. We can give but a few ideas relating to these ceremonies. Following the Apostolic traditions on Holy Thursday, by order of Pope Fabian,[5] the Oils must be blessed each year by the bishops[6] and given to the priests. The old Oils must be burned, for after the new Oils are blessed, the old cannot be used.[7] It is not necessary to take the Oils to be blessed to-day from the last year's crop of olives.[8] The Oils are blessed on Holy Thursday, because the Chrism and the Oil of the catechumens are used in solemn baptism, which is conferred on Holy Saturday, and therefore it is right that they be

---

[1] Benedictus XIV. de Mat. Tenebrarum, n. 9, ad Finem. [2] Ordo Nota Dom. Pal. [3] Mentioned by S. Aug. De Bap. Contra Donat, n. 28. [4] El Porque de las Ceremonias, c. xxx. Missa Solem. [5] 236 to 246 ; [6] Concil. Antis. c. 6. et Tholetan, et cet. c. 20, S. Thomas, lxxii. 8. [7] S. R. C. Sept. 160 1. [8] S. R. C. 22 March, 1862 to Bishop of St. Paul, Min.

blessed two days before, so that they can be distributed through the diocese. "It behooves that the material for the sacraments be blessed the day when the sacrament of the Eucharist was instituted to which all the other sacraments relate,"[1] "because two days before the Pasch, Mary anointed the feet of the Lord."[2]

Everywhere the consecration of the Oils takes place on this day, nor can bishops bless the Oils at any other time,[3] but if there be not enough of the Holy Oils, they can be got from neighboring bishops.[4] When the bishop of the diocese is sick, absent, or for any reason he cannot bless the Oils, he must either invite another bishop to come, or send them to some neighboring bishop to be blessed.[5] When this cannot be done, the Oils of last year may be used, putting in a little less than the consecrated Oil, because this privilege was given to the bishops in the Vatican council by Pope Pius IX. This is what is to be done, for the Oils cannot be consecrated on any other day without a special permission from Rome, while the Holy Oils remaining in the vases in the Cathedral must be burned before the Blessed Sacrament, when the new Oils are consecrated.[6]

The consecration of the Holy Oils should take place in the most beautiful chapel in the Cathedral, if there be one of this kind, otherwise in the sanctuary with the Blessed Sacrament removed to another altar, for the ceremony could not be carried out before our Lord with due reverence. The consecration of the Oils cannot take place in a private chapel in the Episcopal residence,[7] neither in a parish church without sufficient reason, but publicly in the Cathedral,[8] except when for a just reason the bishop lives elsewhere.

In former times, three Masses were said on Holy Thursday, one for the reception of the public penitents, the second for the consecration of the Holy Oils, and the third in honor of the institution of the Blessed Sacrament. At the present time there is only one High Mass offered up to-day,[9] because the piety of the people has grown weak, and they do not keep up the custom of

---

[1] St. Thomas, p. 3. q. 72, a. 12, ad. 3.   [2] St. Isidore, Ep. His. de Eccl. Off. L. i. c. 28.
[3] S. R. C. 23 Sept. 1837, Oriolen I.   [4] S. R. C. 27 Sept. 1864, Niver.   [5] S. R. C. 13 June, 1695, dubia 2.   [6] Pontif. Rom. T. V. in Caena Dom.   [7] S. R. C. 21 June, 1862, Torcel. [8] S. R. C. 23 March, 1669, Brug.   [9] O'Brien, Hist. of the Mass, p. 17.

doing public penance, as in the Apostolic times.[1] During the Mass, the cross on the altar before which the Oils are consecrated, which from the vesper time before Passion Sunday was covered with a violet veil as a sign of penance, is now covered by a white veil as a sign of joy, for on this day we celebrate the institution of the most Holy Eucharist and of the Mass at the Last Supper.

From ancient times the consecration of the Holy Oils takes place at the one Mass in the Cathedral, said by the bishop, and by no one but him can the oils be consecrated. The first to be consecrated is the Oil for the sick. It forms the material for the Sacrament of Extreme Unction, for when any one is in danger of death by sickness, we anoint him with the Holy Oil, blessed this day, according to the words of St. James the Apostle: "Is any man sick among you? Let him bring in the priests of the Church, and let them pray over him, anointing him with oil, in the name of the Lord, and the prayer of faith shall save the sick man ; and the Lord shall raise him up; and if he be in sins, they shall be forgiven him."[2] In former ages the benediction of the Oil for the sick took place at any time during the year; but because it is so like the other Oils, in later times it is blessed on Holy Thursday. For that reason it is not blessed with the other two, but before them.[3]

The greatest of the Holy Oils is the Chrism, a Greek word, which means anointed with oil. From that comes Christ,[4] one of the holy names of our Lord, for in many parts of the Bible he is called the Anointed of the Lord, that is, he was anointed in an invisible way by the Holy Ghost.[5] Following the example of our Saviour, all members of the Church are baptized as he was, in the Jordan, and at their baptism they are anointed like him with Holy Chrism, and again they are anointed with Chrism, at their confirmation.

The third is the Oil of the Catechumens. The Catechumens are those who are preparing to be admitted into the Church by baptism, and are learning the truths of the Christian religion. Although it is not the material of any Sacrament, nevertheless like the other two Oils it

---

[1] Gueranger, la Passion et La Semaine Sainte, p. 401. [2] James v, 14, 15. [3] Gueranger, la l'assion et la Semaine Ste., p. 409. [4] St. Aug. vol. xi. 151, vol. xv. 868, Enar. in Ps. cviii. n. 26. [5] St. Aug. De Trinitate, lxv. n. 46 in fine.

comes down to us from the Apostles. It is named the Oil of the Catechumens, for it is used to anoint their breasts and shoulders, before they are washed in the waters of baptism. It is also used at the ordination of priests, to anoint their hands, and to anoint the heads of emperors and empresses, of kings and of queens, when they are crowned.

Of all the ceremonies of the year, the consecration of the Holy Oils is one of the most beautiful, and the ceremonies are deeply mystical. We can give but a few of them, and for the others we refer the reader to the Pontifical. Twelve priests, representing the twelve Apostles around our Saviour, stand around the bishop, who takes the place of our Lord, and in his name and by his power consecrates the Oils. Seven deacons and seven sub-deacons must be present, signifying the seven deacons chosen by the Apostles.[1] Priests, deacons, and sub-deacons are clothed in their sacred vestments, there to be witnesses of the ceremonies, and in the name of the Church to testify that the Oils are correctly consecrated. In no case will the Church allow the ceremony with a smaller number of clergymen.[2] When a sufficient number are not present, the bishop can command them to come,[3] or call some of the clergy of the Religious Orders.[4] When there are not enough in the whole diocese, only with the permission of the Pope can the ceremony take place.[5] This is to keep to the traditions of the Apostles, and because the Church will not change in her rites and ceremonies.

The clergy, vested in white or golden vestments, in honor of the Blessed Sacrament instituted to-day, go to the Cathedral, where the bishop says the Mass till he comes to the words of the twelfth part of the Canon, "Through whom, O Lord, good things thou doest always create," when he comes down from the altar and takes his seat. One of the sub-deacons goes to the vestry, and taking the vase of oil, he covers it with a violet veil, and carries it to the arch-deacon, who presents it to the bishop, saying : "The oil for the sick."

The vase of oil is brought from the vestry, for in the

---

[1] Acts vi. [2] R. S. C. 9 May, 1606, Lanret. [3] R. S. C. March, 1679, Sur. [4] R. S. C. Nov. 11, 1641, Rith. [5] R. S. C. Jan. 24, 1645 ; Jan. 23, 1644; March 22, 1862.

first ages of the Church the people brought their gifts of oil, bread and wine, to the vestry, from which the oils for consecration were chosen. The oil is carried by the sub-deacon, for he represents the Old Testament, in which the Holy Oils were typified. They must be of the purest olive oil, figured by the olive branch brought to Noah in the ark, and by the dove, a figure of the Holy Ghost overshadowing our Lord at his baptism.[1] The purest olive oil was always burning in the lamp before the Lord in the tabernacle.[2] The hands of the priests of the Israelites, their vestments, the altar of holocaust, the unleavened wafers of bread, the tabernacle of the Lord with all its utensils, the heads of Aaron and of the high priests, the heads of Saul, of David, of Solomon and of all the kings of Israel, were anointed with oil. What does that oil signify but the Holy Ghost,[3] who anointed our blessed Lord? The ceremonies of the Old Law prefigured the Holy Oils in our ceremonies. The sub-deacon figuring the Old Law comes with the vase of oil covered with a violet veil, representing the ceremonies of the consecration of the Oils coming from the Old Testament, wherein our holy rites were as it were covered. The vase of oil is covered with a violet veil to typify penance for our sins. Moses, and Christ, whom he represented, was not anointed with material oil, but like Christ, in an unseen manner.[4] Aaron was anointed with oil, for he was a type of the bishop, who like him, is anointed on his head the day of his consecration. With beautiful prayers, then the bishop consecrates the Oil for the sick.

The bishop, with his ministers, then returns to the altar and continues the Mass. From the earlier ages the clergy have been in the habit of receiving Holy Communion from the hands of the bishop, in remembrance of the Apostles receiving the body and blood of our Lord from his hands at the last supper. No priest is allowed to say a private Mass on Holy Thursday, except it be urgent.[5] The priests wear their stoles while receiving, as a sign of their priesthood. Three chalices have been prepared for the services. One is used for the Mass; one is to receive the second Host, to be kept

---

[1] Math. iii. 16. [2] Exod. xxvii. 20, Levit. xxiv. 2. [3] St. Aug. Enar. in Ps. cviii. n. 26. [4] Durandus, Rationale Div. L. 1. c. viii. n. 2. [5] Gueranger, la Pas. et le Sem. S. p. 424.

in the repository for Good Friday; and the third is for
the washing of the bishop's fingers, before the consecration of the oil for the sick.[1]   Having placed the Host reserved for the morrow in the chalice on the altar, which
has from the beginning of the Mass been lighted up with
a large number of candles, the bishop again comes down
to his seat.   No kiss of peace is given, because with a
kiss to-day, Judas betrayed our Lord.   Having put
incense in the thurible, at the words of the arch-
deacon, the twelve priests and the seven deacons go
to the vestry to get the oil for Holy Chrism and the oil
for the Catechumens to be consecrated while the choir
sings the hymn: "O, Redeemer," etc., composed in the
fifth century, by Fortunatus, bishop of Poitiers.[2]   A sub-
deacon carries the vase of balsam, and two deacons the
two vases of oil.   They all come into the sanctuary,
where the bishop with his ministers have been waiting.

The oils are consecrated during the Mass, for it is
right that these creatures, made holy for the spiritual
good of the people, should be consecrated during the
Mass, wherein are typified the sufferings and death of
our Lord, who died for the people.[3]   The two lights are
carried on each side of the oils to recall the law and the
prophecy of the Old Testament, in which consecrated
oils were used by command of God,[4] while the burning
incense tells of our prayers, which make the Sacraments
given by these Holy Oils, more powerful for our salvation.   The clergy coming, two by two, recall the disciples sent two by two into the cities of Judea to preach
salvation, which is worked by the sacraments given to
the people by the consecrated oils.   Thus the deepest
mysticism and mystery surround these holy rites.   The
vase of oil typifies our Lord himself,[5] for from him comes
the graces which by the sacraments given by these consecrated oils will flow into the souls of the people.[6]   The
vase is carried covered, signifying the clothes he wore.
It is carried on the left arm, for the left is this world in
which our Lord lived. The vase is uncovered at the altar,
for he was stripped of his garments at Calvary, represented

---

[1] De Herdt, Pont. L. III. n. 10. [2] Pontif. Roman. de Of. in Fer. v. c. Dom. ; Gueranger, la Pas. et la Sem. Ste. p. 416.   [3] Durandus, Rationale Div. L. vi. lxxiv. n. 6.
[4] Durand. Ibidem, n. 16. [5] El Porque de las Ceremonias, c. xxx. Bened. de la Pila.
[6] Rupertus Abbas, L. v. de Divinis Of. c. 12.

by the altar.   It is carried between two priests, to tell of
Christ between Moses and Elias on Tabor's mount, in
the transfiguration.

Our Lord chose oil for the materials of the sacraments, because, as by the waters of baptism we are
washed from sin, so by the oils we are given strength
and power.   Oil, in the words of Isidore, comes from the
olive tree, which tells of peace, to tell of the peace of the
soul when free from sin.   It is used as a food to give
strength, and the sacraments given by it gives us spiritual strength; when burned it gives light, for the sacraments give light to our souls.   The ghostly powers of
this oil was foretold by Israel's prophet king, in the
words: "O taste and see that the Lord is sweet,"[1] in the
Sacraments of his church drawing their wondrous
power "from the fountains of the Saviour."[2]   Olive oil is
sweet to the taste, balsam is sweet to the smell, and
these two tell of the sweetness of heavenly wisdom, and
the teachings of faith, which are given in the sacraments
infused into our souls by these Holy Oils.[3]

We read that the Apostles anointed with oil many
that were sick and healed them;[4] that Jesus anointed
the eyes of the man born blind;[5] that according to the
prophecy of Isaiah,[6] our Lord was anointed to preach
the Gospel;[7] that Mary Magdalen anointed his feet before his death;[8] that when they fasted, they were to
anoint their heads;[9] and that with sweetly smelling oils
and spices, they came to anoint the body of our Lord
when laid in the tomb.[10]   From this we know that the
custom of anointing with oil came to us from the Jews
and from the Apostles.

When the oils are brought to him, with beautiful prayers the bishop beseeches God to send down his blessings and his power on the oils.   He mixes the oil and
balsam and prays, that as the human and the divine natures were united in Christ, thus may the union of these
fluids, which represent that union in our Lord, give
grace to man made of soul and body, and that the oil
may give to all the graces of the Holy Ghost. Continuing,
he prays over the Chrism, recalling its figures in the Old

---

[1] Ps. xxxiii. 9. [2] Isa. xii. 3. [3] Durandus, Rationale Div. L. 1. c. vii. et. L. vi. c. lxxiv.
[4] Mark vi. 18. [5] John ix. 6. [6] Is. lxi. 1. [7] Luke iv. 18. [8] Luke vii. 38. [9] Math. vi.
17. [10] Mark xvi. 1.

Testament with which priests, prophets, kings and martyrs were anointed in the old law.

The bishop first, then each of the twelve priests,
breathe three times upon the oil, because it signifies
the Holy Ghost; because it is to receive the Holy Ghost,
who like a wind moved the waters at creation, and who was
sent upon the Apostles in a mighty wind,[1] prefigured
when our Lord breathed upon them.[2]

The clergy breathe three times on the oils, because
the three most holy persons of the Trinity are to work
the wonders of salvation by the sacraments given by
these oils.[3] The oils are addressed three times in the
words, "Hail, Holy Chrism!" "Hail, Holy Oil!" as when
the Apostle St. Andrew was brought to be crucified, he
hailed his cross from afar, saying, "Hail, precious cross."[4]
Three times they are thus saluted, for it is not the oils
precisely which we address, but the power and the virtue of the three times Holy Christ and the Holy Ghost,
who use these Holy Oils as means for the salvation of
mankind. We thus salute them as so many types of
Christ our Lord and of the Holy Ghost.[5] "We must
reverence holy things because of their holiness, for they
are set apart for divine worship, whence the respect
given them by its very nature rests in God.[6]

Balsam is mixed with the Oil of Holy Chrism, for the
sweet smell of the balsam tells of the sweet odor of our
good Christian works.[7] From the earliest ages the precious balsam of Palestine or of the Indies has been used,
but the American balsam will do.[8]

The Oil of Catechumens is used for the blessing of the
baptismal font, in the sacrament of baptism, in consecrating churches and altars in the ordination of priests,
and in the blessing and crowning of kings and queens.
The oil for the sick is used in anointing the sick, when
in danger of death, and in the blessing of bells. Holy
Chrism is used in the sacraments of baptism and confirmation, in the consecration of bishops and of chalices and
patens, and also with the oil of the sick in the blessing of
bells.[9]

---

[1] Acts ii. [2] Durandus, Rationale Div. L. vi. c. lxxiv. n. 20. [3] Durandus, ibidem.
[4] Benedict XIV. De Fest., D. N. J. C., Cap. vi., n. 66. [5] Bellarmin, t. iii., cont. l. 2, c. 18;
Tonrnely de Sac. Confir. A. III., p. 501; El Porque de las Ceremonias, c. xxx. Bened.
de la Pila, etc. [6] Bellotte, p. 791, n. 4. [7] Durandus, Rationale Div. L. i. c. vii., n. 3.
[8] De Hert. [9] Pontif. Rom. S. P. Clementis VIII. et Urban VIII., in Benedicti XIV. De
Festis D. N. J. Christi, c. vi. n. 59.

The Mass of Holy Thursday is in remembrance of the
Last Supper. Following the words of our Lord, "Do this
for a commemoration of me,"[1] we say this Mass to recall to our minds that time when the Master and his disciples eat the paschal lamb to fulfil the law of Moses,
when they lay on couches around the table, according to
the manners of the ancients, when the Lord in wondrous
humility washed his disciples' feet, but above all when
he instituted the holy Mass, ordained his Apostles
priests, and gave his Body and his Blood for the life of
the world. That "large dining hall," wherein these
wonders took place in the time of Christ, is seen to-day
in Jerusalem, and lately the Turks have given leave to
the Christians on a few occasions to offer up the Holy
Sacrifice in the very spot where the first Mass was offered
by the most sacred hands of our Lord himself.

The Mass of Holy Thursday is one of the most solemn
of the year, and was formerly celebrated in the evening;[2]
but because the ceremonies of the blessing of the Holy
Oils last so long, the feast of the Blessed Sacrament, instituted to-day by our Lord, is put off till the feast of
Corpus Christi. The violet vestments of penance and of
sorrow give place to white, in honor of the Blessed Sacrament instituted to-day by our Lord at the last supper.
The angelic hymn, "Glory be to God in the highest,"
silent since Septuagesima Sunday, breaks forth in all its
gladness.[3] The bells,[4] whose joyous tones are hushed
during Holy Week, now for the last time tinkle through
the church or peal from the steeple.[5] The sad and sombre rites commemorating our Saviour's sufferings, give
place to gladsome ceremonies. A light breaks forth
through the gloom of Holy Week, to tell that "when he
had loved his own, who were in the world, he loved them
to the end," by giving himself to them in the Sacrament
of his love, the Blessed Eucharist.

The holy Sacrifice pursues its course. No bell, with
silvery tones to tell us of joy and gladness, will be heard,
till the Angelic Hymn is sung in the Mass of Holy Saturday. The Church, the widowed Church, is weeping
for the death of her spouse. All ceremonies breathe the

---

[1] Luke xxii. 19. [2] S. Augustine VI. Concil. Carthage, etc. [3] El Porque de las Ceremonias, c. xxx. Misa Solan. [4] El Porque de las Ceremonias, c. xxx. [5] O'Brien, Hist.
of the Mass, p. 152.

deepest sorrow for the murder of our beloved. We are drawing near to Calvary. The celebrant at the altar on Holy Thursday consecrates two hosts, one for the sacrifice of to-day, the other for the morrow, for on Good Friday no Mass is offered up through the world. The second host is carried in solemn procession to the place called the Repository, where, amid the burning candles, the blooming flowers, and the adoring people, it is kept till the morrow, when, in another solemn procession, it will be carried to the high altar again, for the ceremonies of the Presanctified.

At Rome, the Station is in the Lateran Basilica, because the ceremonies of the blessing of the Oils, the receiving of the penitents and the washing of the feet, require that they be carried out in the mother Church of Rome and of the world, and such has been the custom since the time when Constantine gave the Lateran Palace as a residence to S. Silvester and to the Popes.[1]

The Epistle is taken from St. Paul to the Corinthians,[2] where he speaks of the Blessed Eucharist, while the Gospel is from St. John, because he speaks of the washing of the disciples' feet[3] at the Last Supper.[4]

During the rest of Lent, vespers or the evening song of praises to the Lord follow after Mass. While the choir is chanting the vesperal service, the celebrant, with the deacon and sub-deacon, take off the holy cloths covering the altars. The altar represents our Lord, and the stripping of the altar tells how he was stripped of his garments when he was put to death.[5] In ancient times they washed the altar. Now in St. Peter's, Rome, the Canons wash the grand altar with seven flagons of wine and water. We find St. Isidore, of Seville, mentions that ceremony in the VIIth century. It is still practiced by the Greeks and by many of the religious orders of the Church.[6] It is in remembrance of our Lord washing the feet of his disciples.

The Popes and bishops from the most remote times,[7] from the very days of the Apostles, wash the feet of twelve[8] or thirteen persons, following the example of the Saviour at the Last Supper.[9] Stripping off their sacer-

---

[1] Les Plus Belles Eglises du Monde, p. 40. [2] II. Cor. xi. [3] El Porque, c. xxx. Miss G. [4] John xiii. [5] Gueranger, La Pas. et La. Sem. Ste., p. 446. [6] Card. Wiseman, Holy Week, p. 107. [7] S. Aug. Epist. lv., n. 23. [8] S. Aug. Epist. lv. n. xxxiii. [9] S. Aug. In Joan, t. lviii. n. 4.

dotal robes[1] and girding themselves with a towel, they wash and kiss the feet of the poor. Such is the example of the humility given by the Pope each Holy Thursday in the Vatican. It has always been a custom of the eastern nations to wear sandals, and after the journey of the day, it is most refreshing to have the feet washed, but when it is done by the host himself, it is considered to be the highest honor one can receive; and therefore we can understand the wonderful humility of our Lord in washing the feet of his disciples. In the beginning of the Christian religion, the washing of the feet was a common custom. St. Paul, writing to Timothy, speaks of the Christian widow, and how she washed the feet of the saints.[2] In the first six centuries, we find the washing of the feet mentioned in the lives of the Saints, in the Homilies of the Fathers, and in the writings of the great men of that olden time. From the monks in the monasteries to the kings upon their thrones, they washed the feet of the poor. The pious Robert, King of France, and great St. Louis, the saintly King of France, washed each year the feet of the beggars. The holy princesses, Margaret of Scotland and Elizabeth of Hungary, yearly performed the ceremony of washing the feet.

The feet of twelve are washed to represent the twelve apostles, but the Pope washes the feet of thirteen, of as many different nations. Some say that the number thirteen represents the complete College of the Apostles, Mathias having been elected in the place of Judas; others, that the thirteenth tells of St. Paul, the Apostle of the nations; still others, with Benedict XIV.,[3] say that Pope Gregory the Great[4] washed each year the feet of twelve poor beggars, and that once thirteen were found in the room without any one knowing how the thirteenth entered. It was an Angel sent by God, to show how he loved the charity and the humility of the great Pope. In remembrance of this miracle, the feet of thirteen are washed. The ceremony of washing the feet takes place with the words of our Lord: "A new commandment I give unto you, that ye love one another,"[5] etc. The word

---

[1] El Porque de las Ceremonias, cxxx. Mandato Fabri Conciones Fer. Quinta in Caen, Dom. Con. i. [2] I. Tim. v. 10. [3] De Fest. D. N. J. Christi, l. i. c. vi.. n. 57. [4] El Porque de las Ceremonias, c. xxx. Mandato. [5] John xiii. 34.

commandment in Latin is mandatum, from that comes one of the names for this day, Maundy Thursday.[1]

In the evening, the Office of the Tenebræ is sung, as on the afternoon before, and the evening often closes with a sermon on the Blessed Eucharist.

IV.—GOOD FRIDAY.

Christ was crucified on the 25th of March,[2] and the Friday on which our Lord died, by all other nations called "Holy," by us from the remotest times it has been named Good.

The robes and vestments, which before were violet, to-day are black. The cardinals change their robes of silk to those of serge. The thrones and the altars are stripped of every ornament, and the floors and seats in the sanctuaries are bare. Sad and sombre are the rites of the Church in celebrating the yearly remembrance of the death and of the funeral of our Lord and Saviour.

Clothed in black vestments, the celebrant and his ministers come forth to the sanctuary without lights or incense. Before the altar they prostrate themselves upon the floor with their faces to the ground in prayer, in memory of our Lord, who, prostrate upon the ground in the garden of Gethsemane,[3] prayed before his passion for the salvation of the race.[4] Going to the corner of the altar, the celebrant reads the prophecy of Osee, the tract following the prayer, and the history of God commanding eating of the paschal lamb,[5] followed by a tract. Then comes the chanting of the history of the passion of our Lord, given by St. John.[6]

On Good Friday the Church offers up her prayers for men of all states and conditions. During the year the Church prays for all men throughout the world, except for heretics, to express her horror of apostacy and to distinguish them from her children. But on this day, forever sanctified by the death of our Lord, who died for all men, she makes no exception, and prays for all, naming heathens, heretics and Jews.[7]

---

[1] El Porque de las Ceremonias, c. xxx. Mandato.   [2] O'Brien, Hist. of the Mass, p. 325.   [3] Luke xxii. 41.   [4] El Porque de las Ceremonias, c. xxx. Viernes Sancto.   [5] Exod. xii.   [6] John xviii. xix.   [7] Butler's Feasts and Fasts, p. 258.

Before the prayers, when the celebrant says, "Let us
pray," the deacon sings, "Let us bend our knees," when
all except the celebrant kneel[1] to adore the Lord who
died for us this day. The next instant the sub-deacon
sings, "Arise," when all rise. The celebrant sings
the prayers.[2] At the prayers for the Jews we do not
bend our knees, because in mockery and in derision they
bent their knees before our Lord before they crucified
him.[3] These prayers were offered to God, each Good
Friday, from the first ages of the Church.[4] Following the example of our Lord, we pray according to the
words of St. Paul, "who in the days of his flesh, with a
strong cry and tears, offering up prayers and supplications to him that was able to save."[5] In one of the prayers, supplications are offered for the Emperor of Germany who in the middle ages received from Rome the
authority to spread the faith in the north of Europe.
Now that prayer is not said, except in those parts subject
to the Austrian empire.[6]

After having prayed for all those not belonging to the
fold of the faith, the Church now turns her thoughts to
her children, showing to them the cross, which is a scan-
dal for the Jews, a folly for the Gentiles,[7] but the glory
of the Christians. Putting off the chasuble, the celebrant takes the cross, which, from the evening before
Passion Sunday, has been covered with a violet veil.
Standing on the floor at the epistle side of the sanctuary,[8] he uncovers the top of the cross, saying, "Behold
the wood of the cross on which the salvation of the
world hung," and the choir sings, "Come, let us adore,"
when all but the celebrant fall on their knees. Coming
up the steps of the altar, on the epistle side, he uncovers
the right arm of the cross, repeating the same words in
a higher key. Going to the middle of the altar, he uncovers the whole cross with the same words in a still
higher tone. The celebrant alone sings the first three
words, while the deacon and sub-deacon aid him in singing the remainder. He lays then the cross in the place

---

[1] Gav. p. iv. tit. ix. in Rub. iii.; Merp. iv. t. ix. n. 15. [2] O'Brien. Hist. of the Mass,
p. 212. [3] Math. xxvii. 29. [4] Gueranger, La Passion et La Semaine Ste., p. 547. [5] Heb.
v. 7. [6] Gueranger, Ibidem, p. 550. [7] I. Cor. i. 23. [8] El Porque de las Ceremonias,
c. xxx. Viernes Sancto.

prepared for it before the altar, and, out of respect,[1] only with his stockings covering his feet, and genuflecting three times on both knees, he comes and kisses the image of our Lord nailed to the cross. All in the sanctuary then go two by two through the same ceremony, while it is customary for the clergy to offer the image of the Crucified to the people at the altar-railing to be kissed.

The origin of this ceremony goes back to the time when St. Helen, the mother of Constantine the Great, in the IVth century, recovered the cross on which Christ was crucified. The sacred relic of the sufferings of the Lord was exposed to the people. When they saw the cross, they fell down in adoration of their Lord, who was crucified on it. It became customary for the clergy to expose it on Good Friday each year in Jerusalem, and the holy city was crowded with pilgrims from all parts of the world during Holy Week. The pilgrims brought to their homes in the different countries the story of the cross, and to those who could not go to Jerusalem the clergy exposed a cross in the different churches of the world on Good Friday. Thus it came to pass that in the VIIth century the image of our crucified Lord was shown to the people in every church throughout the world.[2] It was only an image, but it recalled to them their Lord, who died for them. All the respect they gave it was to him who died for us on the cross, the instrument of salvation.

Such is the history and the reason of the imposing rite of the stripping of the cross on Good Friday. The celebrant takes off his chasuble, which is the vestment for the sacrifice. He strips his feet according to the customs of the Eastern nations, like Moses when he approached the burning bush.[3] He genuflects three times on both knees to honor the three times holy Lord, typified by the crucifix. He kisses the image to show how he loves his Lord, for a kiss is a sign of love.

While this impressive ceremony is being carried out, the choristers sing the words of our Lord, in sad and solemn tones, to the Jews who crucified him.[4]

---

[1] O'Brien, Hist. of the Mass, p. 177. [2] By order of Gregory the Great. El Porque de las Ceremonias, c. xxx. Vier. S. [3] Exod. iii. 5. [4] See Goar. Euchol. Græcorum, p. 126 ; Neal, Holy Eastern Church, vi. p. 367.

"O my people, what did I do to you, or in what did I sadden you? Reply to me."[1]

"I led you from the land of Egypt, and you prepared a cross for your Saviour."

Then one choir says in Greek, "O Holy God."

The other choir replies in Latin, "O Holy God."

In Greek, "Holy and Strong."

In Latin, "Holy and Strong."

In Greek, "Holy and Immortal, have mercy on us."

In Latin, "Holy and Immortal, have mercy on us."

Then the choristers continue:

"Because for forty years I led you through the desert; I fed you with manna; I brought you into a real good land: you prepared a cross for your Saviour."

"Holy God," &c.

"What more should I have done to you which I have not done? For I planted you as my most beautiful vineyard, and you became to me most bitter drink; you gave me vinegar to quench my thirst, and with a lance you pierced the side of your Saviour."

"Holy God," &c.

"For you I struck Egypt in their first born, and you gave me up to be scourged, O my people," &c.

"I brought you from the land of Egypt, Pharaoh being drowned in the Red Sea, and you gave me up to the chief priest, O my people," &c.

"I opened the sea before you, and you opened my side with a lance, O my people," &c.

"I went before you in a pillar of a cloud, and you led me to Pilate's hall, O my people," &c.

"I made manna fall for you in the desert, and you fell on me with blows and scourges, O my people," &c.

"I, from the rock, brought forth for you the waters of salvation, and you brought to me vinegar and gall, O my people," &c.

"For you I struck the kings of the Canaanites, and you struck me with a reed, O my people," &c.

"I gave to you a royal sceptre, and you gave to my head a crown of thorns, O my people," &c.

"I raised you up with great power, and you hung me on the gibbet of the cross, O my people," &c.

When these heart-rending "Reproaches" are ended, if the ceremony of kissing the cross is not finished, the choir sings the celebrated hymn, "O faithful cross," composed by Mamert Claudius, in the VIth century, in honor and in remembrance of the holy cross on which our Lord died.

Then they all form into a procession and go to the "Repository," where the Sacred Host has reposed since the day before. With psalms and hymns they march

---

[1] See El Porque de las Ceremonias, c. xxx. Viern. San.

around the church carrying our Lord, till they come to the altar, where the Mass of the Presanctified is said.[1] It is not a Mass in the true sense, as no consecration takes place, only the Host consecrated the day before is consumed by the celebrant, for to-day the world stands appalled at the remembrance of our Lord's death.[2] Mass is the most joyful ceremony man can perform, but there is no joy in the world to-day, when we celebrate the memory of the crucifixion of the Saviour. A part only of the prayers and the ceremonies of the Mass are to be seen in the services of Good Friday, as it is not becoming to represent, mystically, in the Mass, the death of our Lord whom the Church represents as already dead.[3] In the afternoon and evening the "Tenebræ" are chanted for the last time, and all retire to wait for the ceremonies of Holy Saturday.

Such are the ceremonies with which the Church recalls to the minds of men the tragedy of Calvary. The traditions of the early Christians tell us that the face of the dying Lord was turned toward the west, toward Rome, which was to be forever the city of his choice after he had rejected Jerusalem. Tradition says that when the soldiers dug the hole for the cross, they found a tomb and dug up a skull. It was the skull of Adam. Thus the blood of the second Adam, Christ, crimsoned the bones of the first Adam, and by his death wiped out his sin.[4] We also learn that God commanded the paschal lamb to be eaten on the fourteenth noon of the first month, and Christ was crucified on the fifteenth noon, when the moon was on the opposite side of the earth from the sun, so that unbelievers could not say that the darkness over the whole earth was caused by an eclipse of the sun, by the moon coming between the sun and the earth. Even the celebrated Denys, of Athens, afterwards the disciple of St. Paul, cried out, when he saw the sun darken: "Either the God of nature is dying, or the world is dissolving."[5] Thus, when man refused to believe, nature trembled to its centre, the rocks split, and the dead came forth from their graves to bear witness to the death of the son of God.

---

[1] O'Brien, Hist. of the Mass, p. 12. [2] El Porque de las Ceremonias, c. xxx. Viernes Sancto. [3] St. Thomas, p. 119, s. 83, a. 2. [4] S.S. Basil, Ambrose, Chrysostom, Jerome, Origen, etc. [5] Gueranger, La Pas. et La Sem. Ste. p. 576.

V.—HOLY SATURDAY.

When God finished his work of creation, he rested on the Sabbath day. When he ended his work of redemption, he rested in the tomb.[1] One was but a figure of the other. On Holy Saturday, by our rite and services, we recall the rest of our Lord when dead and laid in the tomb; when his blessed soul went down to the limbo of the holy ones of the Old Testament, to tell them of their redemption.

From the earliest ages the Christians celebrated Holy Saturday. Mass,[2] in ancient times, was not said either on Friday or on Saturday of Holy Week.[3] In these ancient times the services began at three in the afternoon and ended in the night, for the people were accustomed to remain[4] in the church till after midnight. The services then of Holy Saturday belong to Easter eve.[5] This we learn by Apostolic traditions.[6] At that time they used to say Mass in the early morning, about the time of the resurrection of our Lord.[7] When the people gave up the custom of spending the night in the church, and fasting so as to receive the blessed Eucharist at the moment of the resurrection, the services were began in the day, and now they are all held on Saturday morning. Still, these old customs can be seen to-day in the services of the Church. Night is mentioned in place of day.[8] The people of the East follow the ways of the early Christians, and say no Mass to-day; but from the IXth century, when the people began to lose their love of prayer and of fasting, the services were begun earlier and earlier in the day, so that now they are commenced in the morning.

At the time announced, the celebrant, in violet vestments, as a sign of penance, with a deacon, sub-deacon and all the clergy, go outside[9] into the porch of the church, where fire is struck from flint. There he blesses the new fire and the five grains of incense, with the prayers

---

[1] Durandus, Rationale Div. L. vi. c. lxxviii. n. 1. [2] De Consecrat., dist. 3, Sabbato. [3] Decret. Innocen. I. [4] St. Aug. Sermo. ccxxi. in Vig. Pasch. [5] De Consecrat. dist. 6, in Jejuniis. [6] Benedict XIV. De Fest. D. N. J. Christi, De Sab. S. n. 2. [7] Tertul. I. II. ad. Ux. c. 4 ; St. Jerome in Cap. xxv. Math. [8] O'Brien, Hist. of the Mass, p. 18 ; El Porque de las Ceremonias, c. xxx., Sabado Santo. [9] Benedictus XIV. de Fest. D. N. J. Christi Sab. s. n. 50.

given in the Missal. Before this, all the lamps and candles in the church were put out. These ceremonies are deeply mystical. Our Lord says: "I am the light of the world."[1] Light, then, is a type of the son of God. All lights are put out, for he was put to death. The flinty stone, from which the fire is struck, tells us of Christ coming forth from the grave, when he passed through the rock. He is the stone struck by Moses in the desert,[2] "for the rock was Christ;"[3] "the stone which the builders rejected, the same is become the head of the corner,"[4] the stone cut from the mountain without hands, which filled the whole earth.[5] The fire coming forth from the flinty rock tells us of our Lord coming forth from the rock when he rose from the dead—when his body passed through the solid rock.[6] In the Old Testament a light forever burned before the Ark of the Covenant, a figure of the light now ever burning before the Lord upon our altars. All candles and lights in the church must be lighted from the fire blessed on Holy Saturday. That light represents the light of faith burning in our souls. It tells us of the light of heaven revealed by God to man. The lights of the tabernacle and of the temple told of the revelation made to man. All lights are put out in the church before the fire is blessed, to tell of the Old Testament passing away, because it was fulfilled by the death of our Lord.[7] The fire is blessed outside of the church, for the tomb of our Lord was beyond the walls of Jerusalem.[8] The five grains of incense tell of the incense and of the perfumes with which the holy women came to anoint the body of the dead Lord.[9]

When the fire has been blessed with incense and holy water,[10] the deacon takes the long staff, with its three candles in the form of a triangle,[11] and as soon as he comes into the church he lights one of the candles, and in a low tone sings, "The light of Christ," while the choir replies, "Thanks be to God." It tells how God the Father was revealed to man in the beginning of the world. Coming to the middle of the church he lights the second candle,

---

[1] John viii. 12.　[2] Exod. xvii. 6.　[3] I Cor. x. 4.　[4] Math. xxi. 42., Ps. c. xvii. 22.
[5] Dan. ii. 34.　El Porque de las Ceremonias, c. xxx. Sabado Santo.　[6] Math. xxviii. 2.
[7] Durandus, Rationale. Div. L. vi. c. lxxx. n. 1.; Gueranger, La Pas et la Sem. Ste p. 638.　[8] Ibidem, p. 685.　[9] Ibidem, p. 635; El Porque de las Ceremonias. c. xxx. Cirio.
[10] El Porque de las Ceremonias, c. xxx. Sabado Santo.　[11] Benedic. XIV., Ibidem, n. 51.

and sings in a higher tone the same words. It recalls how God the Son was revealed to the Jews by the prophets. Drawing near to the altar, he lights the third candle and sings in a high key the same words. It typifies the revelation of God the Holy Ghost to the world. Thus it tells of the unity and trinity of God revealed at the time of the Apostles.[1]

We cannot find the beginning of these ceremonies. Pope Zachary, in the middle of the VIIIth century, mentions them. Pope Leo IV., in the IXth century, tells us of these rites of Holy Saturday. In some churches they used to bless the fire each day, because in the church all things used in the service of the Lord are blessed.[2] We must conclude with the words of an ancient writer,[3] speaking of this ceremony: "This is the remains of antiquity." No writer gives the origin of the staff with the three candles carried by the deacon. Even Martine says nothing of it; and we conclude that these sacred rites come from the Apostolic times.

When the deacon comes to the sanctuary he blesses the paschal candle. Only bishops and priests can bless. There is but one exception for the deacon on Holy Saturday. The deacon always blesses the paschal candle. This is the reason. The holy women came to the sepulchre and announced the resurrection of Christ, and as St. Augustine[4] and St. Chrysostom say, it was right for woman, who first sinned, to be the first to tell that sin had been wiped out. Thus, the young deacon, who represents the weaker sex, blesses the paschal candle.[5] While all the other clergy are clothed in violet vestments during the blessing of the fire and of the candle, the deacon alone is in white to honor the holy women who told the Apostles of the resurrection of our Lord.

In all the rites and services of the Church, the candle represents our Lord.[6] It must be made of beeswax.[7] The wax from the bodies of virgin bees tells of his body coming from the immaculate body of his Mother. The wick within that candle tells of his holy soul within his body, while the flame typifies his Divinity.[8] In the flame of a

---

[1] Gavantus, El Porque de las Ceremonias, c. xxx. Sabado Santo; Gueranger, Ibidem, pp. 638, 639. [2] Benedictus XIV. de Fest. cviii. n. 50. [3] Pouget, Inst. Cath. T. I. p. 647. [4] St. Aug. Ser. 252, 144 de Temp. T. 5. [5] El Porque de las Ceremonias, c. xxx. Cirio. [6] St. Aug. Sermo. l. de Cero Pasch. n. ii. [7] O'Brien, Hist. of the Mass, p. 182. [8] El Porque de las Cerem. c. xxx. Cirio.

burning bush the Divinity appeared to Moses. In the flame of fiery tongues the Holy Ghost came down upon the Apostles. In the flame of the pillar of fire God appeared and led his people to the promised land.[1]

The paschal candle, before being lighted, tells us of the pillar of cloud[2] which led the children of Israel, and when lighted it represents the pillar of fire.[3] It is lighted from the fire blessed outside the church, to tell of Christ illuminating the world by his doctrine when he rose from the dead. It is blessed by the deacon singing the beautiful words composed by St. Augustine :[4] "O, now rejoice, Angelic hosts." The music was composed by St. Ambrose.[5] Thus, the large candle tells of Christ with the transcendent splendors of the Son of God rising gloriously from the sepulchre.[6] The deacon imbeds in the five holes in the wax the five grains of incense, to tell of the fragrant incenses and spices with which they laid away the body of the murdered Lord.[7] They are put in the form of a cross, to teach us of the five wounds of our Saviour on the cross.

The paschal candle is lighted during the Gospel at all the Masses from Holy Saturday till Ascension Thursday, when it is put out at the end of the Gospel. It is lighted at the Gospel, for it tells of Christ enlightening the world by the light of his Gospel. It is quenched on the day he went up into heaven, to typify that now all revelation is ended. Thus, the paschal candle tells us of Christ rising from the dead.[8]

When the paschal candle is quenched on Ascension Thursday, it is kept till the following Holy Saturday, and the wax, mixed with chrism, is made into the form of little lambs, blessed by the Pope. They are kept till Low-Sunday, when, after Communion, they are given to the people, as a figure of the "Lamb of God who taketh away the sins of the world."[9] The nuns cover the wax with beautiful designs, and the people wear them around their necks. They are known by the name of the "Agnus Dei."

The beginning of the ceremonies of the paschal candle

[1] Rupartus de Divin. Offic. c. xxviii.   [2] El Porque de las Ceremonias, c. xxx. Cirio.
[3] St. Aug. de Cirio. Pasch. n. 11.   [4] O'Brien, Hist. of the Mass, p. 96.   [5] Ibidem.
[6] Concil. Toletan, IV.   [7] El Porque de las Ceremonias, c. xxx. Cirio.   [8] Concil. Toletan.
VI., c. viii. in 633 under Pope Honorius I.   [9] John i. 29.

and of the "Agnus Dei," is lost in the silence of the catacombs, beyond the times of the persecutions. No time can be found when the paschal candle was not blessed in the cathedrals. Toward the beginning of the Vth century Pope Zozimus mentions it, and afterwards Pope Zachary allowed the ceremony to be carried out in small churches.[1]

When the candle is blessed, the celebrant reads twelve lessons from the Old Testament, in honor of the twelve Apostles taught by our Lord, and of the twelve prophets, and of the figures of our holy religion hidden in the Old Testament.[2] During the ceremony of baptizing the newly converted, which took a long time in the days of the Apostles, the clergy used to read twelve parts of the Old Testament to the people, and that was the origin of the twelve lessons read to-day before Mass.[3] In Rome they are read both in Latin and in Greek, to tell that the Pope is the head of both the Latin and Greek Rites. A prayer follows each lesson, and expresses the desire of the Church for her children. Those who are to be baptized are in their places, and the whole ceremony is grave, yet beautiful. The many genuflections, the violet vestments, the air of penance, the burning candles, all proclaim in powerful symbols, signs and ceremonies, that the time has come when the newly baptized will rise with their Lord glorious from the waters of baptism.[4] Such are the ceremonies coming down to us from the times of the Apostles, when all the converts were prepared during long months for their baptism on Holy Saturday.

When the twelve lessons are ended, the celebrant with the clergy go in procession to the baptismal font. Like the pillar of cloud guiding the children of Israel to the promised land, the paschal candle is carried before those who are to be baptized. The promised land was a figure of heaven, the pillar of cloud a type of Christ, who guides us all to heaven. The Holy Chrism and the Oil of the Catechumens are brought to be used in blessing the waters,[5] while the choir sings the Psalms of David. All monuments of the past tell us that the blessing of the

---

[1] Benedict XIV. de Fest. D. N. J. Christi. c. vii. n. 54 ; Molani de Agno Dei. c. vi.
[2] Durandus, Rationale Div. L. vi. c. lxxxi. n. 10. [3] Gueranger, La Pas et la Sem. Ste. p. 648, 649. [4] El Porque de las Ceremonias, c. xxx. Bened. de la Pila. [5] El Porque de las Ceremonias, c. xxx. Benedic. de la Pila.

waters of baptism was instituted by the Apostles. The great Saints and the Fathers of the Church tell of these ceremonies in their writings. On the walls of the catacombs are to be seen pictures of the baptized, likened by the persecuted Christians to the fishes of Christ swimming in the waters of salvation.[1]

With beautiful prayers the waters are blessed. The celebrant stops in his sublime prayers, and, with his right hand, he divides the waters in the form of a cross,[2] to show that from the cross these waters receive their power to wipe out sin.[3] Continuing, he stops again and touches the water. The celebrant represents our Lord, who, when he was baptized, the water, by touching his most holy person, received the power to baptize and wipe out sin.[4] Three crosses are made over the water to tell us that by the work of the three Persons of the Holy Trinity, salvation is given to man in baptism.[5] He divides the water towards the four quarters of the world, to typify that our Lord sent his Apostles into the four quarters of the world to baptize all nations.[6] He breathes three times on the water in the form of a cross, because, when our Lord sent the Holy Ghost, which means, in the ancient language, a breath,[7] upon his Apostles, he breathed upon them. He was the same Holy Spirit who moved over the face of the waters on the morning of the creation,[8] who shook the upper chamber with a mighty wind when he came upon the Apostles, and who now works all these wonders by the waters of baptism. The celebrant breathes three times in the form of a cross, to show that to the sufferings of the cross is joined the work of the holy Trinity in the salvation of the race.[9] Then the paschal candle is immersed three times in the water with the words, "that the Holy Spirit may fill this font with his fullness," as when he came down in the form of a dove on Christ, immersed in the waters of the Jordan, when he came in a cloud in the transfiguration, and when he came upon the Apostles, figured by the paschal candle immersed in the water, while the raising up of the candle

---

[1] See diagrams and copies of pictures in the Catacombs, made by the French Government. [2] El Porque de las Ceremonias, c. xxx. Ben. de la Pila.; St. Aug. Contra Julian. Pelag. n. 42. [3] Gueranger, Ibidem, p. 695. [4] St. Aug. Sermo. xvi. in Circumcis. Dom. n. 3. [5] Catena Aurea Sup. Cap. xvii. Math. [6] XXVIII. 19, Mazzinellus, Off. Major, Hebdom. p. 293. [7] Gueranger, Ibidem, p. 698. [8] Acts ii. 2. [9] El Porque de las Ceremonias, c. xxx. Bened. de la Pila. Gavantus, etc.

tells of baptism raising man from sin to glory.[1] The third
time the celebrant plunges the candle into the water; before taking it out he breathes upon the water in the form
of the Greek letter with which the word Spirit begins in
that language,[2] praying that the water may receive the
whole power of the Holy Spirit. The candle is then
taken out of the water.[3] The candle tells of Christ, the
second person of the Holy Trinity. From him, as well
as from the Father, comes the Holy Ghost, and with the
candle we pray that the same Holy Ghost may come
down into the waters by his power.

When the prayers are ended, the people are sprinkled
with the holy water, and some of it is kept for the people to take to their homes as a remembrance of their
baptism, and to use as holy water.

This is the holy, or the Easter water, but another ceremony is held in order to prepare it for baptism. From
Holy Thursday the Church has guarded the Holy Oils,
and to sanctify still further the water he pours upon it the
Oil of the Catechumens in the form of a cross, telling by
that ceremony that, as the Lord Jesus was anointed by
the Holy Ghost for the redemption of mankind, thus this
water is now anointed with oil for the redemption of all
in baptism. The celebrant then pours upon the waters the
Holy Chrism, which tells of Christ giving to the waters
power unto the remission of sin. He then pours both
the Oils of the Catechumens and the Holy Chrism together
on the waters, in the form of a cross, to typify that they
have received the power of the three Persons of the Trinity[4] to work their wonders in the souls of men when they
are baptized.

After this the Catechumens are baptized when they have
been prepared beforehand for the ceremony. The baptismal rite is followed by the Litany of the Saints, to call
down the aid of all the holy ones of heaven on the newly
baptized, that they may keep the faith given them by
God by this holy sacrament. While the choir sings the
Litany, the clergy prostrate themselves on their faces before the altar to implore the grace of God upon the peo-

---

[1] El Porque de las Ceremonias, c. xxx. Benedic. de la Pila; Durandus, etc.; Gavantus,
etc. [2] El Porque de las Ceremonias, c. xxx Bened. de la Pila. [3] El Porque de las Ceremonias, c. xxx. Bened. de la Pila. [4] El Porque de las Ceremonias. c. xxx. Bened. de
la Pila.

ple and upon those to-day baptized.' In former times, when a great number received the sacrament of baptism, they used to sing the Litany three times. Now, at the words "Sinners," etc., the celebrant and his ministers rise and continue the Litany and the prayers.

The Mass of Holy Saturday now begins. It bears many of the marks of its ancient origin. The altars are covered, for the Church begins to celebrate the glories of the resurrection. Formerly the Mass was begun long before the break of day on Easter morning, and the ceremonies still retain their ancient traits.' The violet vestments worn since Septuagesima Sunday give place to white and gold in honor of the risen Lord. No Introit is said, following the custom before the time of Pope Celestin.' The Mass then has no heading, for our Head lies dead in the grave. The Angelic Hymn, "Glory be to God in the highest,"' is sung, and the bells, the joyful tones of which were heard no more from Holy Thursday, burst forth in all their tinkling tones from the sanctuary, or pealing sounds from the steeples, to tell of the joyful news of the resurrection of our Lord. The Hebrew word " Alleluia—praise ye the Lord,"' is sung by the celebrant three time to praise the three times Holy Lord, who has risen from the grave. No candles are carried at the singing of the Gospel, to typify that the resurrection of the Lord is not yet known, for light represents knowledge.' The Creed is not sung, to tell of the silence of the women who came to anoint our Lord's body.' The Mass is very short, because the children who were to be baptized would be tired out before the end.'

Such are a few ideas of the meanings of the services of Holy Saturday. It is with regret that the writer sees that he cannot, in a book of this kind for the people, give all the meanings of these ceremonies filled with the deepest mysticism. In the early ages of faith, the services used to begin at three in the afternoon and last till the dawn of Easter Sunday. Then there were no Vesper Services, but when the people would not fast, and the services were commenced in the morning, a small Vesper service was given at the end of the Mass.'

---

¹ El Porque de las Ceremonias, c. xxx. Ben. de la Plla. ² Pope Innocent Epert. 11, etc., cap. 4. El Porque. c. xxx. Ben. de la Plla. ³ El Porque de las Cerem. c. xxx. Ben. de la Plla. ⁴ St. Liguori. Caerem. Mis. c. iv. n. 8. ⁵ Butler's Feasts and Fasts, p. 275. ⁶ Durandus, Rationale Div., Ibidem, n. 5. ⁷ Wal. Straho de Rebus Eccl. c. xxii. etc. ⁸ Meratus, p. 1179, Benedictus XIV. de Fest. D. N. J. Christi c. lx. n. 68. ⁹ Gueranger la Pas. et la Sem. Ste. p. 720.

INTERIOR OF ST. MARY MAJOR, ROME.

Chapter VIII.—The Easter Season.

The word Easter comes from the name of the old Teutonic goddess of spring, Ostera, or Eostre, whose feast was celebrated by the Druids and the pagans of the north of Europe during the month of April.[1] Among the people of the south of Europe, from the times of their conversion to the Christian religion, it is called the Pasch, from the Hebrew word which means the Passage of the Red Sea, when the Israelites were delivered from the land of Egypt.[2]

On the fourteenth moon of the month of March, the children of Israel eat their Paschal Lamb in remembrance of their delivery by Moses from the land of Egypt, a type of Christ by whom all men are delivered from the power of the devil.[3] The people of Israel took the blood of the paschal lamb and sprinkled it on the door-posts of their houses, by which they were saved from death, from the hand of the destroying Angel,[4] a type of the blood of Christ by which we are saved from everlasting death.

The Easter Season was instituted by the Apostles.[5] No writer has doubted that such was its origin. The Fathers of the Apostolic age call it the Feast of feasts and the Solemnity of solemnities. In these early times it lasted for a whole week.[6] For that reason the Offices of the Breviary are quite short on Easter week. During each of these days the people were obliged to hear Mass.[7] That continued to be the law till the XIIth century, when the people not attending, the obligation was taken away.

According to the Latin Rite, Easter is celebrated on the first Sunday after the fourteenth moon following the vernal equinox, or following the 21st of March. The Jews

---

[1] Ven. Bede, L. de Rat. Temp. c. 13. [2] St. Aug. Sermo. vll. De Pasch. n. 1. [3] Exod. xii. [4] Benedictus XIV. De Fest. D. N. J. Christi, c. ix. n. 1. [5] St. Augustine. Epl. 54, Gregory Nazian., etc. [6] Benedictus, Ibidem, n. 2. [7] Concil Lugd. Martine de Antiq. Eccl. Diclp. c. 25, n. 1, et seq.; Can. 1. de Consec. Dist. 3.

held their Easter on the fourteenth moon of the month of March.[1] Thus the Christian Easter always falls on Sunday, while the Jewish Easter may come on any day of the week. The time of holding the Easter services is a matter of discipline and not of faith.[2] Discipline can change, faith never, and the Apostles allowed the converted Jews this freedom of discipline to show that the Church did not condemn, but fulfilled the law of Moses. But the Apostles directed Easter to be held on the first Sunday following the fourteenth moon after the vernal equinox, while the Jews held their Easter on the four-teenth moon of the month of Abib or Nisan,[3] corresponding to our March. In Rome, and in all parts of the pagan world, the converts followed the directions of the Apostles regarding the celebration of Easter. So as not to turn the Jews away from the Church, in the first Council of Jerusalem they were commanded only to abstain from things suffocated and from blood, while they could keep many of the ways and customs of the Mosaic law. This was allowed them till the time of the destruction of their city and of their temple in the year seventy, forty years from the death of Christ. The Apostles then saw the prophecy of our Lord and of the prophets fulfilled, that the law of Moses would cease, and that the Jews would be scattered throughout the world. From that time the Jewish ceremonies have been condemned. Two exceptions were made : one regarding to abstinence from things strangled and from blood, the other regarding the celebration of Easter by those who followed the Eastern Rites.

One part of Asia Minor for a long time refused to change from the Jewish to the Christian time, of celebrating Easter. They claimed that St. John, the Evangelist, allowed them the Jewish custom, which history tells us he did, because there were so many converts from the Jews among them.[4] St. John became bishop of Ephesus, and died there in ripe old age, the last of the Apostles, and all loved him and respected what he taught. But they differed from the rest of the Christian world in this matter of celebrating Easter. In 150 Pope St. Ana-

---

[1] Exod. xxii. 6; De Consec. dist. 8 Nosce. et seq. [2] Benedictus XIV. De Fest. D. N. J. Christi, c. ix. n. 5. [3] Exod. xii. 42 ; Num. ix. 12 ; John xix. 31. [4] Gueranger, Le Temps Paschal, p. 5.

cletus sat upon the chair of Peter, and St. Polycarp, the disciple and the successor of St. John, as bishop of Ephesus, came to Rome to see St. Anacletus relative to the celebration of Easter. As it is a matter of discipline, which may change, and not of doctrine, which never changes, St. Polycarp continued to celebrate the feast on the same day as the Jews. In place of any feeling arising between him and the Pope, following the manners of the early Christians, they parted with the kiss of peace,[1] and St. Polycarp departed for Ephesus without settling the matter. Some years passed when Polycrates, the successor of St. Polycarp, with all the bishops of Asia Minor, wrote to Pope St. Victor, asking if Easter could not be celebrated on the same day with the Jews. The Pope gathered all the bishops of the world in a council in Rome, and all were of one mind, that Easter should be held, not on the fourteenth moon of the month of March, like the Jews, but on the first Sunday following the fourteenth moon following the vernal equinox.[2] The same was the decision of many other Councils in various parts of the world. The Council of Ephesus, presided over by Polycrates, alone held out against the whole Church. We see by this how hard it is to change old religious customs.

Thinking that it was time to bring all back to the rule laid down by St. Peter and the other Apostles, so as to break up the Jewish custom allowed by St. John in the church of Ephesus, Pope St. Victor pronounced sentence against the churches of Asia Minor, which separated them from the centre of authority, Rome. That sentence, pronounced only after long trials on the part of Rome to unite all together, excited sorrow in the hearts of many bishops, above all of St. Irenæus, the disciple of St. John and the successor of Lazarus as bishop of Lyons. He asked the Pope not to carry out the sentence against the churches and cut them off from the fold,[3] for, as he said, they acted thus through want of knowledge rather than through stubbornness. The sentence was recalled, and in the year 276 St. Anatolius, bishop of Laodicea, tells us that soon after all the churches of Asia Minor changed from the Jewish to the Christian day of celebrating Easter.

---

[1] Benedictus, Ibidem, n. 5.   [2] De Conscer. Dist. 3, Celebritatem.   [3] Brev. Rom. Of. St. Irenæ.

All the world was then united regarding the time of holding the Easter solemnities. But soon a remarkable turn of affairs took place. Many of the churches of Syria, Sicily and of Mesopotamia, returned to the Jewish time of holding Easter. That change from the Apostolic customs afflicted the Church, and the council of Nice was called. One of the first matters brought up by the bishops was that Easter should be celebrated on Sunday; "all dispute laid aside, the brethren of the East will celebrate Easter on the same day as the Romans, the Alexandrians and all the other faithful."[1] The time of holding Easter was such an important question, that St. Athanasius, afterwards archbishop of Alexandria, tells us that the Council was called for two reasons, to establish unity in the celebration of Easter, and to condemn the errors of Arius, who denied the Divinity of our Lord.[2] At that time Alexandria, of which St. Mark was the first bishop, was celebrated for her learned men. The Council of Nice directed that the bishop of that city was to make out the calculations each year relating to the time of celebrating Easter. The Roman Pontiff wrote to all the churches in the world, which were represented by their bishops in that the first general Council, telling them on what day Easter should be kept. From that time the custom was for many ages for the Pope to address an Encyclical Letter to all the churches of the world each year relating to the celebration of the Easter time.[3] Thus the whole Christian world was again united. But in after years, when the British Isles were converted, some difficulties arose among them relating to Easter, some holding to the custom of the churches of Asia Minor, others, and the greater part, to the time taught by St. Augustine, the Apostle of England, sent by Pope Gregory the Great, and St. Patrick, the Apostle of Ireland, sent by Pope Celestine I.[4] In the Council of Whitby, in 664, they settled the matter by following the Roman Rite.[5]

The Easter, or Paschal Season, begins on Easter Sunday and ends on the Saturday after Pentecost. It is the most holy part of the year, and to this season all the other feasts relate. It is the time of the triumph of the

---

[1] Spicil. Soles, t. iv. p. 541.   [2] Epist. ad Afros Episcopos.   [3] Concil. Galliæ, t. i.
[4] Am. Cycloped. Art. Celestine.   [5] Life of St. Cuthbert, etc.

Son of God.[1] It is the figure of heaven. It is a picture of the glories of the hereafter. On Easter Sunday man, in the person of the Son of God, triumphed over hell, and regained his inheritance lost in Adam.[2] During the last week we have seen in signs, symbols and ceremonies, Christ the man, weak, suffering, dying, dead. During this season we are to see in type, figures and rites, grand and beautiful, the same Christ the Lord, powerful, conquering and triumphant over hell, sin and death, the first-born of these two, as he rises gloriously from the tomb.[3] "For by a man came death, and by a man, the resurrection of the dead. And as in Adam all die; so also, in Christ, all shall be made alive."[4]

To yearly celebrate the resurrection of our Lord is the object of the Easter services. Sin is the death of the soul, and that the people may rise in glory and in triumph from the grave of sin, Septuagesima Time, Lent and Holy Week are given to the people to prepare themselves for the sacraments during the Easter Season. All who have received their first Communion must receive the Holy Eucharist each year during the Easter Time, which in this country lasts from the first Sunday of Lent till Trinity Sunday.

The uncreated wisdom, the Holy Spirit which dwells within the Church and teaches her all things,[5] guided her in celebrating Easter on the Sunday appointed, and not on any day of the week like the Jews. On the first Sunday of creation, God, from everlasting night, brought forth the light which illuminates the world around us. It was but a figure of the Wisdom of the Father, his only begotten Son coming forth from the sepulchre on that first Easter Sunday, when, with the transcendent splendors of the Divinity, he passed through the solid rock. Easter Sunday is the greatest feast of the Church; and the other Sundays of the year are but so many little Easters, coming each week to remind us of our risen Lord.[6] Thus, to break the last link which held the early Christians to the law of the Jews, Easter was fixed on Sunday. The laws of Moses and of the Jewish Sabbath were gone forever,

---

[1] Fabri Conciones Dom. Resurrec. Concio I. [2] Gueranger, Le Temps. p. 1. [3] St. Chrysostom, etc. [4] I. Cor. xv. 21, 22. [5] John xiv. 26. [6] St. Aug. Epist. l. n. 23.

and the laws of Christ and the Christian Sunday took their place.[1]

The Easter Season is like a continual Sunday. For that reason the first week is like a continual Easter, and was once celebrated with great pomp and ceremony.[2] The law of the Church will allow no fasting for forty days from Easter to Ascension Thursday, following the words of the Lord: "Can the children of the marriage fast as long as the bridegroom is with them?"[3]

The most rigid and austere of the religious Orders of the East, going back to the times of the Apostles, keep that rule. The celestial song of the "Alleluia,"[4] is heard continually in the services. All Christians, from the earliest ages, considered the Easter Time as a perpetual series of feasts, as Tertullian tells us.[5] St. Ambrose, instructing the faithful of Milan, says: "If the Jews were not content to celebrate a weekly Sabbath feast, but also a whole Sabbath lasting a year, how much more should we honor the resurrection of our Lord? Thus, we celebrate the fifty days of Pentecost as a part of the Paschal Season.[6] These days are seven whole weeks in length, and Pentecost is the eighth day after.[7] During that time the Church forbids fasting, as on the Sundays of the year, for all these days are like one whole Sunday."[8]

In the Apostolic times the people used to go to Communion each day they heard Mass; for we read that they met daily, * * breaking bread.[9] It made them saints. It gave them strength to bear their persecutions and suffer martyrdom. In after times they became negligent, and did not receive so often, till at length the Church made a law in the beginning of the IVth century, obliging all to receive the Holy Eucharist on Easter Sunday, Pentecost and Christmas.[10]

Two hundred years afterwards we find that those who did not obey that law were not to be considered as Catholics.[11] That remained the rule for many centuries afterwards, when the law was restricted to the Paschal Time alone.[12] We find the same custom carried out in England

[1] I. Council of Jerusalem. [2] Concil. Toletan. VI. in 683 under Pope Honorius I. [3] Mark ii. 19. [4] St. Aug. vol. vi. 299, et Enar. in Psalm CVI. n. 1. [5] De Idolat. c. xiv. [6] St. Aug. Epist. xxxv. n. 21. [7] St. Aug. Sermo. viii. de Decem. Plag. et Præcept. n. 18. [8] St. Ambrose in Luc. l. viii. c. xxv. [9] O'Brien, Hist. of the Mass, p. 371; Acts ii. 46. [10] Concil. Eliber in 305. [11] Concil. Agathen. I. c. xvii. in 506 under Pope Symmachus. [12] Concil. Ratisbon II. in 1524 under Pope Clement VII.

after her conversion by St. Augustine. We find it in the writings of Egbert, archbishop of York.[1] We find it was the rule in France by command of the council of Tours. In some other parts of the Christian world they used to go to Communion on each of the three last days of Holy Week, as well as at Easter. But at length the people became relax and did not keep that law.

Towards the beginning of the XIIIth century, at the call of Pope Innocent III., the IVth Lateran Council met, and, with regret, seeing that the people did no more frequent the table of the Lord, as in the times following the Apostles, the Council decreed that they were obliged to receive the blessed Eucharist only once each year at the Paschal Time.[2] So as to show that the negligence of the people could not go any farther, the Council declares that those who will dare to break that law, shall, while living, be forbidden the Church, and dying, be deprived of Christian burial, as though they had in their lives renounced the Christian religion.[3] To give all a chance to approach the sacraments, afterwards Pope Eugenius IV. allowed the yearly Communion to take place between Palm Sunday and Low Sunday.[4] The same was decreed at another time.[5] For no cause except when exempt by their bishop or parish priest, or ordered to defer it by their confessor, were the people allowed to put off the yearly Communion.[6] At another time they were commanded to receive in their own parish,[7] and the bishop was himself to look after tramps and see they went to the sacraments.[8] Even servants working in the monasteries were obliged to receive in their own parish churches,[9] and when the people were sick, the parish priests were directed to bring them Communion to their houses.[10] In America the Easter Communion can be received from the first Sunday of Lent till Trinity Sunday.[11]

By the ancient writers, the Easter Time is called in Latin, Quinquagesima, and in Greek, Pentecost,[12] both words meaning fifty, because it lasts for fifty days.[13] It is

---

[1] Gueranger, Le Temps Paschal, p 14. [2] In 1215. [3] Gueranger, Le Temps Paschal, p. 14. [4] Const. Fide Digna in 1440. [5] Concil. Colon. I. in 1536, under Pope Paul III. p. 7, c. xix. [6] Concil. Mediola, n. XI. under Pope Pius IV. p. 2, c. iv., in 1565. [7] Concil. Mediol. XII., t. 1, c. ii., in 1569, under Pius V. [8] Ibidem, c. xiv. [9] Concil. Mediolan., XV., p. 1, c. x. [10] See Concil. Trident, S. XXII., c. xi. ; Concil. Mediolan, n. XVI., c. viii., 1582, under Gregory XIII. [11] O'Brien, Hist. of the Mass, p. 372. [12] St. Aug. Sermo. CCX. in Quadragesima, n. 8. [13] See St. Aug. Epist. LV., n. 28.

a continuation of the glories of the resurrection, and signifies the everlasting joys and pleasures awaiting us in
heaven,[1] after the trials and sufferings in this valley of
death through which we must pass, like our Lord.[2]   Each
fiftieth year among the Jews was their year of Jubilee,
when all their debts were blotted out and their slaves were
set at liberty, a figure of our fifty days of Easter Time,
when all our sins are blotted out by our good works during our penance and fasting of the Septuagesima and
Lenten Seasons.   Thus we celebrate two Seasons—one
before Easter, when we do penance, a figure of this world
of penance and of sorrows; the other after Easter, when
we rejoice, a figure of the other world of glory.[3]   From
the first ages of the Church during the first of these holy
Seasons, the people spent their time in the churches on
their bended knees in prayer; but when the Easter Season came, they stood while praying in the church.[4]   Thus,
it is a time of joy, for it tells of the time spent by our Lord
among his Apostles after his rising from the dead.[5]   From
this comes the custom of the people standing at the
prayers at High Masses during the Sundays of the year,
which are all consecrated to the resurrection of Christ
from the dead.[6]   This is mentioned by many of the first
councils and fathers of the early times.

In the Offices and services of the Church the Hebrew
word, "Alleluia," is often sung.[7]   Many writers have given
different meanings of the word,[8] but it seems to mean,
"Praise ye the Lord."   St. John often heard it sung by
Angels before the throne of God.[9]   It tells then of the
joys of heaven.   The last part of the word, "ia," was
never pronounced but by the high priest once each year,
when he went behind the veil into the Holy of Holies,
clothed in all the grandeur of his sacerdotal robes.[10]   "O
happy Alleluia, which we shall one day sing in heaven,"
says St. Augustine.   "Let us also sing here below Alleluia, though we now live in pain and trouble, that we
may sing it there in perfect security."[11]   Thus the penitential Season before Easter represents this life on earth

---

[1] St. Aug., ibidem. [2] Butler's Feasts and Fasts, p. 313. [3] St. Aug. Enarac. in Ps.
cxlviii. n. 1; Durandus, Rationale Div. L. vi. c. lxxxvi, n. 17. [4] St. Aug. Ep., l. 5, n.
28. [5] 75 Dist. Scire. [6] Butler's Feasts and Fasts, p. 311. [7] St. Liguori, De Cærem.
Mis., c. vi. n. 1. [8] See Teaching Truth by Signs and Ceremonies, p. 171. [9] Apoc.
xix, 1. [10] Cornel. Lap. Calmet. Bellarm., etc. [11] Ser. 256.

while the Paschal Season after Easter represents the other life in heaven.

Spiritual happiness fills the souls of those, who, like their Lord, have passed through the sufferings of Lent and Holy Week and risen with him at Easter to the glories of a better and a more perfect life. Of all times of the year this Season is filled with the deepest mysteries. It is the culminating point of the whole year. All which has gone before has been but like so many preparations for the Easter Season. The pious waitings of Advent, the joyful holidays of Christmas, the penances of Septuagesima, the fastings of Lent and the sorrows of Holy Week, all are like so many steps by which we arrive at the sublime mysteries of the Easter Season. To show us the greatness of this time, God gives us two wonderful works in which to see his power—the raising of our Lord from the dead at Easter, and the coming down of the Holy Ghost at Pentecost. Again, as a further showing forth of his power, he gives us the Easter of the Israelites and the Easter of the Christians, the Pentecost of Sinai and the Pentecost of the Church. The Easter of the Israelites, when led by Moses, they passed through the waters of the Dead Sea, was but a figure of the Christians; when led by Christ, they pass through the waters of baptism. The Pentecost of Sinai, when God came down, and in the figure of fire gave his law to the Jews, was but a figure of the Christian Pentecost, when the Holy Ghost came down in the figure of fiery tongues, and wrote his law in the hearts of the Apostles.[1] The law of Moses was but the dim twilight of the morning of the world, till all was lighted up with the splendors of the rising Son of God, when he came forth from the tomb to enlighten the world and to fulfil the figures of the Old Testament.

The human race was dead, dead with the sin of Adam, and to bring them forth from that spiritual death, he came and died, and rose to tell us how to die and how to rise into the happy eternity—into the everlasting life of which our Easter Time is but a figure. The Holy Church then, say the Fathers, wishes us all to rise from sin as he rose from death, and to die no more by doing wrong.

The wonderful wisdom of God, who leads all creatures

---

[1] St. Aug. Contra Faustum, l. xxxii., n. 12.

to the end for which he created them, disposed all nature
in such a way, that the world around us is a figure of the
world of grace. From the reception of the sacraments,
and from the contemplation of the mysteries of the sufferings, death and resurrection of our Lord, our souls are
to begin to grow stronger and stronger in the grace of
God. Nature around shows us that God has made the
world we see to be a figure of the unseen world of grace.
Now, in the spring-time of the year, when we are celebrating the glories of the risen Son of God, the plants and
flowers are springing forth from the ground, the trees are
putting on their leaves, all nature rises from the death of
winter and tells man to rise from the death of sin, from
the sleep of indifference and of neglect, to that other and
to that higher life of grace and of innocence with the glorified Lord. At Christmas Time, the days had just began
to grow longer, while the darkness and the shadows of
deep winter stretched across the earth. All was in harmony with the humble birth of the infant God. But now
when he has gained his triumph over the old enemy of
the human race, when he has risen from the grave to
show how man may rise from sin, the time of the equal
days and nights has passed, and the days grow longer
and longer. Light is a figure of grace in the heart of
man, and the increasing light of the days after Easter,
typifies the increase of grace in the hearts of the people
by the sacraments received at Easter.[1]

God rose from the dead on Sunday, the first day of the
week, the day he created light, and he rested in the
tomb the last day of the week. The day he rested after
the creation, Saturday, tells of the rest of God after the
creation of the material world, while Sunday tells of the
rest of God after the redemption of our race. Thus
Saturday recalls the creation, while Sunday recalls the
redemption; thus speak the great doctors of the Church;
thus Saturday, the Sabbath of the Jews, is gone, and Sunday, the Sabbath of the Christians, has taken its place.
Sunday is but a continual Easter, in remembrance of the
redemption of the world. It was well to keep the Sabbath of the Israelites, but God came and hid the light of

---

[1] Gueranger, Le Temps Paschal, p. 20.

his Divinity under the veil of our human nature, and, after having fulfilled all the types and figures of the law of the Old Testament in his sacred person—after having redeemed the race, he rested on Saturday in the grave. "Let us leave, then, the Jews, the slaves of the love of the things of this world; let them live in the pleasures of their Sabbath, which is but the remembrance of the material creation; filled with the love of earthly things, they knew not the Lord who created the world; they would not receive him because, he said : 'Blessed are the poor.' Our Sabbath is the eighth day, and the first day of creation. Our joy, then, comes not from the created world, but from the redeemed world."[1]

The mystery of seven days, followed by the eighth, called the Octave, is found in a new way in the Easter Season. That holy time is made up of seven weeks making a week of weeks, and the day following is the glorious Sunday of Pentecost. God himself gave these mysterious numbers in the desert of Sinai. In the Pentecost of the children of Israel, fifty days after they celebrated their Easter, they celebrated the feast of Pentecost. God himself gave these mysterious numbers in the coming down of the Holy Ghost on the Apostles, fifty days after our Lord rose from the dead, on the feast of Pentecost. From that the Apostles formed the Easter Season of the Church. Such is its origin, say the greatest writers.[2] "If we multiply seven by seven we find that this holy time is the Sabbath of Sabbaths ; but what makes up the fullness of the eight beatitudes of the Gospel[3] is the eighth day which follows Pentecost Sunday ; that day was Sunday, at the same time the first and the eighth." The Apostles considered these seven weeks so holy that during them they bent not their knees to adore, nor disturbed their happiness by fasting. The same belongs to each Sunday, for that day, by the Gospel, takes the place of Saturday, and the perfection of Saturday belongs to the day we celebrate in feasting and in joy."[4] Thus, as the most holy day of each week is Sunday, the day set apart to the worship of the Lord, who rose that day from the dead, the Easter Season is

---

[1] Rupert. De Divin. Officis., l. vii., c. xix. [2] St. Isidore, Amalarius, Rhaban Maur, etc. [3] Math. v. [4] St. Hilary, Prolog. in Psalmos.

the Sunday of the year, set apart to the remembrance of the resurrection of our Lord.[1]

We find it figured in the law of Moses. Their Pentecost was the fiftieth day after their Easter, and it was the day following the seven weeks. Again, they had their seven weeks of years, and the fiftieth year was their year of jubilee; that was for them a year of rest. Those whose farms and property were lost or sold all were returned; they got again their property, and those who were made slaves were set at liberty. All were figures of the liberty with which God hath made us free, by dying and rising for us from the dead.

No hymn is sung during the first week of the Easter Time, because, although the hymn is a sign of joy, still this season tells us of heaven, the world of bliss beyond the grave. As St. John saw in heaven the Angels and Saints praising God, repeating again and again the word, "Alleluia,"[2] the Church reminds the people of the weakness of earthly hymns compared to the heavenly choirs, to which we are all called. Therefore we sing no hymns but the heavenly song of the "Alleluia" in the Offices of the Breviary.

The color of the vestments is white, to typify the glories of the Lord, clothed with light, rising from the dead, and to tell of the innocence of the souls of the Christians who have fortified themselves in the blood of the lamb, without spot, by receiving the sacraments. The feasts of the higher classes, which could not be celebrated before, because of the ceremonies of Lent, Holy Week, and of Easter Week, will now appear in the Cycle of the year.

Three great mysteries are celebrated during the Easter Season—the Resurrection of our Lord, his Ascension into heaven, and the descent of the Holy Ghost. During the forty centuries before Christ all the wonders of the Lord, to the chosen ones of old, were to prepare the world for these three great events—the showing forth of God's almighty power. Thus, during the year, all the feasts, fasts and the seasons of the religious year have been to prepare man for these three great feasts. The spirits made perfect, who inhabit the

---

[1] Gueranger, Le Temps Paschal, pp. 23, 24.   [2] Apoc. xix. 1, 3, 4, 6.

home of God himself, are wonder struck at the wisdom of God thus repairing the fallen race of sinning Adam.[1] The Easter Season is a part of the Enlightening Life, and we can say that it is the highest and most sublime of any other part of the year. It shows us God in all his glory; it shows us our nature raised up to the highest throne of God in heaven.

I.—EASTER SUNDAY.

Easter, the greatest day of the year, has come. Death, from the day he devoured Abel, had conquered numberless generations of men; death now stretched his dark wings over the tomb of the crucified God and claimed the noble prey. But his victory was short. The blessed soul of Christ went down to the Limbo of the Patriarchs; there to tell them of their deliverance. Friday night, all day Saturday, and Saturday night, the soul of Jesus passed amidst the dead. Men before had risen from the grave by the power of God, but it was only for a time—death came again. But how different with our Lord. He rose the Victor over death, and the grim monster was to have no more dominion over him.

All know the history of the resurrection. The soul of Jesus leaves the place of rest of the ancient Saints; in an instant it has gone again into his sacred body. The blood comes back into his veins; the wounds are healed, and he rises from the stone slab on which he rested; he lays aside the shroud and the garments of the tomb; he folds and lays by the linen garments with which the piety of the women had clothed his body, and at the break of day on Sunday, the first day of the week, with splendors far eclipsing the brightness of the sun, he rises from the dead. As the light passes through the clearest crystal, his body passed through the solid rock, and then the Angel came and rolled away the stone from the mouth of the sepulchre and sat upon it.[2] This is the testimony of all the Fathers writing or preaching on the resurrection of our Lord.

The earth trembled in giving forth her Creator,

---

[1] Hymn Mat. Assen. [2] Math. xviii. 2.

transplendent splendors shone from the glorified body of our Lord; the guards, placed there by the Jews,[1] became the witnesses of the resurrection. The seal upon the tomb and the guards around the grave, in the providence of God, became the means of proving that he really rose from the dead.

The most ancient traditions[2] tell us that he first appeared to his mother. The Gospels say nothing of it, for this apparition did not relate to our salvation like the others, but it was but the duty of the Son to soothe the grief of his Mother. After that he appeared twelve times to his followers, because, as St. Chrysostom says, he was to send his twelve Apostles to preach his death and resurrection to the ends of the earth. But we will refer the reader to the Bible for the history of the resurrection.

The Catholics of Bohemia, Hungary, and of Poland, have continued the customs of the East in passing the whole of Holy Saturday night in prayer in the church, waiting for the morning, the moment of the resurrection, when the Benediction of the Blessed Sacrament is held, wherein the Lord himself blesses his people. In some of the cities of Spain two processions come forth from the church before the rising of the sun on Easter morning. One carries the Blessed Sacrament under a gorgeous canopy of golden cloth, and the other an image of the Virgin. In silence they pass through the streets of the city till the rising of the sun, when they take off the dark veil, which till then covered the statue of the mother, and sing the beautiful hymn, "O, Queen of Heaven, Rejoice." All this is in remembrance of our Lord appearing to his mother when he rose from the dead.

Regarding the origin of the hymn, an ancient tradition tells us that in the days of Gregory the Great a plague broke out in Rome. As in the times of David, the Pope prayed to God for his flock, and ordered all the people to march in a procession, carrying the picture of the Virgin Mother, painted by St. Luke. The great crowds went towards the Basilica of St. Peter's. Coming to the bridge across the Tiber, suddenly a host of Angels were seen above the image, singing the following anthem:

---

[1] Math. xvii. 66.   [2] St. Ambrose, etc.

> "Rejoice, O, then, thou Queen of Heaven,[1]
> Alleluia.
> For he to you to bear was given,
> Alleluia.
> As he said from death has risen,
> Alleluia."
> "O, pray to God we be forgiven,
> Alleluia."

cried out the holy Pontiff, and the exterminating Angel was seen on the summit of Adrian's mausoleum sheathing his destroying sword. From that time Adrian's Tomb has been called the Castle of St. Angelo,[2] and the anthem is said at the end of the Offices of the Breviary during the Easter Season.

Another of the customs of the East was to give the brotherly kiss of peace at the moment when the resurrection was announced. Men and women were each in different places in the church in these times, and there was no danger of temptation. That continued till the XVIth century, when the sexes were no more divided, but families sat together as they do now, when, on account of the abuses and the danger of temptations, the custom of the people saluting each other with a holy kiss was discontinued. As in our times we read that in the IVth and Vth centuries the priests of the country, with crowds of their people, used to come to the cathedrals there with their beloved bishop, to be present at the blessing of the Holy Oils, the baptism of the converts, and the celebration of Easter.[3] The Councils forbid the rich to leave the city for the watering places till after the holidays.[4]

At Rome on Easter Sunday, the Station is in the Basilica of St. Mary Major, that queen of all the churches dedicated to the Queen of Heaven throughout the world. The Mass of Easter is said in her church because, of all the Apostles, and disciples, and the followers of our Lord, she kept the faith when he was dead, and firmly believed that he would rise again from the grave. During the latter ages, when St. Peter's was built, because it is so large as to hold a greater number of people, they now hold the Services there.[5] To-day the holy water is not

---

[1] Translated by the author. [2] Rome, by Dr. Nelligan, p. 241. [3] Gueranger, Le Temps Paschal, p. 188. [4] Concil. Agd. et Orlean. I. iv. Ep. etc. [5] Gueranger, Le Temps Paschal, p. 190.

blessed as on the other Sundays of the year, for it was
blessed on Holy Saturday before at the blessing of the
baptismal font.[1]   In many of the churches of France,
and in some parts of Europe, they sing the beautiful
hymn, composed by Venance Fortunat, Bishop of Poitiers : "Hail, Festal Day, in Every Age so Holy."

The Gospel of to-day is taken from St. Luke, who was
the disciple of St. Peter, and wrote his Gospel at Rome
under the very eyes of the Prince of the Apostles.   In the
book, "Teaching Truth by Signs and Ceremonies," the
author gives the whole services for Easter Sunday, and
the reader is referred to it for an explanation of the
Church and her services.

During the middle ages, while the Pope was reciting
the Secret of the Easter Mass, the two youngest Cardinals, vested in white dalmatics, came and stood at the
two ends of the altar and turned towards the people.
They represented the two Angels who guarded the tomb
of the risen Saviour, when they appeared to the holy
women and told them of the resurrection.   The Cardinals remained there till the words of the Mass, "The
Lamb of God," when the Pope returned to his throne.
After the benediction given by the Pope, he came down
the steps of his throne, his brow crowned with the tiara,
the triple crown; with great ceremony he was carried on
the shoulders of his admiring people to the chief nave
of the Church, where, at a certain place, he came down
and fell upon his bended knees.   One of the attending
clergymen then exposed the wood of the true cross to the
Pontiff and to the people, with, at the same time, the
handkerchief of Veronica, having the picture of the sacred
face of our Lord imprinted on it, when he was on his way
to Calvary.   These ceremonies are to show forth the
wonders of the resurrection by exposing the instruments
of the Passion, while celebrating the glories of his rising
from the dead.   Christianity in the person of its head
thus adores Christ.   Afterwards he is carried to the gal-
lery from which he gives the Apostolic blessing to the
crowds of people assembled below.

For many centuries, while the Pope lived in the Lateran
Palace and celebrated the Easter ceremonies in the

---

[1] Gueranger, Ibidem, p. 191.

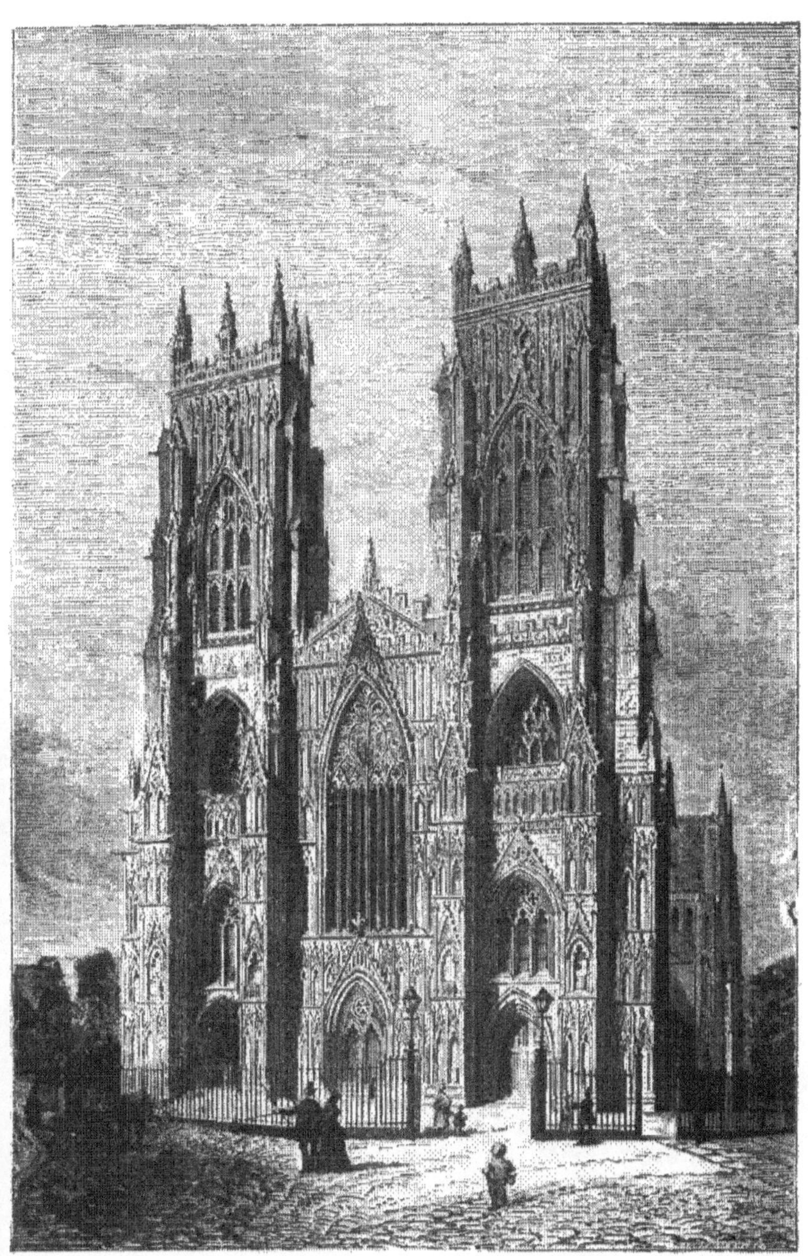

York Minster.

Church of St. Mary Major, after Mass all went into the
Festal Hall, built and decorated by Leo III., where tables were prepared for five Cardinals, five Deacons and
the Dean of the Church, near the Pontiff. They brought
the paschal lamb, and, saying grace, the Pope announced
that the time of fasting was gone, and then served the
others at the table. Grave and simple was the joy with
which that dinner was eaten, while the choir sang, and
they played the music of the ancient Romans which had
come down by tradition. Such are some of the simple
customs of the middle ages.

We have given but a few ideas relating to the resurrection ceremonies of our Lord on the first day of the week,
when he created the light, which was but a material figure of himself, who is "the light of the world," "enlightening every one who cometh into this world." This
thought is beautifully expressed in the Gothic Missal of
Spain, and is found in all the Liturgies of the Church, for
they all agree in celebrating, with the greatest pomp and
ceremony, the day when our Lord rose from the dead.

As Easter is the greatest Sunday, so the week following is the greatest week of the year. In ancient times
the days of this week were kept like one whole feast. In
389 the Emperor Theodosius forbade law courts to be held
during this week. St. Augustine tells us how these days
were to be celebrated.[1] St. Chrysostom says: "During
these seven days you rejoice at hearing the divine instructions of the people ; because of your coming together, we
allow you to come to the spiritual table."[2]   *   *   *   Such
was the desire of the people to see the beauties of the
services, that the churches were crowded on these days.
Many laws were made by the old Councils. In 585 a law
was enacted forbidding all servile works during the week
following Easter.[3] The same was given in the Councils
of Mayence[4] and of Meaux.[5] The same were the commands
of the Spanish and the Greek churches. Charlemagne,
Louis the Pious, and Charles the Bald sanctioned these
laws in their Codes. The Liturgical writers of the XIth
and XIIth centuries, speak of the custom of celebrating
Easter week. Gregory IX. gives it force in his Decrees

---

[1] De Ser. Dom. in Monte.   [2] Hom. V. de Resur.   [3] Concil. Macon.   [4] 813.   [5] 845.

in the XIIIth century. But the people did not keep the days holy any more, as in the times of the followers of the Apostles ; and in 1094 a Council shortened the holidays to Monday and Tuesday after Easter.[1]   Beleth in the XIIth and Durand in the XIIIth centuries, say that this was the custom in their times among the French. Thus, the people became so relax in keeping these days, that in the Concordat between the Holy See and the first Napoleon, the people were allowed to observe only Easter Sunday.[2]

This week is set apart to the care and instruction of the newly baptized, and many of the services of the week allude to their baptismal innocence. During this week no Masses with black vestments are allowed for the dead, except funeral Masses, when the body is present, for we are celebrating the resurrection of our Lord.

At Rome the Station of Monday is held in the great Church of St. Peter. Baptized on Saturday in the Lateran Basilica of the Saviour, they attended the solemnities of Easter, celebrated in the Church of St. Mary Major, and it is but right that they come to show their love and esteem for St. Peter, the Prince of the Apostles. To-day, in the Gospel, is given the history of the three disciples who went to Emmaus, and how our Lord came and joined them on the way, and taught them the figures and the prophecies relating to him in the Old Testament, and they knew him in the breaking of bread.[3]

Tuesday the baptized hear Mass in the Basilica of St. Paul, for their fourth duty was to return their thanks, and offer their love to the Apostle of the nations, the companion of St. Peter, and his associate in martyrdom. Thus, the Station of Tuesday is held in St. Paul's Church in Rome, where his body is kept with holy care. To-day the Church celebrates the time when our Lord appeared to his disciples and said, "Peace be to you,"[4] when he showed them his wounds, when he opened to them the Scriptures, so that they could understand the types and figures of him in the law of Moses, and in the Prophets, and in the Psalms.[5]

On Wednesday the Station is at St. Lawrence's Church, because, in the first ages, baptism was followed so often

---

[1] Concil. Const. [2] In 1801. [3] Luke xxiv. 31. [4] Luke xxiv. 86. [5] Luke xxiv.

by martyrdom, that the baptized came this day to the tomb of this great martyr, to learn heroism for the faith by his example. To-day we read in the Gospel which tells of the time our Lord appeared to his disciples on the shore of the sea of Galilee and told them to throw the net on the right side of the vessel, and they could scarcely draw it to the shore, there were so many fishes.[1]

The newly baptized go on Thursday to the Basilica of the Twelve Apostles, where repose the bodies of the Apostles, SS. Philip and James. The Gospel gives the history of the two Angels appearing to Mary Magdalen, and our Lord coming and showing himself to her.[2]

When Rome was converted from the darkness of paganism to the light of the Gospel, the venerable Pantheon of Agrippa was purified and turned into the Church of St. Mary at the Martyrs. It was given to Pope Boniface IV. by the Emperor Phocas, and ever since it has been dedicated to the Mother of God, and to all the Saints and holy Martyrs. There the Station of Friday is held. There from the VIIth century the baptized come this day to be present at the services of the Church. The Gospel is taken from St. Matthew[3] and gives the history of our Lord after his resurrection, sending forth his Apostles into all nations to preach the Gospel, and to baptize "In the name of the Father, and of the Son, and of the Holy Ghost."[4]

Saturday after Easter is called Low Saturday, because then the newly baptized since Holy Saturday used to wear white garments till the following Saturday, as a sign of the innocence and the purity of their souls after baptism, and that they were not to stain again their conscience with sin.

At Rome the Station to-day is in the Basilica of the Lateran, near Constantine's Baptistry, where they were baptized on Holy Saturday. They unite again in the darkness of the night, and led by the Paschal candle there they put off their white robes, and heard for the first time the whole of the Mass. No other place was so apt to leave a lasting impression on their minds as that Baptistry, where they were washed from sin, in that

---

[1] John xxi. [2] John xx. [3] Math. xxviii. [4] Math. xxviii. 19.

Church, the Mother and the Cathedral of all the churches of Rome and of the world. The Gospel, taken from St. John,[1] tells us of Mary Magdalen coming early in the morning to the sepulchre, and of SS. John and Peter running to the grave to find that their Lord had risen from the dead.

II.—LOW SUNDAY.

The first Sunday after Easter is called Low Sunday, because for the first time the baptized came to the Church without their white robes, which they have worn since their baptism on Holy Saturday.[2] It is also called "Quasimode," from the first word with which the services begin.   In ancient times they named it Close Easter, because it closed the Easter week. It is of such importance that no other feast is ever allowed to be celebrated on this day.

Low Sunday is also the Octave of Easter,[3] and from this day begins the time when the race of Adam is reconciled again to God. Before Christ was the time when the race went farther and farther from God. Except the Jews all the races of men were idolaters. Our Lord came to save them. He paid the price, and that redemption is applied to our souls by the Mass and the sacraments.   From this time to the end of the ecclesiastical year we represent the redemption of the members of the race—called the summer and the autumn time of the year.

During the time of fasting and of penance before Easter, we read the history of the law and the prophecies, which relate to and prepared the world for the coming and the death of Christ, for Advent, Septuagesima Time, Lent and Holy Week, which were but figures of the world before the coming of our Lord. After Easter we read the Acts of the Apostles,[4] but especially the Book of the Apocalypse, for, as the Easter Time typifies the glories of heaven, so the Apocalypse tells us of many visions of our home amidst the skies.[5]

---

[1] John xx.   [2] El Porque de las Ceremonias, c. xii. Sabado Santo.   [3] St. Aug. Sermo CCLIX. in Die Dom. p.st Pasch.   [4] St. Aug. vol. xxi. 122.   [5] Durandus, Rationale Div. l. vl. c. xcvii. n. 3.

Formerly, during Easter Time, servants were accustomed to correct their masters,[1] and a rule was made relating to married people receiving holy Communion at Easter.[2] Farmers were not allowed to work during the three days following Easter, or women spin, or dances held. The converts who were baptized on Holy Saturday, and were well instructed in our holy religion, were confirmed on Low Sunday, and for that ceremony they wore their white garments, because the Angels who appeared at the sepulchre were clothed in white, and because it is the color of innocence and of joy.

From Easter to Low Sunday, for seven days, we celebrate the resurrection of our Lord, for we are to be filled with the seven gifts of the Holy Ghost while in this life, that we may celebrate his glories in heaven. The days of this week are to be taken as one whole day. For that reason, in the Offices and the Services of the Church, this day for this week is mentioned in the Preface and in the Breviary. After these days comes Low Sunday, the Octave of Easter, for after our good lives spent here, when we are filled with the sevenfold gifts of the holy Spirit, comes the everlasting Octave of this life in heaven, where our Easter of praises and thanksgivings will never end. As on Easter Sunday, we say only three Psalms during these seven days, for they tell of the three heavenly virtues of faith, hope and charity infused into the souls of the converted with the seven gifts of the Spirit of God, when they were baptized. Nine lessons are to be said on all the Sundays of the year, but for these reasons an old Council, following the traditions of the Apostles, stated that during these days following Easter only three Lessons are to be said.[3]

Sunday is the Lord's day. That is the day forever dedicated to the resurrection of our Lord, but it is also in a secondary way devoted to the glory and the praises of the Holy Trinity. For that reason three Nocturns are always said, and the Preface of the Holy Trinity sung at the Masses during the Sundays of the year.[4]

The Athanasian creed is not said, for it belongs to faith, but this Time tells us of heaven, where there will be no

---

[1] 12 q. 2, Quest.   [2] De Conc. Dist. 2 Omnis homo.   [3] Concil. Magun.   [4] Ord. R man.

more faith but everlasting charity, the love of God above
all. In the same way we ask not the aid of God's Saints,
for there in heaven we will not want God's aid any more
against temptation.

In Rome on Low Sunday the Station is in the Basilica
of St. Pancrasius in the Via Auralia. Writers do not
tell us why that church was chosen for the Services of
to-day, but some think it was because of the tender age
of fourteen years at which the holy martyr suffered, so
that his example may encourage the newly converted
and baptized to keep the faith through the trials of life.

The Gospel comes from St. John, where he tells us of
our Lord appearing to his Apostles, and saying twice to
them: "Peace be with you." He breathed upon them
and said : "Receive ye the Holy Ghost; whose sins you
shall forgive they are forgiven, and whose sins you shall
retain they are retained,"[1] giving them the power to sit,
and in his name and by his power to forgive sins. Then
he showed his wounds to Thomas, who would not believe.[2]

III.—THE ANNUNCIATION.

On the 25th of March, each year, the Church celebrates
the mystery of the incarnation of our Lord. The origin
of this feast goes back to the time of the Apostles.[3] The
ancient Councils made laws relating to the feast,[4] and the
most ancient writers tell of the mystery and of the feast.[5]

In some of the churches of Europe in the early times,
they celebrated the feast on the 18th of January, in others on the 18th of December, but that was only for a time.
Soon knowing that according to the laws of nature, the
God-child who was born on the 25th of December, was
conceived nine months before on the 25th of March. According to the Latin Rite, from the very beginning of the
Church the feast was always held on the 25th of March.
It happens sometimes that this day falls during the week
before, or the week following, Easter. As at that time
the Church is celebrating either the sufferings of our

---

[1] John xx. 23. [2] John xx. [3] Benedictus XIV. De Festis B. V. Mariae. c. iv. n.
17 ; V. Bede de Locis Sanctis. S. Jerome ad. Marcel. El Porque, Trat. C. c. xiii.,
Boland. [4] Concil. Toletan. Collect. Labb. p. 460. [5] Micrologus, c. xlviii. Rudolphus,
Prop. xvi. etc.

Lord in his passion or his glories after the resurrection, then the ceremonies of the Annunciation are put off till the first Monday after Low Sunday.

This feast has been considered by all Christians as a day of great importance, as to-day the Lord and Creator of all things, took our nature and in the Virgin became man.[1] The conception of Christ took place in a wonderful way, and was above all the powers of nature. In a moment, in the twinkling of an eye, God and man were united, and our nature raised up to the throne of the Divinity. His perfect body was formed from the purest blood of his Mother. At that moment Christ became a priest forever, and a true King of a spiritual and everlasting kingdom. According to St. Thomas the Divinity was united to our nature through his highest manly power; his mind,[2] his Divine mind saw all things, the past, the present, and the future. His human mind was happy in seeing his Divinity face to face. From that moment, then, he had the use of all his faculties, and not like other children who have to wait till they are about seven years of age.[3] With these wondrous gifts and privileges was the conception of Christ beautified, from which one can easily conclude that it was miraculous and above nature.[4]

The Annunciation took place in Joseph's house, where Mary, his wife, lived,[5] at the moment she gave her consent.[6] We cannot tell at what time of the day the Angel came.[7] She was a little girl of fourteen years of age. It was on the 25th of March. The authority of the Church guards the tradition that Christ was conceived, and that he died on the 25th of March.[8] Such is the voice of all the works of the past, the writings of the Greeks, of the Copts, of the Syrians, of the Chaldean Christians, and of all works of past ages.[9] Such is the tradition of the Apostles.[10]

At the Mass the history of the Annunciation, as given by St. Luke, is read,[11] where he speaks of the Angel going in and telling the Blessed Virgin that she would become a mother. Before that she had vowed her virginity to

---

[1] Suarez. t. i. de Relig. l. ii c. 5. [2] St. Thomas, 3 p. q. vi. art. 11. etc. [3] Benedictus XIV. De Fest. B. M. Virginis, c. iii. n. 13. [4] P. Graveso de Myst. et An. Christi, Dis. II. and Benedictus XIII. de B. Virg. Ser. xiv. p. 1. [5] St. Bernard. Hom. iii. sup. Mis [6] Theop. Raynaudus, p. 52; Saxius de Laud. Mariæ, P. I., p. 91, etc. [7] Benedictus XIV. Ibidem, n. 14. [8] St. Augustine de Trinitate. iv. c. 56. [9] Benedictus XIV. Ibidem, n. 14. [10] Bolandists, ad. 25 Martini. [11] Luke i.

God, and she was troubled to hear that she was to become a mother, but when she learned that she would bring forth, and before, and in, and after that birth, she was to always remain a virgin, gave her consent.

On the 25th of April, having left his disciple, St. Evodius, in his place as bishop of Antioch, St. Peter entered the great city of Rome, and there fixed his See as first Pope. From that time the Christians of Rome celebrated his coming by reciting the Litany of the saints during the ten terrible persecutions which followed.[1] A feast in honor of the coming of the Prince of the Apostles used to be celebrated, but often interfering with the services of Low Sunday, it was discontinued.[2] Because the feasts of the Easter Season change each year, the people of Rome recited these Litanies at different times, till Pope Gregory the Great appointed them to be said on the 25th of April.[3] In the same way the feast of the Apostle St. Mark was held at different times on account of so many feasts of Easter coming in this season, till later St. Mark's feast was fixed on the 25th of April. Thus, although one does not relate to the other, we say the Litanies on the feast of St. Mark.[4]

During the first ages the Romans abstained from eating meat on that day, and when the Roman Rite was brought to France by Pepin and Charlemagne, the great Litany of the 25th of April came with it. One of the councils of France forbade all manual labor on that day,[5] but the custom of keeping the day holy is not now observed in any part of the world, because the people became relax. When St. Charles Borromeo became archbishop of Milan he found that the clergy only marched in the procession, and he commanded all the people to be present and to walk in their bare feet.

Monday, Tuesday and Wednesday before Ascension Thursday are called Rogation days, from the Latin, which means a request, a prayer. They are days of penance and of prayer. Why does the Church interrupt the joys of the Easter season by these days of penance and of self-denial? The Holy Ghost, who was sent to

---

[1] Moretti, Do Fest. in Hon. Princip. Apost. Rom. 4.   [2] Sacrameut. Leou.   [3] See El Porquo de las Ceremonias, c. xxi., De las Letanis, etc.   [4] Gueranger, Le Temps Paschal, vol. II. p. 448, et seq.   [5] Council of Aix-la-Chapelle in 836.

remain and forever to be with and guide the Church,
directs these things. They go back to the Vth century.
St. Mamert was then archbishop of Vienna. All kinds
of misfortunes threatened that province of ancient Gaul.
Earthquakes, fires, storms and pestilences afflicted the
people. When the saintly bishop commanded three days
of fasting and of penance to be held before the Ascension,
they ceased as by the power of God. St. Avit, his successor, tells us that these days were everywhere held in
his time.[1] When the Goths, the Huns and the barbarians of the north of Europe and the west of Asia, threatened to devastate the fairest portions of southern Europe, then the three days of Rogation and of prayer before Ascension spread into every part of the Church.
We see that the question was stated in the council of
Orleans,[2] and that they had extended to every part of
the Clovis empire. That assembly of the bishops commanded their people not only to abstain from meat, but
also to fast from food. Later, the council of Tours sanctioned the same law.[3] At that time they used to march
in long processions, beseeching the favors of heaven, and
as they were days kept like Sunday, all the people used
to take part in them. St. Cesarius tells us that the processions sometimes lasted six hours, all the people praying and singing hymns.[4] Before they set out on their
march, they all received ashes on their heads, like on
Ash Wednesday, while the clergy and the people walked
bare-footed, as a sign of fasting and of penance. Histo-
rians tell us that the Emperor Charlemagne, on these
days put away his sandals and went with the common
people from his palace to the church, where the Mass
was said.[5] St. Elizabeth, queen of Hungary, gave the same
example to her people.[6] Toward the end of the VIIIth
century, Rome adopted the custom under the Pontificate
of Leo III. Before that, in the VIIth century, it was
spread into Spain and through the south of Europe.

The Litany of the Saints said on these days goes back
to the earliest times, but we cannot find out the exact
date. The word Litany comes from the Greek, and
means a prayer or a supplication, for by the intercession

---

[1] Hom. de Rogat. [2] Can. xxvii. [3] 567, c. xvii. [4] Ser. 174, Herb. Tur. Mir. l. i.
c. 21. [5] De Reb. Bel. Caroli, Mag. c. xvi. [6] Surais Die 19 Nov.

of the saints, the friends of God, the early Christians, prayed when they wished to receive some special benefit. Again, these days of prayer were held to call down the blessings of heaven on the fruits of the earth. And well are they said in the spring time of the year, when the earth is clothed with verdure and nature puts on its sweetest smiles, the hope of a bountiful harvest.[1] We find some beautiful hymns, composed by the saints of the middle ages, praising God for his benefits, and calling down the grace of God on the people during these three days.[2]

IV.—The Ascension.

On Thursday following the fifth Sunday after Easter, we celebrate the Ascension of our Lord.[3] For forty days after he rose from the dead he remained with his apostles,[4] to teach them that he was truly risen, to explain to them the types and the figures which foretold him in the Old Testament, and to send them forth into the world to preach, to teach and to save the redeemed race. The solemnity of the Ascension was instituted by the apostles[5] on Thursday, for tradition tells us that at noon[6] this day he went up into heaven.[7] The Apostles had gathered all together in the large hall, where the first Mass was said by our Lord the night before he suffered, and he came and sat and eat with them. That upper hall is to be seen to-day in Jerusalem, and now the Turks occasionally allow the Holy Sacrifice to be celebrated within its holy walls. The Saviour led them out beyond the walls of Jerusalem. Five hundred witnesses followed him[8] along the road to Bethany, the length of a Sabbath day's journey, nearly a thousand paces,[9] to the Mount of Olives.[10] From there, before the eyes of all, by his own power, he went up into heaven, and a cloud received him from their sight. That cloud was the souls of the holy ones of the Old Testament, to whom he descended at the moment of his death, to tell them of the joyful news of

---

[1] Gueranger, Temps Paschal, vol. iii. p. 177. [2] Liturg. Gallic. Mamert. of Vienna, etc. [3] Benedictus XIV., De Fest. D. N. J. Christi, c. x. n. 1. [4] Fabri, Con. In Fest, As. Dom. Con. iv. n. 11. [5] St. Aug. vol. xxxviii, 488. [6] Constitnt. Apost. l. v. c. xix. [7] St. Augustine, Epist. xliv. c. i ; Martine, c. xxviii. n. 1. [8] I. Cor. xv. 6. [9] Benedictus XIV. Ibidem, n. 43. [10] Fabri, Conciones, In Fest. Assen. Dom. Con. iv. n. 1.

their redemption.[1] These were the dead who came forth
from the tomb, when the Son of God died on the cross,
and appeared to many in the streets of the holy city.
Then having fulfilled their mission of being present at
the crucifixion of their Lord, whom they had longed to
see, they laid themselves down again in death, till they
will rise again, like all the children of Adam, when called
at the general resurrection at the end of the world.[2]

The writers of the early times tell us that before he
ascended from the earth, he left the marks of his holy
feet in the rock,[3] as the prophet foretold.[4]

Even when Titus took and destroyed Jerusalem, the
imprint of the Lord's feet remained,[5] and over them the
Empress Helena built a beautiful church. From there
she wrote to her son, the Emperor Constantine : "With
worthy devotion, the impressions of our Saviour's feet are
honored."[6]

In memory of the Ascension of our Lord, they used to
have a procession each Thursday, in the first days of the
Church, but afterwards, because the people could not
always come on a week day, Pope Agapitus changed it
to Sunday, when the people could all attend.[7] This procession is spoken of by many writers of the early times,[8]
and appears to have been commenced by the early Christians, to keep the people from attending the pagan procession on this day in honor of Jupiter, and also to bless
the bread and the new fruits of the earth.[9] There is no
fast on the eve of the Ascension, because it falls within
the Easter season.[10]

The paschal candle, which tells of Christ, the light of
the world, is lighted from the time it is blessed on Holy
Saturday, Easter Sunday, the three days following
Easter, at the high Masses of all the Sundays and feasts,
and at the vespers of the Easter season till Ascension
Thursday,[11] when, after the Gospel is finished, it is
quenched, to show that our Lord on this day, as the
light of all men, went up into heaven.[12]

---

[1] Benedictus XIV. Ibidem, n. 49. [2] St. Thomas, 4 Sent. Dist. 43 qu. 1. a. 3 ; St. Augustine, Epist. 164. and nearly all the Fathers. [3] St. Augustine, Tract. 37 s. 4 St. Paullnus Nolanus, Epist. 11. ad Sever. [4] Zach. 14, 4. [5] Balletus, Hist. de Myst. Assen. [6] Euseblus, Vita Constantini, l. iii. c. 42. [7] Durandus, Rationale Div. l. iv. c. vi. n. 21. [8] Greg. Turon. l. v. Hist. Franc, c. 11. [9] Benedictus, Ibidem, n. 59. [10] Gavantus, Sec. vi. de Lit. Maj. c. 17. [11] Decrit. Cong. Rituum of May, 1607. [12] Benedictus XIV. Ibidem, n. 60.

From near Bethania the Lord ascended. And well was it called by this name, which in the Hebrew means obedience, for from that time, the Church was to be formed by the obedience of all to the successors of the Apostles, and without obedience to God and to his church, no one can go to heaven.[1]

The services of to-day are held in Rome, in the great Church of St. Peter. What a happy thought, to unite around the tomb of the Apostles the faithful followers of the Lord, who to-day ascended into heaven, where he sits at the right hand of the Father. For many ages the Pope, with the whole College of Cardinals, went to St. John Lateran to end these holy rites in the Church built by Constantine in honor of the Saviour.

The Gospel of to-day is taken from St. Mark, and tells the history of our blessed Lord going up into heaven in the presence of all his holy followers.

Such are a few thoughts on the feasts of our beloved Saviour, which year by year, and generation after generation, we celebrate. Eighteen hundred years have passed, and still by yearly ceremonies, by rites and services, by the types and figures of our Church, his life, his works, his miracles and his life have been brought before the minds of men. Thus it will be ever after, till the day of doom, till the angel's trumpet calls the dead to rise and come to judgment.

The Sunday following Ascension, at Rome is called Rose Sunday, from the ancient custom of strewing the floors of the churches with roses and flowers in honor of the Lord, who says: "I am the flower of the fields and the lily of the valleys,"[2] who in this time of bright fields and blooming flowers, ascended into heaven. As it falls within the octave of the Ascension, it is called the Sunday within the Octave.

V.—WHITSUNDAY.

Before our Lord went up into heaven, he told his little band of followers to remain in Jerusalem till the coming of the Holy Ghost, who was to fill them with power from

---

[1] Durandus, Rationale Div. l. vi. c. civ. n. 1.   [2] Cant. of Cant. IV., 1.

on high for their sublime mission of converting the world. They returned to the holy city, and for ten days they remained in the upper chamber in the home of Mary, the mother of St. Mark,[1] where the Last Supper was celebrated, where so often the risen Lord appeared to them after his resurrection, and where the Holy Ghost came down upon them.[2] There they were in prayer at nine on Sunday morning, when suddenly they heard a sound like a great wind from heaven. The house trembled while tongues of fire came and sat upon the heads of the whole 120 assembled persons. They were filled with grace, but that is not enough for those who preach the Gospel. They must be filled besides with the gifts of the Holy Ghost, to convert souls to God. The Holy Spirit could come in an unseen manner, but he came in the form of fire, to show that, as before, he came on Christ in the form of a dove at his baptism,[3] so now he comes in the form of fire as a sign of his power, to show that the Church is guided by him in the signs, symbols and the ceremonies of our services. He came in the form of fire, to tell the world that now the Apostles were to renew the earth by the fire of charity. As fire purifies all which passes through it, thus they were to purify the world. He came in the form of tongues, to show that by their preaching they were to renew the world, and that their eloquence and their power over the hearts of men come from the Spirit of God. He came with the sound of a mighty wind, for the word Spirit, in the ancient languages means a breath, a wind, for the Holy Ghost is as the breath of God healing the souls of men.

At that time Jerusalem was one of the most celebrated cities of Asia. Since Solomon raised his mighty temple, the fame of the city and of the sanctuary of the Lord of hosts had gone through the world. The Jews, given to trade, had wandered even to the ends of the earth. They used to come each year to the city of their forefathers to be present at the great festival of Pentecost. Great crowds from all parts of the world were in Jerusalem on that day. They were struck with wonder when they heard the vulgar fishermen of Galilee speaking all the

---

[1] Baronius, Jansenius, Canisius, Menocius, etc. [2] Benedictus XIV., de Fest., D. N. J. Christi, c. xi. n. 17 ; O'Brien, Hist. of the Mass, p. 18, note. [3] Math. iii. 16.

languages of the earth. The gift of tongues was given the Apostles so that they could preach to all nations. They said that they were drunk. Peter, the head, the first Pope—Peter filled with the Holy Ghost—then preached his first sermon, and convinced them that they had not been drinking.[1] On that day he converted and baptized three thousand persons. Peter spoke for all.[2] Before that day they were timid and afraid. They had no strength. They ran away from the sad scene of the crucifixion. They hid themselves in the upper chamber, but from the moment they received the Holy Ghost they became like other men. They were filled with strength from the Spirit of God within them, and died at the hands of the people whom they converted to the Gospel.

Such are but a few of the traditions coming down to us, relating to the great Christian Pentecost, after Easter, the greatest feast of the Church, of which the Jewish Pentecost was but a figure.[3] Fifty days from the time the children of Israel celebrated the ceremony of the eating of the paschal lamb, they held their services of Pentecost, when God gave to Moses his law of the ten commandments, carved on tablets of stone.[4] Fifty days from the resurrection of our Lord, the Holy Ghost gave the law of the New Testament written in the hearts of the Apostles.[5] The law of the Old Testament was given on Sinai's top, amid the winged lightnings. The law of the New Testament was given amid the fiery flame of tongues in the upper chamber. As the Hebrews, after they were delivered from the slavery of Egypt, fifty days after eating the paschal lamb, received the law on Mount Sinai, thus, after the sufferings of our Lord, who was the true Lamb of God who was sacrificed, fifty days after his resurrection the Holy Ghost comes down on the Apostles and on those who believed.[6]

All writers of the past tell us that on Sunday the Holy Ghost came upon the Apostles.[7] On this day the world began; on this day, by the resurrection of Christ, true spiritual life began and death ended; on this day the Apostles received the command to teach all nations, and

[1] Act ii.   [2] St. Chrysostom, Hom. IV. in Act. Apost. c. ii.   [3] Isidore, l. i. de Of. Eccl. c. xxxii.   [4] St. Aug. Contra. Faust, lxxxii. n. 12.   [5] St. Chrysostom.   [6] St. Leo, Ser. lxxiii. de Pent. i. c. 1.   [7] Const. Clement, St. August. Ser. CLIV., de Temp.

to baptize them, as Blessed John, the evangelist, says:[1] "The Lord came and breathed on them, saying: 'Receive ye the Holy Ghost,'" and finally on this day the Holy Ghost came down into the world.[2]

Pentecost has been celebrated by the Church since the days of the Apostles.[3] "From the times of the Apostles the custom began of standing during the services of Easter and of Pentecost," as Blessed Irenæus, the martyr and Bishop of Lyons, says.[4] In the first centuries of the Church, the whole time from Easter to Pentecost was so holy that it was considered like one continual Sunday,[5] but the people were not commanded to cease from work.[6] During these days, from the first Monday after Lowsunday, the Acts of the Apostles are read, for as St. Chrysostom says, there is found a history of their works. Then we read their Epistles, for there we find their words.

The two great days when the converts used to be baptized are Holy Saturday and the eve of Pentecost,[7] and for that reason the services of the Church on these two days are very much alike. Formerly the baptismal font[8] and the paschal candle were blessed on the Saturday before Whitsunday. The converts were baptized on Holy Saturday, to signify that they were buried with Christ, while they were baptized on the eve of Whitsunday, according to the words of our Lord, "You will be baptized by the Holy Ghost,"[9] and following the example of St. Peter, who on Pentecost baptized three thousand persons.[10] They are baptized on Saturday and not on Pentecost Sunday, in imitation of our Lord, who lay buried in the tomb on Saturday. From Easter to Whitsunday, at any time, converts were baptized and confirmed during this season. In some churches of these early times, when they sang the hymn, "Come, O Holy Spirit," trumpet tones imitated the sound of the wind, and tongues of fire were thrown from the roof of the buildings, to re-call the coming of the Holy Ghost on the apostles.[11] This took place especially in Italy.[12] But because these cus-

---

[1] John xx. [2] St. Leo, Epist. xi. alias xviii. ad Clos. c. i. t, Op., p. 220. [3] Justinus, quest. 145. [4] Lib. de Pasch. ; See S. Leo the Great Ser. lxxv. de Pent. i. c. i., p. 155 ; Tertul. De Idol., c. xiv. [5] Concil. Illiber. c. xlii. [6] Benedictus XIV., Ibidem, n. 34. [7] Epist. Siricii ad. Him. Tar. Leon. Mag. Epist. 4 et 80, Gelas. Epist. i. c. 12. [8] El Porque de las Ceremonias, c. iv. [9] Acts i. 5. [10] Acts ii. 41. [11] Durandus, l. vi., c. xvii. [12] Ctserus l. i. de Fest. c. xxviii.

toms used to sometimes frighten the people, they were not continued.[1] The eve of Pentecost is a fast day.[2]

The word Whitsunday comes from the old Saxon word meaning White Sunday, because the newly baptized used to attend the services of this Sunday clothed in their white baptismal robes ; it is also called Pentecost Sunday. The word Pentecost comes from two Greek words, which mean five and ten, that is, fifty, for it always falls on the fiftieth day after Easter.[3] For seven days we celebrate the giving of the Holy Ghost with his sevenfold gifts, although our salvation is the work of the three Persons of the Holy Trinity, for the works of the Trinity are one and the same,[4] but the work of the Trinity in the salvation of the race is never to end. Pentecost has an Octave during the week, like the other great feasts of the year,[5] but the feast of the Holy Trinity falls on the Sunday following. The Matin Office of Pentecost and of the week following[6] have but three Psalms and three lessons, showing the work of our redemption, finished with the coming of the Holy Ghost in the work of the three Persons of the Holy Trinity.[7] In the Holy Scriptures the Holy Ghost is called the Paraclete,[8] from the Greek, meaning our Advocate, our Comforter ; for that reason he was sent to remain with the followers of our Lord forever, and comfort them in this life.

In the middle ages Pentecost was called Rose Easter, and the Sunday before it was called Rose Sunday, because the red roses which, in their simple piety, the people plucked from the fields and decked their churches reminded them of the red fiery tongues in which the Holy Ghost came down on the Apostles. .For the same reason to recall the fiery tongues, the vestments of the clergy to-day are red. In some of the churches of these early times they used to set at liberty in the church white doves, to remind them of the Holy Ghost coming down on our Lord in the form of a dove.[9]

At Rome the Station is held in the Basilica of St. Peter, to recall by these services in the Cathedral of

---

[1] Baillet, Hist. huj. diei S. ii., u. 7. [2] Dist. vi. c. Nosse et Ibidem, c. Scire. [3] St. Aug, Contra. Faust, l., xxxii. n. 12. [4] De Conc. Dist. iv. [5] Pope Clement Extra. De Fer. Capel. [6] Concil. Magunt. et De Consec., dist. 5. [7] Durandus, Rationale Div. l. vi., c. cvii., n. 3. [8] St. Aug. In Joan. Evang. t. lxxiv., n. iv. [9] Durand., Rationale ; Meno. etc.

the world, dedicated to the Prince of the Apostles, his inspired eloquence on that first Pentecost, when he converted the three thousand from the people of Jerusalem.[1] The Pope with the Cardinals then go to the Church of St. John Lateran, the mother of all the churches of Rome and of the world.

At nine in the morning, tradition tells us, the Holy Spirit came down upon the Apostles, and his coming is recalled at this hour in the Hymn of Terce, composed by St. Ambrose, who is also the author of the Hymns of Sext and of None. But to-day this hymn, said each day throughout the year, gives place to another, longer and more beautiful: " O come, Creator Spirit,"[2] which was composed by either the Emperor Charlemagne, Notherus, Robert, King of France, Herman, Contract, or Innocent II. We cannot find out which composed the Hymn said before Gospel: " Come, O Holy Spirit."

The Gospel of the Mass is taken from St. John,[3] and tells how our Lord, before his death, promised to send the Holy Ghost upon his Apostles.

The seven days of Pentecost week are dedicated to the seven gifts of the Holy Ghost. Coming on the Apostles, he gave them three things to remain with them and their successors forever: the eloquence of the pulpit, figured by the fiery tongues; the burning love of souls, typified by the fire, and the power of miracles represented by the great wind. Their eloquence is the " sword of the mouth," their love is the courage to die for God, and their miracles have attracted the eyes of the whole world in every age.[4]

On Monday the Services are held in the Basilica of St. Peter in Chains, called also the Church of Eudoxia, after the Empress who built it. There are guarded with holy care the chains with which Herod bound St. Peter in Jerusalem, and the chains with which he was bound by order of the impious Nero. The people are called to this church, to recall the gift of strength given by the Holy Ghost to the Prince of the Apostles on Pentecost, by which he was able to suffer and to die for the Lord.

---

[1] Acts ii. [2] Veni Creator Spiritus. [3] Gueranger, Le Temps Paschal, vol. iii, p. 397. [4] John iii.

St. Denis in Paris.

Chapter IX.—The After-Pentecost Season.

REASONS RELATING TO THE AFTER-PENTECOST SEASON.

We have finished the Feasts, the Fasts and the Seasons, which each year are held to recall the life, death, resurrection and ascension of our Lord with the coming of the Holy Ghost. The history of the God-man, the wonderful work of the redemption, the glories of the risen Saviour, and the coming down of the Holy Spirit, each year are brought before the world by the rites, the services and the ceremonies of the Church. Take away the Church and her works, and, in one generation, God and all his wonders, performed for man's redemption, would be forgotten. Inspired by the Holy Ghost, the Apostles appointed these chief feasts, festivals and seasons, to be celebrated to keep forever before the world the coming of our Lord and the work of our salvation.

Six months of the year is thus dedicated to the memory of our Saviour, while the six following months are dedicated to the work of God in the souls of men. Thus half the year is spent in celebrating the work of the Son of God when he lived upon this earth, while the other six months are set apart in which to celebrate the working of this redemption in our souls. Nature itself is in harmony with all this, for in the winter season all is cold and dismal; light has left the earth, a figure of the state of the pagan nations when the Lord came to redeem the race. The summer season is the most beautiful part of the year. The earth is green, while flowers cover the fields, all springing forth in bountiful plentiness, a type of the grace of redemption springing up into everlasting life in the souls of men. In the spring time the seed is sown; in the spring time our redemption was sown by the death of our Lord; in the summer the seeds spring forth and grow strong to bear the harvest of the autumn time; in the summer time the grace of God sown in the redemption, springs forth in souls of Adam's children, growing large and strong in godliness to bear the fruit of everlasting life, in the autumn time of eternity, when God will gather into his granary of heaven the souls of the saints, the fruits of redemption.

Thus after the Easter Season we enter a new period of time, which differs from the others. From the beginning of Advent to the coming of the Holy Ghost, the mysteries of our salvation have been unfolded. That time was like a long series of feasts, of fasts, of ceremonies and of services, during which, as in a sublime drama, the work of the redemption of our race was renewed. This latter part of the year is not without its mysteries and its solemnities ; some joyful and glorious, some sweet and touching, all for the good and the growth of Christian holiness in the souls of men, to end at Advent, when again we will begin the same solemnities of another year.

The After-Pentecost Season is longer or shorter than six months, according to the time when Easter falls. This season has come down to us from the times of the Apostles. It is sometimes made up of twenty-eight weeks and sometimes of only twenty-three. The Sundays of this season are called the Sundays after Pentecost. Such are their names in the most ancient books in the olden Missals and in the quaint Sacramentaries of the ages past. Such is their name in the writings of Alcuin in the VIIIth century.[1] In some of the ancient books these Sundays are divided into five series. The first is called the Sundays after Pentecost, the second the Sundays after the Feast of the Apostles,[2] the third the Sundays after St. Lawrence,[3] the fourth the Sundays of the Seventh Month,[4] while the fifth was called the Sundays after St. Michael.[5] These were their names in some of the oldest Missals and books used in the services of the Church from the middle ages till the XVIth century. When Pope Pius V. published his Missal, following the customs of the Apostolic ages, and wiping out the Missals which for more than two hundred years before his time had been changing, the Sundays of this Season appear again with their old title, The Sundays after Pentecost.[6]

---

[1] Com. [2] SS. Peter and Paul, 29th of June. [3] St. Lawrence the Martyr, 10th of August. [4] September. [5] St. Michael the Archangel, 29th September. [6] Domin. post Pentecosten.

That we may well understand the meaning of the time of the year in which we are now, we must remember the other Seasons through which we have passed. Each ceremony, each service was to make its influence felt in our souls. At Christmas, Christ was born in us; in Septuagesima Time he did penance for us; during Lent he fasted to show us an example; at Passion Time he died for us; he rose on Easter that we might rise from the death of sin; he went up into heaven to open to us its gates of everlasting glory, and from the right hand of his Father he sent down the Holy Ghost, the Spirit of truth, to live with us and to abide in our hearts. Thus all was done that Christ might be formed in us.[1] The Holy Ghost then came into the world to live in the hearts and in the souls of men, to help them in their work of saving their souls. That same Spirit of God, who came on our Lord with his sevenfold gifts, comes on each one of us and leads us on to our salvation. That time of the work of the third Person of the Holy Trinity in the world is called the After-Pentecost Season.

Two temples the Holy Ghost inhabits, the Church and the Christian soul. For this was he sent into the world. "I will send you another Paraclete, who will teach you all things and who will abide with you forever."[2] By his strength and by his power, the holy Church, the Bride of the Lamb, goes on in her conquering career, gaining souls to God. Holiness and truth are in her. Unchanging in her teaching received from her founder, Christ; changing in discipline to accommodate herself to the different customs of peoples; kept from error by the Spirit of truth; obedient to her clergy, her commanders, like an army in battle array, she advances in this holy time after Pentecost to the conquest of souls, to battle with the old enemy of our race. Nothing on earth can be compared to her. She is above kings and governments. She is independent of earth. She is the mountain on the top of mountains.[3] Persecuted for a time, yet she is always triumphant. Guided by the Holy Ghost she converts, sanctifies and saves the souls of men. This she always will do till the consummation of this world. This work of the Spouse of Christ is typified by the After-Pente-

---

[1] Gal. iv. 19.   [2] John xiv. 16, 17, 26; xv. 26.   [3] Is. ii. 2.

cost Season. She gathers then the fruit of holy souls. She baptises and guards the child from the moment of its birth. She teaches it her holy doctrine. She guides its stumbling footsteps during life, and at the end she sends the holy souls to heaven to worship God forever. Thus the work of the church is typified by this holy time, the last of the Seasons of the Christian year.

The Christian is a temple of the Holy Ghost; "Know ye not that your members are the temple of the Holy Ghost?"[1] No temple ever built by hand of man can equal the beauties of our bodies. In the beginning, God made man to live within him as in a temple, till sin in the garden drove the Lord away. Man becomes again the temple of his God at his baptism.[2] Then we should be like the Church. We should go on from virtue to virtue, gaining during this Season—gaining in grace and good works before God and man. But there is this difference between the Church and man in being the temples of the Holy Ghost, that while the Church represents in summer time the ages which will come to pass from the days of our Lord to the end of the world, the soul can at the end of this Season begin again the same series of feasts and fasts, of ceremonies and services, of the times and of the Seasons of the year, and thus increase in holiness and in godliness, till at death God calls him to the everlasting glories of heaven.

From the times of the Apostles, the parts of the Holy Bible read in the Offices and in the Services, have been arranged for this time, so as to tell of the works of the Holy Spirit both in the Church and in the soul. The history of the children of Israel is but a figure of the story of the Church[3] and of the Christian soul, and the trials and the battles of the Jews were types of the battles of the Church and of the Christians. From the first Sunday after Pentecost to the beginning of August, we read the four Books of Kings. They are a prophecy of the Church. The kingdom of Israel began by Saul. The Church of God began by the Jews. Saul was rejected by God. The Jews were discarded because they rejected the Saviour; David was chosen in his place. The

---

[1] I. Cor. vi. 19. [2] Cerem. Bapt. in Rituale. [3] St. Aug. Contra. Faust., l. xxii., n. 24, et De Civitas Dei., l. vii. c. 32.

nations were taken in the place of the Jews. David first lived in continual combats and warfare; the Church was first persecuted. At length peace came to Israel. Peace at length was given to the Church by Constantine. Solomon built his magnificent temple; the Church reared her wonderful Cathedrals. For a long time the Jews lived in peace; for many centuries the Church had peace during the middle ages. Of the twelve tribes ten fell away and were lost by Samaria in the north, being separated from the centre of worship at Jerusalem. In the XVIth century the nations of the north of Europe fell away at the reformation and are being lost, for now we see that little by little the revelation of God preserved by tradition is being destroyed among them. . From the death of Solomon began the wars of the Jews with the surrounding nations. Some were good and saintly kings, like Asa, Ezechias and Josias; some were bad infidel kings, like Achab, Manasser and Achaz.

The people of God heard among the hills of Judea the voice of the Lord by the mouth of his prophets, calling them from the worship of idols, calling them to the worship of the Lord. The people of the Church hear the voice of God by the mouth of the clergy, calling them from the vices of this world, which are like so many idols. The Jews heard from the inspired men of old the ruin which would fall on them if they did not return to the religion of their fathers, as now we tell of the ruin of nations and of empires if they serve not the Church.[1] Many times were the Jews punished for their sins. Many times have the Christians fallen because they served not their Lord. Thus the Jews were a figure of the Church, and Jerusalem a type of this world. They listened not to the prophets of the Lord. The Jews were taken captive; Jerusalem was destroyed—figures of the destruction of all things at the last coming of our Lord, at the destruction of the world.

In August we read the Sapiential Books—Proverbs, Ecclesiastes, Wisdom and Ecclesiasticus—because they tell us of the wisdom of God. That wisdom is the Son of God, the "Wisdom of the Father" revealed to man by the guiding influence of the Holy Ghost through the Proph-

---

[1] Isaias lx. 12.

ets and through the Church, and who ever lives in her, and speaks to mankind by the voice of our chief pastor, the Pope.

Man can do nothing of himself for his salvation unless helped by God. Following this grace of God he soon becomes a saint. To give a good example, we read in the month of September the lives of the Saints of the Old Testament, of Tobias, Judith, Esther and Job, in whose souls we see the work of the grace of God. But as towards the end of the world, as foretold by the prophets, the Church will be driven to fight the great battles, which will be raised against her by the persecutions of Anti-Christ, in the month of October we read the history of the last wars of the Jews, and how they conquered their enemies, as given in the books of the Maccabees. As they conquered those who would destroy the nation of the Jews, thus the Church will not be destroyed, but according to the words of our Lord, she will last till the end of the world. "Behold, I am with you always, even to the consummation of the world."[1] Thus the Church, having her founder, Christ, with her, will outlive the persecutions of the last ages of the world. To recall the prophecies of the last days, when the number of the saints will be filled, in the month of November, at the end of the ecclesiastical year, we read the prophets of old—Ezechiel, terrible in his words; Daniel, whose inspired eye reviews the empires, the nations and the peoples of the earth, and the little prophets, who foretell the vengeance of God, the calamities of the latter times, the end of all, the death of the world, and the wonders which will come to pass when the Son of God, in power and in majesty, will come to judge the living and the dead.

Such is the meaning of the After-Pentecost Season, the summer of the Church, when Christian souls flourish in grace, like trees planted by the limpid waters of life flowing from the exhaustless fountains of the crucified Saviour. During this time the vestments are green, to express the hope we have of salvation through our God, when guided by the Holy Ghost at the end of our exile in the heavenly and the everlasting Jerusalem which is above.

---

[1] Math. xxviii. 20.

I.—TRINITY SUNDAY.

The first Sunday after Pentecost is called Trinity Sunday, because it is dedicated to the glory of the most Holy Trinity. From the times of the Apostles, the Christians had a feast set apart in which they recalled the glory and the worship of the Triune God. In some of the churches, in those times, they celebrated that feast the first Sunday before Advent, but the most of the churches, following the traditions of the Apostles, held the festival on the first Sunday after Pentecost.[1] In the first ages, besides these two Sundays mentioned, they devoted each Sunday in the year to the Holy Trinity, till at length the first Sunday after Pentecost was above all others set apart to the special worship of the Trinity,[2] throughout the whole Church.

All worship goes to the Holy Trinity, for when we adore any one of the most Holy Persons, we adore all Three, for they are one God.[3] At the end of all the prayers, in administering the sacraments, at the end of the Psalms, all end with the words, "Glory be to the Father, and to the Son, and to the Holy Ghost." These words were formed by the Apostles.[4] When Arius and his followers in the IVth century denied that Christ was God, equal to the Father in all things, the Nicene Council condemned him, and to the words, "Glory be to the Father," etc., added, "As it was in the beginning, and is now, and will be forever, Amen," to show that Christ was always, is now, and ever will be God.[5] The Saints of these olden times had a special devotion to the Holy Trinity. The remains of that is seen in the services of the Church. Sunday was dedicated to the resurrection of our Lord, but in another manner it was set apart for the glory of the Trinity. For that reason, on Sunday, the office of Matins is always made up of three watches of three lessons each, to honor the three Persons of the blessed Trinity. The Athanesian Creed, which treats of the Three Persons of God, is said at Prime, and the Preface of Trinity Sunday is sung at the Masses of the Sundays of the year when there is no other feast.

---

[1] Pope Alexander II. Decret. Quoniam Tit. de Fer. [2] Pope John XII. [3] Benedictus XIV. De Fest. D. N. Jesu Christi, c. xii., n. 5. [4] Benedictus XIV. Ibidem, n. 7, Kosma, 164. [5] Acta Concil Nic.; O'Brien, Hist. of the Mass, p. 166.

In the VIIIth century we read that the pious Alcuinus, encouraged by St. Boniface, the Apostle of Germany, composed the votive Mass we offer in honor of the Holy Trinity. Later, in 1022, the German bishops pronounced in favor of the devotion to that Mass.[1] Before that time the Belgians had a feast in honor of the Holy Trinity, for the bishop of Liege celebrated a solemn feast in his cathedral in 920, and composed a complete Office for the day. It spread rapidly, especially among the religious Orders during the first years of the XIth century, being fostered by Bernon, Abbot of Reichnaw. We see by one of the old liturgical works of Cluny, that it was celebrated there for a long time before 1091. In 1061, Alexander II. sat upon the Chair of Peter, and sanctioned the celebration of the Feast of the Holy Trinity, which at that time had been spread into every part of the world.

In the beginning of the XIIth century, the prince of liturgical writers, Rupert the Abbot, wrote: "After having celebrated the solemnity of the coming of the Holy Ghost, we sing the glory of the Holy Trinity, in the Office of the following Sunday, and that is very proper, because after the descent of that divine Spirit, began the preaching of our belief, and in baptism is the faith and the confession of the name of the Father, and of the Son, and of the Holy Ghost."[2] In 1162, the glorious martyr, St. Thomas of Canterbury, celebrated the feast of the Holy Trinity in the cathedral on the first Sunday after Pentecost, in memory of his consecration to the episcopacy, which took place on that day. In 1260, the council of Arles, presided over by archbishop Florentin, solemnly sanctioned the feast in France,[3] and added to it an Octave. In the beginning of the XIIIth century, Durand leads us to conclude that a great part of the Christian world kept the feast.[4] Some of the churches of France celebrate twice in the year the feast of the Holy Trinity, on the first Sunday after Pentecost and on the last Sunday before Advent,[5] the remains of very ancient customs.

When Atilla, the "scourge of God," conquered a large part of the Roman empire, he destroyed numberless liturgical works of our holy religion. St. Boniface, archbishop

---

[1] Concil Seligen. [2] De Divinis Officiis l. i. c. i. [3] Can. vi. [4] Rationale Div. l. vi., c. cxiv., l. i. [5] At Narbonne, Mans and Auxerre.

of Metz, asked Alcuinus, the teacher of Charles and of his son Louis, kings of France, to rewrite again these books which had been destroyed. They were approved by the Council of Metz, and the feast of the Holy Trinity was commanded to be celebrated the first Sunday after Pentecost.

Alcuinus wrote a special Mass for Trinity Sunday, which he showed to Pope Alexander, who replied that every day we give glory to the Trinity.[1] The Arians, who denied the Divinity of Christ and the Trinity, having spread, SS. Hilary and Ambrose, with Eusebius, wrote and preached against them, and Gregory the Great commanded the Mass to be sung and churches to be built in honor of the Most Holy Trinity;[2] because, although each Sunday was consecrated to the Trinity in the early days of Christianity, when but few feasts of the saints were celebrated, it was foreseen that as the saints grew in numbers their memory would be celebrated during many Sundays of the year, and that unless a special feast in memory of the Holy Trinity was celebrated, soon the Trinity would not be honored as in former times. For that reason the feast was commanded to be held on the first Sunday after Pentecost.[3]

During this season of the year, except those of the Quater Tenses of September, the Masses have no titles like the great feasts of the other seasons, for they are not of such importance, or they do not go back to the Apostolic times.

II.—CORPUS CHRISTI.

The words Corpus Christi, in Latin, mean the Body of Christ, for in this feast we celebrate the goodness of God in leaving us his Body and his Blood to be our food and drink. From the beginning of the Church, the memory of the institution of the blessed Sacrament was always celebrated on Holy Thursday; but because the ceremonies of the Holy Oils took up the time of the clergy and of the people, they could not celebrate on that day the feast of the most Holy Sacrament.[4]

---

[1] Extra. de Fer., c. ii. [2] Durandus, Rationale Div. l. vi., c. cxiv. n. 6. [3] Gueranger, Le Temps apres La Pent, p. 126. [4] Benedictus XIV. De Fest., D. N. l. Christi, c. xiii. n. 1.

From the beginning the people of the Church poured out their greatest love and adoration to the Blessed Sacrament. We find it mentioned so often in the writings of the Father and of the great Saints of the olden times. No one ever dared to deny the real Presence of Christ upon the altar. till Berengarius,[1] the proud, haughty, vulgar and ignorant heretic, dared, in the face of the whole Catholic world, to deny that truth, taught by all ages from the time of the Apostles, that our Lord was really present in the Eucharist. He said that Christ was present not really, but only in a typical manner.[2] By many Councils, but especially by one held in 1050, his errors were condemned.[3] Once he denied his heresy, but afterwards he returned to the vomit. Again he was condemned, when he again returned to the Catholic fold and died reconciled to the Church.[5]

We have spoken of the procession of the blessed Sacrament, which from the most ancient time takes place after the Mass of Holy Thursday, when it is carried to the repository, there to remain till, in the services of Good Friday, it is carried back to the main altar. On Corpus Christi the Host is again carried in triumph through the church, and in Catholic countries our Lord is borne by the clergy through the streets of the cities. The houses are decorated, the streets strewed with flowers, and the whole people turn out to honor their God.

The custom of carrying the blessed Sacrament in a procession appears to go back to the most ancient times. We cannot find the beginning of the procession of Holy Week, but the procession of Corpus Christi appears to be more recent than the feast itself. Urban IV. speaks of it.[6] Martin V. and Eugenius IV. granted indulgences to those who took part in the processions,[7] which supposes that they were then customary each year. Bosius tells us that in 1404 the Sacrament was carried in procession "as was usual before."[8] We find that ceremony mentioned in a manuscript of the church of Chartres in 1330, in one of the Acts of the Chapters of Tournay in 1325, of Paris in 1320, and these two Councils

---

[1] In the year 1047. [2] Gautier de Præcip. Sectis Hæres Sec. x. et xi. [3] Concil. Rom. under Leo IX. [4] Synod Rom. sub. Greg. VIII. [5] 1088. [6] Bull. Const. [7] 20th May, 1429 : 20th May, 1432. [8] Chron.

SAINT ISAAC OF ST. PETERSBURG.

granted special indulgences to all who would fast on the eve of the feast.[1]

It appears more probable that the Host was not always carried in a solemn procession as to-day, because of the persecutions, but that in some churches It was left on the altar, and there received the adoration of the faithful. In the eleventh century It was sometimes carried in procession on Palm Sunday and on Easter morning. We cannot find out when the custom of carrying the Host in the monstrance began.[2] It is mentioned for the first time in the Council of Cologne.[3] The monstrance was first made like a little turret of gold.[4] In a manuscript Missal of 1374 the letter D, with which the first prayer of Corpus Christi begins, represents a bishop carrying the Host in a turret with four openings. In after times, to give force to the Christian teachings that our Lord is the Son of Justice, which enlighteneth " every man that cometh into this world,"[5] the monstrance was made with rays of gold coming forth from the blessed Sacrament.[6] That can be seen by examining a book called the " Gradual," of the time of Louis XII.,[7] where the first letter of the Mass represents the Host carried by two persons vested in copes, followed by the king and a number of cardinals.[8]

During the procession, the clergy and the people sing hymns and psalms in honor of their Lord. When they march in the streets of Catholic cities, " stations " are prepared in different parts, where they place the Host on altars, and give the benediction to the people. Coming to the church, all is finished with a grand benediction, when the Sacrament is left on the grand altar for eight days to be worshipped and adored by the whole people.[9]

About the year 1230, a nun named Juliana said she had a vision, in which our Lord appeared, and said to her that he wished to have a special feast set apart to the honor of the Blessed Sacrament.[10] She consulted one of the canons of her diocese,[11] who advised her to ask the theologians and bishops. One of her advisers was James P. Trecenis, who afterwards became Pope, under the name of Urban IV. Moved by many reasons,

---

[1] Labb. Concil. t. xi. p. 1680, 1711. [2] See O'Brien, Hist. of the Mass, p. 78. [3] In 1452. [4] O'Brien, Hist. of the Mass, p. 79 [5] John i. 9. [6] O'Brien, Hist. of the Mass, p. 79. [7] 1498-1515. [8] Thiers, Exposit. du S. Sacr., l. ii. c. 2. [9] Gueranger, Le Temps, apres La Pent., p. 323. [10] O'Brien, Hist. of the Mass, p. 78. [11] Laodiensis.

Robert, Bishop of Liege, in a Council, held in 1246, ordered the feast to be held throughout his diocese. Hugo, Provincial of the Dominicans, moved by the prayers of the holy nun, approved of the feast, and when sent by the Holy See as Cardinal and Legate to Belgium, he fostered the feast in that country.[1] The matter was afterwards brought before Urban IV., who, after a long time, commanded the feast to be celebrated throughout the whole Church.[2] Pope Urban IV. died about two months after sending forth the Bull, and his commands were carried out only in the diocese of Liege.

According to the Bull, the feast was to be celebrated on the first Thursday after Trinity Sunday. Clement V., the successor of Urban IV., in the Council of Vienna,[3] confirmed the instructions of his predecessor, and with the consent and at the request of the greater part of the world, represented by the bishops of the Council, he commanded the feast of Corpus Christi to be held on the Thursday after Trinity Sunday throughout the whole world. Clement V. died, and John XXII. took his place on Peter's Chair. By every way he promoted and sanctioned the feast. Martin V. and Eugene IV. granted new indulgences to all who would, in a becoming manner, celebrate the solemnity. The Council of Trent confirmed what was done before, and called it the Triumphant Feast.[4]

Urban IV., before his death, asked the great St. Thomas to write the Office of Corpus Christi. The Saint, whose wonderful mind has enlightened the world, who has been given to all as the greatest of the Doctors of the Church,[5] composed the beautiful Offices of the Mass and Breviary of this feast. According to the words of Urban IV., " the Office of the same solemnity was composed by B. Thomas of Aquin."[6] The day for having the feast was fixed on Thursday, because on Thursday before he died, our Lord instituted the Blessed Eucharist. It was commanded to be held the first Thursday after Trinity Sunday, because the whole Easter Time is dedicated to the resurrection of our Lord, and thus it does not interfere with any of the other feasts of that season.

---

[1] Benedictus XIV. De Fest. J. Christi. c. xiii., n. 3. [2] Bull. Urban II. Aug. 1264. [3] 1311. [4] Sess. xiii., c. 15. [5] Leo XIII. Const. Unigenitus. [6] Bull. Frat. Predicat, t. iii., p. 555.

III.—THE ASSUMPTION.

On the 15th of August the Church celebrates the Feast of the Assumption. Some of the early saints supposed that the Mother of our Lord never died,[1] but that she was taken up body and soul into heaven.[2] Many of them say they doubt her death; others say she did not die;[3] but the common opinion among both the Latins and the Greek Fathers is that she died.[4] The Bible is silent on the matter. The Gospels were written to give a history of our Lord from his conception till his going up into heaven, while the Acts of the Apostles tell us of the lives of some of the followers of our Lord, till they went forth into the different parts of the world to preach the Gospel, in the fourth reign of Nero and the sixty-third year from the birth of Christ. The other parts of the New Testament give some of the doctrines, but not the history of these early days. Following the inspired words : "Who is the man that shall live and not see death,"[5] "It is appointed unto men once to die,"[6] the great writers say she died. Death can be taken in two ways, as the natural end of all living creatures in this world, and as the punishment of sin. She committed no sin, for she was conceived to be the source from which was to come the human nature of the Son of God, and therefore as a sinner she did not die. But she died because she was a creature of this world.[7] This is the common belief of all Christians. As the daughter of Adam she was subject to all the miseries of this life, although without sin, and one of these miseries is death.[8]

The constant and universal tradition of the Church is, that our Lord's Mother died and was buried.[9] Her tomb to-day is pointed out on the side of the Mount of Olives. We know that she lived for many years with the beloved Apostle St. John at Ephesus, and that at length she went to Jerusalem, where she met all the Apostles.[10] There, many years after our Lord's ascension, she died, and they buried her.

---

[1] Serm. S. J. Joannis Damas. Or. 2 de Dor. B. M. V. [2] St. Epiphanius, Hæres., 78. [3] P. Macede de Clav. Petri, t. i. 1. iv., p. 11. [4] Benedictus XIV., De Festis B. M. Virg. c. viii., 1. 2. [5] Ps. lxxxviii, 49. [6] Heb. ix. 27. [7] Benedictus XIV., Ibidem, n. 4. [8] Theop. Reynaudus Dip. Mar. t. vii. n. 5. [9] S. Greg. Sacrament. Tilloment, t. i. n. 17. [10] See The Falling Asleep of Mary and The Passing of Mary among the Apocryphal Gospels, etc.

From the most ancient traditions we learn that Mary left the home of the beloved Apostle St. John at Ephesus and returned to Jerusalem. At that time all the Apostles had preached the Gospel to the ends of the earth. Now, as by the hand of God, they all gathered again in the holy city. Suddenly they heard the voices of angels singing the glories of their Lord. The Virgin Mother of our Lord laid down, and in the midst of the sweetest music ever heard by human ears she went to sleep in the Lord. Her body filled the air with sweetest odor, while the heavenly song still resounded from the invisible choir, and continued for three days after they buried her in the Garden of Gethsemane, in the tomb pointed out to-day. Thomas came after the burial, and asked to look once more on the face of the Lord's Mother. They opened the grave for him, but the body was gone, only her grave clothes were found, which filled the whole place with the sweetest odor. They closed the tomb, and from that time the Apostles taught that her body was taken up into heaven.[1]

We are not sure how old she was when she died. Some say she lived to a good old age,[2] others that she was 57,[3] 59[4] or 60 years of age when she died.[5] While we have the bones and the remains of all the Apostles and the martyrs, while countries and cities have in the past vied with each other in guarding the relics of the saints, no place, city or church has ever claimed to have the body of the Virgin. It is the common belief of all Christians that her remains were taken up into heaven shortly after her death, before her body saw corruption.[6] The doctrine of the Assumption of the Virgin body and soul into heaven has not been defined by the Church, nor is it given in Scriptures, but the time will come when the Church will define it; nevertheless, he who would attack such a pious and religious teaching would be guilty of the greatest temerity.[7] Such is the belief of all the Saints, Fathers, and of all the writers of the Church. The Church will one day define it, therefore it must be now in tradition.

---

[1] Ser. S. Joannis Damas. Or. 2 de Dormit. Dieparae. [2] Andreas Cretensis. [3] Nicephorus Evodii. [4] Epiphanius Const. [5] St. Damascenus Hom. de Dermit. B. Virginis, n. 18. [6] Benedictus XIV. Ibidem. n. 12. [7] See Words of Concil. Toledo in VIIth Century, O. p. 4. St. Aug.; Suarez iii., p. qu. xxxvii. a. 4, disp. 25, s. 2.

From the very earliest times, the Church celebrated the Feast of the Assumption on the 15th of August.[1] This is the day her body is said to have risen from the grave and gone up into heaven. The day of her death is not certain; some say that two days, some three days, others seven or fifteen days before this she died.[2] But most writers think it took place three days before, following the example of her divine Son, who rose on the third day.[3]

We find that this feast was celebrated in the remotest times in the beginning of the Christian religion.[4] Some of the early churches held the Feast on the 18th of January, till at length they followed the customs of the early Christians by celebrating the Assumption on the 15th of August.[5] We find the Saints of the earliest times preached some of their most eloquent sermons and wrote many beautiful things on the services of the Assumption of the Mother of God.

Like the other great feasts of the year, the Assumption has an Eve, when we are to fast, and it is followed by an Octave.[6] It is always a feast of obligation, when we are to stop all servile work and hear Mass, in a word, we are commanded to keep it like Sunday.

The Gospel is taken from St. Luke,[7] where our Lord went into the house of Lazarus, Mary sat at the feet of the Lord and Martha went about her work. Mary, say the great writers, was a figure of the religious life, while Martha was a type of the active life. The religious life is the most perfect; for that reason Mary was praised by her Lord while Martha received a mild chiding, because she was troubled about many things. This Gospel is read to-day, because Mary, the Mother of our Lord, was the first to give women the example of following the religious life. She spent her early days in the temple, she was the first who ever took a vow of chastity, and she was thus the mother and the example of all virgins, who dedicate their virginity to God.

All Saturdays are dedicated to the Mother of God, and on that day her Office is often said, because when our Lord lay dead in the tomb on Saturday, all his followers

---

[1] Can. I. de Consec. Dist. 3, c. ult.; El Porque de las Ceremonias, Trato. Cuarto, c. x.; St. Cyril of Alexandria, etc. [2] Revelat. S. Brigit. l. vii. c. 63 et 26. [3] Benedictus XIV. Ibidem, n. 25. [4] See Reply of Pope Nicolas I. in 858. [5] By order of Pope Sergius, El Porque, T. Cuarto, c. x. [6] Leo IV. an. 347. [7] Luke x.

fled and gave up hope. His Mother alone had faith in his resurrection, and for that reason to remember her faith we celebrate her praises on Saturday.

In the third week of September, following the Feast of the Holy Cross, come the Quater Tenses, or Ember Days of the fall season. Wednesday, Friday and Saturday are fasting days of obligation. They come in the week following the XVIIth Sunday after Pentecost. On Wednesday the Station is in the great Church of St. Mary Major, where the services are held. Friday the Station is at the Church of the Twelve Apostles, where the services are not as long as on the other two days. Saturdays the Station is in the great Church of St. Peter's at Rome, and the ceremony is of considerable length.

IV.—FEAST OF ALL SAINTS.

For four reasons we celebrate the memory of the Saints, that we may honor in them the wonderful works of God, for "God is wonderful in his saints;"[1] that we may consider them as the instruments God used for carrying out his work in the salvation of souls; that we may look on them as the temples of the Holy Ghost, who lived upon this earth, and that we may imitate their good works and thus become saints ourselves.[2]

Numberless are the saints and the martyrs, which the Church proposes to us, that we may honor and imitate them, but they are so numerous, that we cannot celebrate all their memories; but in the Breviary we have the Offices of the principal Saints of God, whose feast is celebrated on the day of their death.

We celebrate each year the memory of all the saints in one great feast, because they are so numerous that we cannot set apart a day for each one during the year, but on this day we make up for all the negligences which we have been guilty of regarding the honor due them, and because by asking the aid of all the saints at the same time, we will be better helped by their united prayers.[3]

The Romans in Pagan times had so many gods that they could not dedicate a day of the year to each of them.

---

[1] Ps. lxviii. 36.   [2] Natalis Alexander de Cultu Sanc s. i. in fine.   [3] Durandus, Rationale Div. l. vii. c. xxxiv. n. 4.

For that reason Marcus Agrippa built a beautiful temple to the honor of Cybeles, the mother of all the gods, which he dedicated to all the divinities of the Roman Empire. For that reason it was called the Pantheon, from two Greek words, meaning all the gods. Time passed, and the Romans were converted from Paganism to Christianity. Pope Boniface IV. obtained the Pantheon from the Emperor Phoca Cæsar, who, as the successor of Constantine at Constantinople, ruled the Roman Empire. Then the celebrated Pagan temple, dedicated to the mother of all the gods and to the false deities of Pagan Rome, was dedicated to the Mother of God and to all the martyrs. The feast was first celebrated in the month of May, and commanded to be celebrated throughout the whole world by Gregory III. ; but, by order of Pope Gregory IV., it was postponed till the 1st of November, because the people were accustomed on this day to bring the fruits of the earth to be offered in the church, and they could more easily get the fruits in the fall than in the spring.

The eve of All Saints is a day of fast as a preparation for the feast itself. The Feast of All the Saints is a holiday of obligation, which must be celebrated like Sunday, by hearing Mass and resting from work.

In the Epistle of the Mass of to-day we read the vision. of heaven seen by St. John, the beloved apostle, in the Island of Patmos, such as he gives us in the Book of the Apocalypse.[1]

The Gospel is taken from St. Matthew, where our Lord preaches his wonderful Sermon on the Mount, and tells of the perfections of the saints, of the eight beatitudes of those who serve God upon this earth, of the sufferings and of the persecutions they will have to go through during this life, and of the rewards they will receive in heaven.[2]

V.—FEAST OF ALL SOULS.

The custom of praying for the dead came from the Apostles. That doctrine is certain. The Old and New Testaments prove that it was a religious belief among the

---

[1] Apoc. vii.   [2] Math. v.

Jews.[1] The early Christians prayed at all times for the repose of their dead friends. We cannot go into the proofs of that doctrine of the Church. It would be out of place in a work of this kind, written to explain the Christian Year.

After celebrating the glories of the saints in heaven, the Church, the following day, on the 2d of November, remembers all her dead, all the souls who have gone before, who are waiting to be delivered from their prison house and to be admitted into the happiness of heaven. It follows from the sweet doctrine of the communion of saints, that the Church is made up of three parts, the saints of earth, the blessed in heaven and the suffering souls of purgatory. That feast was instituted by the Apostles themselves, but the whole Office was revised by Origen.[2]

The object of these services is that the general prayers of the Church may aid those suffering souls with her spiritual benefits, for they cannot in any way help themselves.[3] Its origin goes back to the time of the patriarchs, for we read that when Jacob was dead they wept over him for forty days in Egypt, and when they brought his body to Hebron, there they mourned him seven days. To-day the bodies of the patriarchs are guarded with jealous care by the Turks in the double cave which Abraham bought.[4] Their bodies are never shown to Christians, but a traveller disguised as a Mohammedan succeeded in entering the cave where lie the embalmed bodies of the patriarchs.[5]

Again we read that when Moses died, for thirty days the children of Israel wept over him, the same as they did at the death of Aaron[6] and of Mary, his sister. From this custom of the Jews weeping for thirty days over their dead, the Christian Church has, from its beginning, observed the "Month's Mind," on the thirtieth day after death.[7] From the example of the children of Israel weeping seven days over Jacob in Hebron, we say Mass for the dead on the seventh day, and in remembrance of the three days of our Lord in the tomb, we say Mass on

---

[1] Bouvier. De Praecip. Eccl. Fest. n. 5. Com. Fid. Defunct. [2] Isidore, Lib. de Eccl. Officiis. [3] De Consec. Dist. I. Visum [4] Gen. l. 10. [5] Cuvalier's tom. iii. c. iv. n. 1. [6] O'Brien, Hist. of the Mass, p. 14. [7] Gavantus, p. 1, tit. 5, l. a.

the third day after death.[1] Some of the early Christians used to have Masses said for their dead on the ninth day, but it was forbidden, for the pagans mourned their dead for nine days.[2] The custom of having anniversary Masses for the repose of the dead is also very ancient. The year, as it were, revolving ever into itself, represents eternity into which the souls of the dead have passed. The anniversary for a dead friend can be held as often as we wish, for we cannot tell how long the souls remain in the other life before entering heaven.[3] When the anniversary of a saint falls on a Sunday or a feast day, it is put off till the next day it can be held, but when the anniversary of the dead falls in the same way, it is sometimes said before, so as to receive the benefit of the Mass as soon as we can offer it. On Sundays and feasts we cannot offer up the holy sacrifice for the dead, unless the body is present, because it would draw the people away from the services of the day.

We should pray each day for our dead friends,[4] but on this day, we pray in general for all the dead, for there are many who die without friends, without any one to pray for them, and "their Mother, the Church, takes the place of all these."[5] As in the old law no oil of joy or sweetly smelling incense was offered in the sacrifices for sin, thus as death is a figure of sin in the Offices of the dead, no songs or signs of joy are seen or heard, all is mourning, for death has swallowed up his victims. Thus following the law of Moses the incense is not offered at certain times during the Masses for the dead.

In the early times, when a person was about to die, following the example of St. Martin, he was laid on ashes or on straw. This was not a universal practice. The early writers say that after death the body was washed to signify that it would rise gloriously from the dead on the last day.[6] To follow the example of our Lord they used to sometimes anoint the body of the dead with oil. The custom of saying Psalms for the dead was commanded by some of the early Councils.[7] They also ordered that the body should be carried by

---

[1] Cavalieri, tom. iii. c. iv. n. 1. [2] St. Liguori, De Caer. Missæ, Ap. iv. c. iii. [3] 13 quest. 2 Non æstimamus. [4] Concil. Cabilon. De Consecra. Dist. I. Visum. [5] St. Augustine L. de Cura pro Mortuis, c. ix. [6] Durandus, Rationale Div. l. vii. n. 35. [7] Concil. Toletan, 13 quest. 2 Qui divina.

the members of the same station in life and of the same profession. That was the origin of the pall-bearers.[1]

The people from the most ancient times have been accustomed to make some offerings to their clergy for Masses for their dead friends on the 2d of November. We are not able to find the beginning of that good and holy custom, but we are inclined to believe that it has always been in the Church.

For the services of the dead and for a translation of the celebrated "Dies Iræ," the reader is referred to the book "Teaching Truth by Signs and Ceremonies," where the meaning of the funeral rites will be found.

The Gospel read on the Feast of all the Dead is taken from the Gospel of St. John, where our Lord says the time will come, on the last day, when the dead in their graves will hear his voice, and all will rise from the grave, some into everlasting life in heaven and some into everlasting death in hell. He speaks of the general judgment.

Such is the last of the chief feasts of this Season of the year. On the last Sunday of the year the Church reads at the Mass the Gospel giving the prophecy of our Lord relating to the last and general judgment, for this Season tells of the time of the Church which will close the age of this world by the end of all things. That Gospel is read to bring before the minds of all men their last and final end. Thus the year in the Christian Church is like a sublime arena, whereon the miraculous birth, the holy life, the wonderful works, and the awful death of the Son of God is opened out before the minds of men in mystic rites, in striking figures, in majestic ceremonies, and in beautiful portraits, so that generation after generation comes and goes on the stage of this world ; their creation by God, their fall by Adam, and their redemption by Christ, are each year vividly brought before their eyes.

Pray, reader, that the pen of the writer may, in its own feeble way, continue to show still further the wonderful beauties of the Church of God.

---

[1] De Consec. Dist. I. Sicut Extra. de Obser. Jejun.